An Appearance of Impropriety

BOOKS BY JAYNA BREIGH

The Hunted Heir

An Appearance of Impropriety

An Appearance of Impropriety

A ROMANTIC LEGAL DRAMA

Jayna Breigh

An Appearance of Impropriety: A Romantic Legal Drama
© 2026 by Jana Riediger

Published by Kregel Publications, a division of Kregel Inc., 2450 Oak Industrial Dr. NE, Grand Rapids, MI 49505. www.kregel.com.

All rights reserved. No part of this book may be reproduced; stored in a retrieval system, including but not limited to generative AI training systems; or transmitted in any form or by any means—for example, electronic, mechanical, photocopy, recording, or otherwise—without the publisher's prior written permission or by license agreement. The only exception is brief quotations in printed reviews.

Jayna Breigh is represented by and *An Appearance of Impropriety* is published in association with The Steve Laube Agency, LLC. www.stevelaube.com.

The persons and events portrayed in this work are the creations of the author or are used fictitiously, and any resemblance to persons living or dead is purely coincidental.

Scripture is paraphrased or quoted directly from either the New International Version or the New King James Version of the Bible: The Holy Bible, New International Version®, NIV®. Copyright © 1973, 1978, 1984, 2011 by Biblica, Inc. Used with permission of Zondervan. All rights reserved worldwide. www.zondervan.com. The New King James Version®. Copyright © 1982 by Thomas Nelson. Used by permission. All rights reserved.

Lyrics to "I Surrender All," written by Judson W. Van DeVenter, 1855–1939, first published in *Gospel Songs of Grace and Glory* (Sebring Publishing, 1936), no. 83, are in public domain.

Cover design by Caroline Cahoon

Cataloging-in-Publication data is available from the Library of Congress.

ISBN 978-0-8254-4887-4, print
ISBN 978-0-8254-6377-8, epub
ISBN 978-0-8254-6376-1, Kindle

Printed in the United States of America
26 27 28 29 30 31 32 33 34 35 / 5 4 3 2 1

For CTB and RTC

Chapter 1

Molasses-thick traffic advanced toward downtown Los Angeles in the jerky fits and starts of a cheap carnival ride. California's 110 Freeway wasn't exactly known for its flow, but seriously? Heat crawled up Mahalia Jackson's neck, and her beloved granddaddy's maxim scrolled through her mind. *"Baby girl, if you're on time, you're* already *late. Early* is on time."

She checked the clock on the dash screen, ran her hand up the nape of her neck, and gave a firm squeeze to break up the stress. But the knots only tightened. The application window opened today for the position she'd coveted since she'd ascended to the bench—the next rung on her ladder of success. Arnold Goldstein, her mentor, the man who held the key to her promotion, had pushed off other meetings and squeezed in thirty precious minutes for her in his over-packed schedule. She would have met on a videoconference, but he was old school. Handled important matters face-to-face and only used technology when unavoidable.

A picture formed of him sitting in his office, shaking his head at her tardiness. Coffee growing cold. Gnarled fingers tapping on his desk.

A woman in her position shouldn't be late. Ever. The hairpins in her twisted updo pinched, making her scalp feel like monkeys were grabbing fistfuls of hair and tugging at random.

She chanced a look away from the road toward her GPS to check the projected ETA, but her gaze halted at a snag on the cuff of her lucky jacket. The pantsuit, with its vivid emerald color and cloud-soft silk, served as her go-to pick-me-up. Mahalia's spirits usually lifted as she anticipated compliments on her outfit. Too bad it wasn't working today. Lucky jacket? Nope. Not magical today, especially with traffic at a standstill.

She suppressed a growl and stared at the side-view mirror. A small gap between cars materialized, and she stomped her foot on the accelerator. She squeezed her car into the carpool lane. The blaring collision-avoidance system jerked her attention back to the freeway. The auto-braking engaged, and her head snapped back into the headrest. She missed crashing into the motorcycle in front of her by mere inches. The biker himself wasn't watching the road but had his head trained upward. She tracked the stares of the other distracted drivers around her to a new billboard looming over the freeway.

In the sign's foreground, a man with a shock of thick silver hair stood—arms flexed, bodybuilder style—with his boot planted on the back of a person lying on the asphalt. In the background, a damaged tractor trailer obscured the subcompact squashed beneath it. Car parts, along with vehicle fluids, or worse, covered the roadway.

> **Widowed and destitute because of an accident?**
> **Big insurance company giving you the runaround?**
> **Call 800-555-CA$H.**
> **I Got This!**
> **Jimmy Dean Cash & Associates, PC, Los Angeles**

A dollar sign for the *s*? She snorted. Ambulance chaser, no doubt. And wasn't Jimmy Dean the name of some old-time country singer who had peddled breakfast sausages? That Cash guy was probably using the crazy billboard to generate accidents.

Mahalia refocused on the traffic. The muscles in her long legs cramped in her Eco4/2Microcar, supposedly built for two. The vehicle barely fit one person. She quelled her internal grumbling. With her government-employee salary, the tax break on her zero-emissions car came in handy. Plus, the single-occupant HOV privileges trumped comfort. Congestion eased, and she whizzed by a solo driver in the regular lane. He could be in her lane, too, if he folded himself, origami-style, into a clown car. Another check of Google Maps clocked her recalculated arrival at quarter after. Fifteen minutes late because of gawkers and rubberneckers. Irritation flared again. Her reputation had become the collateral damage of an attention-seeking huckster.

She entered the staff parking lot and slid into a space reserved for electric vehicles. She scurried to the pedestrian zone and started crossing the street at the Walk signal. Halfway across, the driver of a beat-up import yelled at her from his open window.

"Come on, dark woman."

His heavy accent of unknown origin rendered his rude statement poetic. The man lay on his horn as he curtailed his right-hand turn to wait for her.

She slowed her stroll and glared. According to the painted lines on the road and the countdown timer, she had the right of way and ten more seconds to cross. The man retaliated by scooching his vehicle into the crosswalk. *Oh no, he didn't.* She rolled her eyes and slowed her pace. Mr. Beater Car inched closer and honked, taking the turn a nanosecond after Mahalia cleared the bumper.

"Jerk."

Shame stung at how the harsh word had flown from her mouth. Granddaddy Henry had no tolerance for unkind utterances. At least once a week as a small child, he'd reminded her, *"The tongue is a fire . . ."*

Granddaddy was right. The man's words had burned her feelings like paper lit with a match.

Beater Car's rude outburst echoed the skin-tone related slurs hurled at her in childhood. The need people had to point out the obvious—that she was dark—had started inside her own home with Granddaddy Henry and Granny, who had raised her. Granny had called her *"my beautiful coal-black grandbaby"* and told her she was *"pretty . . . for a dark-skinned girl."*

As each foot ascended a worn granite step leading to the front doors of her building, Mahalia pushed away the sting of the man's words and the memories it dredged up by rehashing her oft-repeated mantra. *Prestigious college—check. Ivy League law school—check. Top-drawer law firm—check.*

She entered the courthouse, tossed her keys and phone into a plastic bin, and shoved her briefcase onto the conveyor belt of the X-ray machine. Once clear of the metal detector, she collected her belongings.

"Morning, Deputy Parker." Mahalia mustered a greeting for the deputy staffing the security station.

"Backatcha." He gave a congenial wave. "Want me to make a coffee run for you? Got a break coming up."

"Thanks, but not today. Busy as always. Corporation X versus Corporation Y. Boring."

"Well, hang in there . . ." he said with an upward nod. "Judge Jackson."

There. He'd said it. Her title. Judge P. Mahalia Jackson. Her most prized accomplishment and the sweet honey to her soul. Now at age thirty-six, and with two years behind her on the bench, she retained the title of youngest elected female judge ever in Los Angeles County Superior Court.

Check! Check! Check!

Mahalia pulled her shoulders back, lengthened her stride, and strutted down the courthouse corridor like it was Paris Fashion Week.

Her bravado crashed down at the door to Judge Goldstein's chambers, and trepidation halted her knock. Her mentor since he'd taught her Civil Procedure class, Goldstein had taken her under his wing. Helped her land her first job and treated her like a daughter—including parental scolding and fussing if necessary. He'd seeped into the gaps in her heart, left vacant when Granddaddy Henry died. Unfortunately, like Granddaddy, tardiness sat atop his short list of pet peeves.

Goldstein's impish charm and genuine love for her offset his occasional tirades in this one area. She'd only been late on a handful of occasions—none of them her fault. But today, as she had before, she'd face her scolding like a grown-up. She took a few breaths and worked out a humorous angle on the atrocious billboard to distract the octogenarian from serving up a plateful of wrath.

She braved a brief knock and entered her mentor's chambers, a time capsule from a bygone legal era. Law books and treatises lined three of the four walls. A banker's lamp, shaded by green glass with a gold pull cord, sat on a massive desk reminiscent of the Resolute desk she'd seen on the Smithsonian Channel program *Inside the White House*.

Mahalia eased herself into an indestructible government chair facing him and crossed her legs.

Her mentor trained his rheumy eyes toward her. His smooth, shiny cheeks belied his eighty years. He scowled, appearing to wind up for a rant.

She held up her hands, palms out, as if calming a skittish animal. "I am so sorry. Lookie-loos slowed me down and . . ."

Her words withered away as Goldstein stared at her and gave a dismissive wave. "I will let you off the hook, *zeeskeit*, my Precious Mahalia, because first, we don't have time. Second, you already know what I'm going to say, and we cannot be at cross-purposes if you are to land the position of assistant supervising judge."

Zeeskeit. Sweetheart. Her tense muscles relaxed. His love for her outweighed his ire today. When he used her first name, Precious, or his pocketful of Yiddish endearments, he never failed to charm her, and it signaled her return to his good graces. It meant the world to her that he supported her dreams, back in law school and now. She hoped one day to advance in prestige to a position on the California Court of Appeal. Or maybe, if she played her cards right, she might earn a seat on the federal bench.

He pulled a document from a heap on the edge of his desk and nudged it toward her. "The applications for assistant supervising judge are out. Time for us to strategize."

She scanned the ASJ application and dropped her forehead into her palms. Committee work and community service. She had the former, but only on the Courthouse Facilities Committee. The dumping ground for people who wanted to argue over greenery placement and carpet swatches. As for community service? Batting zero.

A knock sounded at the door. Edith, Goldstein's secretary and the only courthouse employee older than he was, popped her face and her helmet of hair-sprayed brunet curls around the door.

"You told me to remind you about your next meeting. Five minutes."

"Right." Goldstein eased himself to standing, crackles and pops coming from his knees.

"I stacked meetings one after the other. We'll get back to this. Edith will put it on the calendar." He skewered her with his look.

"I'll be on time." She arranged her face to appear chastened.

He patted her on the shoulder with fatherly affection and gestured for her to exit before him.

She had so much to discuss with him this morning, but that billboard... Ugh. She fisted the application and silently recited her mantra.

***

Beyond the windows of Mahalia's office, the setting sun tinted the sky with a dusky rose glow. The clock in the corner read seven thirty and marked another eleven-hour day. *From Here to Eternity*, the title to the old black-and-white movie Granny had loved, described her feelings about all the hours she'd put in. Her vision blurred.

She blinked, pinched the bridge of her nose, and reread the last paragraph of the memorandum of points and authorities in front of her. The convincing arguments and case law in the brief sealed the deal. Now, with a stroke of a pen, millions of dollars would disappear from the bottom line of a balance sheet. Funds scooped from the coffers of one multinational corporation and dumped into the account of another. A dispute over language in a contract. Not life or death. No feeling, no emotion. Only money trading hands because of the verbal boxing skills of snore-inducing lawyers.

There had to be more to life.

To advance her career, she'd sought the complex load of corporate cases, but they were dry and soulless. Now the job of ASJ lay within tantalizing reach, but would one more step up the ladder of success quiet the relentless doubts inside her head? When would she *feel* like she'd made it? Had succeeded? Could relax?

Enough. With a flick of her hand, she banished the melancholy broodings and checked her email one last time. Atop her inbox sat a reminder that she had seven hours of continuing legal education to complete on ethics. The rules were important, but rehashing them was tedious. Still a little over two months left to satisfy the requirement. She'd squeeze it in somehow.

The rest of the emails could wait. She stacked the papers on the side of her desk, then grabbed her briefcase and handbag. No second-guessing. She'd continue the slog and pay the price for her dream career—death by boredom and paper cuts.

Flicking off the lights, she pulled the literal and figurative door closed with a decisive snap behind her. That all-expenses-paid judicial conference in Vail the following week couldn't come fast enough.

The *click-clack* of her heels echoed on the gleaming marble floors as she made her way past the night-shift deputy sheriff, Turner.

"Want an escort tonight, Judge?"

"I'll be fine. Thank you."

"Anytime. No prob."

"I appreciate that, Deputy." She gave a wave.

AN APPEARANCE OF IMPROPRIETY

Mahalia *did* appreciate Turner's offer and his charming smile. Turner had been flirting with her for a while, but she'd mentally sealed that door tighter than the vault at Fort Knox. Her type? Oh yes. Rich brown, tall, and handsome described Turner to a tee. But he worked in the courthouse, which violated The Rule. No coworkers. No lawyers. Too much could go wrong if things soured. Plus, he wasn't the one. Her Midnight Prince held the key to her hope—a longing to be cherished and truly accepted, a dream far deeper and longer yearned for than her ambition to reach the pinnacle of her profession. So why start down a road to nowhere?

She rolled her shoulders and let out a sigh as she pressed the ignition button. She drove home on autopilot, and daydreaming took over. Her prince had a mind as complex as chess and skin the color of the ebony king. He'd be unfazed by her accolades, because he'd have more.

She'd held up her end of the bargain. Climbed the ladder and followed the trail of success blazed for her by her family. Now, with age forty looming, neither an aerospace engineer nor a hedge fund manager with a baritone voice had materialized. She'd prayed for years, then hoped, then wished. God still had not answered her prayer, and now her faith in him and her hope for her dream man remained tethered by the merest gossamer thread. So off to Vail she'd go to spend a weekend with ancient, married judges and their wives. The romance-killing trifecta. Resignation fell over her like a mantle. Was there anything that could happen to her in Vail, surrounded by baby boomers, that would bring her Midnight Prince one inch closer?

Chapter 2

"Mr. Cash," the balding judge intoned, boredom inscribed across his jowly face. "Your witness."

With that, twelve pairs of eyes locked focus on JD Cash. He jammed the tip of his thumb between his teeth, clamped down, but stopped short of ripping off the nail. He hoisted himself from his chair behind the plaintiff's table. The underlit and dated room in the Los Angeles County Superior Courthouse smelled like mustard and pickles, a byproduct of the lunch the jurors had eaten in the adjacent deliberation room. The odor upset his stomach. Worse, the air-conditioning was on the fritz.

Against his better judgment, he'd hired a jury consultant for the case. Never again. Five thousand dollars later, he sported a pink oxford and a three-piece navy suit designed to convey "power." These weren't his usual battle clothes. Not the cut or style he preferred, and he felt stiff and awkward. Like David wearing King Saul's armor. Plus, between his dress shirt, vest, and jacket, he felt as though the humid air was baking him alive.

JD approached the witness stand and stared down the shifty-eyed accident reconstruction specialist fidgeting in front of him. The diminutive Dr. Brady, whose height barely cleared JD's chin, wore a tweed jacket, bow tie, and circular, wire-rimmed glasses mashed up against a thick hedge of eyebrows. With his twitchy movements and magnified eyes, the man reminded JD of the barred owls that haunted the woods back home in North Georgia.

This case required a hard reset. HBA Transit Company had bullied his witnesses all morning. Right now—this moment—he could turn the tide if he dismantled the testimony of this pipsqueak hired gun and boomeranged all liability back onto HBA, where it belonged.

Help, God. The man who was killed by HBA's negligence left behind kids. JD looked over his shoulder. His eyes took in his client, sitting in the front row of the gallery. Towheaded eight-year-old twins sat beside their mother, who clutched a tissue in the hand pressed under her nose.

He skimmed his cross-examination questions one more time and shifted his facial expression from cordial to the "Afghanistan glare" he'd honed on his deployment to the Middle East. He crowded as close as possible to the witness box. Didn't want the jury looking at anything else in the courtroom except his hand-to-hand combat with the alleged expert.

Game on.

"Dr. Brady, you have a PhD in urban transportation planning. Am I correct?" He didn't need the written questions anymore. Adrenaline and hours of preparation had kicked in.

"Yes."

"And your résumé, labeled Plaintiff's Exhibit 32, says you've spent your entire career teaching about traffic management, gridlock reduction, and signage impact on driver confusion?"

Brady's Adam's apple bobbed up and down. "Yes."

"Roundabouts, double diamond interchanges?"

"Yes."

"But you're not an automotive engineer, are you?" JD leaned closer to Brady.

"No."

"Never worked for a trucking manufacturer?"

"No." Sweat dotted the expert's upper lip.

Now it was time to make the little owl unpopular with all the blue-collar folks on the jury—people he'd specifically selected during voir dire. JD locked eyes with the man who'd listed his job as *construction worker* on the juror questionnaire, then turned back to Brady. "Is it true you're charging five hundred dollars an hour for your testimony here today?"

Counsel for HBA sprang to standing. "Objection."

JD arranged his face to appear incredulous, pulled his mouth into a frown, and looked at the jury. "Withdrawn." Counsel for HBA knew the question was standard and acceptable when cross-examining expert witnesses. That was why the man hadn't stated a ground for his objection. No matter. JD had only asked to goad HBA.

The construction worker's lips slanted down. Probably thinking about the fifteen dollars a day Los Angeles County was paying him for missing work and fulfilling his civic duty. Point scored. Time to move on.

He faced the witness box. "Dr. Brady, I see no evidence on your résumé that you've ever done any research on calculating impact speed or vehicle approach energy. Nothing to do with large-scale reconstruction of crash sites. Nothing about the physics or mechanics of tractor-trailer units, or the reliability of energy absorption components in long-haul trucks."

He gave the jury a pointed stare. Wanted them to see he knew his stuff regarding semitruck accidents and the so-called expert didn't. "In fact, isn't this your first case testifying as an accident reconstruction expert?"

A snide smile curled Brady's lip. "Everyone has their first case, Mr. Cash. You yourself had a first case at one point." The doctor straightened in his seat and raised his chin a notch.

JD suppressed a snort. The little weasel was smug. "Yes, and I lost because I was inexperienced and out of my league, like you are today."

Counsel for HBA Transit launched to his feet again. "Objection. Mr. Cash is testifying."

"Sustained. Ladies and gentlemen, Mr. Cash's last statement is stricken from the record and is not evidence." The judge gave a little flutter of his fingers, indicating JD should move his questioning along.

He didn't care if he received a response or not. Throughout his questioning, he'd noticed a couple of jurors nodding in agreement, and one of them even had a slight smile, which she tried to hide by placing her hand over her mouth. He'd made his point.

"Your Honor, I renew my motion to exclude Dr. Brady's testimony," he said.

"Objection." A flurry of paper shuffling and muttering came from the HBA side of the courtroom. Both attorneys at HBA's table were on their feet.

"Approach the bench," the judge ordered.

JD snagged a legal pad and pen and hustled to the front. Counsel for HBA didn't appear as eager to face the judge.

"I'll tell you what, counselors." The judge leveled a calculating look at HBA's senior attorney and addressed them all. "We will adjourn for the day, and I'll defer my ruling on the motion to toss Dr. Brady's testimony until tomorrow at nine. I suggest you go out into the hallway and discuss settlement. If you don't, one of you will be very unhappy when we reconvene."

Bingo. All he had wanted to do was shake the defense's momentum. Now the judge was signaling he might bounce the doctor's testimony and destroy the foundation of HBA's case.

The judge gave a slight nod to Brady. "You may exit the witness stand."

The man stood. His hands trembled, and sweat slicked his brow as he left the stand to take his seat in the gallery. JD imagined a puddle left behind in the chair.

"Ladies and gentlemen"—the judge cast a stern gaze at the jury—"we are adjourned for the day. Remember, do not discuss these proceedings with anyone. Also, do not form an opinion until all the evidence has been presented to you and you are in your deliberations."

The judge descended from the bench and exited through a door on JD's left. The bailiff escorted the jurors from the courtroom via a door on the right.

JD inhaled and let out a stream of air. That had gone well. He leaned over the gallery railing, briefed his client on what he had discussed with counsel for HBA and the judge, and told her he'd call her if he made any headway toward a settlement.

He turned to the table heaped with trial gear. He picked up the first thing handy, a couple of evidence notebooks, and loaded up his rolling bags. Movement caught his eye, and he spied HBA's defense counsel slinking his way. A full day of proceedings had rumpled the worsted wool suit that encased the man's stout body.

"Hey, Cash." The guy's low-pitched voice tremored with worry.

The twerp spoke in a near whisper, so JD folded his six-foot, two-inch frame in half, bending to listen.

"It's been a long day." Stale breath reached JD's nose. "Lots of twists and turns. Let's talk settlement."

He'd taken on their expert witness and ripped him apart. The dude's meltdown on the stand would add a zero behind the dollar amount he'd hoped to recover for his client. "Sure." He jutted out his chin toward the doors at the rear of the courtroom and stalked off down the hallway, leaving HBA's attorney to follow in his wake.

Jayna Breigh

***

Victory. After forty-five minutes of back-and-forth and a couple of phone calls to his own client, JD and HBA had come to a handshake agreement on a settlement figure. The energy rush from settling the case propelled him through the hulking courthouse doors, down the accessibility ramp, and into the parking lot. HBA had caved to all JD's demands, and if everything went as planned, his client would receive a substantial and much-needed payout.

He loaded two dollies' worth of trial paraphernalia into his Wagoneer, climbed inside, and cranked the ignition on the vintage eighties behemoth. He made a call over the Bluetooth speaker installed next to the still-working tape deck.

"Jimmy Dean Cash and Associates. How may I assist you?"

"Monica," he shouted.

"Boss Man." Monica's excitement matched his. "I'm picking up good-news vibes."

"Affirmative." JD's cheeks pulled up with a smile.

The LA skyline had appeared drab and foreboding on his drive to the courthouse that morning. Now the late-afternoon sun sparkled and glinted off the downtown high-rises, a picturesque view to match his mood. "Start drafting up a settlement agreement for the HBA Transit case. They've agreed to our terms."

"Whoop whoop!"

Distracted by Monica's exuberance, he drifted into the adjacent lane. The toot-toot of an electric car jerked him back.

"Hold your horses, Monica. I can't cut a bonus check yet, but soon."

"I haven't had air-conditioning in my house all summer. Not complaining. Only stating facts."

Her words burst his elation like a nail in a tire. Standard procedure was to give bonuses after the firm received payment. He didn't mix money between his personal account, the firm's accounts, or the charitable trust he'd established. Keep the books clean and make an easy paper trail to audit. This, however, qualified as an emergency.

Monica wasn't only an employee but a former client and a grandmother. She was raising a teenager left parentless when a tractor trailer jackknifed on the 5 Freeway. His first case and first courtroom loss. She'd been so instrumental in helping him organize and gather information for trial that he'd taken her on as a quasi-paralegal and secretary all in one. He wanted to take care of her. She and her granddaughter, Julie, had sweltered all summer without air-conditioning? Knives clawed at his gut.

"You should've told me."

"I know. That's why I kept my trap shut. You're an awesome boss. I need to handle my business better."

"Well, always remember we're a family at Cash and Associates. I look out for my people. I got a guy who can fix it, and his prices are reasonable." He made a mental note to connect Monica with his contractor, Emmanuel. No one he referred to the handyman knew that JD's trust subsidized Emmanuel's super-discounted rate. Like the other things the trust did behind the scenes, he'd keep this part of his involvement with his secretary's HVAC crisis to himself.

He heard her sigh.

"You're the best, JD."

"I know. Quit slacking. Back to work."

Monica's peals of laughter rang in his ears as he disconnected the call.

***

At the door to his downtown condominium, JD yanked off the stupid tie the jury consultant had picked out and toed off his Italian oxfords. He couldn't wait to shuck the claustrophobia-inducing suit and send the whole ensemble off to Goodwill. Not his style.

He walked to his kitchen, guided by the waning evening light coming through the floor-to-ceiling windows in the high-rise. Traces of the lemon-scented cleaner his housekeeping service used still lingered in the air. He never let his place get super messy, but the couch needed an occasional touch-up to keep the leather soft. The chrome table and lamps showed every fingerprint, and the few knickknacks collected dust.

He ticked off his list of necessary things to nail down the settlement and secure the funds from HBA. Rhythmic throbbing started behind his right eye, and his elation tripped and fell into a pit of stress. His stomach squeezed, cutting off his train of thought. Monica regularly scolded him for his punishing work hours and the pressure he heaped on himself. "*This workaholic thing's got to stop. You're only thirty-six, but the bags under your eyes add ten years. Plus, your blood pressure's probably so high it could power the coffeepot!*" He flexed his neck back and forth. His vitals were fine, but there was truth in all of Monica's admonitions.

He opened the fridge and pulled out the store-brand jelly and milk. Turning to the sleek mahogany cabinets, he took down the peanut butter and the cheap white bread. He slapped together a PB&J, grabbed a mug, poured a glass of milk, and stood at the counter, savoring the comfort food and praying his headache would stop.

The childhood combo had been his mama's go-to fix-all. He eyed the three-thousand-dollar granite countertop and stainless-steel Sub-Zero. *You could take the boy out of the trailer park . . .*

The smoky roasted flavor of peanuts infused with grapey goodness acted like a time machine, causing his mother's words to drift through his consciousness.

"*Make something of yourself. Don't be like me.*"

"*Go into the bedroom. Turn the TV on good and loud. Don't want you listening to grown folks' talk.*"

Twenty minutes later, she would appear, centering her rail-thin body in the doorway to block him from seeing another loser stumble out of the front door—high, drunk, or both. Her usually porcelain skin would have a gray cast to it. Her blue eyes would be glassy and unfocused. She'd thrust forward a paper plate with a sandwich as a peace offering. "*Toasted the bread this time. Makes it nice and melty.*"

Drugs and poverty had sucked Mama down into a black hole, and he hadn't been able to save her. An all-too-familiar piercing of feline claws stabbed the big toe on his right foot. He wrenched himself back from the depths of childhood. Squinting, he made out the form of his chocolate-colored short-haired cat, Americano, in the dim light. The fuzzy ball of hair, with gray eyes and the attitude of a diva, ignored him or clung to him like gum on a shoe as the whim struck her. Based on the fur he'd found on his bed recently, she'd also resumed napping on his pillow while he was at work, which she *knew* was against the rules.

AN APPEARANCE OF IMPROPRIETY

She pounced on his toes again as he put the condiments away. Americano's antics lifted his mood for a moment. Another pair of socks would have snags in them. He bent and scratched her behind her ears. "You love the toe-pounce game, don't you, girl?" Now that Americano had his full attention, she made an imperious turn and swished her way out of the kitchen.

The sandwich killed the pulsing in his skull, and his traitorous mind marched right back to his waiting to-do list. He trudged down the dim hallway to his home office and flipped on the light. Jumbled stacks of papers sat strewn across his desk, out of place in the utilitarian and otherwise uncluttered space. He checked his watch. Eight o'clock. *Close it down by midnight, Cash.* A groan escaped. Fat chance.

The money didn't matter. All the hours. All the stress. He did it for his clients—the moms, their kids. Whether a settlement or a verdict at trial, every multimillion-dollar result and the various causes that money funded through the trust he'd created in Mama's name showed he'd fulfilled her wishes. Made something of himself.

Could the courtroom wins bring her back? No. The shame of his failure to protect her crowded in on him. He stopped rehashing his bleak childhood and forced himself back to the present. He was doing right by families in need. There was honor in his work. Plus, *no one* could look down on him, because when he strode in to try a case, he had more money in the bank than anyone else in the courtroom. No one could ever treat him like they'd treated Mama or him when he was a kid.

The check he would get from HBA would have six zeros behind it. Did the money make him a better person than other lawyers? No. It didn't. But it brought him respect. He might be trailer trash, but he was stinking-rich trailer trash.

Chapter 3

"All rise, the Honorable Judge P. Mahalia Jackson presiding." The buzz of lawyers trading gossip and war stories quieted to whispers. Deputy Franklin rocked back on his heels and linked his thumbs in his gun belt. "Silence all electronics." His head turned one way, then the other. The deputy surveilled the attorneys crammed on the opposite side of the railed partition that spanned the room, separating the seating gallery from the counsel tables, clerk's desk, and the bench.

Mahalia trained her stare on the morass of besuited lawyers outfitted with their assortment of legal pads, tablets, and briefcases, and slammed her gavel down twice. "Be seated."

She leaned toward the court clerk sitting to her right and whispered, "This is a zoo."

Judge Goldstein's accident on the Vail retreat threw her normal Monday morning docket into near chaos. The rumor mill placed the golden-ager either on the black-diamond slope or the jump area when he'd bruised his coccyx and torn a supporting ligament in his knee. But she'd been in the lodge when he'd come crashing down because of a spill in front of the hot cocoa machine.

Becky, Mahalia's clerk, scurried to the bench and handed her another stack of files.

"Who's that?" Mahalia muttered, nodding toward a wiry man in a rumpled suit who slouched in the back row. His cynical smirk and sharp, restless gaze made him stand out.

"Dinkelman," Becky whispered. "Reporter for the *San Gabriel Daily News*. He likes to stir up conflict and spread rumors." Becky sniffed. "He's

AN APPEARANCE OF IMPROPRIETY

always lurking around on Goldstein's floor, looking for a scoop big enough to get the *LA Times* to notice."

A scoff slipped out before she could stop it. Of course, this was how her morning would go.

"When's Judge Goldstein coming back?" Deputy Franklin asked.

"Not soon enough." The fold-down seats squeaked as the lawyers fidgeted, adjusted their papers, and otherwise waited for her to call court to order. Every seat was taken. "I think I have ten extra cases. Goldstein owes me. Big time."

"You got that right, Your Honor." He torqued up his face with disapproval and gave a knowing nod.

She called the first matter and worked her way through the calendar—getting status updates, setting trial dates, and figuring out where to delegate her mentor's cases. A distracting flash in the gallery kept catching her eye. There it was again. A glint of silver. Whoever he was, the attorney in the back row had an impressive mane of hair. Oh, for her future husband to reach retirement age with such a thick thatch. A sigh escaped. A girl could dream. Smiling to herself, she plowed back into her doubled workload, not looking up from the paperwork to call the next case.

"Number CC082917. *Hunt versus TransNation Trucking Corporation*." She scanned the petitions one more time, the noise of lawyers shuffling papers the only background sound.

"Counselors, are you ready to proceed with . . ." Mahalia lifted her eyes, but the words died off in her throat. Standing before her, not towering fifty feet in the air, was silver-haired, traffic-stopping Billboard Man himself.

"Yes, Your Honor. Jimmy Dean Cash, of Jimmy Dean Cash and Associates, PC, for Plaintiffs Ann Hunt and the Estate of John Hunt, here on a motion for substitution. We intend to replace the prior attorney of record." His voice rumbled into the courtroom at the low octave reserved for life-hardened country singers.

Traffic Stopper, whose tresses had captured her attention all the way from the back of the courtroom, raked his fingers through that thick hair. His hands were pale, but his face had a faint tan, which hinted that he didn't spend all his time in an office, or perhaps he had a sunroof.

Everything about him set him apart from her usual fare of cadaver-like corporate attorneys, a stodgier, less fashionable bunch who wore ultra-conservative attire. Cash sported an impeccable single-breasted charcoal-brown suit with a caramel tie. The tie, dotted with vivid blue, coordinated with a paisley square peeking from the jacket pocket. The ensemble sent up internal flares in that childhood part of her that had yearned to be a fashion designer, not the career professional her family had expected.

He had the confident, erect bearing of someone who'd spent time in the military. He stood immobile before her without a trace of the nerves that plagued insecure lawyers or the impatience that marked attorneys her grandfather would have labeled "big old donkey behinds."

"Max Sidwell, of Sidwell and Hopkins, for TransNation." The attorney standing at the defense table piped up. Sidwell, somewhere between fifty and sixty years old, based on his receding hairline and middle-aged paunch, nervously fingered the pages of the legal pad in his hand. "Your Honor, we filed my client's sworn declaration in this matter under seal. While we don't oppose the motion to change counsel, we object to Mr. Cash's refusal to extend the due date on the discovery requests served by the departing attorney. Our reasons are sensitive, so we ask to discuss this at the bench and not in open court. May we approach?"

Mahalia took a sip of water and cleared her throat. "Step forward, counselors."

Attorney Cash cut his eyes to Sidwell, snatched up his pen and legal pad, and made his way to stand before her.

Up close, she could see that Mr. Cash's gray hair overstated his age by ten . . . scratch that, by fifteen years. He was under forty, not an ancient, overworked trial attorney. Did he resemble Anderson Cooper from CNN? No. He looked nothing like the newscaster. Chris Noth? Nope. Still way too old. Ideas tumbled. Then, click. Early onset gray. His tanned skin had character lines, not wrinkles. Grooves etched the forehead and cheeks on his rugged face, like the cowboys in the old Westerns Granddaddy Henry used to watch on Saturday afternoons. Cash had weathered storms in his life.

Yet there was something else. *What?* He rubbed his eyes, as if clearing a lash. When he opened them, it took a second, but she figured it out. Attorney Cash had the saddest eyes she'd ever seen. As if he'd lived one hundred years of sorrow.

AN APPEARANCE OF IMPROPRIETY

Like a shiny toy, a new lawyer in the courtroom always cut through the tedium, but it was time to corral her mind back to the matter at hand. "You coming, Mr. Sidwell? You're the one who requested this little conference at my bench. We don't have all day." She eyed TransNation's counsel as he struggled to get his paperwork together.

"Sorry, Your Honor."

Her conscience pricked. Her terseness with Sidwell was uncalled for. "That's okay, counselor." There. She'd apologized. Somewhat. "Let's hear your arguments. Sidwell, you go first."

Sidwell's client had a doozy of a reason for wanting privacy. Her eyes pulled wide at the story rushing out of the man's mouth in hushed tones. Not only had what happened in Vegas *not* stayed in Vegas, it had sent two TransNation executive VPs to the emergency room. A trick involving handcuffs, a rookie magician, and superglue had fused the men's hands together at the wrists. The doctors had deployed stitches, antibiotics, and painkillers to make everyone whole again.

The reporter—Dinkelton, or whatever his name was—sat perched on the edge of his chair, neck craned, eyes narrowed, as if he were trying to read her lips. She lowered her voice further and shifted forward to ensure her words didn't carry beyond the assembled attorneys. Deputy Franklin's fake coughing spasm covering his laugh fooled no one. The court reporter sported a beet-colored blush. Sidwell appeared chagrined and strained to keep a straight face while he asked her to swap out deposition witnesses.

Hunt v. TransNation had started with a bang, but Goldstein would recover soon, and she could push this case right back on him. What was it about this case that piqued her interest? A groan welled up inside her. Didn't have to think hard. Her cases were boring. One multinational conglomerate versus another, both represented by stodgy, bloviating attorneys. Maybe it was the chance for a few courtroom fireworks? David and Goliath locked in battle, with a quick-on-his-feet attorney to keep things interesting? *Never going to happen.* Given Goldstein's otherwise hale constitution, he'd recover in record time, and she'd never see Cash again.

She slammed down her gavel. "Call the next case, Deputy Franklin."

"Yes, Your Honor."

Jayna Breigh

***

JD sat in the courthouse hallway, organizing his papers and preparing to leave. The unnatural grayish glow of the bulbs in the ceiling fixtures reflected off the polished floors. Judge Jackson had handed him a win and a loss. She'd granted his motion to substitute in for the previous disaster of an attorney who'd represented the Hunts, but she'd simultaneously granted TransNation's request for more time to respond to his questions and told him to expedite deposing their expert witness. Plus, she had put the case on the fast track for trial.

Jackson was rushing the case along, while TransNation was deploying stall tactics. The company had an army of litigators on this case. He still needed time to go over everything thoroughly, digest the facts, and prepare his plan of attack. Maybe if he pulled a stunt like TransNation and glued himself to a tree or a rock, he could get the case slowed down. Stress flared, and he bit at his thumbnail, but stopped short. He *almost* had the nail-biting controlled.

It would be a rough couple of months. Hadn't had a chance yet to meet with Ann Hunt face-to-face, but he'd committed himself to her cause after listening to her message on his hotline. He'd replayed the recording over and over. The quaver in her voice. The money she'd already shelled out for an attorney who'd never tried a tractor-trailer accident before and was flailing under the crush of paperwork marching in from TransNation's lawyer bots. But what had sealed his fate was the three-second aside Ann had made. He'd heard a kid calling out to her in the background.

"One minute, baby. I'm on the phone," she'd soothed.

He couldn't understand the next words, but it was the voice of a toddler—scared, weepy.

Ann Hunt again. "*I know, sweetie. I miss Daddy too.*"

The heart-jerking exchange between mother and child had hit him like a pile driver to the gut. Instinct kicked in, and he'd decided that moment he'd take the case.

He recalled the hearing with Judge Jackson. *Collected* usually described his mental state in the courtroom. But not today. After figuring out Goldstein's empty courtroom was the wrong place to be and double-timing it to Judge Jackson's courtroom two flights down, he'd been off-kilter the remainder of the morning. It hadn't been his usual floor or his normal crowd.

AN APPEARANCE OF IMPROPRIETY

There'd been harrowing chatter concerning Goldstein, a skiing accident, and a medivac helicopter. The scuttlebutt said other judges would babysit Goldstein's cases until he returned to the bench.

JD's mind also stumbled over the new judge. She was a wild card in terms of judicial temperament. He'd never been in front of her before. But worse, distracting wasn't a strong enough word to describe how she looked. It was like a tractor beam had possessed his eyes, riveting his attention on her. She was flat-out gorgeous.

He'd picked up some Italian when stationed in Italy with the JAG Corps. The word *ebano*, in the lilting tones of the region, had floated through his mind as he'd admired her flawless ebony skin. Her elusive smile gleamed like stars against a matte sky. She'd pulled her braided hair back into a severe bun. The style complemented the delicate sweep of her cheeks. Judge Jackson's standard-issue judicial robe was the opposite of a fashion statement, but she had a lemon sherbet–colored scarf peeking out from under the neckline of the drab garb. The color highlighted the rich tone of her skin and framed her graceful neck.

He grunted. Even if he had one second of free time for a woman—which he absolutely did not—Judge P. Mahalia Jackson was 100 percent, completely and totally off-limits. There would be allegations of impropriety against Judge Jackson if there was even a hint of something between her and someone whose case she presided over. Didn't matter, anyway. He'd sworn off all romantic entanglements years ago. His mama's death at the hands of an abuser while he was still in high school had altered the trajectory of his life. After a tour of duty in Afghanistan, he dedicated himself to fighting for the legal rights of widows and orphans. *Lord, please help me focus.* He hoisted himself, grabbed up his briefcase, and stalked to his car.

***

LA Hearsay Chat Board

4thEstatePitBull: TransNation case already a mess. Jackson's completely out of her depth. Someone tell me I'm not the only one watching this train wreck.

1st&Goal: Will keep my ears open. Sounds like the kind of thing that could blow up.

MotionDenied42: What's the big deal? Trucking companies are always in court for something.

4thEstatePitBull: This is reality-show gold! A "grieving widow" with $$$ in her eyes, a showboat attorney, and a rookie judge.

Chapter 4

JD ZEROED IN on Ann Hunt. She sat on the edge of a tattered sofa bearing the telltale stains of spilled juice boxes and grubby hands. The drive down her street had revealed house after house in tract-home beige. Her interior was the same oatmeal color. She dabbed and re-dabbed a crumpled wad of tissue against her eyes but missed most of the tears dripping down her cheeks.

Ann's harried-mom uniform—faded-black yoga pants and a "Mama Needs Coffee" T-shirt—had seen better days. Toys and discarded children's clothing covered the worn laminate flooring in the cramped living room. She stared off into the distance and ran her hand through shoulder-length, wispy blond hair, which showed two inches of light-brown roots.

"Tell me about your husband, John." JD shifted his notepad to his knee and placed the tip of his pen on the paper. He slowed his breathing and steeled himself for the emotional torrent that might ensue.

Ann fixed her eyes on a point somewhere behind him. "He was my everything." Fresh tears streamed.

"Take your time." He fingered the crease in his slacks. No matter how many living room sessions he conducted, they never got easier. He'd open with softball questions and transition her into discussing the accident that took her husband's life. "Start with his job."

"Johnny—well, I called him Johnny. His name was John. Anyway, Johnny worked at the logistics and distribution center. Right off the interchange." Ann angled toward a toddler bounding into the room. The kid wore nothing more than an unsnapped onesie and a sagging Pull-Up.

"This is my baby boy. Dylan, say hi to Mr. Cash."

The child waddled to him on flat feet and smacked JD's thighs with his small fists.

"Hey there, big fella." JD grasped both the boy's hands in his and jiggled his arms, eliciting a squeal from the child.

"Caylee, come in here. Get your brother."

A tween girl entered the room. Her long brown hair was pushed back severely by a tie-dyed hairband, making her buck teeth more prominent.

JD's heart squeezed. "You have a lovely family."

"Thank you. Where were we?" Ann swept a wrist under her eyes. "Oh yeah, Johnny worked out at the warehouse as an assistant to the graveyard shift supervisor. He'd only had that job for six months."

JD didn't interrupt. He'd let the story unwind at her pace.

"When Johnny landed the position, it allowed me to stay home with Dylan. He'd put in for the shift over a year ago. Things were tight, but he said he'd always wanted me to be here full time for our kids."

A few seconds ticked past in silence. It was time to steer the conversation onto the painful topic. He made sure he faced her square on and uncrossed his ankle from over his knee. "That night." He cleared his throat. "What do you remember?"

"I got a call at four thirty in the morning. That was when Johnny had his usual break . . . although I never understood why they called it a lunch break when it happened two hours before breakfast time. Later a coworker told me Johnny'd headed out to grab his favorite breakfast egg burrito and some coffee." Ann gave a soft snort. "Anyway, the caller's voice was robotic. 'Ma'am, there's been an accident,' he said."

JD trained his eyes to look at a spot between her nose and forehead so she knew she held his full attention but didn't feel he was staring at her. "What did you do next?"

"Woke a neighbor to come over and watch my kids. Then I went to the hospital. Looked for someone to help me, asking anyone I saw if they'd seen my Johnny. A nurse came. She walked me to a door, opened it, and pointed at a chair. I remember I wasn't chilled, but I was shivering. She said somebody would be with me soon. I kept wondering why they wouldn't let me see my husband. How long? No idea. Five minutes, an hour. A lady in a business suit came in, followed by a man with a clergy collar. When I saw him, I knew. They asked me if there was anyone . . ." She choked back a sob. "While I identified my husband's . . ."

AN APPEARANCE OF IMPROPRIETY

He held his hand out to stop her. "We can end here for now." He nodded and looked away, giving her another moment.

Ann's story ripped JD's heart out. There were plenty of reputable trucking companies, but the rotten apples on the road were rolling time bombs.

"Weird thing. He looked asleep. Like he was napping." Pain laced her words. "The trooper told me internal injuries killed him. The trailer of the truck had jackknifed and flipped over the roof of my husband's car. But his face had remained unharmed."

"What else did the officer say?" JD had read the police report, but he wanted to see what other facts she remembered from that time.

"The trooper said the rig hadn't maintained its lane. And he said from the marks on the road, it was obvious the truck was traveling well above the speed limit."

"Have any insurance companies contacted you?"

"Yes, TransNation's insurer called me. They offered us one hundred thousand dollars. I could use money like that, Mr. Cash."

He nodded. "The six-figure offer means they want to stave off a lawsuit, and it's evidence that they're trying to hide more costly liability. I want to help you and your family. These are the kinds of cases I handle." The situation was tragic, but he sensed this time he could nail the company to the wall.

"TransNation's been unsafe for years. Now they've crossed the line into reckless homicide." Surprised to find he was on his feet and pacing, JD halted and faced Ann. "Your husband's accident is not the first involving a TransNation driver. But it may be the worst. I want their trucks off the road. Litigation takes an emotional toll, but I will walk with you through the process." A framed poster hanging on the wall snared his attention. "Footprints in the Sand." He studied the poem superimposed over a photo of a beachfront. Trials ground clients down, and usually someone cried "uncle" before a case made it to a jury. Good to know Ann relied on God for strength.

He removed a business card from his breast pocket and handed it to her. "Here's the name of an organization that can help if you need something to tide you over." The card was for an assistance program for widows and orphans that his charitable trust helped support. "Clothes, grocery money."

Jayna Breigh

Water pooled in Ann's eyes.
"Are you ready to do this together?"
"Yes." Despite her tears, her voice held firm resolve.

***

JD merged his car into traffic on the Santa Monica Freeway. Other cars kept a wide birth from the ancient, imposing Wagoneer he'd purchased after his army tour of duty in Afghanistan. He slid his mom's old Steely Dan cassette tape into the deck. Cases like the Hunts' were the reason he'd gone into private practice. Guys who made careers of the JAG Corps or corporate law had stable, secure jobs with preset trajectories. But his heart gravitated to widows and orphans, so he fronted all the costs himself and bore the risk of failure alone. His mother hadn't been a widow, just defenseless, single, and poor, with a son too weak to protect her.

His thoughts jumped back to junior high, when his mom lay crumpled in the bathroom, wearing a thin-strapped tank. Her pale arms bore greenish, finger-shaped bruises. Someone had grabbed her—hard. They'd squeezed and gripped and pulled. They'd manhandled Mama. She'd done her best to shield JD from the consequences of her own terrible choices and the worthless men who sought her out. And he'd tried to save her. But he'd failed. A domestic abuser had killed her.

Ann Hunt's case was one more chance to make good on the promise he'd made to himself—he'd escaped Spring Creek, and now he was atoning for his many, many failures. Jimmy Dean Cash & Associates was the public face of his work. The charitable trust handled matters via back channels. By his personal reckoning, he was nowhere close to paying his debt to his mom. A debt he owed because he hadn't saved her from herself and her abusers. It was impossible now, but he could and would pay it forward through his clients. A stray thought, sharp and unexpected, hit him—what if he could have a family of his own someday? The image of a house filled with laughter and the kind of stability he'd never known came and went like a flash of light. He chuffed out a rueful sigh. Not in the cards. The strains of the saxophone solo from "Deacon Blues" swelled in the Wagoneer's interior. Could he fulfill his promise to follow Mama's admonition and make something of his life? He'd given up the scotch whisky, but when all the dollars and court cases were tallied, would he be a winner? A loser? Time would tell. JD rolled his window down and cranked up the volume on the theme song for his life.

Chapter 5

MAHALIA ENTERED HER chambers and walked to the mini blinds covering the windows. She twirled the long wand to slant away the glare from the early-morning, late-August sunshine. Stinging heat increased on the fingertips holding her mocha, purchased at the little courthouse kiosk. She placed both the drink and her handbag on her desk.

Taking her seat, she wiggled her mouse. The computer yawned out of sleep mode, and emails loaded.

Another reminder from the Judicial Council to finalize and report the completion of her mandatory continuing education unit on ethics sat bolded and unread in her inbox. "I know . . . I know."

She clicked the next email from Gavel-Link CLE, the provider she was using to fulfill and track her credits.

> Under California Rule of Court 10.469, you must complete 30 hours by October 31. This is to remind you that in your CLE Tracker dashboard, you have finished four of the five online units to satisfy this requirement.
>
> Completed Modules
> 1. Conflicts of Interest
> 2. Ex Parte Communications
> 3. Gifts, Benefits, and Political Contributions
> 4. Use of Social Media and Public Commentary
>
> Outstanding Modules
> 1. Judicial Impartiality and Avoiding Bias

AN APPEARANCE OF IMPROPRIETY

Pffft. She rolled her eyes remembering module number four. There was no way she'd ever have a public social media account that would allow John Q. Citizen to stalk her and come egg her house. She bounced her attention over the remaining words in the email, skipping the details—disqualification . . . confidentiality . . . professionalism. A two-second perusal of her bank account would show there were no outside financial influences or pecuniary gifts affecting her decisions.

She closed that email down, gave her mocha another tiny sip, and opened a missive from her mentor. Judge Goldstein requested she meet with him and do him a "little-bitty" favor. She blinked, and her thoughts U-turned at his words. He hated email and texting, yet here he was trying to hide behind technology. *Sneaky old man.* He wanted to lasso her into juggling his caseload while he was on light duty and blackmail her into babysitting his pet project—the Junior Jurors. His bait, so tantalizing. A plum appointment to his Litigation and Trial Practice Committee. A perfect setup for her dream promotion. The hitch? Billboard Man ran the mock trial program.

The state bar encouraged judges and attorneys to cooperate on community projects, but really? This? From time to time civic work and court proceedings overlapped—no biggie. But she wished Mr. 1-800-Number looked like a two-horned toad and not a model from the Hugo Boss catalog. A groan welled up. She'd fast tracked Billboard Man's case on her active docket, so until Goldstein got back on his feet, she'd be stuck with the larger-than-life Attorney Cash.

Pharrell Williams's earworm from the morning commute danced around in her brain, taunting her. "Happy." Clap, clap, clap. "Happy." Clap, clap. Mahalia shot laser beams of death from her eyes into her computer screen. With luck, they'd travel across Google's servers and pierce Goldstein's heart. She'd submit to his little ploy. Babysit his project while he recovered. But when her stint on this ended, he'd be getting a few choice words from her.

***

"If you want the position, you must play the game." Goldstein looked paler than usual and had gray circles under his eyes. He sat kitty-corner to his desk in an elaborate wheelchair, with his injured leg in a knee-immobilizing brace.

"I know. I know." She flopped back in her seat and huffed. "But for your information, Mr. Cash has a case before me on the bench. Further, how does babysitting elementary school kids translate into becoming assistant supervising judge?"

Goldstein's torso jiggled up and down while he laughed. "Must you always be so . . . so . . ." He moved his hands around in the air, attempting to conjure the word into existence. "*Farbisn*. Only you drive me to Yiddish with your hardheadedness."

His description of her was intractable. Or was it stubborn? Tenacious? No matter. He always sang the same tune.

"What can I say?" Mahalia lifted and dropped her shoulder. "I'm hard to budge."

A woman in her mid-forties shuffled in, balancing a teetering stack of files that she deposited on Goldstein's cluttered desk with care.

"Thanks, Angie."

"Of course, Your Honor."

Angie offered Mahalia a polite, tight-lipped smile before slipping out the door.

"Who was that?" Mahalia asked. The woman's expression had an air to it. Hard bitten? World weary? She wasn't certain how to describe it.

"Ah, yes. Up in the rarified air where you practice, you don't mingle much with the hoi polloi," Goldstein teased. "She's Angie Kane—recently promoted and transferred over from the juvie courthouse near USC. Dependable. Hardworking. She hasn't been here long, but she's lightning fast getting me the files and documents I've requested, and I've seen her here after hours as well."

Maybe the woman had a sick husband at home? Money problems? With over fifteen hundred employees in the courthouse on any given weekday, everyone had a backstory. She dismissed her unease. Goldstein was an excellent judge of character.

Goldstein clapped his hands together. "Now, where was I? Oh yes. They're not elementary kids," he scolded lightly.

An image of a hulking edifice surrounded by a barbed-wire fence, with vast swatches of surface defaced by graffiti, sprung up in her memory. The school garnered coverage at least once a month in the *Times* or on *Eyewitness News*. Failing test scores, gangs. Granddaddy Henry had labored hard to ensure she never attended a place like City of Angels. He'd used his meager pastor's salary and the booth rentals he received from his barbershop to ensure she attended private schools.

Goldstein waggled an arthritis-gnarled finger at her, drawing her back to what he was saying. "Mr. Cash is a nonissue. We have the greatest legal system in the world. It would grind to a halt if attorneys and judges didn't work together on community service projects and other educational activities. He and I have run the program for several years, and he often has cases in my department. Everyone knows how the system works." He gazed off for a moment, then refocused on her. "I trust you and Mr. Cash implicitly. But you're both single, and this courthouse is full of gossips and busybodies. One bit of advice. Stay out of the appearance-of-impropriety zone"—he wiggled his fingers in air quotes—"and you'll have no problems."

Easy peasy. Her long-standing, bright-line rule covered it all—avoid dating courthouse staff, bailiffs, and lawyers. That eliminated almost all eligible men in the building. She'd never had an ethics complaint filed against her and wasn't about to start now. Professionalism was her middle name, and Goldstein knew it—or at least, she thought he did.

Okay, truth be told, after hours spent watching spy thrillers and Westerns on Turner Classic Movies with Granddaddy, she knew what a hardbitten, rugged hero should look like. Cash had the presence and features of stars from Hollywood's golden age, like Rock Hudson and Clark Gable, mixed with those of newer stars like Daniel Craig, but that shouldn't matter.

Did her mentor think she couldn't toe the line? She sucked her teeth. "I'm offended."

The old judge pierced her with his wizened stare and tossed off a dismissive wave. "Mr. Cash is an attorney of the highest ethics and integrity. He picks his clients with care, and his zeal is admirable." He pressed his lips together and gave an affirmative nod. "That one. He's on the angels' side. You will enjoy working with him on the Junior Jurors, and I think you'll learn to exercise your compassion muscle as well."

Goldstein's commercial for Cash insinuated itself into her thoughts.

Good to know he was a man of character, but she didn't want to think about that. She batted her mentor's words away and trotted out her ideal man in her mind's eye. Suave, debonair, and smooth. If Goldstein found someone like that, she might find some trouble to get into and she'd recuse herself immediately.

She dragged her mind back from its little getaway. "Don't you have any other projects I can work on for you?" Some people had a knack for dealing with teens. Granddaddy had corralled, cloistered, and constrained her to ensure that as the pastor's granddaughter, she spent as little time as possible with troubled youth. This whole project lived so far from her comfort zone that it had a different area code.

"Put your thinking cap on, *sheifele*."

Not fair. Old Goldstein had taken off his gloves. Whenever he called her his "little lamb," she thawed. His advice always came from a place of fatherly love.

"You're brilliant. Smarts aren't your problem, Mahalia. But you need to"—he winced—"brush up on your social graces."

He gestured to the ever-present jar of pistachios sitting on the desk, and she grabbed a handful. "Tell me how helping these"—she caught herself before saying *delinquents*—"underprivileged students helps me become assistant supervising judge?" She narrowed her eyes and pursed her lips for good measure.

Goldstein chortled again. He'd seen her heels-dug-in posture before and, as usual, wasn't buying it. "Mahalia, you need to prove that you care about the impact of the judicial system on our city. That you have the right temperament to supervise the judges and the other court staff."

"I have the right temperament."

"I know under that tough-as-nails shell you're a softy." He pinched the bridge of his nose between his fingers, which shoved his eyeglasses up against his bushy brows.

"But let the committee see more . . ."

"Administrative ability?" Mahalia supplied.

"No."

"Mediation skills?"

"No."

AN APPEARANCE OF IMPROPRIETY

"What?" She drew a complete blank.

"Heart."

***

Heart? I'll show you heart. Mahalia yanked open the back door to her chambers. Papers fluttered in protest from the forceful action, startling Becky, who was placing yet more documents on Mahalia's desk. Men didn't have to show heart. Being tough was a point of pride for a male jurist. For a female judge, a show of strength earned you various titles, all beginning with the letter *b*.

She watched as her clerk flitted around her desk. Becky's lips were moving, but no sound came out of her mouth. Was she one of those people who always kept up a running internal monologue? The clerk's nervous energy sometimes grated on Mahalia's nerves, but she gave the woman points for the pewter-colored pantsuit and light pink blouse.

"What was that, Your Honor?" Becky smoothed a clump of hair and fidgeted with a tiny silver cross around her neck.

Mahalia stopped the diatribe she'd been muttering under her breath. She strode to her chair and sat. Becky reached for the knob to retreat to the courtroom.

"You like working for me, right?" Mahalia's words pinned the clerk in place. A gazelle cornered by a lion.

"Um . . ." Becky's eyelids pulled open wide, and she kept darting glances at the door.

"I treat you well, don't I?"

The woman's chest contracted, and she receded into her clothing. "Yes, Your Honor." Becky's voice trilled up, as if she'd asked a question, not answered it.

"You don't seem sure." Mahalia inspected Becky's manicure-challenged finger, fiddling with that cross again.

"I, uh . . ."

"I'd appreciate your candor." Already this wasn't turning out like she'd planned. Her clerk's evasiveness had Mahalia on high alert.

"Well, Your Honor . . ." Becky's throat worked. "Mind if I sit?"

Mahalia arranged her face into a mask of compassion to keep the fire inside from exploding out dragon-style and scorching Becky where she stood. "Make yourself comfortable."

"I find your cases fascinating. Lots of complex proceedings come through here."

"But . . ."

"And I am privileged to work with you . . ." The girl didn't look at her directly.

"But . . ."

"You can be . . ."

"Go on . . ." She'd hurl all patience out the window if Becky didn't get on with it already.

"A little harsh."

"Harsh?" She clenched her jaw and clamped her teeth to hold back a sharp retort. "In. What. Way?"

"Well . . ." The clerk's fingers flew back to her necklace. "There's an expression, 'A gentle word can break a bone.' Or you know, 'You catch more flies with honey than with vinegar.'"

Since words failed her, Mahalia waved her hand around, giving Becky permission to continue.

"You don't smile. You're terse with the lawyers who appear in court. And . . ."

"You've got more?" How could there possibly be more?

"You're a stickler for the tiniest of rules." Her assistant's shoulders dropped from their elevation up near her ears. "But I respect you, ma'am. You are smart, honest, and . . . well, I hope this is useful."

"It is."

"Anything you need, Judge. You can count on me." A shy smile appeared on Becky's lips. "Is that all, Judge Jackson?" Becky sat on the edge of the chair. "I want to help you in any way I can."

"Yes—"

The clerk had made it to the door and yanked it open before she could finish the thought.

"One more thing."

Becky turned back to face her.

AN APPEARANCE OF IMPROPRIETY

"Thanks." The word squeezed out between Mahalia's pursed-together lips.

***

Goldstein's and Becky's words rattled around Mahalia's noggin like two loose marbles as she mounted the dais and took her seat behind the bench. Summer vacations had come to an end, and things ramped up at the courthouse. Now that their July admissions to the bar were behind them, newly minted associates with a few weeks of training under their belts packed the courtroom to appear on low-stakes motions. With all the novices on hand, the docket bordered on a clown show.

Painful self-awareness produced an out-of-body experience. Mahalia measured every word and gesture while interacting with the newbies, and she dialed back the inclination to bark orders like a drill sergeant breaking in new recruits.

"Counselor, *please* don't walk between my bench and the counsel table. That area is called the 'well.'" She made air quotes with her fingers. "And it's off-limits." She aimed a pointed stare at the space in the courtroom separating her from the attorneys.

The ginger-haired newbie attorney quaking behind the table turned beet red.

A cell phone blared.

She pinned another Doogie Howser–aged lawyer with her glare and ratcheted down her ire. "Remember to *please* silence all electronic devices." A flurry of hands jamming into briefcases and purses to turn off ringers ensued. Why could they not remember the simplest of protocols? Didn't they know the rules existed for a reason?

"*Please* do not refer to me as Judge. Call me Your Honor or Judge Jackson."

If another attorney named Jayden, Braydon, or, heaven help her, Justin came before her today, she'd scream. Every time an attorney with a boy-band name stood and addressed her, she imagined him ripping open his button-down and taking a selfie after her ruling.

The day dragged out at the tedious pace of a DMV line. At the stroke of four o'clock, she threw in the towel, smacked down her gavel, and clamped her temples to ease the pounding behind her eyes. If the day's events were any sign, this personality makeover might kill her.

***

Misdemeanor Order Diversion Pursuant to Penal Code § 1001.95

Defendant was charged with cyber harassment under California Penal Code § 653.2.

Pursuant to California Penal Code § 1001.95, the Court hereby orders:

1. Defendant shall participate in the Los Angeles County Superior Court–sponsored Junior Jurors Program, administered by Jimmy Dean Cash, Esq.
2. The diversion period shall be for the remainder of the current school year.
3. Conditions:
    + Defendant must comply with all rules and requirements.
    + Defendant shall submit monthly progress reports.
    + Defendant shall not commit any additional offenses.
4. Upon successful completion of the diversion program, the Court shall dismiss the harassment charge against Defendant.
5. If Defendant fails to comply with the terms of this order, the Court may reinstate criminal proceedings.

IT IS SO ORDERED.

Chapter 6

CALM. JD CLOSED his eyes tight and prayed for calm. The first week of September and his first Junior Jurors meeting of the year started in one hour. Now Judge Goldstein, who regularly lamented about how much he hated texting, had blown up his day with fewer characters than a post on X.

He pulled his phone out of his pocket and swiped up, hoping magic would change the message he'd stared at for a full thirty seconds the first time.

> Mr. Cash, I cannot assist with the Junior Jurors program this term. Glad to report that Judge Mahalia Jackson has agreed to be my replacement. She has a Litigation and Trial Practice Committee meeting and may be late. Sorry this is last minute. These bones are taking their own sweet time to heal.

Since stalling couldn't hold off the future, he hoisted himself into his Wagoneer, slammed the door, and mashed the tape into the deck. He and Goldstein had a rhythm. They'd worked together several times and had already gone over the year's agenda months ago. The rumor mill had clarified that it was merely a garden-variety slip and fall and not a near-death experience. Given Goldstein's age, the two might be the same thing.

He blew out a long breath. He'd done committee work with jurists handling his cases, but never with a woman as breathtaking as Judge Jackson. It wasn't her beauty alone. It was the way she carried herself. The last time he'd felt this drawn to anyone, he'd been a different man—before that night on combat deployment. He would, however, control himself.

Before the firefight, he'd lived his life with one foot planted in the world and, to hedge his bets, the other foot half-heartedly on the ground of shaky faith. His folly had become crystal clear when the carnage of war showed him his mortality. After the haze of the battle had cleared, he'd pledged to lock his life down like a monk and eliminate all the things distracting him from his commitment to the Lord. No booze, no smokes, no women. He was a single breath from eternity, and he would do as God commanded—look after orphans and widows and keep himself from being polluted by the world.

His thoughts spun as he exited his car, gathered his gear from the rear hatch, and navigated to the courthouse on autopilot. How often had Monica told him, "Go home. Get some sleep. You work way too much, and you can't save them all, Boss Man." She urged him to take a vacation. Spend his money on a man toy like a boat, a plane, classic cars. Anything to stop his self-imposed and relentless grind.

Could a multimillion-dollar win bring Mama back? Could it erase the horrors of war from his mind? No, but he would pay it forward. Again and again. Rescuing as many moms and their kids as he could. Fishing the Junior Jurors from the choppy sea of the inner city before life sucked them down in the undertow. The time he sacrificed was worthwhile. It smoothed the way for the kids to have opportunities he'd had to scrape and claw to obtain for himself.

The strategy, simple. Feed them and give fist bumps. He poured love and information into the students. Arranged college scholarships via his charitable trust. This year he'd have to monitor a kid with a diversionary order in force, but he'd only had a handful of washouts since he founded the program. He wasn't worried. At least not about that. It was already dicey mixing academic content and teen drama. Job one—keep everyone in check. Starting with himself. The jinglejangle of "I Walk the Line" by Johnny Cash bounced out of the speakers. Walk the line was an understatement. He'd be on a tightrope juggling bowling balls, between all these kids and his unexpected attraction to Judge Jackson.

A diverse assortment of teens filed into the cavernous courtroom. JD remembered a few from the prior year, and several were new. The girls advanced into the room first. The boys hung back and gawked. There were nervous giggles and outfit adjustments. They weren't the only ones on edge. He checked the time. Judge Jackson could walk in at any second. His gut did a weird clinching thing. He tried multimillion-dollar cases for a living, but somehow her imminent arrival onto his turf had his stomach in knots.

The gallery chairs clacked as this year's crop of participants unfolded them and sat.

As the last kid settled into a chair, JD clapped his hands and rubbed his palms together. "Ladies and gentlemen, welcome to the LA Superior Court Junior Jurors Program. Glad to see some of our returning seniors here."

A petite girl with a prominent nose, large pretty eyes, and a mass of brunet spiraling curls stood and gave a beauty pageant wave to the other students.

"Thank you, Mercedes." The girl was bright. It would be a squeaker, but she might qualify for entry into a Cal State school next fall. He'd scanned her grades and was receiving regular updates from her teachers about her progress.

Mercedes shrugged and squinched her face, as if to brush off the limelight she'd sought.

"Quincy, you're a senior. Why don't you stand up too."

The boy's brown face sported a broody half smile offset by hair standing three inches tall, with zigzag parts cut into the sides. He unfolded his rangy frame from his seat, gave a slight bow, and flopped back down.

"Dig the high-top fade, Quincy." JD nodded in the teen's direction. "For the rest of you who are new, I'm Attorney Jimmy Dean Cash. You can call me Mr. JD, Mr. C, or Mr. Cash. There are two reasons you're here. Either you volunteered for this program, or the school has disciplinary charges against you. Those of you in the latter category aren't here because you're dumb—you're here because your teachers see something in you. Potential that you're letting slip away."

"Hear that? You're not dumb—you got potential." A pale teen in a

T-shirt and hoodie slapped the back of the head of the boy beside him. A few moments of roughhousing erupted.

"Settle down, guys. Settle down. Anyway, as I was saying, the program is a crash course in understanding our civil judicial system, and you'll take part in a mock trial."

Head Slapper sucked his teeth and plopped down onto his seat. Several other students on that side of the room hunched together, looking at something held in one girl's lap.

JD strolled toward the klatch and came to a halt, towering over them. "Rule number one—no phones." He gave a fixed stare until a graceful Black girl with thick braids and a confident smile dropped the phone into her purse. He motioned to her with his hand. "What's your name?"

"Aisha. And these are my girls, Destinee and Brittany." She pointed to her crew.

Brittany's wavy hair contained various shades of blond. She sported a braid that fell off to the side, adorned with a feather. Destinee, with a medium-brown complexion, wore large hoop earrings. Her puffy blouse was splattered with every color of the rainbow. Teen fashion never ceased to amaze.

"Nice to meet you. And thank you, Aisha, for putting your phone away."

He pivoted and strode back toward the center of the room. "Rule number two—we will respect each other at all times."

From the rear of the courtroom, a snort sounded. JD whipped his head around, but the culprit wasn't obvious.

"Gentlemen, your names, please."

The boys slouched and posed.

JD sucked in his lips to hold back a smile. Knew exactly what it was like to be sixteen, seventeen and trying to impress girls with ginned-up machismo.

"I'm José." The teen wore a green-and-white-checked flannel, blue jeans, and coordinating green-and-white high-top Chuck Taylors.

Internal alarm bells rang. José had been flagged by the principal as a student who walked a fine line, his charm masking a history of close calls. In addition, José's clothes had a gang vibe. "José, those aren't the colors of your set, are they? Because no gang colors allowed in here." The no-gang-colors rule was nonnegotiable. The penalty, immediate expulsion. Couldn't risk the safety of the other students.

"Nah, man. Green means you're neutral, dude. A hustler," José intoned in a melodic voice. "I'm all about the papers, like you. Cash money, baby." José gave the kid next to him an elaborate handshake involving slapping palms and wiggling fingertips.

"Good to know on both counts. Stick with this program and you could earn a respectable living." JD tipped his chin up, gesturing for the kid next to José to go next.

That boy tossed up a peace sign. "Devin." He made a face full of smolder, and several girls giggled.

Kyle, a senior and a candidate for intensive dermatology, spoke up next. His student records documented a near perfect SAT score but also a penchant for hacking into computer systems.

"I'm Langston." The legs of the soft-spoken bean pole sprawled into the aisle. He had to be at least six-foot five or six. His file said he was a starter on the school's basketball team. Childcare for three siblings created an attendance problem.

"Tanner, with a *T*" sat to Langston's right, looking like he starred in a movie with werewolves and vampires. He flashed a smooth grin and adjusted the pins on his letterman jacket. Something about him seemed overly practiced. JD regarded Tanner's jocular self-confidence. His file said he was in line for a full-ride football scholarship and had potential endorsement deals in the works. The boy and his coach had committed to his attendance at the meetings. JD genuinely hoped Tanner could juggle his time so that it all worked out. Hopefully, neither he nor any of the other kids would give JD any trouble this year.

"Rule number three—have fun."

"Now there's a rule I can obey," Devin, the head slapper, said.

In the corner, the boys gave each other dap and fist bumps. JD failed at his attempt to suppress his grin.

"Throughout this program you will need to take notes so you can prepare for your mock trial. Quincy, please come up here and help me pass out the notebooks and pens."

JD walked to the front of the room. "First question. Do you know the names of the parties in a civil lawsuit?"

No one had their hand up. "Okay, I'll draft one of you if no one takes a shot at answering."

"The plaintiff and the defendant?" Destinee's voice warbled higher.

"Correct. It's not like *NCIS* or *Law & Order*. A civil suit is not about criminals and prosecutors. Instead, it solves problems by having one person give another person money."

"See, that's what I'm talking about." José tossed his thoughts into JD's monologue.

"And who decides the winner and loser of a civil case?"

"The jury," someone shouted.

JD turned to the interactive whiteboard behind him and tapped it a few times to pull up his notes on the large screen. He wrote "plaintiff," "defendant," and "jury" on the board.

"I am a plaintiffs attorney. My clients sue trucking companies that have injured people in accidents."

"Yeah, I've seen your billboard." José snickered. "Tacky."

"Saw it too—800-555-CASH. I got this," Langston called out.

"You may call it tacky, but I say it's worth every cent I paid, since you've got it memorized."

"You ain't wrong about that, Mr. C," Destinee said.

He waited a beat for the fun to die down. "Most cases take months to get to trial because you have to gather evidence to determine how much money you think the defendant should pay your client. The name for the investigative process is *discovery*. Write that word down."

"I get it. I get it." Brittany bubbled with enthusiasm. "You're trying to *discover* what happened."

He never tired of the lightbulb moment on the kids' faces. "That's right. Okay, write this down too. In the beginning of a lawsuit, determining two crucial things is essential. First, whether there are any documents that support your case. Second, if there are any witnesses."

Mercedes furiously scribbled notes, and Quincy seemed locked in.

Their focus encouraged him. He tapped the edge of the whiteboard absently with his fingertips, his mind flipping through ways to challenge them further.

"Is this where subpoenas come in?"

AN APPEARANCE OF IMPROPRIETY

JD scrutinized Kyle. With Kyle's hacking history, the boy might have seen a subpoena or two already. "Excellent question. Almost. Let me walk you through the steps."

He swiped open a tab on his phone and cast the notes so they displayed on the board. "Here's discovery in a nutshell. I send questions that ask who, what, where, when, why. Who knows any relevant facts about this case? Produce for me the documents supporting these facts. What things are you willing to admit are true up front? The other side must provide answers to your inquiries, give you requested documents, and either confirm or refute the relevant facts."

"So boring." José made snoring noises.

"Yes, it can be tedious," JD admitted. "Once your opponent has responded to all your written questions and given you the documents you asked for, you subpoena all the witnesses they've identified to testify under oath about the documents and to flesh out answers to your questions. It's called a deposition." He wrote "deposition" on the board.

"This is how you prep a case for trial. You take all the factual evidence the other side gives you—deposition testimony from defense witnesses, any pertinent documents they've turned over—and combine it with what you've learned from your client. Next, you assemble the relevant statutes and case law that support the legal basis for your claim. Finally, you compare your facts with the law. If the facts and law match, and if the jury agrees with you, you will win."

It was hard work, but putting in the extra hours on discovery paid off in the courtroom. No lawyer wanted a document he hadn't seen before or a witness pulled out of the hat at the last minute.

He flicked his cuff back and checked the time. When would Judge Jackson arrive? He hadn't experienced anticipation like this since that girl had agreed to meet him in the yearbook darkroom his tenth-grade year. She'd always smelled like Love's Baby Soft, what all the girls wore back then, and he'd only worked up enough courage to hold her hand that day.

"Mr. Cash?" Mercedes asked.

"Right, where was I?" *Get your head in the game, man.* He'd negotiated with terrorists in Afghanistan, for Pete's sake. Certainly he could handle a pretty co-facilitator. He adjusted his sitting position on the side of the counsel table. One foot on the floor, one leg dangling. "You look for people who are lying, whose deposition testimony doesn't match what the documents are telling you. Discovery bores lots of attorneys, but I think it's like working a puzzle."

Faces brightened and eyes lit up. Warmth permeated his chest and reminded him to concentrate on his real purpose tonight.

"So you're like a detective, ain't that right, Mr. C?" Quincy asked.

"Yes. Like a detective. But also like a scientist, a professor, even an actor. A talented lawyer sifts through the evidence. He sometimes must understand scientific facts, then turn around and write legal briefs. At the end, during the trial, he puts on a show for the jury, like a director, producer, and actor all merged into one."

"Like Tyler Perry. He writes the movies, stars in them, directs them, produces them. You got a Madea dress somewhere?" Aisha asked.

A stir arose from the students. He looked at his watch for the three hundredth time. Movement at the entrance to the courtroom caught his eye, and he spied Judge Jackson as she eased into the back. She was strikingly tall, and as she scanned the room, he realized that the robes had hidden a willowy figure—at present decked out in an emerald-green pantsuit with a pink blouse. The strong, clashing colors would overpower other women, but they made her features stand out like a classic Technicolor movie.

She'd stacked her hair in a topknot, and elongated geometric earrings accented her neck. Her shoes were ridiculous, clocking in at four inches or more. If she stood beside him, they'd be eye to eye.

He forced his mouth shut and coughed. She looked straight at him and smiled, forcing him to drag air into his lungs to talk. "We covered a lot."

"Yeah, I'm starving too," Quincy said.

Mercedes raised her hand. "Wait, where's musty old Judge Goldstein? Shouldn't he be here by now?"

"That comment wasn't necessary, Mercedes."

"Sorry, Mr. Cash." She slunk down in her seat.

"But now that you mentioned it"—JD motioned toward Judge Jackson—"Judge Mahalia Jackson will be with us while Judge Goldstein recovers from an injury. She's just joined us. I'll have her come forward, and you all can greet her while we have dinner." He pointed to the spread of sandwiches, chips, and drinks. "Fuel to help you finish your homework."

Mahalia half glided, half strutted to the front. Admiration shone on the girls' faces, and a few sat up, as if Mahalia's mere presence changed the way they perceived themselves. The outright stares and drooling by the guys might offset the benefit. He'd have to work on that. She stopped beside him and gave a professional nod to the students.

"First, I want to introduce you all to the judge. Judge Jackson is one of LA's youngest judges, and she's quite an accomplished woman."

A round of applause ensued, and there was one catcall.

"Settle down, Quincy. You and your parents signed off on the rules for the program when you joined. What's rule number one for guys?"

José stood. "We're gentlemen at all times."

"That's right, José."

"What's rule number two?" He pinned José with his stare.

Without a word, José hooked his thumbs in his belt loops and yanked his pants up. "No sagging your pants."

Quincy pointed at José. "Aw, snap. He roasted you, dude, without saying a word."

"Shut up, Quincy."

Tanner giggled like a six-year-old girl.

"Calm down, gentlemen." JD tensed his face so the kids wouldn't see him grinning at their antics.

"Glad to be here . . ." Judge Jackson stumbled over her words. ". . . ladies and gentlemen. I look forward to getting to know each of you."

Ladies and gentlemen? His malarkey detector went on high alert. Picked up that she didn't mean one bit of what she'd said. The stiff posture. The rigid face. She had so many tells that he'd clean her clock if she played poker. Had Goldstein tangled him up in a crazy spiderweb of resentment? If she'd been strong-armed, she might take it out on him or the kids. Or worse, his clients.

He ran through the parade of horribles trotted out in Torts class back in law school. The worst of the worst-case scenarios. Judges were human. Not everything in the law was black and white. If a ruling in his case came down to the judge's discretion, he wanted the judge to have a favorable opinion toward him and his clients. One false move might tank his lawsuit *and* the program. His priority now? Making sure the judge was happy and comfortable being on this service project.

He motioned toward the sandwiches and chips. "Don't forget to sign the attendance sheet to receive credit for today. Grab what you want, and I'll see you all next week."

The students filed past him on the way to the snack table. A cluster chatted with one another. Most kept their distance from Mahalia, but a few ventured to engage her in conversation. Even though he'd grown up small-town poor, and these kids were urban poor, their horizons were just as limited. Fierce protectiveness crashed over him. He'd simply need to balance his interactions with the judge carefully—in and out of the courtroom. Failure on either front wasn't an option.

***

Two girls sidled up to Mahalia, one on each side. It was rare that any female in a room stood at her height. What these two lacked in stature, however, they made up for in street assurance.

The one with a quirky sense of fashion involving feathers looked her up and down. "Great outfit. Those colors look good on you."

"Thank you."

"Do you make a lot of money being a judge?" This one had braids.

"Why don't you tell me your names first."

"I'm Aisha, and this is Destinee."

"Glad to meet both of you ladies."

The girls gave each other quizzical looks.

Her lack of comfort with teens must be showing. She'd always been driven in school and kept herself apart. Not because she didn't want friends. But family expectations overshadowed everything. Plus, there was her coloring, her height. She'd grown into her own as she got older, but she had missed a lot of youthful interactions. She knew she should connect with the teens, but her brain wouldn't engage.

Mahalia switched gears, and she tried to ratchet down the formality. "Well, to answer your question, being a judge is a public service job. It pays more than other jobs in government, but while a judge is on the bench, it's not about the money."

It was late. She was tired, and she'd come ill prepared. Time to push off the interrogation to another day. "Why don't we get to know each other better at the next meeting? Mr. Cash looks ready to go." She gestured in Cash's direction.

"Alright, Your Honor. Catch you later."

Mahalia gave a wave and an inward sigh of relief. She watched the backs of the girls as they filed out of the courtroom.

"That wasn't so bad, was it, Your Honor?" Cash's rumbling bass voice stood in sharp contrast to the magpie-like chatter emanating from the corridor.

"No. It wasn't." They had behaved well and were not the miscreants she'd expected. Shake her family tree and Quincys, Destinees, and Aishas would rain down. Teens from working-class homes, struggling schools, limited horizons. These kids weren't alien to her but were more like first cousins once removed.

But her branch—the Jackson branch—had pruned the deadwood and vines, leaving what were, according to Granddaddy, only the successful, thriving branches. Granddaddy and Uncle Harold tended those branches with love. Her grandfather had kept her as far away as possible from anyone who might taint her. He didn't want any slipups to hinder his line's reign in the educated "Afro elite," as he called it.

She associated only with her Uncle Harold's children. She and her cousins Martin and Leontyne huddled close together when at family events to avoid being bullied for their over-the-top aspirational names.

As she helped JD clean up the remnants of dinner, her consideration returned to the students. They were such a diverse bunch. Black, Hispanic, White. Dark. Light. The sting came back. Martin and Leontyne were light-tan colored. Their mother, Aunt Lena, had been lighter than that. Mama was a pinch darker than Aunt Lena.

Then there was Mahalia. Granddaddy's genes had combined with those of her absent father to create a color as inky as a starless night. She'd endured having her nose pinched and being told to tuck her lips in by Granddaddy's hundred-year-old mother, Great-Granny Bertha. Great-Granny wasn't happy that she had a great-granddaughter who pulled stares and negative comments about her deep-hued skin from the other deaconesses at church.

Granddaddy had worked hard to ensure the success of the future generations of his family. But there had been that one tare among the wheat. Mama. The wild child who'd gotten herself pregnant at age sixteen. Oh, they'd ushered her back into the fold. He didn't kick her out upon discovering her sin. But with the same iron determination with which he ruled his congregation, Granddaddy had laid down the law.

He and Granny would raise Mahalia as their own. He'd provide a private education and the finest life he could scrape together pastoring and running the barbershop. Mahalia's mother was always welcome to visit. But to return home permanently, she had to repent of her ways and be in church. Every Sunday.

Mama had agreed, and over time she'd finished college and become a teacher. A respectable profession. The trio lived a life dedicated to advancing Mahalia as far as they could. Granddaddy had not lived to see her become a judge but had seen her law school graduation. Beside his wheelchair sat her mother, plus Uncle Harold and his kids, Leontyne and Martin, who'd become an engineer and physician, respectively.

Mahalia dropped the last bit of trash into the receptacle and gathered her purse and briefcase.

"Your Honor." JD's voice brought her back to the present. "Like I was saying, I'll walk you to your car. It's late, and the parking deck will be empty." Hesitation sprang up. Her general policy was to refuse offers like this. Didn't want to provide any fodder for the courthouse gossip mill. But tonight was different. She and Mr. Cash were two professionals working on a community service project. They were peers. Colleagues. A security walk to the car was appropriate—no impropriety.

"Sure, I'd appreciate that, Mr. Cash."

They walked to the elevator, and she cast about for small talk while they waited. "How long have you been in practice?"

His gray hair and haunted eyes didn't match his fit physique. He could be anywhere from thirty to fifty.

JD tilted his head back and closed his eyes. "Basic training right after high school, then straight to Afghanistan. Reserves during college, and law school after that. Four years in JAG. Been in solo private practice since . . ." He held up a hand and counted off on his fingers. "About five and a half years. I'm thirty-six."

"Me too."

As she understood from Goldstein, he wasn't scraping by with low-ball settlements from insurance carriers. He'd won numerous multimillion-dollar verdicts. Was that true? Why was she so curious about him anyway?

"With contingent cases, isn't it feast or famine?" Ugh. She wished she could suck the words back inside. "Sorry. Don't answer that."

"No worries. It's all pretty much out there with the public trial verdicts. My clients are widows and orphans. Money can't bring back a family member. But add up loss of future earnings and loss of companionship, and tack on punitive damages . . . the verdicts are in the multimillion-dollar range." He shrugged.

She schooled her facial expression. All of that in thirty-six years? Given his military service, education, and net worth, it was like he'd jammed two lifetimes into one.

The elevator dinged, startling her out of her musings.

***

The doors on the old Otis elevator rattled shut. JD punched the button for the lobby, and the conveyance groaned and creaked its way down from the fourth floor. Apprehension crossed Judge Jackson's expression as she faced the glowing panel of lights marking their descent, and a light sheen of sweat broke out on her brow.

"I've never liked this thing. Grandfathered in. Historical architecture and whatnot." She pressed the back of her hand to her brow a few times. "Most days I take the stairs to the second floor, where my chambers are." Her voice was steady, but she straightened her back and exhaled.

"Well, it says right here, 'Inspected by Peter Vanderklump.' Rumor has it, he's the best." He tossed her a smile to loosen her up, and she lowered her shoulders.

She'd handled herself well in small talk with the kids. She'd smiled and nodded where appropriate. But her smile seemed forced, and her hand had drifted to the back of her neck several times, squeezing, as if to relieve tension. Teenagers weren't for everybody. Churlish one minute, needy the next.

Her background was a complete mystery. Who her people were. How she'd come up. She reminded him of the elite attorneys at the huge firms he often dueled with. Sophisticated and well spoken. Polished.

The Junior Jurors, and JD himself, seemed light years from Judge Jackson. They'd thrown out improper questions, but she'd been tactful and gracious with them. And they'd also tried to connect with her in a way they hadn't with the good-natured grandpa Goldstein. Perhaps it was providential that Arnold had assigned a successful African American judge. Didn't know why he hadn't come up with the idea himself.

At the lobby level, the elevator gave a little bounce, and the doors jerked open. The strain on Judge Jackson's face did not ease until she exited and was on the steady floor of the lobby.

"After you, Your Honor." He wheeled out his trial bags, which held the leftovers of catered food and utensils he'd taken into the courtroom.

"Night, Franklin," Judge Jackson called out.

The deputy did a double take.

JD suppressed a smirk and let Franklin off the hook. "Did all the Junior Jurors leave?"

Franklin pulled a face. "You working on that now, Your Honor? Not Judge Goldstein?"

"Yes. For now. Mr. Cash is walking me to my car."

Unless he was mistaken, Franklin's posture relaxed, but his glower at JD only softened to law-enforcement neutral.

"Alright. See you tomorrow, Your Honor." The officer broke off his death stare at JD.

They made their way across the street. The night air was typical for Los Angeles fall. Low-eighties temps and no rain in sight. A night where a gentleman would remove his jacket and place it over his lady's shoulders. His train of thought caught him off guard. He put the mental brakes on—hard—and reversed course.

At the parking deck, Judge Jackson gestured. "This is me."

JD choked back a guffaw when she pointed him toward the spaces reserved for electric cars. He hadn't known her long at all, but she had every appearance of a woman who'd wear real fur, eat rare steak, and drive a Porsche 911.

She gave an indignant sniff. "There are always spots available, and I can park close to the building."

He raised his hands in surrender. "I didn't say a word, Your Honor." Uncomfortable silence stretched and stretched.

"Well, Mr. Cash, I'm sure I'll see you in court soon."

"That you will. I'll wait till you drive off." Not a date. A professional courtesy for a legal colleague. Yet his insides twisted like a high school boy on his way to the prom.

Judge Jackson entered the Hot Wheels–sized car with royal grace and drove off with the eerie whir of all electric cars.

She was stunning, brilliant, gracious, and allergic to elevators. He was in trouble.

Chapter 7

JD WOULD SEE Judge Jackson today. Based on the preliminary order the clerk Becky had emailed him, she would consider and deny his motion. But he *would* see her, and that was enough to make the battle he'd fought on the 210 Freeway after a client meeting worth it. Now sitting in the courtroom, he rehearsed his talking points for the morning's hearing.

Unexpected speed bumps kept popping up in the TransNation case, throwing off his normal pretrial prep. He'd already played endless rounds of phone tag with Max Sidwell, attempting to arrange depositions, and had filed today's briefs to shift the dynamics of the case in his favor. Sidwell had opted for "jerk mode." Today JD would let TransNation know that if Sidwell wanted to play hardball, hardball he'd get. JD wanted to teach Sidwell a lesson. Namely, that continual opposition would be excruciating and expensive. He might go down in flames today, but he'd take Sidwell down with him.

Bright spot of the day—Judge Jackson remained on his case, for now. This was enough to make the otherwise unremarkable institutional beige courtroom sparkle with color and numb the pain created by the fold-down theater-style chairs in the gallery.

Lowly car-crash cases seldom ascended to the rarified air of the complex-litigation floor. He'd never seen this many high-end suits and solid-leather briefcases in one room. He pulled a face. When clients paid by the hour, the number of hours increased. He spied Dinkelman hunched in a back-row corner. The overhead lighting glinted off the bald spot barely concealed by his wispy comb-over. This floor wasn't his usual beat, but Dinkelman was a pit bull when it came to a story.

The chair beside him creaked, and JD looked over. There was a glimpse of pink that perked him up in a courtroom full of gray suits. An attractive, curvaceous blonde.

Her attention bounced off his hands and face, and a multi-watt smile appeared.

"This seat taken?"

Based on her accent, she was a Southern transplant, like him. "It is now." JD moved his briefcase and legal pad to make more room.

The blonde stuck out her hand. "Casey Chapman." She cocked her head to the side, waiting for a return greeting.

"Where are my manners? Jimmy Dean Cash. Pleasure to meet you."

Casey held on to his hand for a beat past professional. "A Southern gentleman, I see."

"North Georgia born and raised."

"I'm an Alabama girl myself. Roll Tide. But now that I know you're from Georgia, I don't think we can be friends."

JD forced out a laugh. "I won't hold the fact that you're a Bama fan against you." She was pretty, no question. Forward, but pretty.

"All rise," the bailiff called out.

Judge Jackson made her way through a door next to the bench. Her perusal scanned the courtroom, and she grabbed her gavel to call the session to order.

Casey angled toward him and began whispering. "Jackson is a witch. Drives all the cases through her docket at breakneck speed."

The gallery was filling up. No time to switch seats now. Although he didn't appreciate Casey calling Mahalia a witch, he let it slide. He'd watched Mahalia handle other cases. Didn't know all the details, but she was always professional and down-the-line fair.

The bailiff called Casey's case. She slipped him a business card as she stood and whispered, "Watch how it's done." She walked to the counsel table at the front, hips swaying. JD saw handwriting scribbled on the card. "Call me." Brazen.

Seconds after Casey took her place before the bench and stated her name and that of her client for the record, a train wreck ensued. She interrupted and contradicted Judge Jackson at every turn, oblivious to the storm cloud brewing on the judge's face. He suppressed a wince.

Jayna Breigh

***

Was Attorney Chapman baiting her? Okay, she wore a fierce pink pantsuit—a good tactical move. Power suits threw the men off. But her sharp gaze made it clear she wasn't here to play nice. Kudos for the effort, but she wasn't getting what she came for. And it had nothing to do with the fact that Mahalia had seen her slide Cash a business card.

"Counselor, I am only granting you partial relief today. Not everything. Go out in the hallway and try to settle this, because it stinks all around. If it settles, come back in here, and we'll put it on the record."

"Yes, Your Honor." A chorus of acquiescence went up from the line of attorneys in front of her, with Chapman adding an eye roll.

Mahalia inhaled sharply and huffed the air out. Not letting that woman get under her skin. Cash was on deck. His look was impeccable. Not a suit, but a sports jacket and slacks. It was classy and exuded confidence. And a paisley tie? Too bad his motion was going down like the *Titanic*.

"Bailiff, please call the next item on the docket."

"Case Number CC082917, *Hunt versus TransNation Trucking Corporation*."

"Jimmy Dean Cash for Plaintiffs Ann Hunt and the Estate of John Hunt.

"Max Sidwell, of Sidwell and Hopkins, for TransNation."

She shot a quick glance at Jimmy Dean Cash. That name. What a mouthful. Like hers. He was several notches up from the blue-haired, staid morticians who populated her usual calendar. After figuring out he was Billboard Man, she'd expected a cornpone hillbilly act to match the tacky sign, but he was professional and well spoken.

The court reporter's steno machine spit out a thin tape of transcription documenting every word.

"Counsel, I've read your briefs. I am not happy with your stall and delay tactics, Mr. Sidwell, but you are within bounds. Mr. Cash, if you want to make his witnesses testify on your timetable, you need to ramp up the pressure."

"Got it, Your Honor." Sidwell aimed a stare at Cash and sneered.

"I'll tell you what I will do, however." The facts gave her wiggle room. She'd toss Cash a bone. "If you have to come back in here against Mr. Sidwell, I will impose monetary sanctions on his client, as well as Mr. Sidwell and his firm."

AN APPEARANCE OF IMPROPRIETY

"Your Honor, thank you."

Sidwell blanched. "But, Your Honor, there's no basis for that."

"It's not a ruling for today, but you're on notice, Mr. Sidwell." She slammed the gavel down. "Next case."

Cash and Sidwell moved toward the back doors, and the disheveled reporter stood and headed for the exit as well. What was going on? The only reporters who ever came to her courtroom were the starched-and-pressed correspondents from the business wires. Was there something she should know about the case between TransNation and the Hunts?

Was he here because of her? If so, why?

***

JD had another motion in an hour on an old case that kept circling the drain, refusing to go away. Eating would have to be on the fly, so off to the food trucks. Hopefully, a shady spot on a bench would materialize. As he exited the courthouse and headed for Taco Alfresco, the glorious Los Angeles sun beat down on him. He was never sorry he'd left Georgia—just felt free out here. Less judgment based on your background and who your "people" were. His money, not his pedigree, opened doors. The trailer park was far behind.

He took a seat beside a copse of dwarf palms. Short enough that birds couldn't perch above him and poop in his hair—he hoped. He caught a flash of pink in his peripheral vision.

"We meet again." Casey settled on the edge of the concrete bench and crossed her shapely legs at the knee. He recognized the scent of Chanel No. 5. What red-blooded man wouldn't?

"This keeps me from having to embarrass myself by asking you out to lunch." She pulled a bundle out of a sack and unwrapped a hot dog with mustard. She nibbled and chewed like a mouse.

There went his few moments of solitude. Not that she wasn't pretty. She was beautiful. But her direct approach was off-putting. He knew enough to be polite, though. "So what brings a Southern belle like you way out here to the West Coast?"

"Same as any girl. The sun. Weather. The shopping. It was all so dull,

dull, dull in my little town back home. I think you know what I mean." She arched a brow as she appraised his attire.

Dull wasn't the right word, but he caught her drift. His hometown, Spring Creek, was nothing but a dead end. Even the name led nowhere—to a runoff ditch, not water. He'd pulled the rip cord on that as soon as he could by enlisting in the army right after high school. The only person tying him to home had been his high school sweetheart, Tammy, but after he'd enlisted, she'd let him go. He'd never had a reason to return after that.

Casey chattered on. Her Alabama lilt was melodic, but he tuned out. His attention drifted from Casey and landed on a bright-orange jacket worn by a statuesque beauty. Judge Jackson stood there, out of her robe, the vivid color striking against her ebony skin.

He made to leave, but something Casey said stopped him short. "I'm sorry. I missed that."

"I was commenting on the judge over there." Casey hitched her thumb in Judge Jackson's direction. "She's a little full of herself. I mean, I looked at her judicial profile. She's not that impressive."

Oh. She had his full attention now.

"You have a problem with the judge's credentials?" JD clenched his teeth.

"I'm sure she's smart, but she's so young. You know, just wondering if the people elected the most qualified person for her position on the bench."

Enough. His whole life he'd been prejudged because of where he was from and his strong Southern accent. "Got another hearing in fifteen. Have a great afternoon, Casey."

He walked away without looking back.

***

LA Hearsay Chat Board

BamaBelle: Jackson in rare form today. Power tripping much?

4thEstatePitBull: And the threat of sanctions against Sidwell. Yikes! A shot across the bow.

AN APPEARANCE OF IMPROPRIETY

Chapter13King: TransNation's angling for bankruptcy to dodge liability. Family will get zilch.

4thEstatePitBull: @BamaBelle you've got a front-row seat to the drama. Don't hesitate to share if you catch anything worth a headline.

ShadowDocket: Don't you guys have anything better to do?

Chapter 8

THE DISTINCTIVE SCREECH and repetitive *twang-thwack* of a basketball game in progress greeted JD at the door of the Athletic Club of Los Angeles gymnasium. He almost never missed the extended bimonthly court time with his team, Nothing But Net, if he could help it. Pounding the hardwood. The running, the sweating, the satisfying swoosh of the ball in the hoop. It all helped him work off the restless energy that dogged him the other hours of the day. *Cheaper than therapy.*

He spied his three-on-three teammates in the corner. DeMarcus Johnson, a brand-spanking-new partner at his law firm, sported his ubiquitous Princeton basketball sweatshirt and a signet ring so huge it looked like a door knocker. A reformed ladies' man, the six-foot-four All American point guard had met his match in his fiancée, private investigator Nona Taylor, and would soon be married. He also had a deadly outside jumper.

"N-B-N's in the house," DeMarcus bellowed from between his cupped hands.

JD tipped his chin up and smiled as he approached the men.

Ben Kincaide, fellow attorney and teammate number two, smirked. "Always with the trash talk, DeMarcus. I let my skills do the talking." He clicked the rhombus-shaped attachment he used for basketball onto the prosthetic on his left arm.

With his boyish charm and an accurate layup, Ben always knocked DeMarcus's inflated ego down a peg or two when it got out of hand. And combined, the two were comedy gold.

"Psyops," DeMarcus said. "I'm living in their heads rent-free."

JD bent his leg at the knee, grabbed his ankle, and stretched out his quads. "DeMarcus, your cockiness knows no bounds."

AN APPEARANCE OF IMPROPRIETY

"That is correct. Neither does my hoop game. That's why you recruited me."

"Can't deny the truth of that." JD shucked his outerwear, tossed his keys, phone, and wallet in a heap with his teammates' paraphernalia, and jogged to their reserved half-court to warm up.

He dribbled the ball a few times and passed it to DeMarcus.

"So what's the deal with Judge Mahalia Jackson?" JD tried to keep his tone professional. "Either of you ever appear before her?" He sank his jumper, and DeMarcus rotated to the top of the key.

"Good judge. Young as far as experience goes, so not a real long paper trail on her decisions. As a matter of fact, last week there was a gossip hit piece about her on the 'Legal Special-Tea' page of the *San Gabriel Daily News*." DeMarcus cracked his knuckles and flexed his neck back and forth. "An anonymous source said they don't like Judge Jackson's temperament. Called her 'The Ice Queen in room 214.' Said, 'If you cross her, she'll chew you up one side and down the other.' Never had it done to me, but I've seen it. All I can say is, ouch." DeMarcus's free throw swished through the net without touching the rim. He rotated out.

That didn't resonate with JD's experience with Judge Jackson. "I haven't seen the article. But from my experience in court, she seems fair and straight down the line."

"She's easy on the eyes too." Ben tossed the ball. Missed by a mile.

DeMarcus snorted.

"She's 'dark and comely,'" JD said.

"Dark and comely. What are you talking about?"

Ben's lips tipped up into a smirk. "It's from the Bible. You need more actual church and less Sunday gospel brunch in your life."

"I go to church." DeMarcus pulled a one-sided smile and bobbed his head up and down. "From time to time."

"Bro, funerals and weddings don't count." Ben rolled his eyes. "I'm kidding. I know you've been taking your faith more seriously."

"She heard my motion last week." JD shrugged. Played it cool. "I lost, but it still turned out well enough for me. She's filling in for Goldstein. Don't know how long she'll hold the case." JD's throw thudded as it bounced off the rim. As he shuffled out of the key, he tossed off, "She single? Married?"

DeMarcus made his next shot. His hand suspended in the air in a hook shape as he hopped on one foot. "Never touched the rim, fellas." He stared at JD, a glint in his eye. "Why do you want to know?"

"I'm curious."

"Yeah, she's single." Ben tried a step back, and the shot landed. He rotated spaces. "What legal strategy do you have that involves her marital status?"

His face flushed with heat, and he stood still. "Not a strategy. Just wondering." His free throw wobbled around the rim and dropped through. Why was he wondering?

"If you say so." Ben's eyes glinted with amusement.

"I've seen Judge Jackson's kitchen, so we're close. Like that." Ben crossed his fingers. "I can give you inside intel if you'd like." Ben winked at DeMarcus.

"Wait, you've been to the judge's house?"

"No. I've seen her kitchen. She has been to *my* house though." Ben snickered.

"You told me you'd dated a Black woman before, JD." DeMarcus's eyes crinkled, and his chest heaved up and down as he laughed.

"I have ... I ... I did. Before I got shipped off to the Middle East," JD stuttered.

"My wife Cassandy and Mahalia use the same hairstylist," Ben said. "She's godmother to my kids. In fact, she recused herself from all my firm's future cases."

JD was still a little confused about the whole kitchen discussion. He smushed up his face.

"Dude, 'the kitchen' is what Black women call the hair at the nape of the neck," DeMarcus volunteered.

"Oh." JD didn't enjoy feeling stupid. His time in the military had given him some insight into Black culture, but it hadn't prepared him for the intricacies of hair and beauty practices.

Raucous smack talk echoed in the gymnasium. Hoop Prosecutors jogged onto the court. Despite his best efforts to the contrary, his thoughts, of late, kept circling back to Judge Jackson. His Afghanistan vow remained firm, but the pull he felt for her left him wrestling with emotions he thought were long buried. He put a pin in it for now and made a mental note to follow up with Ben on the godmother issue—and Judge Jackson's personal life.

AN APPEARANCE OF IMPROPRIETY

***

JD wrapped a towel around his waist and moved to his locker. Hoop Prosecutors had received their customary beatdown from NBN. He twisted his torso clockwise and counterclockwise. Might need an Icy Hot patch when he got home. Not a spring chicken anymore. He'd giggled when Mama used that expression. She'd make a little clucking noise. The smile fell from his lips. *Mama.*

DeMarcus opened the cubby beside JD's, and the distinctive men's gym smell gave way to DeMarcus's potent aftershave.

"Would you quit already with that cologne?" He waved a hand in front of his nose.

DeMarcus worked his polo on and donned his slacks. "The ladies dig the Drakkar Noir, and that's all that matters."

Ben's head angled out from around the adjacent row of lockers. "Don't you mean the grandmothers?"

"Whatever. My fiancée loves it." DeMarcus flung his damp towel toward Ben's face, and his Princeton signet ring glinted in the light.

JD hated signet rings. A high-class way to put your credentials in other people's faces without having to say the words. DeMarcus's ring, paired with the mention of his engagement, called to mind Ashlyn's delicate gold band—a Smith College ring on her pinky. Ashlyn, his law school . . . *girlfriend* wasn't exactly the right word. At the time, her father served as the junior senator from Georgia.

Before he knew Ashlyn, he'd never heard of Smith, or the Seven Sisters, or the Little Three. The closest institution of higher learning to his town had been a trade school for AC and auto repair. One of many firsts with her. She had a flowing mane straight out of a Pantene shampoo commercial, and her cashmere sweaters and wool slacks stood in contrast to the other sweatshirted, ponytailed second-years.

She'd sidled up to him one crisp fall day after Corporations class and invited him out for coffee. In retrospect, the trappings were what had smitten him. She'd driven a Saab 9-3. Something he'd never seen before in Spring Creek, where Ford F-150s with lifts tore up and down Main Street. When she introduced him around in her circles, he became intoxicated with all the possibilities and set aside his pledge of solitude, thinking she would be his future wife.

They shifted to exclusive after a few months, but nothing heavy. He played his cards close to the vest. Painted a picture of Spring Creek that left out the grit and highlighted the quirky characters living life at the poverty level. She found his rough manners charming at first. But reality crashed in—the yawning chasm between them exposed with innocent questions, like "Can you run back into the house and bring my purse from off the divan?"

He'd been gutting it out in a rented room in a ratty fraternity house, while Ashlyn was paying a mortgage and building equity on a duplex.

He entered her place, looked everywhere. The kitchen counters. The dining room table. On top of something he'd have called a hutch. She came back inside when he didn't return after five minutes. The little purse sat on a decorative couch in the living room. *Why didn't she say "ridiculous little couch"?*

Moments like that continued to pop up, unmasking his ignorance and laying bare the class gap between them.

"Which one is the shrimp fork?"

"No, I've never had coq au vin before."

"I got it secondhand."

His lack of knowledge was a sticky spiderweb. Killing it in the classroom, but with his foot stuffed in his mouth every time he was out with Ashlyn.

The final straw? Alumni weekend.

The senator, Ashlyn's father, arrived at the gala affair with Mrs. Senator on his arm. Their tanned, camera-ready exteriors and dignified way of talking put JD off-kilter.

"Father, this is James Cash, a classmate."

The sharp left turn from "boyfriend," which was how she referred to him among their friends, to "classmate" gave him whiplash. Plus, he'd never gone by James a day in his life. Wasn't anywhere on his birth certificate.

"Nice to meet you. What year are you?"

"I'm a Three L, sir. Going to the JAG school adjacent to the University of Virginia after this."

"Fine school. Excellent reputation."

AN APPEARANCE OF IMPROPRIETY

JD stood there in thrift-store loafers that pinched his big toe, clasping his hands behind his back, military-style, to hide the fraying on the cuffs of his borrowed blue blazer.

"And where were you reared?" Mrs. Senator piped up. She was the time-machine version of Ashlyn. She wore her still-blond hair coiffed in an age-appropriate shorter cut. If her genes dominated, Ashlyn would only grow more beautiful with time.

"I'm from Spring Creek, ma'am."

A muscle ticked in the senator's cheek. "I see." He traded an indecipherable look with Ashlyn. "Well, I've been to your part of the state many times on the campaign trail. Think I got a free breakfast program started there, and some methadone clinics."

JD didn't even have a reply to those comments. An awkward silence hung in the air.

Mrs. Senator looked about. "Dear, isn't that Judge Simpson over there? He's waving us over."

JD looked in the direction to which Mrs. Senator was gesturing. There was no one hailing them from that corner of the pavilion.

"Well, if you'll excuse us." The senator and his wife vanished like a wisp of smoke, leaving JD there with a deflated Ashlyn.

Their relationship hadn't lasted another month.

Ashlyn had been his one slipup. He'd felt belittled by the condescension from the hoity-toity class and had flagellated himself for allowing the trappings of high society to entice him. After the Ashlyn debacle, he'd doubled down on his vow and hadn't had a slipup since.

A locker clanked shut, jerking JD back to the musty room. He smoothed his hand down the front of his suit and nodded to himself. Armani, like Harry, the Duke of Sussex. After Ashlyn, he'd kept his eyes open and his mouth closed. Observing. Cataloging. Trying to understand the hidden rules of class. The subtle tells. He wanted to switch in and out of their world at will.

His efforts had paid off. Now he understood his opponents' vanities and the weak points in their egos, so he could pressure those points or flatter them—whatever was necessary to secure the best outcome for his clients. But inside he also understood the people who sought out his services. How the courtroom intimidated them. How the process could make them feel like marks in a rigged poker game. He was in his opponents' world, but not of it.

Ben pulled up short at the door. "Back to the office?"

He banished his introspection to the memory hole and in his mind scanned his to-do list. His life verse popped into his head. *Religion that God our Father accepts as pure and faultless is this; to look after orphans and widows in their distress* . . . "Yep. Grind time."

Chapter 9

THE DRY LATE-SEPTEMBER air followed Mahalia inside as she hoisted open the industrial door of Riveted. The high-concept farm-to-table eatery was famous for its organic, cruelty-free menu options. Tucked in a converted loft space in West Hollywood, the restaurant flaunted a five-star rating. Riveted catered to the professional crowd, whose posh designer outfits stood in sharp contrast to the concrete floor and exposed, rusted ironworks.

Two weeks had flown by, what with her new assignment to the Litigation and Trial Practice Committee, plus learning the ropes for Junior Jurors. A little harried and out of breath, she spied a mirror tucked in a corner, which beckoned her for a lipstick check. After a grueling day at the courthouse, schmoozing was the last thing she wanted to do. She twisted her head from side to side to work off the tension. Goldstein's words continued to sizzle and ping inside her, like popcorn cooking in a microwave. She had to show "heart." Play the game and check the boxes to win the position of assistant supervising judge.

The charcoal and stone colors of the design reflected from behind her in the mirror, and her stomach clenched at the aroma of the signature beef stew.

She jammed her hand down in her bag and pulled out her tube of Dynasty Red, noting it was near empty. She closed her eyes and enjoyed the trademark tropical scent of the Fashion Fair cosmetic line—old-lady makeup, her stylist, Deon, called it. But Fashion Fair always had shades that complemented her skin tone. She slicked on a coat and smoothed her eyebrows with her fingertip. Attendance at a Golden Roses gathering mandated a flawless appearance.

Jayna Breigh

Mahalia had checked out its history before joining. Founded in the 1930s, when Black women were excluded from the other elite women's organizations in Los Angeles, the Golden Roses was a civic organization designed to encourage philanthropy, artistic endeavors, and upward family mobility. In its early days, leadership had been notorious for its preference for women no darker than a paper bag. Times had changed, but the current Golden Roses were often the daughters and granddaughters of the founders—families that had all intermarried for the connections.

Granddaddy Henry and Granny were the children of sharecroppers who'd made the move westward during the Jim Crow era's Great Migration. Granddaddy had kept many of his back-home ways. His back-home religion. When election time had come around and Mahalia had campaigned for judge, practicality had won the tug-of-war over pride. She'd been elected, in part, because she'd joined the Golden Roses and tapped into the rich vein of connections and finances guarded with zeal by the Los Angeles elite.

What would Granddaddy say if he saw her now?

She shook off the melancholy. In a room full of so many preeminent women, no one gave her preferential treatment in the Golden Roses because she was a judge. She'd earned her spot. Fairness ruled the day as they doled out cattiness and boorish behavior. Still, the chip remained on her shoulder, which she pulled back as she strode into the meeting room next to the lobby.

The Neiman Marcus pantsuit parade was on full display. She smoothed a hand over her nape and upward to make sure her natural, two-strand twist updo didn't have any frizzy stragglers.

The gathering of women from the Los Angeles upper crust pushed every insecurity button she had and pulled every stop, like she was the old Hammond organ at Granddaddy's church. She perused the room. Tonight, as usual, she was the darkest woman at the event.

A waiter tried to squeeze between her and the backside of a woman she'd never met. She used the opening to snag a glass of zinfandel from his tray and made a beeline for an unoccupied table in the back of the room.

"Judge Jackson, so good to see you." Golden Roses president Estelle

AN APPEARANCE OF IMPROPRIETY

Thomas sidled over, bent, and greeted Mahalia with double cheek air kisses. She sat in the chair next to Mahalia, put her elbows on the table, and hunched in toward her.

Since Estelle rarely graced Mahalia with her presence, she suspected the woman wanted something.

"I must introduce you to my cousin Darrell Williams." An anxious smile peeked out as Estelle ran her blush-colored gel nails through her tresses. "He's in finance in Atlanta. Condo in Buckhead. A little pied-à-terre here in the Hollywood Hills. Plus, he went to Morehouse. His divorce isn't final, but any day now." She held up both her hands, crossed her fingers, and waggled them around.

Estelle pulled her phone out of a small clutch and scrolled to a picture of a squat man twenty years Mahalia's senior. He looked like an exotic bird, with a protruding belly and tufts of hair obscuring his ears. Estelle vibrated with excitement, like she'd offered Mahalia a free trip to the Grand Caymans.

"Finance, you say?" Mahalia surveilled the room, looking for an escape hatch.

"He's the accountant for Big-Q. You've heard of him, right?" Estelle's eyes sparkled with her proximity to the financier for D-list celebrities. "I mean, his profession is a little *Real Housewives*." She gave a sniff. "But he also has corporate clients."

Oh no. An entertainment accountant? The Midnight Prince did not work for pop stars or rappers or TV actors. That was not the life she envisioned for herself.

"Is it okay if I give him your number?"

It was hard to make direct eye contact with Estelle, who wore the expression of a quiz show host. She gestured and nodded, telegraphing that granting access to a Golden Roses–approved man would be akin to giving a five-year-old a pony.

Mahalia schooled her face and opted for a nuclear weapon. "You know what the Good Book says." She lilted her voice upward for effect. "Dating is not an option until the divorce is final." *Or Hades freezes over.*

Estelle's face drooped for a millisecond. But she recovered. "I know an attorney who's recently finalized his second divorce. No pesky wife to get in your way. I've heard through the grapevine that he's in your courthouse on a regular basis." Estelle held her eyes wide and blinked a few times.

An attorney in the same courthouse? A nonstarter. How would it look if she turned her workplace into a fishing hole for a future husband? Unbidden, Attorney Cash's face floated through her mind. Looks aside, he was a gifted and caring teacher. The way he broke down the complexities of the litigation process for the kids and used analogies to help them grasp the concepts. She shooed his sad eyes away. She wanted a man who didn't have a lawyer brain so they would complement each other, not compete.

"What can I say, Estelle? I don't think it will work out. Rules of ethics and such." Okay, an exaggeration. Yes, judges had to avoid the appearance of impropriety, but personal reasons stood behind most of her obstacles to dating an attorney. There were work-arounds, including stepping down from a case and handing it off to someone else. Frankly, no need existed to let Estelle in on any aspect of her dating life.

Batting zero, Estelle waved her hand toward Dr. Denise Braxton across the room and dropped her voice to a conspiratorial whisper. "I think Dr. Braxton's daughter is single."

The face of the shy, pretty girl who'd accompanied her mother to a few meetings came back to her. Couldn't be older than twenty-four. Any mother who'd unleash a man eligible for AARP on a daughter her age should be ashamed.

"*She* might *appreciate* a man like Darrell." Estelle droned on. "It will be perfect. They can tie the knot right after she completes her residency." Estelle gave a last dismissive look at Mahalia and flounced off toward Denise.

Estelle got under her skin. The niggling unease caused her musings to flip to the criticisms from Judge Goldstein and Becky. *No heart. A stickler. Hardheaded. No nonsense.* Didn't they know? She wouldn't be where she was if she hadn't shielded herself with an impenetrable mental and emotional force field. The attacks came from all sides. Underestimated because she was a woman. Viewed as unqualified because of her age. Treated as a second-class citizen by some inside her own community because of her high concentration of melanin.

Mahalia remembered reading in a magazine that a music superstar's own father said his daughter had a leg up in Hollywood because of her light complexion. A "helpful" college roommate had once offered Mahalia a tube of skin bleach after she'd complained she couldn't find a boyfriend.

A sharp pain pulsed in her temple, and the negative self-talk spiral began—*unattractive, unwanted, unwelcome.*

No. She willed herself to stop and switch her mental station to the words that embodied her self-worth, but a different streak of words fell across her mind from out of nowhere, like a falling star.

Yet indeed I also count all things loss for the excellence of the knowledge of Christ Jesus my Lord, for whom I have suffered the loss of all things, and count them as rubbish, that I may gain Christ.

Where did that verse come from? It had been a while since she'd picked up her Bible. Granddaddy Henry must have transmitted it down from heaven using kingdom Bluetooth. A sob caught in her throat as the Golden Roses swirled around her, eating canapes and sipping chardonnay.

Granddaddy. He would scold her if he were here. *"God doesn't need a computer, baby girl. If the Word is in your mind, the Holy Spirit put it there."*

She'd loved it when he'd say the "naughty words" in the Bible. "Dung, dung, dung," she'd chant, wringing peals of mirth from Leontyne and Martin. Her cousins would take it further and further, whispering verses referencing hell and damnation, scandalizing themselves with the forbidden nature of it all.

Somehow in this moment, hearing Granddaddy in her ear, preaching that verse about the excellency of Christ, both soothed and terrified her. What did all her accomplishments mean? Granddaddy had always been so proud of her, but every conversation with him ended with him asking if she'd joined a church or read her Bible.

"Sweet Mahalia baby," his comforting voice would flow out. *"For what profit is it to a man if he gains the whole world, and loses his own soul?"*

She'd always found a way to brush off his admonitions.

He'd let her deflect but always retorted, *"I'm not giving up on you yet, Mahalia. The Word has a way of getting down deep inside of you, working. Even when you aren't thinking about it."*

The clink of knives tapping against wine goblets, signaling time to quiet and begin the meeting, found her with moisture in her eyes, threatening to spill. She swiped a knuckle under her bottom lids, straightened her spine, and watched the woman at the dais. She forced out the bittersweet memories of Granddaddy and supplanted them with her mantra. Prestigious college. Ivy League law school. Top-drawer law firm. And she added her new hoped-for position—assistant supervising judge.

Chapter 10

MAHALIA EYED THE printout of her calendar for the week. Good thing she'd come in at six thirty rather than her usual seven o'clock. Her phone dinged with a notification from Judicial CLE Tracker needling her about the outstanding ethics requirement. Her October 31 completion deadline, less than two weeks away, hung over her head like a wrecking ball. She could have finished all of it weeks ago in the one-and-done seminar when she'd gone to Vail. But no. Luxury had lured her into the dark playground of procrastination, so she'd prioritized spa treatments instead. No more. She would finish the remaining hours today even if she had to stay until midnight.

She took a sip of her morning English breakfast tea and singed her lip. She opened Gavel-Link and clicked on the CLE Tracker app. A notification popped up telling her she had to update before it would load. *Figures.* Dropping her shoulders, she forced herself to relax. She'd made her itchy, hard bed, and now she'd have to sleep in it. The app finished updating, and she tested her tea. Still too hot.

The canons from the California Rules of Court populated her screen.

> A judge must expect to be the subject of constant public scrutiny. A judge must therefore accept restrictions on the judge's conduct that might be viewed as burdensome by other members of the community and should do so freely and willingly.

> The prohibition against behaving with impropriety, or the appearance of impropriety, applies to both the professional and personal conduct of a judge.

Jayna Breigh

> A judge shall not allow family, social, political, or other relationships to influence the judge's judicial conduct or judgment, nor shall a judge convey or permit others to convey the impression that any individual is in a special position to influence the judge.

Reality settled in as she dunked her tea bag in the water. Yes, it was a hassle to do the CLE hours, but the guardrails were in place for a reason. She had yet to meet a judge in person who wasn't an ethical and fair jurist. But there were those who didn't follow the rules, and sometimes they showed up in public discipline postings on the Commission on Judicial Performance's web page—or worse, on *Eyewitness News*.

Their exploits were a cautionary tale and stiff warning to her and others. Things as petty as deflating the tire of a car parked in their personal space. Text messages sent during trial, mocking witnesses before the bench. A judge who funneled money to herself via back channels from cases she'd presided over. Affairs, fixed traffic tickets, harassment.

Underneath the robe, judges were humans, like the people sitting in the gallery in front of them. Subject to the same foibles and vices. The judicial system in America was a standard for justice around the world but still ultimately overseen by mere mortals. She shifted her mind from thinking about the hassle of finishing the hours to focusing on the questions and reminding herself of the rationale behind the requirement.

> Review the following hypothetical and answer the questions below about a judge's obligations regarding disqualification and disclosure of potential conflicts of interest:
>
> Judge Blue coaches kids in a youth soccer league. Attorney Smith has a child on the team. Attorney Smith is also trying a case before Judge Blue.

She had never seen a hypothetical about legitimate community service work. She sat straighter in her chair. While the Junior Jurors program wasn't a youth sports league, parallels popped off the screen in 3D.

AN APPEARANCE OF IMPROPRIETY

1. True or False—Judge Blue must disclose his/her association.

2. True or False—Judge Blue must objectively analyze whether someone reasonably aware of the facts will doubt his/her ability to be impartial in the case . . .

Did any of these apply to her interactions with the kids? With Attorney Cash? In her time on the bench, she'd never encountered an ethics predicament. The complex corporate cases she presided over were far outside the mundanity of her daily life. Her teeny-tiny 401(k) was invested in mutual funds and managed by a broker, so she wasn't required to recuse herself from hearing cases about multinational corporations.

She googled the fact pattern, and a Committee on Judicial Ethics Opinion popped up.

> If the attorney served as the team parent for the sports team and had close and frequent interactions with the judge regarding the team, or if the families of the team members, including the attorney, regularly met for meals with the judge after team practices, a person aware of these facts might reasonably form the impression that the judge and the attorney had a more significant social relationship that would cause the judge to favor the attorney or to be in a position to be influenced by the attorney.

Yes, she presided over the TransNation lawsuit, but none of the students were Mr. Cash's biological children. She wasn't having meals with him. No contact outside the context of the mock trial meetings. Zero social relationship. The fact pattern was similar to, but not on all fours with, her involvement with the Junior Jurors—so no need to worry, right?

An email notification pinged. She minimized her CLE module and opened her official account. She had no idea who ShadowDocket@ZMail.com was, but the email had cleared the courthouse security software, so she clicked it open. She struggled to make sense of what was displayed on the screen. No words, only what looked like a screenshot of someone holding a phone displaying an Instagram post. She looked closer. The post showed an image of her in her judicial robes, standing impossibly close to JD Cash in a courtroom hallway. Their gazes were locked in what appeared to be a tender, almost intimate moment. She scrolled down to the caption. "We'd ship this all day long . . . #CoupleGoals #FanArt."

This moment had never happened in real life. Where did it come from? Her stomach churned. She examined the image again. The waxen skin and eight-fingered hands screamed phony and AI generated, but fake or not, it could cause chaos in her career.

She stared at the screen and noticed a note on the bottom of the email. "I've taken care of this. The post is down, and it won't happen again. Help is closer than you think."

Mahalia's mind raced. Was a friend behind the scenes stepping in—or was someone watching her too closely for comfort? A quote from the Rules of Court she'd read earlier flashed in her mind. *"A judge must expect to be the subject of constant public scrutiny."*

Nothing in her CLE training prepared her to deal with an anonymous, bogus photograph. Should she report it? To whom? She'd get yanked off the TransNation case. The sender had assured her that the post had been removed, but what if someone else had seen it? How could she know Shadow-Docket was trustworthy? Her prayer life was almost nonexistent, but the words slipped out instinctively . . . *Lord, please help me.*

Chapter 11

STEWART'S AUTOBODY COLLISION Repair held the remains of John Hunt's totaled SUV. As JD entered the bay holding the wreckage, the sweet chemical aroma of engine coolant wrapped around him. Below-average temperatures for mid-October caused a slight nip in the unheated space, and he shoved his hands deep into his pockets. In the car, rounded pellets of safety glass littered the seats and carpet, and deflated front and side airbags sagged across the interior.

JD circled the vehicle in slow motion. The battleship-gray exterior, last year's hottest vehicle color, bore red and white streaks on one side and on the crumpled roof from the impact with the TransNation truck. Scars marred one door where the Jaws of Life had ripped it open.

A sharp stabbing sensation sliced through JD's stomach. This was why he tried cases. Not for the money. He stood in front of the car where John Hunt had left his wife and children until they'd meet again in eternity. JD believed in God's sovereignty. The Lord held the next breath of every man in his hands. But if a corporation's recklessness and utter indifference directly caused such a horrific tragedy, that company should pay.

JD's goal with this case was nailing the hide of every member of the board to the wall. The pervasive culture of corner cutting and safety violations turned TransNation's fleet into eighteen-wheeled time bombs on the nations' freeways. He didn't want to take down some middle management flunky. The heads of CEO Richard Snevelton and his main lackey, CFO Vernon Pilfrey, should be on a pike.

JD would dig and dig and dig until he found that one document, that one witness, to connect Snevelton and Pilfrey to the accident. Those two men had pushed the TransNation drivers to operate at unsafe fatigue levels, falsify logbooks, and defer necessary repairs, all to save pennies per miles traveled.

***

Three days later JD surveyed the Sidwell & Hopkins conference room, the image of John Hunt's car still seared in his mind. The drawn drapes, heavy rug, and cloth seating lent a funereal feel to the room, cloaking it in the hushed silence of a mausoleum. An elongated table sat in the room's center. Sodas, fresh fruit, and pastries were on a console. Given the faint nutty smell, he surmised the white carafe held coffee, not OJ. A stack of sticky notes and a cupful of pens, both embossed with the firm's name, sat in the center of the table.

He shook his head. Big firms always made a grandiose show of hospitality to flex their power and to signal to the little guys that money was no object. Later the firms folded the cost for all the plush amenities and overstaffing into the rate the partners charged the clients. JD kept his operation lean. He'd ditched his tie in the car to distance himself from the power suits and intimidation tactics he'd assumed Sidwell and his firm planned to roll out. He wanted to put the witness at ease.

The court reporter sat at the head of the table, with her steno machine tucked near her knees on its little stand. JD commandeered the seat to her right. Seated across from him was the star witness of the day, Walt McClatchy. JD swallowed hard. The scarred pink skin on Mr. McClatchy's face angered JD, as did the cast on the man's arm. He was still recovering from a second reconstructive surgery. TransNation's reckless management inflicted suffering on the employees, not just innocent motorists.

A few seats down from McClatchy, Max Sidwell and an anonymous assistant huddled together, whispering. The classic senior partner–junior associate pairing piled up billable hours on TransNation's account.

JD took a deep inhale. He glanced down at the outline of questions in his notebook to center himself on his chief objectives—to get McClatchy to cut off any remaining feelings of loyalty to TransNation and to encourage him to ally himself with the Hunts. No going for the jugular today. The goal was to coax as much out of this man as possible so he could hoist TransNation on its own petard.

AN APPEARANCE OF IMPROPRIETY

He turned to the court reporter. "I'm ready to begin."

"Mr. McClatchy, please raise your hand to be sworn in." The stenographer raised her own hand for McClatchy to imitate.

McClatchy's face bore deep wrinkles, no doubt sun damage from years on the road. He wore a blue-and-red-checked flannel shirt with a white undershirt visible under the collar. Tufts of grandpa-like white hairs dusted his forearms. McClatchy, the man whose rig had crushed John Hunt's vehicle and killed him, raised his hand and took the oath.

Sidwell spoke up. "Look, Cash, for the record, and before we get started, I am renewing our objection to McClatchy's deposition on the ground that he signed a comprehensive nondisclosure agreement as a part of his separation from TransNation."

"Too bad, Mr. Sidwell. You lost on summary judgment when you argued the NDA barred some of our claims, and the court said we can proceed with the deposition."

"Let the record reflect that I'm still objecting, to preserve my client's rights, and we will pursue this matter further."

"You do what you feel you have to, Mr. Sidwell." JD gave Sidwell a curt nod and centered his attention back on his witness. "First, Mr. McClatchy, thank you for being here. I wish this had never happened to you. This accident devastated many lives."

"The Lord gave, and the Lord has taken away; blessed be the name of the Lord." McClatchy didn't break his gaze away from JD.

The familiar jolt of electricity that accompanied a connection with a fellow believer surged down his spine.

"Well, let's get started." JD scanned his first page of questions. "How long have you been with TransNation?"

"Oh, I've been with 'em 'bout twenty years."

"Walk me through the steps for entering your time into the system."

"Well, I log on to the company's website, enter my password, enter the times. When I'm ready to sign off, I click Done."

The unique bumping sound made by the keys on the stenographer's machine thudded in the otherwise hushed room. Sidwell and his minion waited to protest any question they deemed objectionable.

"I'm handing you what I've marked as Exhibit 1, a printout of your time sheet for the day of the accident. Have you ever seen this before?" He moved the paper toward McClatchy.

McClatchy studied the paper and placed it on the table.

"Mr. McClatchy—"

He held up an index finger on his good arm, putting off JD's question, and used that hand to fish his cheaters out of his breast pocket. He finagled the stems open, situated the readers on the tip of his nose, and resumed his perusal of the exhibit.

"Can't say as I've ever seen this before."

JD's brows drew together. "If you will read the top, it has your name, do you see that?"

"Sure do."

"Do you also see the date? And the number of hours driven?"

"Yes, I see all of that. But I've never seen this document before."

"Well, is it an accurate document? Does it reflect your hours driven on that day?"

"No, it does not."

"Now wait a minute," Sidwell bellowed, his face purple. "What kind of trick are you pulling? Did you switch out the documents and show him something we didn't provide to you?" Sidwell held out his hand, making a beckoning motion. "Give me that." He snatched the exhibit out of McClatchy's hand. His brows drew up, and he turned the paper over. Examined the back. Turned it to the front again. He rounded on Mr. McClatchy. "Look at the document again. Your boss gave it to me, and I turned it over to Mr. Cash. The document is a business record from TransNation. On the bottom it has our Bates stamp number TN00267. The initials 'TN' mean TransNation delivered the documents to the Cash law firm."

"Never seen it." McClatchy didn't even bother to check the document again.

JD handed McClatchy a second piece of paper. "This is Exhibit 2. A time sheet for the day before the accident. Bates stamp number TN00268. Recognize this document?"

"Mister, you can keep pulling pieces of paper out of your little stack. Not a one of them is going to be accurate."

AN APPEARANCE OF IMPROPRIETY

"I call for an immediate adjournment to give me time to talk to the witness."

"Not so fast, Sidwell." JD gave the jerk a scowl. "Mr. McClatchy, why are you so sure these are not your time sheets?"

"Because TransNation has been lowballing my time sheets for years."

JD's insides bayed and howled like dogs on a scent back home. There had to be something here to break the case open. *Please.*

"I'd be very careful right here, Mr. McClatchy. Any allegations of fraud may come right back to you." Sidwell's voice was hard and clipped.

"Stop trying to intimidate the witness," JD snapped at Sidwell.

"Mr. McClatchy, do you agree that these are the time sheets from Trans-Nation?"

"Sure do, but these aren't the hours I entered."

"How do you know?" JD was on the edge of his seat. The attorneys for TransNation were scribbling notes and giving one another worried looks.

"Because these"—McClatchy reached into the sling holding his injured arm—"are my handwritten time logs." McClatchy set a beat-up accordion file on the table with a thwack.

"Can you prove these are your time records?"

"My wife calls me a pack rat."

"And what is in that file?"

"I keep track of my own time in an old-fashioned log. As I drive along, I jot my time on little scraps of paper—when I clock in and when I clock out. Candy wrappers, the back of a receipt, whatever. When I get home, I transfer it to my handwritten logbook.

"This here is my logbook for the month of the accident. I also kept all those little jots and tittles in a shoebox. I've got reams of them. Slapped a note with the year on the box and stored them away. So I've got the logbook, and I've got the backup to the logbook."

JD rocked back in his chair. The revelation by the self-professed hoarder swung the momentum in JD's favor.

Apoplexy contorted Sidwell's face, and he pointed at JD. "We've never seen this logbook. We have no way of determining if what's in it is even accurate. The company keeps track of your time electronically. We want an immediate postponement so we can review it." Sidwell punctuated his words by jabbing the table.

"Nope. My deposition. My rules." JD composed his face into a stone mask. "You can subpoena him yourself if you'd like. However, today we're going to figure out how deep this little rabbit hole of lies goes."

His gaze moved to the clock on the conference room wall. Time to speed things up so he could make it back to the office, pack up his gear, and get over to the courthouse for tonight's trial competition prep. He laced his fingers together, flipped his hands, and cracked his knuckles.

Chapter 12

AFTERNOON AUTUMN SUN warmed Mahalia's skin as she scurried to the little coffee shop across the street from the courthouse. She checked her watch. Twenty minutes to enjoy a break and get back in time for a late mediation session. She relished the chance to stretch her legs and gaze at the bright cloudless sky before she had to return to her windowless courtroom.

This caffeine jolt had to sustain her past the mediation and into the evening since tonight's Junior Jurors meeting tacked an additional two hours on to her already long day. Funny. The meetings with the teens forced her outside her comfort zone, but somehow, under Attorney Cash's gentle leading, she enjoyed them. Thinking of him reminded her of the phony AI-generated picture, which in turn caused a twist of anxiety in her stomach. She'd used amateur sleuthing skills to see if the fake image of her staring with longing into Cash's eyes had been posted anywhere else. As far as she could determine, she was in the clear. But someone could be waiting in the grass, ready to strike like a coiled snake. Should she mention it to Cash tonight?

Pushing back the mental discomfort, she crossed the threshold of the shop, and Duke Ellington's "Take the 'A' Train" filled her ears. A loud gurgle emanated from her stomach. Apparently her post-lunch docket had burned through all the calories from the Cobb salad she'd noshed on at her desk while reading motions.

She ordered a large mocha with an extra pump of syrup and, caving to temptation, purchased a hot cinnamon bun as well. Her phone vibrated in the pocket of her skirt, and she moved aside to let the next customer order. Fishing around, she located her phone and freed it from the bunches of material. A text from Judge Goldstein.

Jayna Breigh

> Good news. You're off the TransNation case. Still need you to handle the Junior Jurors. It will look good in your bid to make ASJ. Sorry for texting. Busy day.

Goldstein was *so* not sorry. He called whenever and wherever he liked when it suited him. She'd seen articles about the TransNation tractor-trailer case in the *San Gabriel Daily News*, the *LA Times*, and online. In fact, the case might affect trucking up and down the West Coast. Ugh. It rankled that she'd be losing such a high-profile lawsuit, but nothing she could do about it now. She sucked her teeth. She'd have a talk with her mentor about hiding behind the very technology he claimed to abhor.

A trio of small vibrations pulled her mind from stewing over Goldstein back to the phone in her hand. A text from Cash.

> Wildfire jumped the 5 Freeway. Stuck in Santa Clarita. Alternate routes to downtown jammed. Can you handle meeting tonight solo?

Consternation pulled her forehead and brows together. All relaxation from attempting a coffee break took flight.

"Large extra-hot mocha with an extra pump of mocha," a barista barked out as he adjusted his slouchy beanie with one hand and slid her drink across the bar with the other.

She jammed her phone back into her pocket. After snagging a cup sleeve, she slid it onto the scorching drink.

The barista held up a hand to arrest her progress, grabbed a bag with handles, and passed it to her.

Treat secured, she exited the shop, her eyes scanning for a seat. Her only option was a long table with one other occupant in front of the store's

AN APPEARANCE OF IMPROPRIETY

plate-glass window. It would have to do. She angled herself away from her tablemate and faced a flower box full of drought-resistant succulents.

She retrieved the phone and took a tentative sip of her scorching mocha as she reviewed Cash's message again. They'd touched base on tonight's lesson—coincidently, an in-depth look at the judge's role in the courtroom. Worst-case scenario, she could riff and tell war stories to fill the time. All those teenagers in one place, however. A chill ran across her shoulders. Babies she could handle. Preschoolers, fine. She'd had so much practice with her godchildren that it came second nature. But teenagers? Didn't consider herself a teen kind of person. She'd spent those years with her nose in a book, at church, in piano lessons, and doing anything else Granddaddy could think of that would further her in the eyes of society.

Her brain toyed with an excuse to back out, but before she could respond, her phone vibrated in her hand again, with a text from Cash.

> If it's any inducement, Your Honor, my assistant, Monica, will set up the food and can email you a copy of my notes. Not to twist your arm, but I might not reach all the kids to cancel. Some can't afford phones. Would hate for one to show up and no one's there. 😟 😟 😟

A smile tugged at her lips, and she clicked around her phone with her thumbs.

> Blackmail much, Mr. Cash?

> Old-fashioned litigator negotiation tactics and undying gratitude.

Jayna Breigh

She raised her head toward the sky again. Her soul felt parched, as if swept by a hot, dry Santa Ana wind. Judge Goldstein's words stomped around on her conscience. She had a heart, but it had a force field around it. Armor that she'd layered on year after year in her climb up the steep mountain of success. Slights, barbs, questions about her competence. Questions about her attractiveness. Questions about her credentials. She held herself in reserve to preserve her professionalism and to maintain her sanity.

An image of her clerk, Becky, flitted through Mahalia's mind. Her assistant's face screwed up in grim determination, talking to herself under her breath as she scuttled around Mahalia's chambers, movements tight and controlled. She liked and respected Becky, and Mahalia thought she had her clerk's respect as well. But she knew she was closed off around the woman. As a judge, who Mahalia was on the inside and who she presented to the outside world were two different people. Was she wounding those who deserved a glimpse of the inner Mahalia? Was her impenetrable professional persona costing her potential opportunities?

A solo stint with the teens would shake things up and give her compassion muscle some exercise. She typed on her phone's keyboard and pressed Send before she could regret her actions.

Fine. I can handle it.

***

The courtroom set aside for tonight's meeting stood ready for the influx of hungry, chatty teens about to descend. Nothing remained for her to do. Sandwiches, bags of chips, and bottles of water and Gatorade Zero lined a small table at the back of the courtroom, compliments of Attorney Cash's assistant.

Monica had pulled a feast out of Cash's ridiculous trial-gear caddies. The woman, clad in a hip-length tunic and sensible Naturalizer loafers, exuded middle-aged efficiency. A reserved, sweet girl—her granddaughter—worked alongside her. Monica's chatter had filled the space as she bustled around setting up, her admiration for her boss shining through in every word.

She'd told Mahalia about the case that had brought her to Cash's office,

AN APPEARANCE OF IMPROPRIETY

the tragic loss of her own daughter, and the beautiful teen she now cared for. Monica was a one-woman cheering squad for Cash. He gave regular bonuses, she noted, and had even accompanied Monica and her granddaughter to a daddy-daughter dance, standing in as a surrogate father.

Monica had not taken a breath or stopped talking until she'd set everything up and tucked the rolling bags out of the way. "No need for you to clean up, Your Honor. I'll hang out in the back until the meeting is over to handle everything"—she held up her arms and snapped her fingers—"and whisk it away."

It would be wonderful to have someone in her corner like Monica. ShadowDocket's words returned to her. *"Help is closer than you think."* Was there somebody fighting for her?

She shifted back to the task at hand. About ten minutes remained until the teens filed in. Might as well start conversing with a young person now. Monica's granddaughter looked about thirteen. Harmless enough. She cast about her mind for a conversation starter with the girl. "Julie." She hesitated. She thought Monica had called the girl Julie. Oh well, press on. "What's your favorite thing about school?"

The brows above the girl's expressive eyes crinkled, as if she were in thought, and a sparkle shone. "I love English and reading." Spots of pink tinged Julie's cheeks.

"What are you reading now?" Books. Safe territory. Mahalia had loved English and reading as a child as well. The escape to worlds beyond her neighborhood. Adventure, romance. Sometimes a little fright, but then she'd always be sorry after—sleeping with the lights on and flinching at every creak in the floorboards.

"We're reading *The Giver*. We just finished *The Westing Game*."

"I haven't heard of those. I remember *Romeo and Juliet* and *1984* from high school." Granddaddy Henry found *1984* scandalous and had pitched a fit when he'd learned what was in it. She'd told him, "This isn't the 1930s, Granddaddy." He'd harrumphed around the house and threatened to run for the school board, but eventually he calmed down.

"I liked *Romeo and Juliet*." A soft smile played on the girl's face.

See there, talking to a teen's not that hard. She could do this. The meeting would be fine.

The doors of the courtroom banged open, and a mass of students tumbled in. Maybe everything wouldn't be fine. What had she gotten herself into?

***

"You guys did a good job." Mahalia brought the evening's session to a close earlier than the usual ending time. The teens had mostly stayed on task and listened to her talk. The boys had all sat clustered together, and some interrupted with noises and jokes. She didn't have all the names down yet, but she'd thought Tanner, some other boy, and Kyle passed a cell phone between themselves, held low near their laps. When she'd threatened to report it to Attorney Cash, the one with the letterman jacket paled and stowed it.

The session had turned out to be less interactive and more lecture, but she'd stumbled through. "We've got some time, so eat some food and ask me questions..." What? Why did she open the floor to questions from teenagers?

She worked her way from the front of the courtroom and headed to the bunch standing around the spread.

"Your Honor, what happened to Mr. Cash?"

Mahalia scanned the clump of kids for the speaker. The blond-haired girl had a braided ponytail with feathers woven into it. The girl's name danced on the tip of Mahalia's tongue.

"There's a fire in Ventura County. He asked me to step in."

Anxiety pinched the girl's face. "Do you think he'll be okay?" Her hands fidgeted.

"He's not near the fire. Just stuck in the traffic."

The girl's shoulders dropped from their tight clench, and she stepped closer. "Do you like working with Mr. Cash?"

It wouldn't be right to continue talking without knowing who the girl was. "Please tell me your name again..."

"Brittany, Your Honor."

"Well, of course, Brittany, I enjoy working on this program with Mr. Cash. The judicial system is more than trials and hearings. It's one of the things that makes our country what it is. The right to a jury trial, the right against self-incrimination. These things are in our Constitution. The populace needs to understand how the system works."

AN APPEARANCE OF IMPROPRIETY

"Populace?"

A loud snort came from the section of the food table holding turkey sandwiches, putting Mahalia on alert.

"Nobody's ever called me a popu-whatchamacallit before. Sounds like a bunch of rules and regulations."

She squinted. Now certainty clicked in. "Tanner with a *T*." She gave the boy a look she hoped would rein in any planned outbreak of foolishness. "What I meant by the word is, people who live here and participate in our system, our economy. All the people who make up the fabric of America." Even to her own ears, she sounded duller than a C-SPAN lecture. *Loosen up. Where's all that heart you say you have?*

"You are all going to be adults soon. Bills, jobs, kids."

"I already got a job."

"And you are . . ." She put a small wince on her face as an apology.

"José." He wore a green hoodie embossed with a soccer ball and the words *Selección Nacional de México* in large white letters across his chest. "I got a job at the bodega around the corner. I stock the shelves and sweep up."

"Yeah, and give girls free candy."

"Don't hate the player—hate the game." José held out his hand, and the boy who towered over the others gave him a three-part handshake, ending on a snap of the fingers as their hands pulled apart.

The students finished up their food. Movement caught her eye, and she waved to Monica, who'd packed up and was hustling out with her granddaughter.

"Aw man."

Mahalia turned toward Brittany. Worry stamped the girl's face, and her lips pulled down.

"Everything okay?" Apprehension tugged at Mahalia's brain.

"My mom's running twenty minutes late. She's supposed to give Mercedes a ride too. Can you take us?"

Ugh. No way to fit both girls in her Eco4/2Microcar. "I wish I could. I've got a two-seater." Mahalia turned to see the last of the other students leaving the courtroom. She couldn't stick two minors in an Uber and wave goodbye. Her options diminished to one. "I don't mind waiting. It's not a problem." She gave them a smile to ease their worry.

Brittany's expression lifted.

She gestured with her hands, and the girls each took a seat in the gallery. Mahalia sat across the aisle from them and dug her phone out of her handbag. A nice free moment to see if the price had dropped on those strappy lace-up sandals she had her eye on.

Several minutes ticked by. She placed her phone back into her bag and focused on the girls.

"Sweet phone, girl. When'd you get that?" Brittany asked Mercedes.

"Got it Monday."

"Your mom working more overtime?"

"Nah."

Mahalia glanced up.

An odd look passed over Mercedes's face. "Nothing like that."

"Gimme." Brittany snatched the phone away from Mercedes and gave a whistle. "This is nice." She knocked her shoulder against Mercedes "Spill the tea."

Given the look on Mercedes's face, Mahalia wanted to hear the inside scoop as well. She focused on sitting still so her presence wouldn't draw the girls' attention.

Wine colored splotches stained Mercedes's cheeks. "I don't want to say." She dropped her head. "A dude gave it to me."

"Girl, why'd some guy hand over a phone? No questions asked?"

"We started talkin' on Insta after he liked some of my pics. Next thing I know, he's handing me a phone."

"He's in your DMs, and out of nowhere he handed you an eight-hundred-dollar iPhone?"

Brittany's sharp look and raised brows mirrored Mahalia's incredulity.

"I don't know. I think I said something about my phone storage being full and having to delete one app to use another. He gave me this phone the other day in the hall."

Brittany's jocular expression soured. "Girl, that sounds shady. You sure about this?"

"Why?"

"What if he stole it?" Brittany pulled her lids back and cocked her head at Mercedes.

AN APPEARANCE OF IMPROPRIETY

"He didn't steal—" Mercedes huffed.

"You don't know that."

Mercedes crossed her arms over her chest. "Someone told me he's got some NIL money coming in."

"For real? I'd heard there were a couple of kids who might get name, image, and likeness deals if they make it to college." Brittany's eyes were wide. "I think . . ." She held up her hand. "Langston, plus two other dudes on the basketball team are good enough for college sponsorship deals. Someone on the girls' basketball team. There's Tanner and another guy on the football team." She held up a finger for each name. "I hear he's got a sneaker deal in the works for when he signs with a college."

"It's true. D-1 schools here in California, and even some on the East Coast, are trying to sign Tanner," Mercedes said.

"Those basketball guys are cool, but, girl, if it's Tanner, you'd better give it back. I've heard things . . ." Brittany pursed her lips, like she'd eaten sour candy.

"What have you heard?"

Brittany cut her eyes to Mahalia. "Never mind what I've heard. Judge Jackson, what do you think? Does this sound legit?"

Mahalia had never practiced law in the area, but a few facts still stuck from that third-year entertainment and sports law class. "The law may have changed on this because of the new name, image, and likeness rules for the NCAA, but whoever gave it to you should still be careful. It's not a free-for-all. There are still regulations on boosters and recruitment. He could jeopardize his chances for a scholarship."

"Girl, you better find out. You don't need this kind of trouble."

"It's an expensive gift, Mercedes." Mahalia looked the teen in her eyes. "Please be careful. Sometimes girls and guys aren't on the same wavelength. There can be misunderstandings about intentions." She didn't want to be oblique, but Mercedes wasn't her daughter, and she didn't know which lines were appropriate to cross.

Brittany's phone rang out with the loud sound of a marimba and halted the conversation. "That's my mom."

After exiting the courtroom and stepping into the quiet, echoey hallway, the girls headed toward the elevator.

"Do you mind if we take the stairs? It's faster."

"No prob, Judge," Brittany said. She bounded toward the stairs with way too much energy for this time in the evening, her sneakers squeaking on the polished floor. Brittany skipped down the stairs, while Mercedes stayed behind with Mahalia.

Mercedes turned to her. "You're easy to talk to, Judge."

Was Mercedes pulling her leg?

"You listen and don't freak out like my mom and Brittany do."

"Well . . ." Incredulous, she choked on her words. "I'm glad I could help. Anytime."

At the lobby the girls rushed out and hopped into a waiting car. The passenger side window opened. Mercedes stuck her arm out and gave Mahalia a shy wave.

Mahalia headed for the entrance nearest her parking deck. Ahead of her was a familiar form in a letterman jacket. "Tanner?" This didn't make any sense. "What are you still doing here?"

"My mom's taking me home."

"This late? I thought all of you had already left."

"She works here." Tanner pointed to a woman emerging from a door that led to the first-floor file room."

"See you later, Judge."

Tanner's mom did not lift her head to greet Mahalia, but for some reason she seemed familiar. Tanner and his mother hustled out the front door without a backward glance.

The lack of a greeting felt intentional. Why would someone in the file room feel the need to be impolite? Had she offended the woman at some point?

Mahalia strode to the exit for the parking deck. Why was a varsity football player who had a parent with a good job at the courthouse in the Junior Juror program? If Tanner was doing well enough to have an NIL deal, why was he spending his precious spare time on the mock trial team? Shouldn't he be at practice? She reminded herself that Langston was a varsity basketball player, and he attended the Junior Jurors as well.

The questions swirled like a stirred pot of soup.

There had been a bright spot this evening. Mercedes's brief words touched something deep inside of her. That a teen found her helpful, and a good sounding board, might be the best compliment she'd received all year. She felt capable in a way that had nothing to do with being a judge. The words validated her. As if she'd been asked to join the cool kids at lunch, something that had never occurred when she was Mercedes's age. Thoughts of the expensive iPhone crashed back in. Disorientation and satisfaction overwhelmed her simultaneously.

***

Comments on Instagram Post

HighlightKing: UR new phone's fire. You like it?

ChicChica: Yep. No more "storage full" drama.

HighlightKing: You see my pics?

ChicChica: UR buff. Those 2 x Day practices are working.

HighlightKing: Gotta keep it tight. So are you some dude's lock screen?

ChicChica: Nope. Solo for now.

HighlightKing: Bet. Send me some DMs. Tonight.

Chapter 13

THE NEXT WEEK, Mahalia took in the chattering adolescents in amazement. The end of October marked five weeks into her stint, and after the first bumpy sessions, she'd hit her stride with the kids. She rustled up small talk with the guys and chatted about fashion and hairstyles with the girls. Nothing life changing or earth shattering, but she no longer felt stiff and clunky around the students, like the Tin Man from *The Wizard of Oz*.

Cash stood near some boys in a deep discussion. He'd ditched his tie and coat and had folded back the sleeves on his gray dress shirt. His watch face flashed in the overhead light, the large dial so rugged and sturdy that it might have been something he used in the military. The slim fit of his darker gray slacks, with a razor-sharp crease, gave him a timeless masculine elegance.

End-of-session chatter faded as the kids meandered from the courtroom.

"Judge Jackson, I'm so sorry to do this to you, but do you mind giving Mercedes a ride home? It's a bit of an emergency. Brittany couldn't make it, and Mercedes's mom can't get off work. I have a policy of not driving the kids by myself."

Cash trained his eyes on her, and her heart did a weird flip-flop thing. *Oh my. Not good.* She shook off the butterflies. Besides, how could she refuse to take a student home if it was a genuine emergency? Plus, she and Mercedes had bonded, hadn't they? The short ride only gave enough time for pleasantries. She could handle it. "Yes, I've got room for one passenger in my car. Mercedes, text your mom to get her permission."

A few moments later Mahalia and Mercedes exited the courtroom, and JD snapped the lights off behind them. The trio entered the elevator, maneuvering around JD's trial bags, and Mahalia's stomach twisted. Something about this elevator always made her anxious. She swept the thought out of her mind like someone brushing crumbs off a table.

Cash angled his head toward Mercedes. "You getting excited about the mock trial?"

"I am, Mr. C. Working on this has shown me I like organizing things. Right now I'm in charge of the exhibits, but I'm hoping to have a seat at counsel table during the competition."

Cash gave her a fatherly smile. "We'll see. I haven't decided yet."

The elevator reached the ground floor with its characteristic bounce, and Mahalia took a large step to exit as quickly as her legs could propel her. The rapid snap, snap, snap of her heels on the gleaming floor of the courthouse entryway exposed her anxiety, and she slowed her pace.

Tanner appeared from the door near the file room.

"Is your mom inside, Tanner?"

The stern tone of Cash's voice caught her off guard.

"Yes, sir."

"Alright. No wandering around the building after hours. Rejoin her. See you at the next meeting."

She looked at Cash surreptitiously to see what lay behind his tone, but his face was a neutral mask. He looked her way, and a smile replaced the undecipherable expression.

They reached the doors on the side of the building where her car was garaged, and Cash somehow held the door for her and Mercedes and negotiated his gear outside at the same time. The balmy night air smelled slightly of bus exhaust.

"We've got it from here, Mr. Cash." Mahalia attempted to dismiss him to load his massive vehicle with his paraphernalia.

"No can do, Your Honor. I'll see you two to that Matchbox you call a car."

A snort escaped from Mercedes. "He roasted you good, Judge."

She trained her gaze on Cash and sent him pointy little daggers of ire.

"It gets the job done."

"That it does, Your Honor."

Mercedes entered on the passenger side, and Mahalia slid in on her side as Cash held the door for her.

He burst out laughing. "Sorry, Your Honor. Forgot you're sensitive about your golf cart . . . I mean, electric car." His downturned eyes gleamed with humor.

"I'll see you at the next meeting, Mr. Cash."

Cash saluted as she backed her car out. She instructed Mercedes on how to pair her phone and enter the address into the navigation system while watching Cash retreat in her rearview mirror. At the security booth, she swiped her badge, and the arm lifted. The glow of Mercedes's gifted-to-her phone emanated from her side of the car. Mahalia looked at the GPS and flicked on her blinker to make the first right. She reached her hand out to turn on music to fill the awkward silence.

"Your Honor, um, can I ask you something?" Mercedes's hushed voice lacked its usual confidence.

Mahalia pulled her hand back from the stereo controls. "Of course."

The GPS emitted a beep, directing her to take the next turn, and silence returned to the car. Mercedes sniffled.

Mahalia glanced over and saw tears on the girl's cheeks. "Mercedes, you're scaring me. What's going on?"

The infernal GPS beeped again, and she pulled the car over to a side street. Her eyes scanned the neighborhood. Not the safest place to park the car. Across the street, a strip mall beckoned with a sign for a twenty-four-hour doughnut shop. She parked in front, and the sugary sweet smell of pastries drifted into the car's interior.

She killed the ignition and turned to the teen. "What's really going on?"

"You and Brittany told me to give this phone back, but I didn't listen."

"Is it stolen? Are you in trouble?"

"No, it's not that." Mercedes sniffed and swiped her hand under her nose. "I didn't think about it. I mean, it was cool, you know?"

"Who gave you the phone, Mercedes?"

Mercedes hung her head, tears dripping from her eyes to her lap. "If I say something . . ."

"It's okay, Mercedes. You can trust me."

"If I say something, he could lose everything."

Mahalia sat, giving the girl space to tell the story.

"He'd kind of flirted. Told me I was pretty. Made me smile at school. But he's been texting me every day now. So many texts."

AN APPEARANCE OF IMPROPRIETY

"And?" Mahalia kept her voice soft and even, but anxiety pulled at her insides.

"He keeps asking to come over to my house. Asking for pictures. Sending me pictures. He keeps saying things. Things that make me feel bad. Said I should have known what the deal was when he gave me the phone." Mercedes threw her hands up to her face and sobbed.

Nothing about being a judge who handled dry corporate matters had prepared Mahalia for this. She wasn't a family court judge. She'd been a low-drama teenager, as had her cousins. Everyone on the straight and narrow. The best grades. The best behavior. Sheltered from any kind of situation that might draw her off the path to the golden ticket waiting at the end of the journey.

She hearkened back to her days in the legal practice. Ask questions. See what she could learn.

"May I see those pictures?" She held her breath. *Please, please don't let there be anything that rises to the level of a prosecutable offense.* Mahalia held the phone as if it might burn her skin off and scrolled up. *Tanner.* Football workout photos and lots of sweat. Selfies in the bathroom mirror. Sultry stares. She felt icky seeing Tanner in shirtless pictures, and his come-hither looks made her skin crawl. Tanner wanted pictures of Mercedes in a bathing suit. He'd suggested he wanted her to send pictures wearing even less.

Mahalia wasn't a mom, but her instincts told her this clearly was a matter for the girl's family. "What does your mother say, Mercedes?"

"If my mom knew I was talking to a boy like this, she'd lose it. She had me so young. Told me if I ever did anything like that, I'd learn the hard way, like she had." Mercedes started crying again. "I'm afraid she'll kick me out if she sees this."

The confines of her Eco4/2 had them sitting so close that Mahalia felt as though she and Mercedes stood stuffed together inside a phone booth. She doubted Mercedes's mother would kick her out over text messages. But as Mercedes's anguish filled the interior, Mahalia scoured her brain for an answer.

The look Cash had given Tanner in the hallway. What was that about? She needed to talk to Cash before she advised Mercedes.

The girl sniffled.

"Don't answer his messages. Will you see him in school tomorrow?"

"No, not if I eat lunch in the B cafeteria."

"Good. We'll work this out, Mercedes. I promise."

A drowning sensation overcame her. She was out of her depth. If she were Mercedes's mom, would she expect a call? Was that even Mahalia's place? Cash's reaction to seeing Tanner had been off. She didn't know what to do.

"*Mahalia baby, you know what the old hymn says. 'Take it to the Lord in prayer.'*" Granddaddy's frequent admonition sounded as fresh to her mind as if he had at that moment whispered it in her ear.

"Give me twenty-four hours to figure this out, and I'll be in touch." She squeezed her eyes shut and sent up an SOS.

***

Instagram DMs from HighlightKing to ChicChica

HighlightKing: You there?

HighlightKing: I know you're online.

HighlightKing: Why won't you answer me?

ChicChica: Please stop.

HighlightKing: I'm not stopping. I'm so into you.

HighlightKing: Why were you with the judge?

HighlightKing: You're messing with me. Don't.

Chapter 14

THE EERIE SILENCE of the courthouse on a weekend offered no distraction from the heaviness in JD's chest as he prepared for another session with the kids. Judge Goldstein had some paperwork to catch up on and had ushered him in as a favor before heading out for physical therapy. JD wheeled his exhibit binders and mock trial gear into the courthouse elevator and jabbed at the close door button a few times for good measure.

He'd squeezed in this post-Thanksgiving, pre-Christmas Saturday session with the students. He hoped none of the teens would play hooky. He wouldn't see them again until mid-January, so every second counted. The doors took their own sweet time closing, and the car lurched upward. A few seconds into its ascent, the elevator rocked from side to side, clanging against the walls of the shaft. Not so much slamming, but more like a boat bumping against a dock in gentle ocean waves.

The decision to remove Tanner from the Junior Jurors program still left an ache in his gut, but after discussing things with Judge Jackson, he knew he'd made the right call. It wasn't only about the rules. He'd told Tanner and all the kids the first day he could see their potential. Tanner had been a leader on the football field. But potential wasn't enough when weighed against the damage he'd caused. JD had suffered a migraine for two days after informing Tanner he was contacting the juvenile court immediately to recommend termination of the diversion agreement. His heart wrenched anew as he remembered Tanner's mom sobbing on the phone. The kid would lose NIL opportunities and scholarship offers, but he'd also made the choices that led to his circumstances.

JD trundled his exhibit dolly into the courtroom. Monica had arranged for catering to bring in boxed meals for the kids, and they would arrive in five minutes. There was still time to scoot back downstairs to open the door for the delivery guy and run back upstairs and organize all the exhibits and props.

Somehow Judge Jackson had made herself available for a Saturday session as well. They'd kept everything professional, so much so he didn't even know if she had to alter her weekend plans with someone special to be here today. A sinking sensation dropped through his middle. He gave himself a mental shake. This was neither the time nor the place to dissect Judge Jackson's romantic status.

Yet despite the mental effort, he was having trouble keeping his heart from its pull toward her. *There. He'd admitted it.* She tried to camouflage it, but he could sense her inner struggle with self-acceptance. They both had the need to prove themselves. When she had been elected, she was the youngest judge on the bench, and she was a woman. He came from nothing. No people. No money. The kinship he felt with the judge, combined with Monica's increasing efforts to get him to cut back on his punishing hours, was eroding the foundations of his pledge to himself. For the first time since the brief, ill-advised hiatus from his vow in law school, he felt the desire to rearrange the priorities in his life. It was disorienting and exhilarating.

***

The cavernous empty halls of the courthouse were a welcome respite to the usual bustle in the building. Mahalia had clocked countless Saturday and Sunday hours trying to stay ahead of her caseload, and the solitude helped keep her on task. She fiddled with the sleeve on her morning mocha to keep from singeing her fingers as her comfortable wedged heels carried her up the stairs. She was still a little spooked by the small tremblers over the last few days. Maybe someday she'd get used to the idea of the earth trying to shake itself to pieces, but she doubted it.

Mahalia entered the courtroom, where JD's impressive preparations were on full display. X-rays, phony medical records, a handout with an infographic of trial objections, and a neat stack of legal pads set the stage for the kids. JD frowned at the table, as though he wasn't quite pleased with the full-immersion trial experience he was providing.

AN APPEARANCE OF IMPROPRIETY

As students jostled through the door, JD put down a stack of papers and chuckled, doling out high fives and fist bumps as the kids milled around him.

The touch of melancholy she'd seen around his eyes the first time he'd appeared in court remained. What an interesting man. Out of judicial curiosity, she'd gone online to check the *Times'* coverage of the TransNation case. The pundit consensus leaned in Cash's favor.

"Alright, take a seat," he said. "We've got a lot of ground to cover today."

"Should we wait for Tanner?" Aisha blurted out.

"Tanner is no longer in the program," JD said, his tone firm enough to discourage any follow-up questions.

Some of the girls exchanged quick glances among themselves.

"Let's focus on today's lesson." JD paced at the front of the courtroom. "Over the last couple of weeks, we discussed all the players in a trial—the judge, the plaintiff's attorney, the defense team. Today we'll start with the job of plaintiff's attorney and do a pretend direct examination."

Mahalia watched the kids engrossed in JD's directions until an annoying phone buzzed. Aisha swiped around the screen and put the phone back in her purse.

He has them hanging on his every word.

"The plaintiff's attorney is the reason everyone's in the courtroom. His or her client is the one who sued and started the court proceedings. This lawyer is like a movie director. The words come out of the mouths of the actors, or in this case the witnesses. The job of the plaintiff's attorney is to convey the vision, pick the angles, and maintain the pace so that the court believes the plaintiff's version of the story."

Mahalia wished her law professors had explained trial procedure with such clarity. JD would make a wonderful professor. Like iPhone's Siri rousing from slumber to answer a question no one asked, her brain rattled off words—kind, compassionate, gorgeous.

Whoa, sister! She forced her attention back to what JD was saying.

"This afternoon José and Aisha will be the plaintiff's attorney and witness. I'll let you two decide who does what."

"Uh, Mr. Cash, you *know* I'm playing the plaintiff's attorney because I got it goin' on." Aisha gave Destinee a high five, the rhinestones and glitter in her dayglow-pink nail extensions sparkling as they caught the light.

José rolled his eyes.

JD chuckled. "I will act as the defense attorney and try to keep you and your witness from telling your story by objecting to the witness's testimony. And Judge Jackson will be on the bench to hear my objections and decide if they have any merit." JD gestured to Mahalia, and she ascended to the bench.

***

The students were doing an outstanding job acting as witnesses and attorneys. JD rotated through several of the boys and girls, trying to give everyone a chance. Pride burned in the back of his eyes. Judge Jackson was also getting into it. Giving him sass from the bench when he objected. The kids loved the banter between him and the Judge. He liked it more.

"Okay, everybody. We're finished for the day. Well done. If you want anything else to eat, grab a box on your way out."

The young ladies made their way to Judge Jackson, standing near her in awe.

"We sure hope you'll be here next semester, Your Honor. No offense to Judge Goldstein." Mercedes jerked a hand up and fiddled with her hair, the bashful gesture out of character with her normal demeanor. "Not dissing you either, Mr. Cash, but it's great having a woman judge show us how it's done." The gaggle of girls nodded in agreement.

"As it turns out, Judge Goldstein is not returning to the program this year, so you get your wish."

"You're stuck with me." Mahalia's shoulders hitched up slightly, then fell. Her smile held apprehension, but her words rang with sincerity.

"Girl power rocks." Destinee threw a fist in the air, and her hoop earrings wiggled.

"Okay, okay." JD laughed. "You guys get on out of here. Catch your rides. Buddy up if you're taking the bus or walking."

JD began packing up his exhibits. "Thank you again for taking over for Judge Goldstein, Your Honor."

"Please, at this point, when it's only the two of us, call me Mahalia."

"Mahalia it is." JD was used to calling judges by their first names on committees and at social gatherings. He loved the way her name rolled off his tongue. He'd have to watch himself.

"Let me help you take everything to your car," Mahalia offered.

"I can handle it."

"Many hands make light work."

Chivalry warred with the desire to spend a few more moments with her and crashed down in flaming defeat. "If you insist."

A comfortable silence settled as they packed up the few remaining lunches, exhibits, and miscellaneous papers into JD's menagerie of rolling caddies.

"My, my, counselor, you have an impressive amount of exhibit transportation gear."

Mahalia's mockery made him smile. "Some men are into cars as their wheels. I'm into dollies."

They squeezed themselves into the elevator, and JD hit the Lobby button.

"I'll walk you to your car. It's the weekend, and I want to make sure you're safe."

"No need. I'm a big girl."

"Yes, but you've forgotten rule number one."

Mahalia pursed her lips. "I know. You are a gentleman at all times."

As the words left her mouth, the elevator jolted. Mahalia's hand reached out and clutched his arm.

He covered her hand with his own and gave a gentle squeeze. "Almost down to the lobby. No need to worry."

The elevator lurched and clanged against the walls of the shaft. There was a sickening screech of metal scraping metal. The car swayed from side to side, followed by an abrupt drop. Mahalia's scream rang in his ears as her arms flew around him. He yanked her body closer to his and braced for impact.

The lights in the car flickered and died, and the elevator plunged into darkness.

Chapter 15

As the elevator jerked to a stop, terror clawed up Mahalia's throat. Her clenched teeth and jaw held it back. A clammy chill swept over her, bringing a total-body shiver in its wake. Mahalia struggled to compose herself as terror warred within her. Her better judgment told her to release JD from her vice grip, but willpower alone could not make her fingers disengage.

"It will be okay." JD's voice rumbled in her ear like distant thunder. "The emergency systems worked like they should. We'll be out of here in no time."

Her body shook. All attempts to suppress the quavers failed.

"Shh, it's okay. I've got you. We're safe." JD was running his hands over her back in slow, rhythmic circles.

The elevator listed from side to side. She tightened her grip around his midsection.

JD released his arms and moved to step back from her.

She clutched at him more tightly. "What are you doing?"

"I'm right here." He pressed the Emergency button. Three times. No one responded.

"Don't leave me." Her voice was shrill to her own ears.

"I won't. Trying to find my phone so we can call for help. Why don't you dig your phone out too?"

With reluctance, she untangled herself and found her purse to scrounge inside for her phone. There was a glow of light as JD unlocked his cell.

"All I'm getting is a busy signal. Try yours."

"Same."

"Let me see if I can pry the doors open." JD strained against the joint in the doors with no success.

The elevator was dark except for the faint glow from JD's phone.

AN APPEARANCE OF IMPROPRIETY

Lightheadedness overcame her, and she struggled to slow her breathing. She worked her tongue to generate moisture to swallow back the fear, but her mouth remained parched and tasted like metal.

"Might as well get comfortable until we can reach someone by phone. I think we were almost down to the lobby. We're not in danger. Elevators have multiple layers of safety built in."

He sounded certain. She wasn't so sure. The elevator swayed again.

By the glow of JD's cell phone, she watched as he maneuvered the trial caddies around the elevator to create a makeshift seating arrangement.

"Here, sit." He took her hands and guided her to a sturdy trial bag. He sat on another bag beside her.

"I'll add a timer on my phone to go off every twenty minutes. We'll try making calls when it chimes, but let's not use our phones in between, to save the batteries."

"How are you staying so calm?" A shiver racked her frame. She scooted herself closer to JD until the sides of their legs and their shoulders were touching.

"A tour in Afghanistan will do that for you." His tone was rueful.

***

Fear radiated off Mahalia and hit him in waves. He knew the smell. The feel of it. The sporadic micro-shivers of her body. The earthy scent of fabric dampened by perspiration, and the staleness in the air from her shallow mouth breathing. The sensations had imprinted themselves on him during his tour of duty.

He had some familiarity with other legal subspecialties, like products liability and manufacturer defect cases. Elevator safety precautions could fail, and there was no guarantee JD and Mahalia could, in fact, survive if they were stuck more than two stories up and the elevator took a further plunge.

Still, he'd been in tighter spots in combat. He'd enlisted straight out of high school and, after basic, had been shipped out for Operation Enduring Freedom. He'd spent the time sweaty, thirsty, and scared.

His mind reeled back to Afghanistan. Sarge had given a quick briefing about the location, layout, and potential complications before they headed out. The target was a mid-tier insurgent fingered for the IED attacks along the supply route. Thin cloud cover helped dim the moonlight as his squad entered the village. The layout matched the intel—two dozen low mud-brick homes clustered around the tiny central mosque and a water well. Sarge made a sweeping motion with his arm. The unit moved in stack formation, rifles up, all slightly crouched, one man close behind the next. From the wall of an outlying utility building, they worked their way into the village. The baying of goats and sheep masked the crunch of boots on dry dirt. The reassuring weight of his M4 carbine in his hands steadied his nerves.

A sudden burst of gunfire cracked from a rooftop, tightening the squad against a wall. Dust and debris filled the air, and various animals began baying and snorting.

"Country Boy! Direction?" cracked over his earpiece.

"Three o'clock. Rooftop." Adrenaline surged, increasing his heart rate. Every sound around him magnified, and his vision sharpened.

"Take cover," Sarge barked out.

Sweat trickled down his back, stinging his skin as he angled out to return fire, the acrid tang of gunpowder mixing with the scent of baked earth.

A whooshing sound, and then a blast exploded somewhere to his left, rattling his teeth and filling the air with the stench of burned metal and smoke.

"We're pinned down. RPG, rooftop, six o'clock!" Sarge swore in JD's earpiece. "Split up! Alpha team, circle left behind the mosque. Bravo, flank right and take him out—move, move!"

JD prayed as his squad, at Sarge's command, advanced toward the village center. Time blurred. His mind cycled through prayer in time with the rhythm of moving, aiming, firing—each motion a step further from the poverty he'd sworn to escape and closer to God.

***

A rolling aftershock returned his mind to the interior of the elevator. God had rescued him in Afghanistan, and he could rescue them now. And just like in Afghanistan, JD needed to focus on the matter at hand. Job one—keep Mahalia calm. Instincts kicked in, and he stretched out his arm, wrapping it around her.

"Is this okay, Mahalia?"

"Y . . . yes." The halting word squeezed out from between her teeth, which chattered in his ear.

He used his hand to make slow, methodical passes up and down her arm to ward off panic. To soothe and reassure her.

The fragility of her slight frame surprised him. A need to protect her at all costs roared and howled through him. *Shift gears. Keep her talking.* "Tell me something memorable from your childhood."

"Wh . . . what?"

"You know, your childhood. You were a child once, right?" He gave her a squeeze. "Okay, I'll go first." He reclined against the elevator wall and drew Mahalia closer, tucking her head against him. The metal handrail that circled the elevator car felt hard against his shoulder blades.

"I grew up poor. Trailer trash."

Mahalia drew in a sharp breath.

"It was what it was."

She nestled in closer, seeming to calm a fraction.

"Anyway, at one point, my mom cleaned offices in Westerville a few miles over. This was before big companies gobbled up mom-and-pop cleaning services. Compared to LA, Westerville's a pinprick on the map. Five miles from our house, but to us it was the big city." How young he'd been. And even though his childhood had been hard, he'd been sheltered by geography. A city like Los Angeles had felt as far away as Jupiter.

"The buildings there looked like skyscrapers to me. Not a one over ten stories tall. My mother took me to work with her once. I helped her empty wastebaskets. Ran back and forth emptying foam cups of coffee into the sink. Dusted plants.

"Mama sent me to this one office where there was a guy still working. He tells me to come in. I grab the wastebasket to empty it. He held me up, told me to sit. Papers covered the desk. There were bookcases floor to ceiling, wall to wall. With his wrinkled shirt and tie pulled to the side, it was clear this man worked hard."

"So I ask what he does. He says, and I'll never forget this, 'I help people hurt by huge companies. I represent underdogs. I try to make things better for people who can't help themselves.'" JD leaned back and closed his eyes.

"I asked him how he did that. He pointed at the shelves lining his room. 'With these books.' Then he tapped his temple. 'And with this.'"

None of the men who'd visited with Mama had done white-collar work. And there was no shame in blue-collar work, but this was the first man he'd ever seen who made a living with his mind.

"And that's the most memorable moment from your childhood?" Mahalia asked. Her voice hushed.

"Yup. I was ten. Started me thinking about how to use books and knowledge to leverage me and Mama out of the trailer park. I'd never seen books as powerful, but that guy told me law books and what was in them could change lives. That's why I started Junior Jurors. I wanted to take kids who believed using their fists or their bodies was the only way to have power. Point them to an alternate path." His stomach turned and momentary anger flared, remembering the men who'd used their fists against Mama.

Mahalia sighed. "Well, no question you've done that. Those kids hang on your every word."

"I try. I keep it real with them. Let them know about how I grew up and how I escaped."

He wouldn't mention the courtroom drama that had forever sealed his decision to become an attorney. Frozen in the quickset cement of his young psyche. Sixth grade. The day Mama had taken him to court to watch her testify about her injuries from a slip-and-fall accident.

That entire school year had been a nightmare. Not because of Mama's injuries but because she'd gotten hooked on OxyContin. When she couldn't get pain pills anymore, she'd moved on to home-cooked meth.

Chad, the scum Mama was dating, was two or three steps up the food chain from Mama's usual dregs. He'd located a quack chiropractor and a "writing doctor." The first to secure a questionable diagnosis and the second to keep Mama quiet and happy with endless, unnecessary prescriptions. He'd also located the contingent-fee personal injury attorney Mama used to sue the hardware store.

Chad sat behind Mama in the visitor's gallery of the courtroom, waiting for her to testify. The weasel lawyer representing her was a drinking buddy of Chad's, Billy Baggerly. He had slicked-back dirty hair, a pockmarked face, and a beer belly that strained the buttons on his cheap, shiny suit.

The attorney for Neighborhood Hardware, a national chain of mini Home Depot–like stores, sat at the table next to Billy's. JD had been awestruck by the tailored suit. The shoes polished to a high gloss. His hair, his watch, even his ink pen were all finer than anything JD had ever seen. Rumor in the trailer park had it that he'd flown in on a private jet from Dallas and rented a suite of rooms an hour from the courthouse, in the fancy Marriott.

The judge looked imposing from his perch above the courtroom. A black robe covered his frame, and an armed bailiff stood to the side in front of the bench. During the proceedings, the judge slammed his gavel down several times in response to objections and statements made by the attorneys.

On the side opposite the bailiff was the jury box. There twelve citizens sat ready to hear every word Mama said, weighing whether she was telling the truth or lying.

The pomp, the seriousness, and the power in the room all riveted him to his chair.

The bailiff called Mama's name, and she took the steps to the witness box.

"Raise your right hand."

Mama raised her shaking hand. Her thin dress, purchased the day before for five dollars at the Salvation Army, was unable to conceal the tremors of fear racking her body.

"Do you solemnly swear or affirm that the testimony you are about to give in this case shall be the truth, the whole truth, and nothing but the truth? So help you God."

"I do."

Mr. Baggerly's questions were straightforward. "How did you fall? Did you see any signs or cones telling you the floor was wet? Were any employees nearby with mops or rags?" It took him less than five minutes to question Mama.

The attorney for Neighborhood Hardware had risen to his feet like a flag being hoisted up a pole. The tall man spoke with clear, crisp diction. "Ms. Cash, four weeks before your alleged accident, you had to do thirty days of community service for drunk and disorderly conduct, didn't you?"

Baggerly popped out of his seat. "Objection, relevance."

"Sustained," the judge said.

"In fact, you were drunk the day of the alleged accident, weren't you?"

Billy popped up again. "Objection, relevance and inflammatory."

"Not so fast, Mr. Baggerly. Overruled."

"I wasn't drunk."

"But you had been drinking that day, hadn't you?"

"I had a little something with my hot wings."

"A little something, you say. When I call Jake Walker to testify, he will swear you and your partner in crime sat in his bar and drank three beers apiece at eleven o'clock in the morning, won't he?"

"Objection to the characterization."

"Sustained. Ladies and gentlemen of the jury, this is a civil court. There is no criminal action pending. Other than that, she can answer the question."

"I can hold my liquor." A blush stained Mama's cheeks.

"And you shopped at Neighborhood Hardware after three beers and now allege there was a puddle in the gardening section. Isn't that your claim?"

"Yes."

"But our security tape doesn't show a puddle, does it?"

"No idea what's on your video."

"Well, I'll tell you. We see your friend Chad leading the employee who works in home and garden over to look at potting soil in the back corner. Isn't that correct?"

"I was busy looking at plants."

"And that was your goal the whole time, wasn't it? To have Chad distract the only employee so you could stage a fall?"

"No."

Neighborhood Hardware's attorney strode with confidence to his table and snatched up a stack of papers. "Your Honor, these are Defense Exhibits 4 through 8. May we approach the witness?"

"You may."

AN APPEARANCE OF IMPROPRIETY

Counsel for Neighborhood Hardware laid two documents in front of Mama. "Do you recognize what's in these pictures?"

"Yes. The first is the front, and the other is the back of my trailer."

"Now Exhibits 6, 7, and 8. Do you recognize these?"

"They are the other trailers in my trailer park."

"Ms. Cash, there is not a single stick of landscaping in that trailer park, is there? Not one bush, not one potted plant, not one daisy?"

"I . . ."

"Objection, compound and badgering," Baggerly said in a defeated tone.

The judge kept his attention fixed on Mama. "Overruled. This is cross-examination."

Counsel for Neighborhood Hardware moved closer to the witness box, picked up the exhibits, and waved them around. "Yet you're asking the jury to believe that you were planning on purchasing a five-hundred-dollar Japanese maple to plant in front of your single-wide trailer?"

"I was only looking."

"Right." The attorney's face contorted with disgust as he stalked to his seat.

Mama looked like she didn't have a friend in the world, up there all by herself.

Everyone in the courtroom had had so much power. The judge, the hardware store attorney, even that weasel Baggerly. JD had decided that day that he wanted the same level of respect. Wanted people to listen to him and believe him. He'd also decided that nobody would do to someone else's mother what he'd seen done to Mama. She'd gotten herself in over her head with the jerk of the week. Rather than protect her, the dirtbag had roped Mama into a fraudulent scheme. He'd used violent, abusive behavior to trap Mama into a corner and make her do things she didn't want to do.

JD had witnessed that corporate defense lawyer take Mama apart word by word. No one in that courtroom had done a thing to stop it. Just like JD hadn't stopped the men who'd beaten Mama. He'd vowed that day to become a lawyer to help women who made poor decisions because they felt trapped. With his practice, in some small way, he could intervene before other moms fell into desperation.

Jayna Breigh

A jarring reminder timer clanged out, yanking him back to the confines of the elevator and dragging him out of his dead-end past.

***

Safe. Secure. The only thoughts inside with JD's arm around her. His presence countered the pitching of the elevator from aftershocks. With his side pressed to hers, she could feel the vibration of his rumbling voice. The sensation soothed her, and she'd held back sharp, pricking tears as he told his story. He removed his arm to check the phone, and her anxiety returned.

"Still busy. I set another timer."

She nestled back in when he rearranged his arm around her.

"We still have a mess of boxed lunches. We can eat the perishable food now and leave the other things in case we, uh . . ." The noise made by his swallowing echoed off the walls. ". . . overnight it here."

She got it. He was trying not to scare her. "Sure. I'll turn on my phone's flashlight and hold it up while you get the food."

JD divvied out sandwiches and cleared his throat. "Let's share a bottle of the water and leave some in reserve. We'll stay hydrated without drinking so much that sanitation becomes a problem."

"If I'm ever trapped in an elevator again, remind me to make sure that it's with an army JAG lawyer."

His chuckle was soft. "Well, we do what we can."

He shifted beside her. "Do you mind if I say grace before we eat?"

"Not at all." She tried to mask the surprise in her voice.

The hand that closed over hers was giant, firm, and reassuring.

"Dear Lord, we need you now, but you already know that. Please keep us safe and calm. Be with the kids. I pray they all made it home safely. And thank you for arranging for us to have food and to have gotten stuck together and not apart. We trust this situation to your care. In Jesus's name we pray."

At her "Amen," his hand gave hers a gentle squeeze.

She unwrapped the sandwich, surprised to find she had an appetite. "Is it me, or is this the best ham and cheese you've ever had in your life?"

"Gratitude. Sometimes it's the simple things."

AN APPEARANCE OF IMPROPRIETY

She nodded as she took another bite, then swallowed a small sip of water. "You pray like a preacher's son."

"Don't think anyone would use my daddy's name and the word *preacher* in the same sentence unless it was at his funeral. I never met him, but he raised Cain around our town till drinking and driving wrapped him around a telephone pole."

Her face flamed. "I'm sorry . . . that slipped out."

"I knew what you meant. Anyway, you've heard the expression 'no atheists in foxholes'? Applies to me. Got saved in Afghanistan. The chaplain corps has all types, and our base had a great one—serious about his faith and not afraid of hard topics. If he couldn't answer my question, he came back with the answer the next week."

The trial bag creaked under her weight. Something plopped onto her lap. "Chips?"

"Thank you." She opened the bag and dug in. The carb load of the salty potato chips provided a dopamine hit.

"The fear of death clung to me while I was over there. So much carnage. Gave me an eternal perspective. Now I try to focus on all the unseen realities instead of the fleeting here and now."

The crinkle of snack bags and crunching filled the elevator.

"Wow. You are not the man I thought you were."

"Are you flattering me, or should I clutch my pearls, Your Honor?"

A giggle slipped out. He was so different from what she'd expected. "I saw your billboard over the freeway. Animal-skin boots. Blood. I said to myself, whoever that guy is, he's the cheesiest low-rent lawyer out there."

"Ouch. That hurts, Mahalia."

"I don't mean it. It just doesn't match the man sitting in this elevator."

"I'm not trying to reach Beverly Hills clients. I'm the lawyer of last resort for people who live on the margins, like I did. Trailer parks. Down and out. The people who need me see my billboard and know I'm like them."

"Hmm."

"I *had* to go to the military to pay for college. No legacy hand-ups. I got rid of most of the drawl, kept what worked. Got fancy suits, but I will *never* forget what it's like to eat free breakfast and lunch at school and a scoop of peanut butter for dinner. Tennis shoes with duct tape on them. Cold blowing through the cracks in the walls. Drug deals at our door. For a time we didn't even have an entire trailer—just a rented bedroom we paid for by the week. School was my only escape."

"That had to be hard." Mahalia knew the words weren't enough. But it was all she had to offer this complex man who had turned out to be so solid and authentic. "Isn't there someone waiting for your call? Freaking out that you're not where you're supposed to be and calling 911 to get you out of here?" Why was she even asking? He was a lawyer and, worse, practiced law on her home turf. He wasn't what she'd been envisioning all these years. *Three strikes.*

Oh well, too late to take it back now. She squeezed her eyes shut, steeling herself for his reaction but hoping he'd let the question slide.

Chapter 16

Periodic popping noises and a creak like a building settling pierced the silence in the elevator. The warm but not uncomfortable air bore the subtle scent of tropical fruit that he'd come to associate with Mahalia.

She'd asked if anyone was waiting for him. Was she fishing to find out if he was single? His intuition told him he wasn't her type, but just in case . . . "The only woman waiting for me is my cat, Americano."

"A cat lover? Next you'll tell me you moonlight in the LA Philharmonic." Her tinkling laugh warmed his insides.

"It's ironic. I consider myself a dog lover. I hate cats. Moody, bossy, and spoiled. She was a gift from a grateful client. I can't help it. She bewitched me. Has me wrapped around her paw. Sometimes love comes when you least expect it, upending your expectations." He shrugged. "And is there a Mr. Judge Mahalia Jackson rushing over here to claw you out brick by brick if he has to?"

She tensed beside him. "No. Not yet, but. . ." Her response drifted out in a soft sigh.

Her answer came off hopeful, but this was not the time, nor the place to have thoughts about dating. He had to lock both his emotions and his attraction in a cage, at least until he and the judge had their feet on terra firma.

The timer bing-bonged on his phone, breaking the intimacy of the moment. He tried 911 again, and a whoop escaped when the call gave a ring, not a rapid dial tone. He punched the Speaker button.

"Nine one one, please state your emergency." The terse, emotionless voice of the operator crackled over the staticky connection.

Jayna Breigh

"This is Attorney JD Cash, and Judge Mahalia Jackson is with me. We're trapped in an elevator at the downtown Los Angeles County Courthouse."

"Are you injured?"

"No."

"Is there anyone else in the elevator with you?"

"No."

"Do either of you suffer from a medical condition that may flare up if you have to stay put for a while?"

JD turned in Mahalia's direction. "Judge?"

"No."

"No, neither of us has any condition that will require treatment in the next twenty-four hours." *Except having to use the facilities.*

"Please hold." More broken, disjointed noises and clacking sounded from the phone for what seemed like an eternity. "Are you still there?"

"Yes, we are."

"Mr. Cash, the quake's left LA Fire and Rescue swamped, but we'll send someone out as soon as we can. Sometime tonight. Hopefully, no later than tomorrow morning. I've consulted with the city engineer's emergency team. They've confirmed that the elevators in the courthouse can withstand aftershocks of this magnitude, and you shouldn't be in any danger."

"Thank you for your help. We'll hold tight." JD moved to push the End button, but the call disconnected with a click on the operator's end.

He flicked the cuff back on his sleeve, and a greenish glow emanated from his wrist. The session tonight had ended at seven o'clock, and his watch read ten thirty. For over three hours he'd tap-danced around the biggest thing going on in his life—the TransNation case. Even though Goldstein had taken back the reigns, as long as TransNation retained the option of appealing Mahalia's rulings, discussion of the case was off-limits. They'd covered the weather and every other generic chitchat topic. He'd run out of safe-ground material. He'd bust out an old night patrol time killer.

"Let's play a game." He resettled on the trial bag to make himself more comfortable. "Pull out your absolute worst dating story ever, and I'll tell you mine. Nothing's off-limits."

"So many horrible dates, so little time. Where to begin?"

Her words vibrated through him.

AN APPEARANCE OF IMPROPRIETY

***

JD's body heat filled the compartment. The rhythmic swaying of the elevator car with each aftershock lulled Mahalia into a weird calm. He was so easy to talk to. Genuine. They talked as if they'd known each other for years.

She shifted on her small perch.

"Got a cramp?"

"Seat's a little hard."

JD moved around, and fabric rustled. "Here, stand up for a second."

She complied.

"You can sit again."

When she did, there was material cushioning her backside. "Thanks."

"I've secured your comfort. The time for stalling is over, Judge. You were saying?"

A groan welled up. "Should I start with the security guard I once had lunch with, whom I watched eat a sandwich dripping with mayonnaise and then paid two hundred dollars to never call me again?"

"Man."

"Oh, there's more."

"Do go on." JD's voice held amusement, but not at her expense.

"One guy lectured me on the impropriety of offering to go Dutch on a date and then spent the entire time we were together with his fly down."

"Yikes. You didn't tell him XYZPDQ? That's standard elementary school etiquette where I come from."

"Not as quick on my feet with the schoolyard quips, I guess." A smile pulled from deep inside at his humor.

"Are there more?"

"Oh yes. In college I had a job in the business office at an auto dealership. There was an insistent porter."

"Porter?"

"Someone who washes cars and drives them around to the service center."

"Got it."

"He spent the first week asking me out, but I lied and said I couldn't because I had to watch my favorite soap opera in the break room every single day without fail. To make the lie real, I sat fixed in front of that TV every day all summer."

"Torture."

"The joke was on me. Do you know what happens if you watch a soap opera every day?"

"No. What?"

"You become addicted. Took me years to kick the habit."

"Don't know if I can top any of these stories."

"I doubt you can either. A prisoner wanted to write me. Not technically a date, I guess."

"Yikes."

"There was the waiter in Jamaica who wrote and proposed marriage in his first letter." Mahalia pushed out a rueful laugh. "I know a scam when I see one. Oh, and I forgot. While in law school with the most eligible dating pool I would ever have, I didn't have a single date."

"I can't believe that."

"No, it's true. Not one."

He gave a whistle. "Wow."

"So here I am, a sitting judge, and my dating past is littered with car porters, security guards, failed setups, and assorted good guys with less than zero going on in their lives. I don't know why I went on those dead-end dates. Maybe I thought if I kissed a few toads . . ."

"So," he fished, "you've never had a steady beau?"

She sighed. "Only an endless series of first, sometimes second, dates. There are men who find my color 'exotic.'"

JD started to cough. He probably hadn't been expecting that comment.

"Don't worry—that's also a nonissue. Once they find out that having a dark complexion doesn't make me desperate, those guys run."

"I don't get it, Your Honor."

"Ah. Colorism is one of the hidden secrets of the Black world. Women like me wait at the back of the line." She gave a shrug. "I've yet to find the forever brother of my dreams."

The darkness inside the elevator car was acting like a truth serum. The Midnight Prince didn't have to be a *brother*. The idea popped into her head like a flash from a camera. She switched gears. "What's your story? You've got the whole military-hero thing going for you. Why is there no Mrs. JAG?"

"Mrs. JAG. Funny, Your Honor." He listed to the side when she punched his arm. "I've been told I have a chip on my shoulder."

"I don't believe it." Nothing about him indicated he had a negative disposition of any kind.

"A few times."

He'd been nothing but professional in the courtroom. Strong. Determined. What was that all about? Was there a Mr. Hyde behind his upright Dr. Jekyll persona?

"Lived in trailer homes and cheap motels. A car. Used the military and its benefits to claw my way up from being poor. Didn't matter. There is always someone around who won't let me forget where I came from."

"Wouldn't have guessed."

"Yeah, the dirty little secret on my side of town is that classism is alive and well."

"Hmmm." She bit back a retort.

"Although some people act differently, God doesn't have heaven sectioned out by race, class, or anything else. But it still gets to me."

"Yes, but back to Mrs. JAG." Mahalia laughed.

"Well, because of my faith, I have certain other standards. Promises I've made to myself and try to keep. Plus, once women learn I'm a filthy-rich trial lawyer, the opportunists come out."

"Did you say filthy rich?" His deadpan sense of humor lightened her insides, distracting her from the creaking elevator.

"It's a minefield of gold diggers out there."

"Man, we're two pieces of work."

"That we are, Your Honor."

"Okay, we're finished with the dating horror stories," JD said. "It's twenty questions time."

"Ugh." A groan escaped. "Are you always this full of energy?"

"Nope. Pure adrenaline is fueling me." JD yawned, and the noise sounded like creaking hinges. "When we get out of here, I'm crashing. On night patrol I had to come up with something to keep my partner and myself awake."

125

"Got it."

"For the record, you just used up one of your twenty questions. Better make the rest count."

"Are you serious?"

"Deadly. Eighteen left."

"Grrrrr." His game almost made her forget she was trapped in an elevator. Mahalia laughed. "Okay, I've got one."

"Shoot."

"When did your hair turn gray?"

JD took a sharp intake of breath. "Wow. That's personal. I'm wounded."

She winced. "Sorry."

"I'm kidding." JD's laugh bounced off the walls.

"You're horrible."

"Yes, but lovable."

Wait, what? She'd move right past that comment.

"I started going gray in the military, even before I made it to college. Fully gray by twenty-five."

"I'm sure people gave you grief about it."

"Nah, it works for me, I guess."

You got that right. "Okay, your turn. Ask me a question."

"Birth order?"

"First, last, and only." The familiar ache pulsed in Mahalia's heart with that reminder. "My grandparents helped fill that void. My mother eventually settled down when I was in my late teens. She tried to position herself in society among the affluent Black bourgeoisie. My stepfather climbed the corporate ladder. I love my family, but there was a role they wanted me to fulfill, and I've done my duty. From a material perspective, I never wanted for anything though."

"But emotionally?"

"That counts as a question, you know?" Mahalia snickered.

"You lost a question too. That sentence was interrogative."

"That's why I never date lawyers. You can't have any fun with them." *Wait. Why was she talking about dating?* Maybe it was because she yearned for this sort of mental exchange. The crossing of swords in jest.

She rushed her words out, hoping he hadn't caught her slip. "Being raised by a pastor is challenging, but I cherish my memories of my grandparents. Granddaddy Henry passed about five years ago."

"I'm sorry for your loss." His genuine condolences soothed the momentary pang, which always flared at the mention of her grandfather.

"My turn." She brushed away the tender, emotional moment. "Favorite movie?"

He made a scoffing noise. "Not even a real question. I was a JAG lawyer. Everyone knows the answer is *A Few Good Men*. I expected better." His snort of derision was comical. "Okay, least favorite male fashion trend?"

"The Abe Lincoln. Hands down."

"The hat?"

"Ha, that was a question."

"Touché."

"No, beards without mustaches. A man needs to give that look careful consideration. You can count all the men who can pull it off on one finger. Abe Lincoln."

"Note to self . . ." JD pitched his voice like he was dictating a memo. "Scrap plans to cultivate a beard like Honest Abe."

He gave a hearty laugh, which warmed and permeated the pitch-black elevator and made Mahalia's stomach contract. She hoped playing twenty questions would hush the whispers from her bladder.

"My turn. Full name."

"Jimmy Dean Cash. Two first names, no middle name."

"Are you named after anyone?"

"Yes. Cash is our actual family name, like Johnny Cash. Mama loved that. The first name is after another country singer, Jimmy Dean."

A grown man who called his mother Mama. How sweet.

"You blew two questions with that one. Your current tally stands at eight."

Mahalia threw a joking elbow into JD's ribs. *That ought to shut him up.*

"You know, Mama told me back when I was in elementary school that when a girl play socks you, it's because she likes you. I think she was right, because the last girl who hit me tried to kiss me behind the monkey bars two days later."

"Counselor, it appears your ego is as massive as your billboard over the freeway."

"It might be, but the truth's the truth."

Was he right? Did she want to kiss him? *Can't go there.*

"What's your birth order?" It surprised her how interested she was in his background.

"Well, the most truthful way to answer that is to say I am my mother's only child, but my father had many children, some older and some younger."

"Point of information." Mahalia didn't want to blow one of her precious dwindling questions, so she wanted to ask the gaming committee to issue a ruling.

"The chair recognizes Judge Jackson."

"If I ask you to elaborate, does that count as an additional question?"

"Hmm. The chair will allow follow-up without penalty. This question only."

"Was it hard?" She swallowed. "Being so poor?" Her voice was near inaudible, even to her own ears.

JD moved beside her. "Hey, can we sit back-to-back? The bar on the elevator wall is killing me."

Mahalia only hesitated for a beat. "Sure."

She stood. The scrape of JD rearranging the trial bags was the only sound.

"Okay, use your hand to find it so you don't fall."

Mahalia situated herself on the bag again.

"Here I come. Lean back. If we balance right, it should work for both of us."

She settled against his broad back, and a pine scent mixed in with what could only be described as m-a-n enveloped her. She registered slight movement against her spine as he adjusted.

"Is that comfortable?" His voice resonated throughout her torso.

Wonderful. "Yes." Despite the periodic aftershocks and the darkness, fear no longer held her captive.

***

Maybe she would forget her question about his childhood. The poverty. That was fine with him. He didn't want to rehash any of that. It wasn't because it was painful. Okay, it was. But he was taking the Apostle Paul approach. It was all behind him. For. Good. He'd moved thousands of miles away from that life, those people, and he never wanted to see them again. Ever.

California was a place where a man could reinvent himself. Thomas Cruise Mapother IV became Tom Cruise. Dwayne Johnson morphed into the Rock.

The drugs, the beatings, the fear that had dogged him every step of his childhood. The helplessness. His inability to pull his mother out of the quicksand that sucked them both under. All in the past. The only things he'd allowed to survive were the memories of happier times. Mama's love. Her music. The songs locked his feelings in a memory jar. He could listen to them again and again to feel close to her.

He'd skip right past that. "We've got a few more hours. What's your life story? You hinted that you were a preacher's kid."

"A preacher's grandkid—almost the same thing. But church doesn't move me the same as it did when I was a child listening to my grandfather preach. I don't feel like God is talking to me anymore."

"You should come to my church sometime. It's different. You might like it."

She stiffened against him.

"After there's no possibility of an appeal and all our Junior Jurors work is done . . ." He stopped short of mentioning the TransNation case by name.

Her shoulders, still pressed against him, relaxed. "I might take you up on that."

***

Mahalia swiped open her phone and stole a peek—12:18 in the morning. The elevator jerked again. Still on the trial bag, she gasped, turned, and clutched at JD. No. Not now. A shudder racked her. She must retain the modicum of dignity that her office as judge required, even in these circumstances.

The cocoon-like intimacy of the elevator was on a path neither of them could afford to go down. The stress was messing with her, ramping up her anxiety.

She missed Granddaddy. She didn't have a husband or kids. Was her house still standing? She'd climbed to the pinnacle of her profession only to find it a barren wasteland. She was doing everything alone. Pride forced her to pry her fingers off JD and start her mantra. *Prestigious college. Check.* She shoved the fear back with her accomplishments and her stature in the legal community. *But is that all you are?* Why was she having these doubts?

"Hey, it'll be okay." JD's voice soothed her.

Her introspection spun out from this ordeal and into the future. What would it be like to have this gentle, brilliant man love her? *What?* Fear had driven her to the brink of insanity.

She inhaled. Once. Twice. Then she coughed over the lump in her throat. "I'm fine. Tired of waiting here. This whole"—she waved her hands, like she might conjure words—"this whole thing has me on edge."

"I've seen you under pressure in court. You can handle this."

But could she? Fatigue and the desire for connection and safety overwhelmed her.

I want to kiss him.

Was she having a nervous breakdown? A panic attack? She barely knew this man outside of court. A manic desire to laugh pushed up and attraction churned, short-circuiting her reason. This made no sense. Not the timing, the circumstances, or the person. A rolling aftershock collided the walls of the elevator against the shaft, and rationality fled.

Bang! Bang! Bang!

She jerked herself ramrod straight while jackhammer-like pings rang through the elevator's interior, yanking her mind back to their immediate crisis.

"LA County Fire Department. You in there, Judge Jackson?"

"We're . . ." She struggled to get her voice to work. "We're in here." She cleared the crackle in her throat, like she needed a bit of water to erase the last few hours of fear . . . and the fact that she'd wanted to kiss JD.

Metal on metal made scraping noises, and the indistinct voice commands over a two-way radio broke into the elevator. The moment the doors opened, two pops of light flashed in the interior, blinding her for a moment.

AN APPEARANCE OF IMPROPRIETY

What in the world?

She tried to adjust her eyes as the firemen helped her out. Another burst of light.

"What is that?" Fatigue and fury spewed the words out. She squinted to discern body shapes in the dim lobby. Her limbs shook, and she willed herself into composure while an EMT helped her navigate the three-foot gap between the elevator floor and the ground.

***

Firefighters assisted JD with unloading his trial bags and stepping out of the elevator.

Emergency lights and lanterns placed by the rescue squad shadowed the lobby and gave it a haunted-house appearance. Two paramedics led him and Mahalia to a bench in front of the security station and asked the standard questions.

"I'm fine. No. No injuries," Mahalia said, looking as disoriented as he felt. Someone shoved her handbag toward her.

"May we check your blood pressure, Judge?"

She gave a stiff nod.

JD watched as a paramedic wrapped a blood pressure cuff around her arm and began inflating. Another did the same for him.

Like a specter, Dinkelman emerged from the wings.

"Your Honor, Jim Dinkelman, *San Gabriel Daily News*. Are you hurt?"

Why was Dinkelman even talking to her?

"Aren't you hearing the TransNation case?"

"Dinkelman, this isn't the time or the place." At this infernal hour, the man was worried about a case Judge Jackson *wasn't* presiding over? "Call my office in the morning. Let the EMTs clear Judge Jackson so she can go home." Anger simmered in his gut at the disrespect.

The paramedic shone a light in Mahalia's eyes again, and Dinkelman pressed closer and got into her personal space, a trace of desperation on his features.

"Just a few more questions, Your Honor."

"Sorry, Judge." Another rescue worker intervened and yanked Dinkelman's arm. "That's it. No more ride-alongs for you. Out!" The man shoved the reporter toward the door.

Dinkelman gave JD one last look as he exited.

"Mr. Cash, you both look fine. We're gonna do a quick building sweep." The firefighters and EMTs trudged toward the stairs.

Exhaustion crashed in on JD. "Let's get you to your car."

At the parking garage, Dinkelman slithered from behind a pillar. A flickering fluorescent light revealed the desperation and animus on his face.

Somewhere inside JD a switch flipped. Dinkelman was a man harassing a woman. Not on JD's watch. The simmering anger boiled.

"Dinkelman, we were stuck here for over six hours. We're both done talking."

The reporter lurched in Mahalia's direction, his camera raised. "One more picture." He tripped over one of JD's trial bags, knocking into her.

Mahalia's purse dropped from her shoulder, and the contents clattered as it spilled across the concrete.

She gasped and wobbled in her heels.

Off-balance, Dinkelman plowed into Mahalia. She went down—hard. Dinkelman landed on top of her with a thud.

Red streaks of rage blurred JD's vision. "Get off the judge, Dinkelman." He grabbed the reporter by the scruff and yanked him upright. The smell of perspiration and expired deodorant almost gagged him.

Dinkelman flailed and jerked to free himself, and with a crack, his elbow connected with JD's cheekbone. Pain pulsed across JD's face.

"Back off, Cash," Dinkelman spat out, his breath stale.

JD looked at Mahalia. Their gazes tangled. The moisture in her eyes rent him in two.

Dinkelman freed himself from JD's grasp and, instead of helping Mahalia, he popped off more pictures. "Remember, she is a public figure. I have the right to ask questions and take pictures." He looked back at JD and sneered.

JD had seen that twisted look before in the faces of men who had used and beaten Mama. His restraint was on a razor's edge. Summoning every ounce of self-control, he stepped forward, bypassing the reporter, and crouched to help Mahalia gather her things and rise.

AN APPEARANCE OF IMPROPRIETY

"Still no comment, Your Honor?" Another pop of light pierced the darkness. Dinkelman had moved in even closer.

JD sprang up from his crouch beside Mahalia to tell the jerk to step back. Instead, the top of his head collided with Dinkelman's face with a sickening crack.

Chapter 17

Two a.m. and JD drove home on the eerily silent streets. Seven hours from the plunge that had trapped him in the elevator with Mahalia. His head ached from where it had connected with Dinkelman's skull, and his face throbbed where the twerp had clocked him in the cheek while flailing around. Neither he nor Dinkelman had thrown intentional punches, but they'd both gotten banged up in the scuffle.

A spot of good news, though—no signs of damage to the streets or buildings on his way home. Still, he drove with caution in case liquefaction had created unexpected sinkholes. Streetlights continued to burn. All the power poles remained upright. He parked and made his way to his condo. He'd extracted a promise from Mahalia that she'd call as soon as she reached her house, but he'd heard nothing yet.

He opened his front door. Americano yowled and pounced on his shoes, demanding affection. JD scooped up the trembling cat and cuddled her close.

"Poor baby." He kicked his shoes off and padded to the kitchen to check her food. Untouched. A puddle of sloshed-out liquid circled her water bowl.

He worked his way around the rest of his apartment. TV remote on the floor. The picture of Mama lay tipped over on the bookcase. That was it. "You never know about an earthquake, do you, Americano?"

Americano purred and burrowed closer in response.

His cell phone rang, loud and insistent in the dim apartment. Americano clawed his chest at the disruption. "Ow." He shifted her to one arm and caught the call on the third ring.

"Yello."

"Mr. Cash? JD?"

AN APPEARANCE OF IMPROPRIETY

He'd know that honey-sweet voice anywhere. "Your Honor. You're home."

There was a pause.

"I'm okay. My place is a mess. Pipes burst. I turned off the water, but my house is flooded."

"Oh man. I'm so sorry."

"Couldn't reach my insurance company."

"Not surprised." He chuckled. "I deal with them every day. Scum suckers."

"Yes, well. Um, could I ask a big favor?"

"Anything." Seconds passed in silence.

"You said you live downtown. My place is all wet. I can't take any more... I don't have anywhere else to go."

Everything inside JD stilled. Like a night on patrol when something felt off. Like the moment in the courtroom when the witness's answer could crater or make his case. He reminded himself to breathe.

She sniffed. "May I come over?"

The teary sound of her voice and the fact that she had nowhere else to go activated his protective instincts. His mouth engaged before his brain. "Of course." He gave her the address and signed off.

"Looks like we're having company, girl."

Americano *hated* company.

***

Mahalia packed some essentials, and thirty minutes later she gave a gentle rap of her knuckles on JD's door. It opened with a gust of air, and a crisp pine scent surrounded her. A few water droplets dripped from JD's slicked-back silver mane. He wore a well-worn navy-colored jersey T-shirt emblazoned with "JAG Softball," and gray sweats covered his long legs. Giant, pale man-feet stuck out from the bottom of the pants, and he sported a purple bruise on his cheek. JD's expression was kind but guarded. The fuzzy chocolate-brown cat tucked under his arm gave her the stink eye.

"Come in."

She stepped into the entryway with the hobo bag she'd sloshed into her bedroom to find, and JD shut the door behind her.

135

She turned and faced him. "I called around, but all hotels within a reasonable distance are already full of earthquake refugees." A shudder racked her. She lifted her head to gaze at the ceiling and kneaded her neck with her hand.

"My dearest friends don't have power, and their hands are full wrangling little children. I even tried Judge Goldstein." Loneliness pressed on her. What she wouldn't give to have her mentor's dear wife fluttering around her right now and Goldstein bolstering her with his Yiddish endearments. "He's safe in Palm Springs, celebrating his anniversary."

Busy signals had greeted her when she'd reached out to some other acquaintances. Tears threatened to spill, and she huffed out a groan. The irony—he'd been her last desperate call, and somehow the line had connected.

A semblance of composure returned. "May I?" She reached out to scratch under Americano's chin, hoping to make a peace offering. The cat purred under her ministrations. Inside, a knot of anxiety loosened a fraction.

"I was going to"—JD stopped, marvel in his eyes as Americano rubbed herself against Mahalia's outstretched hand—"put Americano up in my room because she's antisocial and a little psycho. Looks like she likes you though. That's a first."

He put Americano down and led the way to the living room.

Americano made a beeline for her feet, rubbing and purring as she wound her way around her ankles.

"It's a couch, but it's comfortable." He pointed to a huge sectional that looked like it would cradle and cushion every tired muscle in her body.

"I can't tell you how much I appreciate you for letting me stay." Tears threatened to spill. Again.

JD looked away and stared into the distance.

"We're . . ." He appraised her. His searching expression was unreadable. "Foxhole friends now."

"Foxhole friends?"

"You've heard the expression 'no atheists in foxholes.' Foxholes also produce fast friends."

The melancholy pools of his eyes were near obsidian. They transfixed her. Made her want to remove the pain and replace the sadness with sunshine.

AN APPEARANCE OF IMPROPRIETY

She squeezed her eyes shut. He was so tactful. By declaring them friends, he allowed her to save face.

"Shower's down the hall. I'll make tea while you freshen up."

Her throat was dry. "Thanks," she mouthed.

In the bathroom, Mahalia inhaled. It was as if JD were right beside her. The wood tones calmed her. He'd placed a towel and face cloth beside the sink. She pulled out her shower cap and sloughed her clothes.

Under the water the fatigue of the day caught up to her, and the tears fell. Years of schooling followed by climbing to establish her career had frayed her connection with girlfriends, and there was no man she could lean on. She was a mess. Granddaddy couldn't help her now. Her eyes prickled at the thought of him. He'd have told her she needed to get back in church. *"To rub up against some saints. Let 'em love on you."* She felt overwhelmed. Tired of carrying all her life's responsibilities on her own. She put her bath gel down and reached for JD's in the corner. The rich masculine scent rose in the lather, and she let the tears flow like rain. She promised herself she'd go to church the first chance she got. That thought gave way as an IMAX movie of a life with JD invaded her mind without invitation.

***

Complicated described this thing with Judge Jackson. Yes, an earthquake, flooded house, and zero hotel rooms was an emergency. She had nowhere else to go. But their interaction would still be grist for the courthouse gossip mill if word ever got out she'd spent the night. She wasn't on his case anymore, but some of her rulings were appealable. A dirt-slinging attorney for TransNation might make career-tarnishing insinuations about the appearance of impropriety. And Dinkelman? He'd snapped at least a dozen pictures. Who knew what trash he'd publish. The mere idea of someone smearing Mahalia made him want to smash things.

He swiped his hand over his face and blew out a breath, aware that powerful attraction fueled his Tarzan-like turmoil. *I'll deal with it tomorrow.* He reached into the cabinet and pulled down his "Boss Man" mug, a gift from Monica.

Americano, tired of waiting in front of the bathroom door for Mahalia, made herself a tripping hazard in the kitchen.

"I like her too, girl." There. He'd said it aloud, even if it was to a cat. But it couldn't go anywhere. His insides wrenched. In mere moments, a good-looking, brilliant woman would emerge fresh from the shower to sleep in his house. His conscience stabbed like an ice pick behind his eyes.

The timer on the microwave gave a ding. He put the mug on the coffee table along with two chamomile tea bags.

His steps quickened down the hall. He plucked an extra sweatshirt out of his drawer and grabbed the bedding, tossing both onto the couch before he bolted back to his room, as if Potiphar's wife chased after him.

Maybe he'd have clarity in the morning? Fat chance.

***

Sunlight streamed into the living room. Mahalia and Americano both stretched. The finicky cat had kept her company all night, lying beside her, purring and snuggling. Calming her nerves, the same way Americano's owner soothed her. She ran her hands down the front of the sweatshirt she'd thrown on over her PJs. It engulfed her. The upside-down letters on the front spelled out ARMY. She pulled the neck of the sweatshirt up to her nose, taking in the scent of Gain detergent and pine. She did a mental shake to return to reality.

Her eyes took in the sparsely decorated, dark-toned room. The coffee table. The large TV enshrined in an entertainment center. The overall effect was sleek and minimalist. She threw her legs over the side of the couch, stood, and walked to the media shelving dominating the wall, Americano on her heels. A record player with an actual LP poised to play sat front and center. She inched closer. Steely Dan. *Who?* She drew a blank. Tucked in a corner of the shelf, an award from the military.

Displayed in a silver frame was a faded photo with a thick white border. A Polaroid. Granddaddy had had the same instant camera. She would beg to be the one to fan the photos so she could watch them develop before her eyes.

A boy with a tangle of brown hair falling over his downturned eyes looked up with complete adoration into the face of a young blond woman, who had him wrapped in her arms. Mahalia closed her eyes and sighed.

AN APPEARANCE OF IMPROPRIETY

Granddaddy had given her that kind of love. Prickles of conscience brought the snooping to an end.

The distinctive smoky aroma of breakfast meat drew her to the kitchen, where she found a bagel beside the toaster, jam and butter on the counter, and bacon on a plate. There was also a note. "Went to church. Hope it's still standing." He'd drawn a smiley face.

When had he done all this? Either he was as stealthy as a ninja or she'd been dead to the world. A tug inside her urged her to stay and be there when he got back, but she knew there'd be nothing but disaster waiting for her if she did.

Americano followed Mahalia to the bathroom and performed figure eights around her feet as she dressed and packed. Her mind flashed back to the surge of emotion she'd felt in the elevator that left her questioning her life priorities. She used all her mental might to shove the memory aside, reminding herself she needed to shield her heart against Cash. Her no-lawyer rule made sense. The adversarial way lawyers viewed things. The parsing of words and defending of positions. She wanted a man whose mind sparked new thoughts and ideas inside her. After so many years spent pursuing the law, she wanted to come home to a breath of fresh air, not shop talk. Yet with JD, their interactions pulsated with an undercurrent of resonance and understanding. His slow, persistent flow of chivalry threatened to erode her rule. If her treacherous heart kept it up, even a titanium shield might not be strong enough to protect her and keep her from throwing away her dreams.

She scribbled a thank-you note on the same piece of paper beneath his handwriting and trudged to the door to go home and clean up the mess at her house as fast as her feet could carry her.

***

He hadn't seen Mahalia's toy car in the parking garage. Good. Americano greeted him at the door. "Hey, girl." Americano clamored into his arms. Church this morning had been a respite. The building had sustained only minor cosmetic damage, and almost every seat was full during the eight o'clock service.

He had to get his head screwed on straight about Mahalia. No. Judge

Jackson. That was one thing he'd decided during prayer at church. Stick to *Judge* or *Your Honor*—for now. It had all come together by the time the praise team played the last song. He had to put his feelings on ice. She'd rotated off the TransNation case, but he didn't want to give the trucking company a reason to poke around her prior rulings. They'd lose any motion, but a fight could drag things out, and the Hunt family deserved compensation and closure. He also didn't want that shark Dinkelman sensing even a whiff of a potential personal relationship between him and a judge to spill gallons of ink over. Plus, he still needed to keep it professional for the mock trial competition. Once those things ended, he'd explore something more.

He sauntered to the couch. She'd folded the bedding in a neat stack. On top was his sweatshirt. He held it up to his face and took a prolonged breath. Then he tossed the sweatshirt onto the couch, as if it burned his hands. He scooped up the bedding and walked toward the closet housing the washer and dryer. *Deal with that later.* It might throw his life out of whack if he continued to contemplate the sweatshirt and the woman who'd been snuggled up all night wearing it.

Americano yowled, and JD returned to the kitchen to refresh her water bowl and put out her favorite treats. He turned to the sink and hummed "A Mighty Fortress Is Our God" as he washed the coffee cup left behind by not only the youngest but the most beautiful judge in Los Angeles.

***

LA Hearsay Chat Board

4thEstatePitBull: So guess who broke my nose. Mr. 1-800.

ShadowDocket: What did you do this time, Dink?

4thEstatePitBull: What did I do? My job! Questioning people who don't want to answer.

ShadowDocket: You mean poking a bear?

AN APPEARANCE OF IMPROPRIETY

4thEstatePitBull: I'm just saying something happened in that elevator. Trapped for hours. Mr. Silver Hair all flustered. Her Royal Highness . . . emotional.

ShadowDocket: Because they were TRAPPED IN AN ELEVATOR.

4thEstatePitBull: I'm not a spider, but my senses are tingling. Connect the dots, people.

1st&Goal: DM me. I have something you need to know.

4thEstatePitBull: Heading to the DMs now.

ShadowDocket: Careers are on the line. Watch yourselves.

Chapter 18

It was almost seven o'clock in the evening at Deon's Salon and Spa, and the Wednesday crush jammed the space to capacity. Mahalia was glad to get back into her routine now that Christmas and New Year's—the great court calendar disrupters—were behind her. Deon's shop was a place of refuge, and she closed her eyes while the shampoo girl, Lakeysha, worked some jasmine-scented elixir onto her scalp. It had been several weeks since she'd last seen JD. With no Junior Juror meetings over the holiday break, there was no excuse to reach out. She had tried—unsuccessfully—to banish the memory of their hours trapped in the intimate confines of the elevator. Perhaps Lakeysha's magical fingers could knead away the hollow spot in her heart.

All the other regulars were in their standard positions. LaTisha, Deon's five-fifteen, was sitting in the owner's chair, getting the last touches on her flat-ironed style. Carol, who came in at six, squirmed under the blast of heat emanating from the dryer. Cassandy Kincaide, a young attorney Mahalia had befriended and the mother to the most precious godchildren she could ever have asked for, had on a deep-conditioning heating cap.

Mahalia coveted the few hours every week the salon afforded. The latest tea, commiseration, current affairs. All within earshot.

Deon held court in his studio. Rotating his clients from service to service, getting them in and out on time, like an air traffic controller bringing in 737s at LAX.

"How are my babies?" Mahalia raised her voice over the general din, turning her head in Cassandy's direction.

"Rambunctious as always and asking almost every day to see their Tee-Tee MayMay."

AN APPEARANCE OF IMPROPRIETY

"I can't imagine why." Hearing the nickname warmed Mahalia's heart. Cassandy's boy Jojo had christened her with it when he couldn't pronounce *Auntie* or *Mahalia*. Although Jojo and his twin brother had since graduated to *Auntie MayMay*, their toddler sister still called her *TeeTee*.

A smile pulled from deep inside.

"You can't imagine why?" Cassandy snorted. "Maybe because of the party-sized bag of Skittles and the endless supply of Thomas the Train cars you magically have in your purse whenever you come to the house. You're worse than the old ladies at church."

Warmth spread through Mahalia's heart. She loved Cassandy and Ben's little ones with the fierceness of a lioness for her cubs.

Plenty of women in the salon were holding it down. Single moms, working married women. Never-marrieds like her. Lakeysha's massaging touch on her scalp worked its usual magic as the tension from the day swirled down the drain.

***

Ninety minutes later Deon locked the door behind the departing back of a customer, leaving Mahalia as the last client standing. She'd wanted curls in her updo, so she still had some time left under the dryer. She loved being last and cherished her private conversations with Deon. He was a good stylist—but a better therapist.

"Deon, I cannot tell you how much I look forward to my regular appointment." She spoke up so he could hear her. He motioned for her to lift the hood and free herself from the sirocco-like wind making her sweat.

"Of course. Don't tell anyone, but you're my favorite client." He winked.

"You're a mess, Deon. And I still can't fix that ticket for your cousin Ray Ray."

"Judge, I've actually been needing to ask you a favor for the last couple of weeks. And not about Ray Ray's traffic citation. He finished his community service on that three weeks ago."

She groaned. "Deon, for the man with the growing hands . . . anything."

"My wife's brother is coming into town and . . ."

"Deeee-onnnn!"

"Before you get upset..."

"I told you. I. Don't. Do. Setups."

Mahalia loved her stylist. The fact that he had transitioned her from chemically straightened hair back to her natural glorious coils in a seamless and professional manner was reason enough to at least hear him out.

"Look, he could be the one."

"What?"

"We've talked about it over the years. What you want in a man. He's an architect. Has his own firm in Chicago. Civic minded."

"Was he ever married?"

"No. Not divorced. He clocked so many hours building his business that he never made time for working on a serious relationship. Sounds like someone else I know." Deon caught her gaze in the mirror and gave a pointed look. "Next thing he knew he was getting ready to cross forty."

"So he's a little older than I am?"

"Yes, but what's five or six years?"

"Not much."

He removed the last of the perm rods and fluffed and arranged the thick twists piled up high on her head.

"Looks good, if I say so myself." He spun her around to face the mirror.

"Oh, Deon, I love it." Mahalia turned her head left and right, admiring the regal look of the twisted updo.

"So you'll go on a date with him? Dinner, maybe a movie. Something simple."

The possibilities tumbled in her brain like clothes in a dryer. Deon was offering her a chance to get back on track to finding her Midnight Prince. If Deon's description was accurate, this man checked *all* the boxes. JD was a wonderful man of integrity, but he was a nonstarter for several reasons. First, dating him violated her rule. Besides, the optics didn't look good since she had presided over his case. That aside, it wasn't even clear he was interested.

Hope at the new direction her life could take bubbled up, but she tamped down any outward sign of enthusiasm. "Yes." Mahalia's sigh was for effect only. "Go ahead—give him my number." This might be the thing to keep her thoughts off the soulful-eyed, husky-voiced attorney plaguing her dreams at night. Her mind drifted to composing professional yet flirty text messages she could send to Deon's brother-in-law once he contacted her.

***

At home, she slipped off her work attire, and her phone chimed. *Unknown caller, Chicago, Illinois.* Deon hadn't wasted one second. Probably afraid she'd get cold feet. *Don't appear too eager? Let it roll to voicemail?* She chided herself. *Don't start with games from the beginning.* Besides, it was a setup. No need to be coy.

"Hello."

"Mahalia?" The voice was businesslike in tone, but smooth, like warm caramel.

"This is she."

"This is Melvin Williams, Deon's brother-in-law. Glad to connect with you."

"Yes."

Melvin chuckled. "This is a bit awkward. I've never used a matchmaker before, but I'd love it if we could see each other the next time I'm in LA. Deon has been after me for a while to agree to call you. He made such a persuasive case this last time that I told myself I'd be a fool not to want to talk to a woman who is as beautiful and intelligent as he says you are."

Okay, that was smooth. The man knew how to give a compliment without coming off as corny.

"Thank you, Melvin. Deon has spoken highly of you as well. My schedule is pretty busy." Giddy hope pressed at the seams of her heart, and sweat slicked her palms.

"I'll put my thinking cap on and come up with something that works for both of us," Melvin said. "Take a look at your calendar and text me back with dates two to three weeks out. I'll work it out so my next trip to LA overlaps somehow."

"I'd love that." *Is this really happening?*

"Perfect. Before I let you go, I was wondering if you knew Eddie Lawrence. He was in your class at law school.

"As a matter of fact, I do."

"He's my frat brother. Pledged the fraternity a year behind me."

Mahalia's face was tight from smiling. Melvin was easy to talk to. Names of common acquaintances and professional affiliations kept popping up. Favorite vacation spots. She felt that power-couple vibe. His family wasn't from South Carolina, but Alabama. Same difference in terms of history. Melvin asked for a selfie. She balked. She wasn't a selfie kind of gal. Her historic win as the youngest female judge ever elected to the Los Angeles County Superior Court had been written up in the *Times*, accompanied by a photo. He could live with what search engines provided for now. He didn't push.

"Well, Judge Jackson, you are a hundred times more impressive than Deon said you were. I can't wait for us to meet."

"I'm looking forward to it as well."

"See you soon."

"Bye." Mahalia pushed End. Maybe God was finally answering her prayers. She swished away the mental image of the sad-eyed cowboy. Was her Mr. Perfect right around the corner?

***

West Coast Gridiron Weekly Chat Board

OddsMaker: Kane's fall from grace #brutal. D1s hyped him 4 the Heisman. Now? Radioactive.

ClubDad21: He was a two-way guy with QB instincts? That's unicorn stuff.

OddsMaker: But a record? Coaches won't touch that. PR's too messy.

ClubDad21: Wild how quick it fell apart. What's the real 411?

HighlightKing: Shut up! U don't know what ur talking about! ☠

Chapter 19

JD stood at the gate of a ratty mini-storage business encircled by a fence topped with barbed wire and guarded by a neglected pit bull. Somewhere inside awaited a treasure trove of documents exposed by McClatchy's deposition. TransNation had squirreled them away under the innocuous title of "Warranty Files and Vehicle Manuals." He zipped up his pullover to ward off the chill brought in by the January El Niña.

Sidwell had feigned ignorance and blamed mistakes by low-level employees for his client's failure to turn the documents over. A fresh subpoena and a heated exchange with Sidwell, including a reminder about the outstanding threat to impose hefty monetary sanctions, had proven necessary before TransNation granted today's inspection.

A man with a grease-streaked face and coveralls reeking of sweat and tobacco stood in front of JD. The name stitched on the oval patch on his uniform read "Boyd," but his posture said "Couldn't care less." Boyd turned and walked away. He gave a grunt for JD to follow. They made their way over a path of cracked asphalt through a labyrinth of stucco-covered units fronted by orange roll-up doors. Boyd stopped, pulled a rumpled sheet of paper out of his shirt pocket, and ran a dirty finger down the paper. He lifted his chin at JD.

"This is it." Boyd undid the lock and rolled open the door.

The musty odor of damp cardboard and the distinctive scent of rodent droppings escaped from the unit. Bile rose in JD's throat.

"You wanted our records for the past ten years? Have at it." Boyd's mirthless grin revealed nicotine-stained teeth in need of several applications of Crest Whitestrips. JD flicked on the flashlight he'd grabbed from his glove box and aimed the light toward the back wall. The dim beam revealed a storage unit packed to near bursting. The yellowed boxes showed signs of water damage, and a few had clear evidence of mold.

"By the way, nothing leaves the premises. Boss said you review 'em here or bring in a copy service to copy 'em here."

Fine. If TransNation wanted to play hardball, he would beat them at their own game. A couple of his Junior Juror students wanted to earn money and get real-world experience. With Christmas break in their rearview mirrors, their schedules should be back to normal. He'd send in a photocopying service and order them not to leave one scrap of paper unscanned or copied. He and his Junior Jurors would comb through each box of copies page by page. Nothing said real-life litigation experience like a good old-fashioned document review. His gut told him TransNation was hiding something big. He'd have to excavate until he found out what it was.

***

A week later in a loaner conference room, five Junior Jurors sat crammed between over fifty boxes of documents. Not a bad turnout for eight o'clock on a Saturday morning. He'd call today a win-win for himself and the students. He could pay them less than he would pay a temporary attorney. On the flip side, they'd get cash for helping him review the mountain of evidence.

He observed his crew. They'd come ready to work. Aisha's extra-long Doritos-colored nails might slow her down as she flipped through the documents. But at least she'd dressed in relaxed overalls, even if they had ridiculous rips at the knees. Kyle's geek T-shirt read "Enigma Buster." Langston sported his usual athletic gear, and Destinee's pullover had holes at the wrists that she'd poked her thumbs through. Devin sat hunched over in a corner, still sleep-groggy.

Today's teen fashions would be his childhood shame—frayed, torn clothing with missing buttons. For him it hadn't been a fashion choice but straight-up poverty. Even on a Saturday, he tried to dress business casual. His gray henley and pressed khakis . . . practically a tuxedo next to what the kids had on.

When the time came for the awards ceremony, he'd make sure his team had clothes as nice as the students' from Pacific Palisades so their confidence wouldn't take a hit. Anything to give these kids a fighting chance.

He clapped his hands once and rubbed his palms together. "Time to get started. Welcome to the most glamorous part of lawyering." JD pointed to the tables stacked with bankers' boxes. "Document review."

"You said there'd be McMuffins." Devin's voice came out in a growl. His smolder apparently didn't activate this early in the morning.

"And that you'd pay us." Aisha rubbed her thumb and fingers together in the universal symbol for money, and her friends murmured in approval.

"Yes, there'll be McMuffins and money. But first, the ground rules. Don't get food on the documents. Especially you, Langston, because I'm guessing you're going to eat about six of them."

"You know it, Mr. Cash." Humor lit up Langston's face. His size 14 feet clogged the space around his chair.

"This is a critical part of the legal process called *discovery*."

"Didn't we talk about this before? Something about depositions and interrogatories?" Devin perked up.

"Yes, we did. What we have in this room are documents that Trans-Nation gave to me."

"What's that stink?" Destinee held her nose and squished her eyes closed. Her oversized hoop earrings swung like playground equipment.

"The original documents were in a storage shed for a couple of years. These are copies, made from the originals. There might be mouse poop, dust, and other residual gunk from being copied in the same room. I guess that's what you're smelling."

"Uh, pee-yew. I'm out of here." Destinee stood.

"You're getting twenty dollars an hour." Kyle flashed a look at Destinee. "Way more than you make at Pick-'n-Shop. Plus, I drove, so you're not going anywhere."

"Don't worry." JD gestured to supplies in the corner. "I always bring face masks and gloves for document review. You never can tell what you'll find."

JD pointed to a side table overflowing with McDonald's bags. "Grab some food so Langston doesn't pass out, and I'll fill you in."

The kids pawed over the food and traded around until everyone had something they wanted.

"First you need to understand that you're acting as my assistants. That means the attorney work-product rule shields everything that goes on in this room. Don't discuss what we do with anyone not present here today. Got it?"

He tried to look each one in the eye as they gave a round of yeses.

It would be great if Mahalia could see the kids hard at work on a real case. She was a part of their progress. He should've been fully focused on the task at hand, but his brain kept looping back to her and the elevator. A moment of something... he didn't know what... had passed between them. Was it a fear response? Or something more?

JD shoved away the thoughts and shifted into mission mode, the way he had in the military—compartmentalize, focus, execute. No time to dwell.

"Next, I've assigned each of you to a table. On the table you'll find a sheet of paper with your name and a list of the specific categories of information you'll be searching for in your boxes—names, dates, times. When you come across the information listed on the sheet of paper, put a fluorescent green Post-it Note on it so it sticks out. Once you tag the document, refile the paper where you found it."

He scanned the room. "Everybody understand?"

"So, Mr. C, for real, this is what lawyers spend their time doing? Looking through stinky boxes of old documents with rat..."

JD threw up his hand. "Stop right there, Kyle. Keep it clean. And yes, this is part of a trial lawyer's job. Prosecutors investigate crime scenes, autopsy reports, ballistics. If you're an attorney—like me—who handles auto accidents involving big companies you examine drivers' logs, GPS data, drug tests, and inspection reports."

"Bo-ring." Kyle gave an enormous yawn.

"You can choose to think of it that way. But I think of it as being like a treasure hunt. Buried somewhere in these boxes are the answers to questions I have about this case. I need you guys to help me find them."

"I get it." Langston nodded.

"If you find something that seems odd, out of place, or fishy, call me over to review it before you tag it. Understand?"

By late afternoon, the stuffy space smelled like pizza and Old Spice deodorant sticks. The Junior Jurors' diligence impressed him. They'd stepped up and taken their responsibilities seriously. Even Langston stuck to it when he wasn't flirting or peeking at ESPN on his phone.

JD checked the time. Not including lunch break, they'd been working for four hours. Based on the number of boxes they'd already completed, he calculated at least two more hours today and another two Saturdays to finish the review.

"Mr. Cash, Mr. Cash." Kyle gave a frantic wave of his hand. "Didn't you say you were looking for information about computers?"

"Yes. I asked TransNation to hand over any information saved on any of their computers that pertained to John Hunt."

"And right here on this piece of paper you gave me, it says you asked them to give you all the documents by the beginning of December. Is that right?"

JD rose from the table from where he was also reviewing documents and walked over to Kyle.

"TransNation told me they didn't have any computer records relating to the requests I sent them. What do you have there?"

"Well, I found this. I think it's a receipt. TransNation gave away ten computers to a place called KCCI. That stands for Kids Camp Charity International. We used to go there when I was little. We learned about coding, and they let us create our own video games."

JD read the receipt. "They gave all these computers away so they wouldn't have to disclose their existence when their responses to my requests for production were due. Those dirty . . ."

"Hey, hey, Mr. C. Language!" Destinee giggled.

"I was going to say 'dogs,' Destinee."

This might be the thing to break the case wide open. "Okay, Kyle and Devin. You're off document review. Time for a field trip." JD rushed toward the door of the conference room. He palmed his phone and tossed it to Kyle. "Your job is to pull up directions to KCCI. We're paying them a visit."

"Sweet. This is real lawyer stuff, isn't it?"

"Yes, it is, Kyle."

Destinee gave Kyle and Devin high fives.

JD turned to the rest of the students in the room. "Do you think you guys can handle the review while I'm away for a couple of hours?"

"We got this, Boss." Langston gave an upward nod. He turned back to Destinee and Aisha. "You heard, ladies. I'm in charge now."

Aisha gave Langston a light slap on the back of his head. "Only 'cause I'm letting you be in charge."

Amusement at the kids' banter floated inside him. JD grabbed his messenger bag and hustled from the conference room. This could be good.

***

JD pulled his Wagoneer into a tight parking spot at a nondescript strip mall in the sleepy suburb of Granada Hills. The long row of storefronts hosted a cell phone store, a nail place, and a DUI / defensive driving school. "Devin, wait in the car. No need for all of us to go in. We'll grab you if we need to haul anything out. Kyle, you come with me." He killed the engine and shoved open the Wagoneer door, not even waiting for Kyle to follow. He scanned the storefront signs for Kids Camp Charity International, locating it three doors down.

Glancing back over his shoulder, JD's impatience flared as Kyle extricated himself from the seat belt. He slowed his pace from flat-out storming the castle to a jog. His gut screamed that KCCI held the smoking gun in his case. JD yanked open the door, and Kyle tumbled in behind him.

"You must be Mr. Cash." A woman in her early seventies with an exaggerated smile stood and greeted him with the over-enunciation of a kindergarten teacher. "I'm Rhoda McNally, the director of this center. We spoke on the phone. You said it was urgent." She extended her hand to shake, grasping JD's hand, then Kyle's. The wooden bracelets that festooned her wrists clattered like dice thrown on a table.

JD willed himself to composure and slowed down his movements. He didn't want to come off as a lunatic. "I understand your charity received computers from TransNation Trucking Corporation."

"Indeed. Quite a generous and, might I say, unexpected donation."

He sized up Mrs. McNally. She wore chunky clogs and a tan pantsuit that were stylish but no-nonsense. She hadn't dyed her graying hair. Practical. He opted for the direct approach. "I need you to give me all of those computers today."

AN APPEARANCE OF IMPROPRIETY

The woman smoothed her tresses. "Well, this is very . . ." She flopped her hands around. "Unusual. Why should I do that for you, Mr. Cash?"

"A TransNation truck killed my client's husband in a horrific accident." He plunged ahead. "I believe that those ten computers the company gave you may contain information relevant to my client's case."

"Oh my." Mrs. McNally wrung her hands, setting the bracelets off again.

"Now, I could go to all the trouble of serving you with a subpoena, but that would take a lot of time. Time I don't have. I hope you can help me do this." JD gave her his most winning smile.

Kyle stood bouncing from foot to foot, and Mrs. McNally blinked her rounded eyes at him, saying nothing.

JD jammed his thumb between his teeth but forced his hand down while reeling in his impatience. Okay, he needed another line of attack. Straight bribery usually worked. "What would you say if I told you I would buy all new computers for your kids here to replace what I am taking, plus tablets for each student? All tablets would have a year's worth of paid internet access."

Mrs. McNally's lips formed an O, and a gleam came into her eyes. "Now I remember why you're so familiar. You're that 1-800-555-CASH man, aren't you?"

"Guilty as charged." JD could sense victory. But the price might be high.

"We need an upgrade to our internet. Fiber is available, but I want Starlink. Been wanting a subscription to this Python educational coding software too. This is a charity for children . . ." Mrs. McNally's words trailed off. She gave him a tight-lipped smile, like a cat with a mouse clamped behind its teeth.

JD was a tough negotiator, but this old woman was a pro. "Fine. I could arrange that by the end of the week. I simply need to have the computers today. Also, since you are providing them to me without a subpoena, I will email a document for you to sign under penalty of perjury attesting to what you are turning over to me."

She dipped her chin. "I am on board with all of that. I'll take you right to them." She turned and marched toward a door. Before opening it, she picked up a flyer off a desk and gave it to JD.

"And here is an invitation to our semiformal charity ball that happens in August. I'm sure you'd be glad to sponsor a table. Great publicity." She smiled her Cheshire cat grin and opened the door. "Right this way, Mr. Cash."

Jayna Breigh

Several hours later, JD sat in his office with a computer from KCCI on a makeshift table and a tech whiz named Edgar in the chair beside him. Edgar's expertise included white hat hacking and data recovery.

Edgar was an answer to prayer. After JD, Kyle, and Devin had crammed the Wagoneer with the computers and taken them back to JD's office, JD had fired one up and tried to search it. Nothing. At all. He'd called in a huge favor from his JAG buddy, Pete, at the Department of Defense, who'd connected him with Edgar.

Edgar wore black jeans, beat-up combat boots, and a weather-beaten T-shirt with a picture of the submarine *Nautilus* with the name "Captain Nemo" under it. He had jet-black dyed hair and nickel-sized things in each ear. JD tried not to judge a book by the cover, but . . .

Edgar fidgeted and bounced in his seat as he clickety-clacked on the keyboard.

"This is amateur hour going on here," Edgar muttered, more to himself than to JD. "Idiots didn't use BleachBit to scrub the computers." He snorted.

JD inched his chair back to give Edgar room to work. Besides, there was no point in listening. Edgar's words were gibberish to JD.

Edgar mumbled something, and JD moved in closer to see what was on the screen.

"In fact, they didn't wipe them at all. Guess they figured that giving them away would make the information disappear."

Edgar continued clacking away with a vengeance, and the minutes ticking by dragged out.

"Cracked it."

JD checked his watch. Had it been half an hour?

"The company is clearly run by boomers who don't want to keep track of complicated passwords." Edgar pointed to the screen. "I've analyzed the metadata, and I've gotten positive results for the search term 'clock out.' I found emails between the president of TransNation and the chairman of the board." Edgar gave a little whistle, popped each knuckle on his left hand, and scooted his seat over so that JD could sit closer to the monitor.

"This email here is between the TransNation tech department and the president of the company." Edgar tapped a finger on the screen.

AN APPEARANCE OF IMPROPRIETY

"Can we tie this email to the CEO?"

"Yes, we can. I uncovered the blind copy of this email to him."

JD peered at the screen. "I can't read it."

"Here, let me try to convert it." Edgar's fingers danced over the keyboard for five minutes straight.

"Got it."

JD's eyes scanned down the email, and he read the message under his breath. "'All drivers are to clock out when refueling, eating, and performing minor maintenance. These activities do not count for DOT purposes as a part of the total drive time for the day.'"

This was flatly untrue, and ordering drivers to clock out was illegal. JD squinted in concentration.

"'We've circumvented the tamper-proof systems and have jail broken the electronic logging devices installed on our vehicles. Now whenever a vehicle is not in motion for two minutes, the software will clock the driver out.'"

Edgar gave a little whistle. "Wow. That means . . ."

"Exactly," JD said.

JD slapped Edgar on the back, and Edgar gave a wince. He'd found the hard evidence JD had hoped to find. "Can you print out these emails for me?"

"You got it."

"I might hire you full time."

"You can't afford me."

"After this case, I might be able to."

***

Text Message Exchange

Tanner:
Only D2 schools still in the mix. Cash and that judge screwed me over.

RaisingKane:
IKR? For a misdemeanor w/ community service.

Tanner:
Yeah, but it's still on my record. Coaches said they don't need problems to explain.

RaisingKane:
We need that NIL $$$. I'm gonna reach out to that reporter.

***

Text Message Exchange

Michelle:
Why won't you tell the judge what's going on behind her back?

Becky:
Some people don't realize they need help, y'know?

Michelle:
But this stuff is serious!

Becky:
She'd tell me, politely, to butt out. How's your judge doing?

AN APPEARANCE OF IMPROPRIETY

Michelle:
A nasty custody hearing yesterday. A 4 y/o. I hate custody cases.

Becky:
🙏🙏🙏

Michelle:
You think Judge G knows?

Becky:
She keeps people out. Can't explain it, but I *know* I'm her clerk for a reason!

Michelle:
See you at lunchtime prayer tomorrow?

Becky:
Yep 🖤

Chapter 20

MAHALIA PULLED HER car into the semicircular driveway of the Laguna Cove Seaside Resort. A boutique hotel nestled off the scenic South Coast Highway, the Cove promised ocean views and five-star dining featuring ingredients farmed with sustainable practices. She rolled her window down while she waited for the valet to come. For late January the temps were cooler than she'd anticipated. She drew in a deep breath of briny ocean air and rummaged in her mind, trying to remember if she'd packed a cover-up.

Where had the time gone? Had it only been a month since she'd begun communicating with Melvin via phone and video calls? Now only one night's sleep stood between her and what might be her last first date. Melvin, a legitimate contender for the title of Midnight Prince, would land at Orange County's John Wayne Airport tomorrow afternoon to accompany her to her favorite Southland attraction, the Millennial Masterpieces en Vie.

A young man in a red vest and white shirt sidled up and opened her car door. "Get your bags, ma'am?"

"I can get it." She pressed the button to open the back hatch, handed the valet her fob as she exited, and plucked her overnight bag from the back of the car.

In half a dozen long strides, she entered the lobby. The soothing neutral palette of boho chic leather furniture, bamboo-framed mirrors, and brass accessories greeted her. An immense philodendron with velvety green leaves brought soothing tranquility to the atrium.

"Good evening, ma'am." A trim, tan gentleman with stylish black hair and trendy rectangular glasses gave her a wan smile.

Consternation niggled at her. The usual concierge, Richard, was not on

AN APPEARANCE OF IMPROPRIETY

duty. He always made the logistics of her stay seamless. Her tradition of Laguna Niguel getaways provided her with a respite to look forward to two or three times a year. Her normal excitement and anticipation dampened without her vacation guru on hand.

She exhaled a sharp breath and forced herself to readjust her attitude. This was a monumental vacay—the first time she would share her special getaway with someone. She and Melvin often discussed art, but he'd never seen a tableau vivant. Since the man was traveling halfway across the United States to see her, she hoped he'd think the show was worth the logistical hurdles.

Not-Richard handed her the keys to her room and blandly wished her an enjoyable stay.

Once in the room, she dropped her bags on the desk in the corner, kicked off the chunky wedge sandals that coordinated with her cinnamon-colored gauchos, and stretched out face up on the bed. Richard always made sure she had a vase of flowers, lavender or jasmine. No flowers today. Turning her head, she gazed out the sliding glass doors at the seafoam green waves washing up from the pristine beach. Stress leeched from her bones with each retreat of the surf.

The melancholy face and gentle smile of Attorney Cash floated into her mind. His way of holding a door for the students—for her. His insistence on walking her to the car because it was after hours. His habit of standing there waiting until she drove off. She wasn't a damsel in distress, but she'd grown accustomed to his ways. He'd defended her after Dinkelman assaulted her and had taken her into his own home, no questions asked, after the earthquake. His demeanor toward her and the Junior Jurors said "I'd take a bullet for each one of you." Protectiveness emanated from every pore. He reminded her of Granddaddy Henry. An old-fashioned man in the best way possible.

What was she doing? Her errant thoughts needed immediate corralling. Melvin would be here in under twenty-four hours. She felt like she was cheating on him and they'd never even been in the same zip code.

Her phone played the distinctive ringtone she'd given Melvin—the Florida A&M University fight song. The rumble of tubas banished thoughts of Cash from her mind like sending a naughty puppy to a corner.

She pressed Talk. "Hi, Melvin."

"Well, hello, Your Honor." Melvin's voice floated from her phone with the sweetness of toffee ice cream topping. He sounded as if he stood in a cavernous conference room with other conversations swirling around him.

"Perfect timing. I'm in my room. Are you on a break?" He'd told her his firm had a pitch session with government officials about a revitalization project near downtown Phoenix.

"Yes. Wanted to update you. My flight lands in Orange County at four thirty. I'll rent a car and connect with you at the restaurant."

"Excellent. Our reservations are at six, and the show starts at eight thirty."

"Mahalia, I can't tell you how much I've been looking forward to this evening."

Heat rose in her cheeks. No question Melvin's logistical backflips to make it to this first date qualified as a Hollywood-style grand gesture. After several weeks of attempting to coordinate calendars, he'd squeezed in a Sunday evening visit following a Saturday meeting in Phoenix. After the show they'd part ways. He'd drive his rental car to LAX in time to catch the last flight to O'Hare, and she'd head home to sneak in a few hours of sleep before work.

She gave him five mental gold stars for his persistence.

"Got to run. Client meeting back in session. Until tomorrow." He clicked off.

One free night to herself. A long nap held great appeal. A walk on the beach? Mani-pedi already covered in anticipation of the date. She closed her eyes, and thoughts of Cash returned. She took out her phone, opened it to a picture of Melvin, and focused on it before closing her eyes again.

***

Random buzzing somewhere nearby awoke Mahalia. Eyes still closed, she stretched out an arm and felt around on the bed for the cause of the annoying vibrations.

"Hello?" Sleep clogged her voice.

"Yes, hello, is this Judge Mahalia Jackson?"

She righted herself and rubbed the sleep out of her eyes. "Who is this please?"

"Judge, this is Adel Smith. I'm Kyle's mother." A tinge of panic laced the woman's words.

"Who?"

"Kyle. He's in your Junior Jurors program."

Her brain continued to flail. The image of a T-shirt with the name of a scientist on it clarified her thoughts. "Yes . . . Kyle . . ." Her recall activated. "How can I help you?"

"I would have talked to Mr. Cash, but he's not answering . . ." Sniffles punctuated the woman's words.

All the kids had her work cell phone number for emergencies, since they met after hours. She must have forgotten to turn off the call-forwarding feature. Judges on corporate matters didn't handle personal problems. No one ever cried over a contract dispute in her courtroom. She pulled compassion from deep within to ensure her tone was gentle, not officious. "How can I help you?"

"Kyle got caught tagging a building with graffiti. I bailed him out. It's a first offense, but the police are talking jail time." A sob accompanied the worried mom's words.

Details about Kyle sharpened into focus. JD had singled the boy out as a candidate for Caltech if his grades and test scores stayed on track. Why was a boy like Kyle tagging buildings?

"He's home with me now, but I don't know where to turn or what to do."

Mahalia scanned her mind for any pertinent law dealing with vandalism. It had been years since she'd crammed in all the criminal law and procedure for the bar exam. A point clicked. "Tagging is a misdemeanor if the damage is under four hundred dollars. It rises to a felony if the property damage is greater than that. Maximum jail time about three years."

Kyle's mother inhaled. "Is there anything you can do?"

The boy's future lay in the balance. She looked at the waves again. Her impromptu nap had frittered away the chance of a beachside walk. And now this call. Oh well, maybe tomorrow there'd be time to squeeze in a stroll on the sand. Besides, wasn't she volunteering with the Junior Jurors to help kids like Kyle?

"May I speak with your son?"

"Oh, Judge, thank you so much."

"Kyle." Mrs. Smith's voice cracked out like rifle fire. "Come here now. Judge Jackson's on the phone."

The sound of heavy footfalls echoed through the phone followed by muffled words. "Why'd you call the judge? I told you I can handle it."

"You'd handle it all the way to a year or two in prison. College? *Poof.* Gone. Take the phone now, and my next call is to your uncle . . ."

More muffled sounds. "Your Honor."

"Kyle . . ."

***

By the time she ended her call, her stomach was spasming with hunger, and she hustled to the downstairs restaurant. The moment the waiter spotted her, he led her to her normal spot, seated her, and sent in her order.

Somehow circumstances had injected Attorney Cash into her perfect weekend. His face and voice already popped up in her thoughts at uninvited times, but now she had an imperative reason to speak with him. However, it would have to wait until she'd eaten.

In what felt like no time at all, her server arrived at the table with her meal—a mouthwatering garlic shrimp slider on a brioche bun basted with butter. Mahalia inhaled and took a bite. The mouthfeel of the juicy shrimp and the delicate saltiness of the warm butter pulled a satisfied groan from deep inside of her.

She took another bite and a swig of sparkling water to fortify herself. Satiated enough that she wouldn't be tempted to bite anyone's head off, she dialed Cash.

"Your Honor, is everything okay?" A strong note of concern threaded Cash's voice.

"Yes. Of course." His timbre caught her off guard but also assured her she'd made the right decision to call him. "It's about Kyle Smith."

"What's wrong?" His manner remained on high alert.

"The police picked him up for tagging a corner store. The owner wants to press charges. Damages exceed four hundred dollars, so there's possible jail time."

"That doesn't sound like Kyle at all . . ."

"He's being bullied by some guys on the football team because he's smart. They call him Professor X. Some kind of Superman thing I don't understand."

JD let out a short, humorless laugh. "Professor X is in the Marvel universe . . . Never mind. Of course it's football players." He exhaled sharply, like he was holding something back. "Yeah . . . that tracks. Go on."

"He held out for a while, but they kept the pressure up. Asking him to cheat. They also framed him for a prank at school. He got a one-day suspension for that. He said he did it to prove he wasn't a computer geek who had no rizz with the girls and played weird fantasy board games."

A rueful exclamation hummed in her ear. "Every one of those things is true about Kyle, which is why he'll thrive if he can get into Caltech. That's his tribe."

"I think you're right. My thought is for you to find someone to go in pro bono to represent Kyle and have them offer to enter a plea deal. No jail time. Twenty hours of community service, including painting and repairing the wall he damaged and expungement of his record after successful completion."

Cash remained silent.

"You can put in a recommendation letter for him, but I can't. Just refreshed myself on the canons about that for my CLE. Not allowed . . ."

"Your Honor, is this how you spend your Saturday nights?"

She groaned. "No. I'm on a staycation down in Laguna Niguel."

"You're getting a much-needed break, and you're calling me to solve a kid's problem. That's dedication. Don't worry about Kyle."

His compliment flowed into the dry cracks of her heart. She wasn't a soulless law zombie doomed to roam the earth alone and unloved . . . *Wait!* Her thoughts of love were supposed to be for the perfect man who possessed the specific qualities on the list she'd refined over the years. Right?

Her wayward ruminations flustered her. "I need to get . . ."

"I'll take it from here."

Their words tumbled over each other.

"I was saying I can handle the logistics of this from here on out. You have a great getaway, Judge." The phone went dead.

Jayna Breigh

The abrupt ending felt awkward and distant. She stared at her half-finished food. The thought of eating the remains now turned her stomach. She told the host to charge the meal to her room and headed down the hallway, consumed with thoughts of the ever-gallant Mr. Cash—fixer of problems, caretaker of kids, complimenter of judges.

Her involvement with him and his Junior Jurors made her want to be a better person. He made her feel more caring and compassionate than she'd thought she could be. Several times during the Junior Jurors meeting, when she'd interacted with the students, she'd caught him regarding her, his eyes filled with warmth and encouragement. His look seemed to say, "You've got this."

Once inside her room, she headed to the deluxe spa bathroom to clear Cash's visage from her mind. One more sleep and the Midnight Prince might arrive. One more sleep. She started the shower and turned the temperature to ice cold to shock her brain into obedience.

***

Ten o'clock in the morning. Silver-tinted sunlight streamed through the room's mini blind slats without mercy. But that hadn't been what had awakened her. She'd been up for hours and had tossed and turned all night. Helping Kyle had been the right thing to do, yet as the time on the clock crept by at a turtle's pace from 1:00 a.m. to 5:00 a.m. to 9:00 a.m., her thoughts had turned from the Millennial Masterpieces en Vie, and her first encounter with Melvin, to jokes and talks with the students and their ringleader, JD Cash. Try as she might to keep those thoughts at bay, some deadpan quip he'd made would return to her memory. Some response of deep respect and admiration from the kids.

She might have caught a few snatches of sleep, but not many. She yawned and dragged herself from bed, determined to fill the hours until her date with pampering and relaxation. *A long walk on the beach, a late lunch, and peeking in at my favorite boutiques.*

Rejuvenated by a day of leisure, she checked her watch. The plane carrying her hoped-for Midnight Prince would arrive soon, and she had an hour to finish getting ready and meet him at the restaurant. She checked her ensemble in the mirror for the fifteen hundredth time. A mint-green pantsuit

AN APPEARANCE OF IMPROPRIETY

featuring a sleeveless V-neck top and wide-legged pants that stopped at the ankle. Silver kitten heels, a chunky silver bracelet, and triangular silver earrings to set off the outfit. In case it got cold, she'd drape herself in a sheer black-and-mint-green-checked shawl. She dashed to the bathroom, dipped her finger into the jar of edge-control gel, and slicked it one more time over the willful and prone-to-stray hairs at her temple and nape. Glancing at her reflection, her sheer-tinted lips smiled, and the dusted-with-minimal-shimmer eyes looked happy.

She hustled from her room, buoyed by the prospect of going on her last first date.

Thankfully, the drive to the restaurant was uneventful. Laguna traffic sometimes had weird jams when tourists and sightseers descended.

She entered the restaurant lobby, and Melvin stood there with an air of expectancy. *Wow.* The selfies and FaceTime calls did not do him justice. He wasn't a pretty boy, but a handsome man. His haircut was fresh. Stylish, but not trendy. His outfit, the perfect ensemble for a late-January event—a caramel-colored tweed jacket, a harvest-orange turtleneck, and slacks. Melvin knew how to dress to impress. So far, he was checking all the right boxes.

"Mahalia." His voice sounded deeper and softer than on the phone. He smiled, and one dimple appeared high on his cheek.

She hesitated for a moment, and then they reached for each other in a quick, awkward hug. No fireworks, but it was sweet.

Melvin broke the brief embrace and scratched his chin. "This moment has been a long time coming, but definitely worth it."

Her cheeks tightened, and she hoped her grin wasn't cheesy. "I agree."

"Shall we?" He held out his arm and escorted her inside to eat.

***

Dinner had been a blur, and she needed time to process it as they headed to the Millennial Masterpieces en Vie. She attempted drive-time conversation, but the ride to the venue was filled with interruptions from the GPS. She knew the way blindfolded but tabled her inclination to mute the sound and navigate for Melvin. No need to come across as bossy when Waze was doing fine. Weren't driving directions something couples fought over?

Melvin slid the car into a parking spot and turned to her. "We made it. If I can navigate a new city on a first date, I think I'm up for any challenge." He raised his brows.

His candor humored and charmed her. "Driving test, pass."

Their intermingled laughter broke the ice as they exited the car and headed for the entrance. After a brief shuffling in her purse for the tickets, they entered the venue and found their seats at the Millennial Masterpieces en Vie.

They were three rows back, dead center. She checked him out from the side of her eye, hoping she wasn't too obvious. *How to describe him?* The word soccer-dad-handsome came to mind. A man who'd garner second looks when he pulled up in his SUV to pick up his 2.5 kids from swim practice or volleyball. Other moms would talk behind their hands and send her sharp glances. She reined in a smile. Why had her brain fast-forwarded itself so far into the future?

They shared an armrest, and after a moment he draped his arm over the back of her chair. Possessive, but not touching. She'd expected some sort of sensation from their closeness—a spark or jolt. But all vital signs remained steady.

"So explain it again," Melvin asked, his tone confused.

"I was baffled my first time too." The Millennial Masterpieces en Vie created some sort of optical illusion that tricked the brain and eyes. Using lighting, makeup, costumes, and other artistic tricks, the sets and performers filled the stage with what looked like duplicates of master paintings and sculptures. It was as if she'd turned a corner at a park and stumbled upon an enchanted real-life painting. Each tableau vibrated with vitality yet was motionless and still. There was no good way to explain it until you'd seen it. "Just wait—when they change from one painting to the next, your brain will figure it out."

The lights dimmed, and she mentally scrolled through highlights from dinner with Melvin. In her mind she always figured that she'd remember the minutest detail of her first date with The One, but her brain reconstructed only brief snatches. Melvin's well-manicured hands. A deep dimple. The salt-and-pepper hair at his temples, receding just enough to give him a dignified air. Melvin was good looking. His golden-ebony face and matching eyes put the two of them in the same skin-tone family—the dark-brown side of the spectrum.

AN APPEARANCE OF IMPROPRIETY

She'd let him do most of the talking at dinner, trying to take the measure of the man. He held memberships to both the Art Institute of Chicago and the Museum of Contemporary Art. While his tastes gravitated toward Jean-Michel Basquiat's esthetic of primitivism, hers tilted toward neo-impressionists, like Seurat. The conversation was intellectual, but she didn't feel a tug of connection.

Over lemon-seasoned chicken, roasted potatoes, and passion-fruit iced tea, he'd filled her in on his profession. "As an architect I resonate with modernists, including Frank Lloyd Wright and Chicago's own Louis Henry Sullivan, father of the modern skyscraper. I try to bring their modernist influences into my designs."

His knowledge of building form and balance had been exhaustive but not scintillating. As far as first-date small talk, she'd grade him a solid B minus.

She gave him a sidelong appraisal, and he turned and met her gaze. Then the master of ceremonies took the stage. "The Millennial Masterpieces en Vie has been an Orange Coast tradition for decades, with cast members as young as four and as old as eighty. With each tableau vivant, we strive to take you inside the art piece itself. Join us this evening as we bring masterpieces to life. No flash photography, and enjoy the show."

The curtains parted, the music swelled, and a life-sized recreation of Edward Hopper's *Nighthawks* graced the stage—the somber gray-green tones, the lines of the counter, the utter aloneness of the four people inside the café on a dark solitary night. She held her breath for ninety whole seconds. The performers broke their stances, and the scene morphed, through stage craft, into *Breezing Up* by Homer. The palette mirrored Hopper's greens and blues. Four young boys lounged on a sailboat in choppy water, as if they hadn't a trouble in the world. Emotive background music heightened her senses. She felt as though she were in the sea with the boys.

Melvin handed her a set of compact binoculars. The close-up view enabled by the field glasses and their third-row seats revealed the inhales and exhales of the living mannequins behind the illusions. But the makeup and lighting still rendered the tableau exquisite.

The curtain closed, and *Snap the Whip* appeared when it reopened. How the festival organizers got the young boys to stand still for even thirty seconds never ceased to amaze her. As with the painting itself, the tableau captured and froze in place the velocity of the boys' schoolyard game and their attempts to shake loose the child on the end of the whip.

Had JD been a rough-and-tumble kid like the ones in the painting? She held in a huff of air and wrangled her thoughts back to Melvin and the tableau.

Intermission began, and she found herself enlivened. She peered at Melvin in the glow of the rising house lights. Did he feel it too? Did the beauty and energy captivate him?

"Can we stretch our legs? I'd love to see if there's a plaque naming the architectural firm. The layout and acoustics in here are fantastic." He held out his arm.

All the beauty and artistry they'd witnessed, and he wanted to talk about construction? She had said she wanted someone whose mind was different from hers, right? Plus, first dates were always awkward.

They ascended the steps and headed in the direction of the information booth. She excused herself. In the ladies' room, she studied her reflection. The moment she'd hoped for and prayed about for years had finally arrived, yet her face did not glow with radiant joy. Random thoughts about Kyle's predicament and Langston's week-long absence from practice to look after his sick little sister interwove themselves with scenes from Jean-François Millet's *The Gleaners*. People doing backbreaking work to sustain themselves by harvesting wheat. The Junior Jurors working hard to elevate themselves—something not expected in their neighborhood. Cash wormed his way into her brain again as well. Just as the original artists whose paintings made up the Millennial Masterpieces had labored, Cash toiled for hours one lawsuit at a time, with meticulous work, to construct cases that helped widows and kids left without fathers.

The lights flashed in the bathroom, and she scurried to join Melvin. He stood waiting off to the side, arm extended.

"Shall we." His warm smile banished the remnants of her renegade thoughts.

***

Melvin linked his pinky with hers as he walked her to her vehicle. They strolled side by side in silence. At her car, he faced her square on. Neat brows, straight white teeth. He met every casting-call requirement for grade A husband material.

"Mahalia, I had such a lovely time with you tonight." He gave a small squeeze to her pinky, still linked with his. "Our schedules are crazy, but can we arrange something in person again soon?"

Letting her gaze scan his face, she peered into his eyes. No fireworks. No skippity heartbeats. Only an incredibly handsome man with an impeccable résumé.

She gave his pinky a return squeeze.

He raised the back of her hand to his lips and kissed it. His mustache left a pleasant tickle. He tucked her in her car, and in her rearview mirror she watched him wave as she drove away.

Too late at night to take the Coast Highway, so boring 5 Freeway it would be. On the drive home, her thoughts were drawn to the perennial closing masterpiece of the tableau, da Vinci's *The Last Supper*. Christ's outstretched hands. Sinners and a betrayer at the table beside him. Granddaddy Henry's words . . . *"You either stand with him or fall alone."* Unexpected deflation settled over her. In her climbing and striving, she'd pushed God into a far back corner of her mind. How long had it been since she'd devoted any time to . . . well, anything having to do with God? Prayer? Not even a quick Psalm to start the day. She shoved the thoughts about eternal matters aside and flicked on a melancholy eighties love-song station to match her mood and keep her awake as she drove home.

***

Text Message Exchange

Tanner:
Dude, U seen Fight Club?

Kyle:
Who hasn't?

Jayna Breigh

Tanner:

You broke the rules.

Kyle:

That's not true.

Tanner:

#SnitchesGetStitches.

Kyle:

What do you want?

Tanner:

CalUni got hit with 3 decommits. I'm back in. Need that algebra grade up.

Kyle:

I'll do the algebra for 100% immunity from the whole team.

Tanner:

Also, I met this sweet hottie 🔥 Want to surprise her with flowers. Gimme the name again of that site U use where you can find anybody.

Kyle:

After this we're even. Period.

Tanner:

Absolutely.

Chapter 21

Mahalia pulled a hanger bearing a blouse off the rod, held it under her neck, and looked at herself in the mirror. So hard to decide. Dress, skirt, slacks? Something red or pink as a nod to the approach of Valentine's Day? She turned this way and that, studying her reflection. Over time Cassandy, mother to her beloved godchildren, had wheedled and cajoled her to come to their new church for a visit. Mahalia had tried Cassandy's former staid, no-clapping church once and never gone back.

But she had promised herself the night she'd escaped the elevator that she'd go to church at her next opportunity. A sigh drifted out. She'd put off her promise more than eight weeks now, but Cassandy had played dirty and resorted to straight extortion, offering up time with her children in exchange. Cassandy *knew* Mahalia was complete putty in her godchildren's sticky little hands.

Time to pay up. Better not be a crazy place where the women all looked the same. Or worse, one of those churches with a coffee bar and a pastor who drove a Lamborghini.

She smiled, thinking of her godchildren. But church? Her lips pulled down. If there was something harder than being a preacher's kid, it was being a preacher's grandchild.

Granddaddy had held an iron grip on the helm of Greater Mount Sinai Baptist. Layer after layer of formality, ritual, and tradition encased everything inside, including her body. The collars of her pristine church dresses had shrunk around her neck, and the elastic of her frilly socks had cut into her ankles.

She'd sit, itchy, hot, and bored, for several hours, neck craned. Worse, ensconced on the first red velvet pew in the church, she and all her darkness were on display. Her one moment of respite was the satisfying swish as she swung her patent-leather-clad feet back and forth.

"Sit up straight. Wake up." The admonitions flew fast and furious.

Sweat had made little trails down the back of her neck from the judgmental stares of those watching to detect any fidgeting or dozing.

The ding of her coffee maker drove away the past. She strode into the kitchen to pour a cup and steady her nerves. At least the kids would be there.

Cassandy had told her one of Ben's buddies from basketball might join them at church. *Better not be a setup.* Things with Melvin continued to progress via technology. He'd sent a box of milk chocolate turtles from Margie's Candies—a Chicago staple, he'd assured her. Sweet. Not super exciting, but a definite upward trend. When she worked hard at it, she could keep Cash-related remembrances at bay for hours at a time. She didn't need Cassandy throwing someone else into the mix to further complicate her life.

She riffled through more hangers, deciding on a Jacqueline Kennedy Onassis–inspired coral-and-cream dress, with a pinched-waist jacket. You could never go wrong with an outfit that looked like something owned by JKO. She accented her attire with coral-colored, rose-shaped earrings, large pearls, and coral-and-cream spectator pumps. She didn't know what to expect. She was ready. Except not. She needed her Bible.

Fifteen minutes later, every drawer opened and closed, still no sign of it. Had it been that long?

Once in a blue moon she'd search for a verse on her phone to get her through the day, but how long had it been since she'd read her Bible? Really read it? *Too long.* On those few occasions she'd made it to church, she'd come late to skip the announcements or left before the benediction to beat the traffic. Probably hadn't sat through a full service in ten years.

A distinctive knock—"shave and a haircut, two bits"—reverberated through her home.

"Come on in, Ben." Her pulse quickened. Car rides with her godchildren always lifted her spirits. Their endless questions, the ridiculous kids' songs their parents played. A jangly guitar and a woman making roaring sounds and belting out the lyrics to "We Are the Dinosaurs" filtered through her mind. The sticky, wet kisses they planted on her cheeks.

AN APPEARANCE OF IMPROPRIETY

The heavy tread of male footsteps echoed off the hardwood floors.

"Are we running late?" She rushed around, searching for her watch.

She heard a weird couple of coughs. And a throat clearing, like an attempt to dislodge a chunk of dry bread from an airway.

"Ben and Cassandy are running late. I got roped in at the last minute."

She'd recognize the voice echoing off her wood floors and vibrating down her spine anywhere. She'd spent almost seven hours in an elevator being soothed and cared for by the owner of that voice.

Not. Ben.

JD.

He gave more coughs.

"Something about having trouble reinstalling a car seat. Once Cassandy said 'car seat,' I blanked out. May as well been discussing nuclear physics."

Spasms clenched her stomach, and clamminess dampened her forehead with perspiration.

JD Cash stood in her living room. Why?

She rubbed her wet palms down the flare of her skirt, smoothing imaginary wrinkles. He'd waltzed into her home. Unexpected. Uninvited. Her firm rules, her bright lines, her treacherous emotional firewall were in danger of imminent breach.

"I wasn't expecting you." Understatement of the year. She rummaged through her memory to piece together the colossal communication breakdown that led to this awkward situation. Realization hit. She'd never mentioned the TransNation case or the mock trial program to Cassandy. Plus, Ben and Cassandy had their hands full. Common sense told her details might slip through the cracks with three kids and a busy law practice.

She continued stalling. Squeezing every muscle and fiber of her being into compliance.

"This is a mystery for me too, Your Honor. I have no idea what happened here. Way I figure it, no harm, no foul. It's only church."

Only church?

More random foot-shuffling noises, followed by rattling. Was he rifling through her drawers?

"You live on a great street. I like your place. Cozy." He sounded at ease. Composed. Not at all thrown off by this bizarre turn of events.

She grappled for a coherent response. "It's tiny, but you know what they say . . ."

"Location, location, location," he chimed in.

You've got to go out there. Now she was simply hiding.

"You almost ready?" JD's voice filled every crevice of her cottage.

"Coming."

She rounded the corner from her bedroom, and there he stood. His presence overpowered the compact living room. The most handsome man she had ever seen. He had tamed his silver glory, George Clooney–style, with a side part and pomade. The collar of a dress shirt peeked from beneath a crew-neck sweater. He'd offset the formality of his top half with well-worn jeans, and he twirled a pair of Ray-Ban Aviators.

"Mercy."

"What was that, Your Honor?"

"Nothing." Seeing him there with those eyes trained on her, calm and peace washed over her. What would it be like to date JD?

Wait, date? What? This could not be a date. Not now. Not ever. Rules. Melvin. Goals. Mantra. Her brain fired off non sequiturs, anything to regain its equilibrium. Besides, how could going to church be considered a date? *You're a judge. Use reasoning.* Fact: Sitting beside someone in a pew in no way violated the Code of Judicial Conduct, especially if you weren't overseeing one of their cases. Fact: Judges could attend church like every other citizen. Final fact: Didn't the First Amendment to the Constitution guarantee her the right to freely practice her religion? Airtight arguments. It was all a huge misunderstanding. She would not be violating any laws, rules, protocols, or procedures. And she would not be on a date.

***

"That's quite a car you have there." Mahalia looked askance at the Wagoneer.

JD's insides scrambled like fighter jets. Thirty minutes earlier, Ben had called in a panic. Said they were running late. Needed him to pick up a

AN APPEARANCE OF IMPROPRIETY

friend Cassandy had invited. Had given him an address. A toddler had screamed into the phone, like they were being stung by a hive of bees, and the call dropped. He'd texted "Roger that" and jetted out.

If a Martian had called out to him to enter the house, he would have been less stunned than when he'd heard Mahalia's honeyed voice welcome him in. God didn't make mistakes, but this . . . He couldn't comprehend the providence behind *this*.

JD held out his hand to help Mahalia climb up into his Wagoneer. With difficulty, he made himself release her hand and tucked her skirt into the vehicle before closing the door. A soft floral scent wafted out as he did. Barely there. Intoxicating.

No way to get out of this thing gracefully. She was at the helm of her own judicial career. They weren't violating any rules, and if she didn't view it as compromising her stature as a jurist, he'd go with her judgment. He rounded the rear bumper. Concentrating in church would require every ounce of internal discipline. *Got to shift gears.* He slammed the door and cranked up his car.

Nonsensical words and sentences pinged in his brain as he tried to come up with a way to lighten the atmosphere.

"So . . . I want to introduce you to someone."

"No need. I probably won't know anyone at the church."

"No, no." He slapped the dash and stroked it. "May I present to you, Gerty? She's my first love. I've had her since college. Over two hundred thousand miles and she's never let me down." Based on her expression, the Wagoneer did not impress her.

"Gerty. A solid, old-fashioned name for a behemoth of a station wagon."

"Careful—you'll hurt Gerty's feelings, Judge. She's not a station wagon. She's a Wagoneer." He drew a hand from left to right out in front of him so she could take in the grandeur of his vehicle.

"Well, um, nice to meet you, Gerty." She smiled. Her eyes sparkled, and behind them was something he couldn't read.

"A little road music. Push the center button, please."

"A tape deck?" Her voice trailed higher.

"Yes, ma'am, and I've got a crate full of mix tapes at home to go along with it."

She pushed the button, and the distinctive stylings of the Brooklyn Tabernacle Choir played in the background.

"I'm impressed. You've got good taste in gospel music. One of my grandmother's favorites."

He placed a hand over his heart. "And I'm humbled."

She laughed. The lightness of it unburdened him. They listened to the music in silence for a few minutes as he pulled onto the highway.

Mahalia's face looked as if she'd drifted to another world.

"What are your brilliant neurons pondering?"

She worried her bottom lip with her teeth. "Okay, I'll let you in on a secret." She angled toward the center of the car, taking him by surprise. "I don't have a Gerty, but I *do* have a beloved possession that I've had since college as well. Swear not to make fun of me."

He ran his finger over his lips, like a zipper pull.

"Bunny slippers. They were a Christmas gift from Granny. She was so proud of me following our family traditions. Going off to college." She turned toward the window. "She told me they would keep my toes warm 'way up north.'"

"So what does your grandmother think about the fact that you're a judge? She must love that." He pivoted his head, hoping to catch a glimpse of her face. She still looked out the window.

There was a sniff, and Mahalia's voice came out in a near whisper. "She passed away before I made it to the bench. She never would give up those menthols, and that and diabetes ate her alive. I've had those slippers resoled twice already. The shoe guy told me there's not enough slipper left to do it a third time."

This time when he looked over, her eyes glistened. She raised her hand and wiped an eye. He caught that hand on its way back down and gave a gentle squeeze. He lingered with their fingers intertwined for a moment, then withdrew. Simply two human beings sharing a moment. Nothing unprofessional about offering another human compassion, right?

This complex woman was filling gaps in his soul he hadn't realized he even had. He steeled himself so he could compartmentalize. Church today would be what it would be. For now, time to seal the hatch on what was lurking deep inside, or it might melt down like a nuclear reactor, leaving devastation in its wake.

Chapter 22

Mahalia stared out the passenger window as the Wagoneer pulled into an industrial office park full of logistics warehouses and single-story buildings. "Interesting place for a church." The moment of comfort he'd offered had temporarily eased the ache from the fresh remembrance of Granny's death, but her emotions remained on edge.

"Well, the rent is cheap, and we only use the space for our Sunday meeting. We do our outreach where people are—coffee shops, strip clubs, Home Depot. Doesn't matter."

Mahalia reared back. "Did you just gloss over the words 'strip club'?"

JD laughed. "That's a ladies-only ministry. Those women are brave. What testimonies. Hurting people are everywhere."

Mahalia could not imagine her grandfather, Reverend Henry L. Jackson, DMin, *ever* having a strip club ministry at his church. The deaconesses in their color-coordinated ensembles marching into Ticklers? *I don't think so.*

Cassandy and Ben stood in the lobby, waiting for them. Two wiggling dervishes by their sides and a toddler in Cassandy's arms. Ben trained his eyes on Mahalia and then on JD. His eyes darted back in her direction. His eyebrows shot up toward his hairline, and a flush, the color of his copper-colored hair, tinged his cheeks.

Ben held his arms up, as if Mahalia had a gun trained on him. "Mahalia, I'm so sorry . . ."

She held up her own hand to stop him. She'd decided in the car to let him off the hook. One look at her two frenetic godsons and Cassandy's happy but haggard face told the story.

"Don't even worry about it, Ben. It's only church." She peeked over at JD, and he gave her a brief nod of affirmation. Cassandy stepped forward

AN APPEARANCE OF IMPROPRIETY

and swept Mahalia into a hug, squashing between them the toddler, who squealed with delight.

"When's the last time we saw you?" Cassandy pulled back, a broad smile lighting up her face. "The kids miss Auntie MayMay. They ask about you all the time." Cassandy wore her easy-care braid extensions pulled back in a ponytail. The style accentuated her pretty face and warm-brown skin. Banished were the heels Cassandy had worn as an attorney—traded in for the cutest Mary Janes, along with leggings and a chunky sweater. Tears pricked Mahalia's eyes. Motherhood suited her sweet friend.

"Somehow, Judge Goldstein and Mr. Cash roped me into the Junior Jurors program." She made a face. "Once the mock trial is over, I'll have free time to visit my babies."

Ben leaned in for a cheek kiss. His voice dropped to a whisper. "Thanks for not ratting out my mistake to Cassandy."

Mahalia smiled and pinched his cheek.

The klatch of adults and kids made their way past a double doorway into the sanctuary, and Cassandy peeled off to drop off the kids in their classrooms. The cavernous warehouse space resembled a Costco-sized coffeehouse with folding chairs. Whereas an altar stood at the front of Greater Mount Sinai Baptist, here stood a backdrop of distressed-wood paneling on wheels. The pulpit was a music stand. Tucked in a corner, stage left, was an acoustic trio playing hymns that Mahalia barely recognized, since they weren't bellowing out of an organ accompanied by a crescendo of piano riffs.

"This is a very international church." She looked around at the diverse congregation—accents from Africa, Central America, and Asia filled the air, plus she noted Americans of every flavor as well.

They entered their row, and Mahalia ended up with Cassandy on one side and JD on the other. JD man-spread one leg into the aisle beside him and ran his long arm behind both her seat and Cassandy's. He used his reach to tap Cassandy. Cassandy turned his way. He leaned across Mahalia's view. "Ask that husband of yours if we are still on for basketball next week."

Mahalia scrunched back in her seat. JD dominated her personal space. *Soap and pomade.* Reminded her of Granddaddy's barbershop. Tears stung the back of her eyes. There was something going on with her today. Being with JD and sitting in church pulled up raw feelings and emotion she didn't understand.

She watched as a late-thirties-looking man, wearing jeans and a plaid button-down, jogged from the wings of the warehouse to stand in front of the makeshift pulpit. He adjusted a nearly invisible earpiece/microphone combo and introduced himself as Steve.

"Just Steve," who apparently had no ecclesiastical title and probably had no academic letters behind his name either, pointed to a screen that had surreptitiously appeared out of nowhere when Mahalia had blinked. The screen splashed in dynamic graphics the title of the series he was preaching—"Discerning God's Will and Call for Your Life," from Revelation 3. How many times had Granddaddy preached from this same passage? She could remember it clearly. *So then, because you are lukewarm, and neither cold nor hot, I will vomit you out of My mouth.*

"Such an intense verse for this time in the morning." Steve generated a few chuckles with his comment. "Some translations say 'spit,' but the gross word 'vomit' is in the original Greek."

Granddaddy Henry had roared, in his baritone, *"Christ would vomit out the lukewarm Laodiceans because of their self-sufficiency, pride, and materialism."* He'd warned her so many times about worldliness, fearing that was her tendency. But was it wrong to have a dream?

She'd only said the words "Midnight Prince" aloud one time in her life. After that, she'd kept it private. Locked inside. Sure, she'd mentioned what she was looking for to a few friends back in college. The must-haves for a guy to grab her interest and hold it. But the name for the total package stayed walled up behind dashed hopes and long-unanswered prayers. The idea of letting anyone know about the Prince Charming of her dreams left her raw and insecure. While Steve warmed up the crowd with more dad jokes, her concentration drifted, turning to the day her vision had come into focus.

***

"Come help Granny set up for fellowship, baby."

Finally a big girl, seven years old. Finally old enough to help in the kitchen, with its massive stove and sweltering heat. Mahalia twirled, her

AN APPEARANCE OF IMPROPRIETY

princess dress fanning out. She was careful not to brush her skirt against the hot appliance.

This day the deaconesses all wore matching white dresses, with red carnations on their lapels. They scurried around in aprons, checking on cornbread in the oven and greens on the stove. The sound of their voices singing Dottie Peoples's song "On Time God"—about Job, the fiery furnace, and Pharaoh's armies—filled the air with melody.

"You're in charge of the salt and pepper today," Granny told her. "Plus, get the hot sauce. Use the cart and load it up from the pantry. After that, push the cart around to the tables to lay everything out."

Mahalia hummed along to the tune that flowed around the bustling ladies, harmonizing and moving from table to table. Each received a set of matching shakers. She did another twirl or two to admire the flare of her skirt. Next, a double check to ensure the shakers aligned precisely with the artificial tulips and plastic baby's breath in little vases on the tables.

She tucked the empty cart away in the utility closet and skipped back to Granny, heart bursting with pride. She peeked her head around the kitchen door. "Come see. Come see." She bounced on her toes, waiting for Granny to tell her what an excellent job she'd done.

Her grandmother rounded the corner and looked at the first table. Her brows pulled down. She walked to the next table. Her forehead creased, and she darted her eyes around, glancing from table to table. "Baby, how come you didn't put a salt and a pepper on each table, like I told you? You got some tables with two salts and some with two peppers. Don't see any tables with one of each."

"They're getting married, Granny."

"They're getting married?"

"Yes, one's a boy. One's a girl. Salt with salt. Pepper with pepper. White with white. Black with black."

Granny's lids pulled wide. She sat in a nearby chair, held her arms out, and pulled Mahalia in.

"Baby, where did you get such a notion?"

"In the movies, Prince Charming always rescues the princess. The prince and the princess always look alike. Then they get married." Why couldn't Granny see how much sense this made?

"But, baby..."

"And you have to match. If you are dark like me, your husband has to be dark. If you're like caramel candy like Auntie Phyllis, your husband has to be like caramel candy."

"That's not true, sweetheart."

"Is too. You and Granddaddy, you're both like chocolate candy bars. And the pink people are always with the pink people. That's how it is on TV and in the movies."

Granny squeezed her in close.

"I can't wait. My Midnight Prince—that's what I'm going to call him—I can't wait for him to come on his big horse and take me away to his castle."

Granny said nothing, but there was wetness between their two pressed-together cheeks.

Her grandmother held Mahalia close to her bosom for a few moments. When her silent tears stopped, Granny had set her straight on spices and real life. Told her it was all the seasonings blended and mixed together—salt, pepper, garlic, and onions—that made a meal and life flavorful. *"Jesus loves the little children, all the children of the world."* Granny had crooned to her.

Her grandmother had made her point clear. And she'd been right. But deep inside, Mahalia still carried a wound. A wound inflicted by family. A wound from friends and acquaintances. She wanted a Midnight Prince because she knew a man with the same wounds would know without asking. He would see it on her downcast face. In the slump of her shoulders. A day when someone else called her "dark woman." And he would wrap her in his arms and make everything all right.

She'd let go of some of her childish misconceptions that day. But she'd also learned a lesson. Keep your hurts and most-cherished dreams locked up inside, and don't confess them to anyone. Not even Granny.

***

The cries of a wailing baby echoed in the large space, pulling Mahalia's mind back from the pain she'd inflicted on her grandmother.

"Do you want to know what God's will is?" Steve paced behind his little podium. "I can finish this whole thing up in under fifteen minutes."

AN APPEARANCE OF IMPROPRIETY

Fifteen minutes. Right. One *song* could go on for fifteen minutes at Granddaddy's church. This she had to hear. She readjusted herself in her seat.

"Fielding tough questions is part of my job. Why does God allow suffering? What can I do to save my marriage? Is there life on other planets?"

The crowd laughed.

"That last question is a fan fave from the middle schoolers." Steve held up his hands in contrition.

Mahalia rolled her eyes, thinking how Granddaddy Henry would institute church discipline, followed by ex-communication, at the mere mention of space aliens inside his sanctuary.

"Okay, hear me out," Steve said once the laughter died down. "Here's the number one question I get—'What is God's will for my life?'"

"Our lifespan is eighty, maybe ninety years. Sadly, some people get less. It rushes by in the blink of an eye, and that's why this question is so pressing."

Mahalia sneaked a glance at JD. No need to question whether he was living life as God wanted. Purpose oozed out of his every pore. Not so with her. She cycled through scattershot prayers, bargaining, and feelings of defeat, trying to discern whether she was on the right path for her career and her future husband, but she never received a definitive direction.

One graphic on the screen dissolved into another, and she returned her attention to the sermon.

"People desire clarity about the calling on their lives. This job or that job? Marry Samantha or Meghan? UCLA or USC? We want the fine print, like those user agreements on apps that we all click but nobody reads."

She sat straighter. The hipster pastor had jokes, but he was landing on the one question she'd asked herself a million times. She crossed her arms with skepticism. Did he have the answers?

Steve switched to his next graphic. "We pray God shines a spotlight so we'll know. Proof beyond a reasonable doubt. Zero ambiguity."

He stepped out from behind the podium. "I'm here to tell you, we don't have to look for signs, lights in the sky, or dry fleeces. God says, 'Do not merely listen to the word . . . Do what it says.' Straight and to the point. Are you freelancing in your life? Making up your own rules? Or are you following his Word?

"Want more?" The next slide displayed a series of verses. "Be holy. Love."

He used his fingers to tick off his points. "Be sanctified. Declare God's glory. Be clear minded. Use your spiritual gifts. And offer hospitality. These things are God's specific will for each of us."

She heard the words he was saying, but she wanted . . . more somehow.

"What about this verse? 'Live in harmony with one another.' Or this one? 'Be sympathetic . . . be compassionate and humble. Do not repay evil with evil or insult with insult. On the contrary, repay evil with blessing, because to this you were called so that you may inherit a blessing.'"

He opened a bottle of water and took a long swig. "The word 'called' is literally right in the verse. Are you doing these things?"

The slick graphics presentation morphed again, and Steve rattled off more verses and points in rapid succession.

A groan sounded from somewhere in the warehouse.

"I hear you." He threw his hands in the air and stomped on the stage. Ripples of laughter filled the room.

"You're upset because all I am saying is to pray, read the Bible, and seek wise counsel. I understand this is reductionistic, but I promised fifteen minutes."

It was as if Steve had read her mind. It seemed like a cookie-cutter answer.

"Can God do things beyond our understanding? Unexpectedly? Even miraculously? Sure! But he doesn't expect us to twist ourselves into knots trying to figure him out when he's provided sixty-six books that go into exhaustive detail. Consult the manual. Seek wise counsel. If you are already doing all that, pray and do what you think is best. God is sovereign. He loves his children. Whatever God decrees to happen will come to pass, and he's got it under control. So relax."

Steve grasped the podium with both hands. "Let's pray."

Steve had been true to his word. Total sermon time—thirty minutes. Wow. Granddaddy would be winding up his introduction and settling in for another hour.

After one more mellow selection by the trio and no collection plate, Mahalia rose and forced her feet to take her out of the sanctuary. Words from Granddaddy Henry and Steve swirled together inside of her. Did she even know what her principles were anymore?

AN APPEARANCE OF IMPROPRIETY

She had gone as far as she was going to go with God, and she was sitting down in the center of the road, refusing to go any further. Her prized man had not appeared despite her hard work in college and law school. He didn't come when she'd ascended to the bench as one of the youngest jurists in the county.

She stood near the top. So close to the pinnacle—but were these dreams and aspirations God's will for her life? Was Melvin? Was God asking her to give up her dream? Her deepest longing? As she strolled to the Wagoneer, the questions dogged her steps like a puppy on the feet of a new owner.

Chapter 23

JD PROPPED OPEN the door for Mahalia to enter ahead of him into S'Getti, Soup & Salad. The sweet tang of garlicky marinara permeated the entryway. Red-and-white-checked curtains adorned the windows facing the street entrance. Three parallel steam tables stood behind the pay-before-you-eat cashier. He spotted a pasta bar, a salad bar, and a dessert table, all crowded with people.

"Girl You Know It's True," by the crash-and-burn duo Milli Vanilli, blasted from the sound system, and there were kids in every crevice. JD cocked his eyebrow at Mahalia. "Come here often, Judge?" Didn't seem like her kind of place at all.

She smiled through a grimace. "Not if I don't have to, but my godchildren love it, and their parents find it convenient, so I indulge them."

Ben entered with the twins in tow, while Cassandy clutched their little girl, Mia.

"Sorry it took so long to get here. Left the diaper bag at the church. Had to circle back." Cassandy puffed out some air, trying to move a braid that had fallen over her eye.

Mahalia held out her arms, commandeering Mia and wrapping her up. She snuggled her nose in the little girl's tawny locks.

"There's my little honey bear. Give TeeTee MayMay some sugar." Mahalia rubbed noses with the girl, who squealed in delight.

Mia put a pudgy palm on each of Mahalia's cheeks and kissed her squarely on the mouth.

"Love you, TeeTee MayMay."

"I love you too, honey bear."

AN APPEARANCE OF IMPROPRIETY

A little boy no older than five darted out from beside Ben and tugged on the full skirt of Mahalia's dress.

"Auntie MayMay, I loss a tooth." The words lisped out.

JD's guess today was that Mahalia was talking to Jojo, not Joshua. Still couldn't tell them apart. Both twins were Ben's spitting image, or would be if Ben had lain out all summer working on his tan.

The second twin popped up on Mahalia's other side, lips pulled back, teeth bared like a hyena. "Me too, Auntie."

"Well, boys, we'll have to talk about this when we sit down. TeeTee MayMay might give you each a dollar." The boys let out a collective screech and began some sort of frenetic dance. Mahalia graced the boys with a smile full of love. He'd never seen her maternal side before, but as he observed her with them, his chest tightened. When she let herself, the judge loved deeply and completely.

"Shall we?" Ben angled his head toward a long table sufficient to fit the traveling circus of four adults and three children.

JD hung back to allow Ben, Cassandy, Mahalia, and the kids to press ahead of him through the throng and secure their seating.

A young lady dressed in the classic red T-shirt and white apron of an Italian-restaurant employee approached from a corner of the room. "Will you need a high chair?"

"Please," Cassandy said.

Mahalia repositioned Mia in her arms and bounced her up and down to soothe her fussy murmurings.

"Mahalia, do you mind sitting here while Ben and I go make some plates for ourselves and the kids? I'll make sure we bring you some of that lasagna you love."

"Of course. Everything's under control."

"Should I stay here and help you, Judge?" JD eyed the twins, who were laboring over the coloring sheets Cassandy had pulled from the overstuffed diaper bag.

Mahalia fed little Mia Cheerios one at a time. "I've got this covered. The harried parents could probably use a hand juggling all the plates."

"I'm on it." *This is married life with kids.* JD stepped in beside Cassandy at the pasta bar. "What can I do?"

187

"If you could hold the plates, I'll scoop up the noodles, sauce, and garlic bread for the boys."

"Got it." He balanced Jojo's plate on his left arm like a seasoned waiter and held Joshua's plate in his left hand. With his right, he carefully made a plate for himself, making sure to keep his other arm steady.

Ben held one plate ready for Cassandy to dish up Mia's food. He supported it with his prosthesis.

After Cassandy had made all the children's plates, she dispatched the menfolk back to the table to serve the kids. She followed behind with plates for herself and Ben, and a generous slice of lasagna noodles oozing cheese and sauce for Mahalia.

"Prayer time, boys." Cassandy set the plates on the table.

"Your turn to lead, Jojo." Cassandy reached out, and everyone around the table joined hands.

"God is great, God is good, and we thank him for our food. Amen."

Heads lifted, and JD's friends helped their kids with forks and tucked napkins under chins. A knot tightened in his throat as he watched Ben and Cassandy navigate the logistics of feeding themselves and three hungry children, communicating to each other with gentle glances and slight gestures. Mahalia was right in the mix, wiping sauce from messy hands, laughing at knock-knock jokes, and admonishing the boys with her sharp stare when a noodle fight broke out.

A spoonful of sauce flew by JD and landed on Mahalia's top.

"Who did that?" Mahalia's eyes flashed fire. Her tone was stern.

Mia's hands, covered in sauce, waved around. Given what he'd witnessed in her courtroom, JD waited for Mahalia to explode.

"TeeTee MayMay's going to get you." Mahalia grabbed both the little girl's hands in her own and wiped all the sauce off. She pretended to eat the girl's fingers and made little growling noises. "I'm going to eat you all up."

Mia squealed with laughter.

Fascination and surprise pulled at JD's gut. Mahalia's uninhibited joy with the children overflowed, washing over him as well. Crinkles formed beside her eyes and an easy grin graced her face as she enjoyed the kids from somewhere deep inside herself. Gone was the always-put-together fashionista and in-charge judge. She was molded and squished like putty in the hands of those kids.

JD's future unfolded in front of his eyes. If he wasn't careful, this brilliant, beautiful, amazing woman might capture his heart—one chorus of "Itsy Bitsy Spider" at a time.

Chapter 24

STANDING IN THE parking lot of S'Getti, Soup & Salad, Mahalia gave kisses all around to her godchildren and waved goodbye to Cassandy, Ben, and the kids. JD waited at the passenger side of the Wagoneer, holding the door open for her. She brushed past him to sit, his clean scent bringing heat to her face as she remembered being enveloped in his shower gel.

JD hummed along with the ancient tape whirling in the deck, sparing Mahalia the necessity of making chitchat. She didn't have it in her. While JD maneuvered the hulking vehicle into traffic, a swirl of emotions banged and clamored inside her, vying for examination.

She took in his profile. JD's work with the students built structure and meaning into the lives of the kids. He showed them a path out of the dead-end futures their neighborhood had waiting for them. Putting his own reputation on the line, he'd written a poignant college recommendation for Kyle, detailing his triumph over relentless bullying and asserting that it made him a strong candidate for admission.

The Wagoneer hit a pothole and jostled her. She ran a hand down the front of her outfit. She'd have to send the whole thing to the cleaners because of the drool and food stains.

The ticktock of her biological clock overpowered the soft music JD played. Sitting at lunch laughing, talking, and loving on her godchildren had filled the cracks in her heart with happiness. Like JD, Ben, and Cassandy were building something real. Pouring their lives into their little people who needed them and loved them. Paying it forward.

Jackson women excelled—the expectation was chiseled in stone. Being a successful judge was what she'd wanted all her life. *Wasn't it?*

AN APPEARANCE OF IMPROPRIETY

What would happen if all the climbing of the ladder of success ended with her ladder propped against the wrong wall?

Points from Steve's sermon popped into her consciousness, chipping away at the edifice of her dream. Clarity emerged. All her climbing and striving had been for her own glorification. Black-tie soirees. Galas. Kudos. And a dashing husband to love her. Not one thought of God or what he might want from her.

But sitting here in JD's massive wagon, the car swaying and the tires humming on the asphalt, she felt mountain ranges of doubt rising up before her. A sermon, a lunch with squirming and food-covered children, and now a car ride beside a man driven by a fierce code of chivalry. That was all it took to leave her feeling like a hollow papier-mâché doll, devoid of any character, personality, or substance.

"I . . ." She swallowed hard. "I want to close my eyes for a bit." She turned her head toward the window and leaned back. Behind her closed lids, the war inside her raged hot and fierce.

***

JD longed to pry inside Mahalia's brain and learn what lay behind the cycle of emotions that had played across her face before she hid it from him.

The collar of her now disheveled outfit bore the complete outline of a small marinara-sauce handprint left there by Mia while she clung to the judge in an embrace full of love. Mahalia had never been more beautiful.

JD averted his gaze from the space between Mahalia's collar and her upswept hair. He should not think about any of her body parts, even innocuous ones like her neck or . . . He bounced his eyes away from their perusal of her tapered legs. *Eyes straight ahead, soldier.* He fastened his hands to the steering wheel at ten and two.

Motherhood looked good on Mahalia. This afternoon he'd watched her juggle a toddler and twirl pasta at the same time. There had been a lightness to her countenance amid the chaos. Her normal air of brusque confidence had mellowed before the children vying for Auntie MayMay's smooches. She focused on the kids and engaged them. They made her laugh. It was as though Courtroom Mahalia didn't exist.

He got it. She was the mother lioness. Fierce over her territory and her cubs.

He pulled up in front of Mahalia's house. He didn't want her to leave with nothing said between them. "Did you enjoy church?"

"The sermon gave me a lot to think about." She remained facing the window.

"Agreed. Everything ready for the next Junior Jurors meeting?"

"I think so."

She continued giving him the brush-off. He swallowed hard, not wanting to watch her walk up the pathway and through the door. "Well, it was a lovely afternoon, Your Honor. Of course, you can call or text if you have questions about the upcoming competition."

He wanted to do something else with his mouth besides blabber. His palm itched to slide along the back of her neck and draw her to himself so he could place his lips on hers.

"Of course. I'll see you soon." Mahalia reached for the door handle.

JD hurried to exit the car and make it around to open Mahalia's door.

He stood there holding it ajar, feeling like a fool. Nothing he could think of to say or do was appropriate or professional in any way.

He palmed the back of his neck. "Have a wonderful afternoon, Judge."

"Thank you, Mr. Cash."

JD shut the door and leaned against it as he watched her willowy legs propel her to the front door. She put the key in the lock and let herself in without a backward glance.

He was toast. A goner—in total freefall without a parachute.

***

Mahalia stripped off the dress she'd worn to church and donned her slouch-about-the-house clothes. She crawled on top of her bed and covered her eyes with her arm.

A swarm of bees buzzed under her chest—emotions she couldn't rein in. God's will for her? Mere hours ago, she'd been crystal clear about her life's direction. Stupid Steve and his short sermon had stirred up a dust cloud full of questions, and the mantle of success she had wrapped around herself provided no comfort.

AN APPEARANCE OF IMPROPRIETY

Steve had said God wanted personal sacrifices—holiness, submission—not her checklist of success. Now second thoughts about her career choices whirled around in a bitter stew seasoned by the hurt she had nursed her whole life over the colorist barbs and jabs.

Where did Melvin fit into God's plans? In her mind, his image gave way to that of a silver-haired, melancholy cowboy. She willed JD's visage away, reframing her thoughts. Romance with him was a nonstarter because of her no-lawyer rule, but she could still view him as an excellent example with his commitment to Junior Jurors.

Resolve set in. She wouldn't totally overhaul her life. She'd implement minor adjustments. A tune-up. Tweaks. Maybe make an effort to go to church more regularly. As for giving back, she'd commit more than her time to the Junior Jurors program—she'd give it her heart. Extend herself.

And Melvin? She clicked off his good qualities in her mind. She'd focus on prioritizing their long-distance relationship.

Misgivings niggled, but she cycled her mantra through her brain, shooing away Steve's words, willing herself to believe this course correction would get her back on the right path.

Chapter 25

MARCH MADNESS DESCRIBED JD's life right now. The date for the mock trial hurtled closer and closer. He *had* to see Mahalia to coordinate her responsibilities for the tournament. Unfortunately, stacked-up cases slammed her docket, and they couldn't agree on a time during the week to arrange a get-together. So tonight, Saturday evening, was the only viable option.

He'd come up with three places they could eat. His office? How would it appear if she emerged from his office at nine o'clock at night? His condo? Even worse.

He settled on a little place in the Valley called San Fernando Seafood Grill. Nondescript on the outside, but locals knew the establishment served the best shrimp scampi in Southern California. Booths made up the bulk of the seating, but one long family-style table ran down the center to accommodate larger parties. It would work perfectly. With all their papers and trial notebooks spread around, no one could mistake their dinner for anything other than a business meeting—which, he repeated to himself, it was.

As he waited for Mahalia, JD scanned his phone for the East Coast basketball scores. He quickly put it down when he heard the bell above the front door give an old-fashioned ding-a-ling.

Mahalia entered, and his ribs squeezed in on his lungs as he admired her willowy figure. Stunning, as always. She was swathed in a zigzag-patterned dress that wrapped around and tied in the front. She also wore her standard-issue skyscraper-high pumps. He choked back a chuckle.

She glided to the table.

"Could you have picked a place farther from the courthouse or either of our houses for us to meet?" Mahalia's sparkling eyes held mirth, not anger, and he relaxed.

AN APPEARANCE OF IMPROPRIETY

"Hey, I hear defending champ Sherman Oaks Prep has spies everywhere. All it takes is one Instagram photo of our trial outline and *bam*, we've lost the whole thing."

Mahalia gave him that rich laugh that filled his insides with peace.

"Alright, counselor. We're going to eat first, right? You can't drag a girl to the farthest edge of LA county at seven in the evening and give her bird food."

"Got it covered. I took the liberty of ordering, especially since there are only three ingredients in all the food—shrimp, fish, or clams."

"Who can mess up an order of shrimp scampi?"

Her words were light, but Mahalia lifted a hand to knead the back of her neck.

"Rough day?"

The look in her eyes asked "Can I trust you?"

JD smiled. "Foxhole friends. Remember? What happens on the Otis elevator stays on the Otis elevator."

She relaxed before him and released a long exhale. "Okay, here's the thing—"

"Mr. Cash." A rotund, middle-aged man wearing a chef's coat approached. He held a platter of scampi, cheese biscuits, and salad, all stacked on a round tray perched on his shoulder.

"You going to drop it, Vinnie?"

"I've got it, Mr. Cash. And this lovely lady is?" Vinnie's round, rosy cheeks capped his toothy smile.

The heat rushing to JD's face made his forehead sweat. Vinnie thought this was a date. "Vinnie, this is Judge Mahalia Jackson."

Vinnie set the platters down, arranged them, and gave a gallant little bow. "A pleasure, Your Honor. Any friend of Mr. Cash is a friend of mine."

"We're here working on a court assignment," Mahalia said, her back straight.

"Of course."

Before JD could object, Vinnie produced a long lighter from his apron pocket and lit the votive candle on the center of the table.

"Sorry about that." He wanted her to know he did not view this as a date.

"Of course."

Jayna Breigh

"Mind if I pray?"

As JD lowered his head, he saw Mahalia's hand outstretched on the table. He interlaced their fingers and felt a contented rightness settle in his heart. He had no idea how or when he was planning to pursue Mahalia, but it was going to happen. He would start as friends.

***

Mahalia jerked her head up after the grace. Grabbing his hand had been reflexive. Years of training at Granddaddy's table. She glanced around the room. The place was almost empty. Besides, who could have a problem with prayer?

She'd almost told JD about all the judges out to stop her from obtaining the assistant supervising judge position. Some were themselves chasing the crown. Others had thrown their support to different candidates. Colleagues, huddled together in the courthouse cafeteria over tasteless turkey sandwiches, would stop talking when she approached. In the stairwell, she'd heard a bailiff and a clerk whispering about a secret Facebook group shared by a cliquish cadre of her peers. Alliances were forming behind various contenders. She normally marched to the tune of her own drum and hadn't realized how fast the winds of politics could shift.

Thankfully, Vinnie's spot-on timing had interrupted before she ran off her mouth and crossed the professional line. Was it too much to hope he'd moved on from his question?

JD held his fork in his left hand, European-style, and shoved a huge shrimp into his mouth. With his eyes closed, he scrunched up his face and nodded several times. "Is this good or what?"

She took a diminutive bite. "Delicious."

"See there, I wouldn't steer you wrong." JD set his fork down, and a serious expression settled over his face. "So back to what's going on with you."

Mahalia dabbed at her mouth with her napkin and let out a long stream of air. It would be wonderful to share her burden with someone. But . . .

He gave her an exit and redirected the conversation to timeline issues for the mock trial meet. By the time the cheesecake and coffee arrived, they'd completed the plan for the upcoming competition, and the knot of stress in Mahalia's midsection had loosened.

She peeked at him while he finished his coffee. His eyes regarded her, holding the gravitas that always encircled him. A glob of whipped cream clung to his cheek beside his lip, an odd juxtaposition to his sorrowful eyes. *What had hurt him so?* Maternal instinct, or an instinct even more primal, kicked in. On impulse, Mahalia grabbed her napkin and raised it, moving her hand toward his lips. Screaming alarm bells went off, and her arm suddenly felt awkward and heavy. She dropped it down.

"You've got some . . ." She pointed at her own mouth, pantomiming.

JD wiped his lips, finally getting the cream off.

Their gazes locked, and a frisson of contentment settled over Mahalia.

"I can't . . . I'm not comfortable telling you what's going on, but thanks for being willing to listen." The words had tumbled from her without permission, but there they were.

"Anytime, Judge." He gave a slight shrug.

Vinnie approached and handed the check to JD. "You two can stay a bit longer. Everybody else, they've got to go."

Mahalia opened her briefcase and placed her mock trial documents inside. Vinnie was shooing two women, a blonde and a brunette, out the front door. Nice of Vinnie to give her and JD extra time to wrap things up. Something about the blonde's long wavy hair seemed familiar, but she brushed the idea from her head. She didn't know anybody on this side of town.

***

"Alright, Americano, off the counter. I'm too tired for this tonight." JD wanted to crash into bed. The carb load from Vinnie's delicious pasta was pulling his eyelids down.

The feline shot him the side-eye while JD reached for the squirt bottle. "I'm working on replacing you."

Americano yowled with indignation and showed him her backside as she slunk down the hall to his bedroom to take a nap . . . probably on his pillow.

He'd built the cold, lonely castle in his legal empire brick by brick by putting in sixty-plus-hour workweeks and sticking to his vow.

Something Monica had said earlier on a phone call pricked him. *"You need to slow down. When's the last time you've had some fun?"*

The answer? Never. He'd hit the ground running after his enlistment ended and hadn't looked back.

But was that true now? He had fun when he was with Mahalia. But she also had depth and character. She was like a lioness on the bench. But when she was with the high schoolers, she was a different person. Gentle and encouraging. And even though she'd been strong-armed into the whole thing, she did it with enthusiasm and grace. It had been a revelation watching her with her godchildren. She was a hidden jewel cloistered up there in her courtroom. A virtuous woman whose price was far above rubies.

What about his vow to himself? He'd made it of his own volition, and it had served him well. Had kept him from throwing his life away on sensual pleasures. He might even have dodged lung cancer or cirrhosis of the liver. But he'd been a believer long enough to know the vow wasn't what saved him from any of those things. It was God who had saved him, sustained him, protected him. And sometimes God called people to make unexpected changes.

He drew a deep breath in. Held it for a beat and exhaled. *To everything there is a season.* Was it time to recant his self-imposed promise? To shed the monk-like solitude and open himself up to the possibility of a wife and a family? The thought caused adrenaline to rush through him, as though he were standing on the edge of a cliff waiting to dive off. Mahalia had awakened him as a man. Had reanimated a part of him that had lain dormant for years. His mental chains fell off, and the door was flung open wide.

Right now, with the TransNation case still up in the air, a relationship felt impossible. But he was confident that if the circumstances could work out, they'd be right for each other. She just didn't know it yet.

***

LA Hearsay DMs

4thEstatePitBull: Fact check this. Want to send to my editor for a greenlight on the story.

AN APPEARANCE OF IMPROPRIETY

Confidential sources indicate that attorney Jimmy Dean Cash had dinner at the San Fernando Seafood Grill with Judge Mahalia Jackson last week. The source says the two sat by candlelight, deep in conversation, and that Cash paid for the meal. Given Judge Jackson's earlier involvement in the TransNation hearing, these facts warrant closer investigation.

BamaBelle: Looks good, but hold for now. Working a different angle.

Chapter 26

A WEEK LATER Mahalia sat in Judge Goldstein's office, nursing a pounding headache. She hoisted a cup of chamomile peppermint tea to her lips, hoping the alleged science about herbs that the barista had droned on about had the power to relieve the pain. As usual, Goldstein's eyes twinkled like an elf. It was *far* too early in the morning for twinkling.

"What's the status on your application?" Her mentor rummaged around on his desk for something.

"You know I turned that in months ago." When she'd finished the application, Mahalia had closed her eyes, said a little prayer, and clicked Send. Yet oddly, her hopes and dreams didn't flash in vivid color but were gray and formless.

"Right, right. So you did. I wanted to show you something." The judge located a wrinkled document near the bottom of a stack.

Sweat prickled her neck as she fixated on the printout in Goldstein's hands.

The judge drew a finger down the first page, flipped it over, and ran the finger down the second page.

"Here it is." He jabbed the document a couple of times. "You see the box where it says 'appeals rate'?" He slid the paper toward her.

She glanced at it. "Yes. So?"

"Your percentage is pretty high. A lot of attorneys appeal your decisions."

"They do. But I've told you my theory about that. First, I'm a female judge. And . . ."

The judge cut her off with a wave of his hand.

Mahalia pressed on. "Look how many of my decisions stand. The appeals court overturns less than two percent."

"You're right. But several of the judges on the committee are worrywarts."

AN APPEARANCE OF IMPROPRIETY

"Worried about what?" Her insides tightened.

"The TransNation case." Goldstein held her pinned to her seat with his wizened stare.

"What about it? That hot potato's been back in your lap for a while now. Not my problem anymore." Mahalia released her grip on the paper and smoothed out the wrinkles.

Goldstein tossed a newspaper onto the center of his desk. Mahalia grabbed it up.

An Appearance of Impropriety?

It was a close call for Los Angeles County judge Mahalia Jackson—trapped in an elevator overnight after it plunged one story following the 5.2 magnitude quake centered in the Valley. Inside the elevator with her for almost seven hours was flamboyant trial attorney Jimmy Dean Cash. Neither Jackson nor Cash was injured, but Judge Jackson appeared shaken, and Cash looked the worse for wear. There was no word from either about how they spent the hours trapped inside.

When contacted for comment, attorneys for TransNation offered this statement: "Obviously this was a terrifying emergency. However, it is our duty to represent our clients zealously. Should we find that TransNation's rights have been compromised in any way, we will take the necessary legal steps. Like everyone else in the Los Angeles County Bar, we are thankful Judge Jackson and Mr. Cash were successfully rescued."

She turned the paper over at the fold. Dinkelman's overexposed photo, taken seconds after the firefighters had pried open the elevator doors, resembled a paparazzo shot of two Hollywood stars ambushed coming out of a hotel after a tryst. One of her hands shielded her face, and her outfit was askew. Cash looked wide eyed and haggard.

A growl emanated from inside Mahalia's belly. Spikes of heat tore at her, and on its heels, icy fear. The TransNation quote didn't outright cite any impropriety, but the words held insinuation.

"Never saw this article. Nobody reads that rag anyway. Besides, this paper is old news. You dumped that case in my lap, and it boomeranged back to you before the earthquake even happened." Her frustration boiled over onto her old mentor. "So what? I heard a couple of pretrial motions, but nothing that would alter the case substantively."

"About that . . ." Goldstein let out a sigh. "There's more."

"More?" Mahalia forced her voice down from a screech.

"You're well aware I pay no heed to courthouse rumors and scuttlebutt," Goldstein said. "But the TransNation case is big. All over the news, and it's being watched closely. The CEO is a major donor to many politicians in the city and on the national level. And Cash is on every bus stop and billboard from Santa Clarita to San Bernardino. There are a lot of eyes on you and—"

"Spit it out." She cut him off. "What are people saying?"

"At this point only one person has said something, at least as far as I can tell. But that person's saying you were not neutral during the time you were handling the case."

Mahalia's heart felt as if a giant hand had worked into her chest and was squeezing. She squashed down the lurching anxiety rising in her stomach. She straightened her spine. No. She would not flinch. She'd crossed no lines. She and Mr. Cash had not discussed one aspect of the case. Despite how inappropriate the rescue photo looked, she had never breached the Code of Judicial Ethics.

"What . . . who started this rumor?"

"There was an anonymous complaint. Someone mentioned that the case may be subject to reversal on appeal because of your behavior."

She'd never gone easy on JD because of the one Junior Jurors meeting that had happened before Goldstein had regained the helm of the case. The two times he'd appeared before her, she'd been fair and even handed. Whoever was spreading these lies had some other ax to grind.

"What behavior? Is this complaint in writing?"

Judge Goldstein gave a weary sigh. "No. Cocktail-party chatter."

"Then why are you bringing this to me?" Mahalia threw her hands in the air. "I work hard to maintain my reputation. To have an unsubstantiated rumor, not even in writing, threaten my chances . . . well, that . . ." She bit back a harsh word. She wouldn't let this anonymous piece of dirt drag her down with him. Or her?

"I understand, *bubbeleh*. I'm only saying watch yourself. I wanted to give you a heads up. Make sure you can defend everything you've ever done in and out of your courtroom."

"I understand."

Goldstein slipped his reading glasses down his nose and trained his filmy eyes on her. "I'm counting on it."

***

Mahalia sat in her chambers with her chair facing the window and stared. Southern California had been under drought conditions for over two years, and pop-up fires continued to throw smoke into the air. The resulting haze obscured the mountains most days, but today's shifting winds meant the range stood out in sharp relief against the crystal-clear sky. Majestic peaks twenty miles from her office appeared to be mere blocks away. Her thinking, however, was still shrouded in smog.

Goldstein's confidence in her had always been like wind in her sails, but with his reputation on the line for backing her bid for ASJ, her desire to make him proud caused squeezing pressure across her forehead.

Nothing had happened between herself and JD that could be grounds for an appeal. Two hearings? One that made JD the attorney of record. Nothing there. Okay, she respected him. Even admired him. But that differed from an appearance of impropriety.

Had she come close? Her mind returned to the elevator the night of the earthquake. Yes, she'd come close. But she had not crossed the line, and neither had he. Besides, she had not backed off one inch on The Rule or on the hope for a Midnight Prince. Yes, JD was considerate, gentle, caring. Brilliant. But other than a cordial and professional relationship, they had no relationship of any kind. Sure, every time she was near him, she felt swaddled in a security blanket. He cast the same magical spell at every meeting with the students. It wasn't about her. His personal code commanded fierce loyalty and respect from everyone whose life he touched. With JD in charge, everyone knew everything was going to be all right.

Jayna Breigh

She had another date with Melvin coming up soon. They hadn't been together in person since the Millennial Masterpieces en Vie. But they had conquered the intricacies of syncing schedules across two time zones for video calls. They also had exchanged dozens of text messages. Quick snatches of conversation here and there. While Chicago to LA was a long commute for a date, things were progressing like . . . She struggled for a word. A conveyor belt? Steady pace. Nothing exciting. Melvin was a nice guy who checked all the right boxes, but her brain kept holding JD up as a side-by-side comparison, and it was no contest.

Stop! She'd build a mental encasement tall enough to dam out any untoward thoughts about Attorney Cash, and she'd starve her mental wanderings of all oxygen and light until they withered and died.

***

LA Hearsay DMs

1st&Goal: Can you use the pic? It's clearly AI, but is there something here?

4thEstatePitBull: It's useful. The appearance of impropriety is based on what others think. Even misperceptions. I can toss out a ton of questions about the "why" behind it.

1st&Goal: Finally got my hands on that other thing. A friend over in the juvie court filing room owed me big time. It's the confidential report the white-haired weasel filed. High and Mighty is mentioned as one of the sources that got my kid kicked out. I will only give it to you if you can shield me using your reporter privilege.

4thEstatePitBull: Perfect. Send it. Even the Supreme Court has leaks and no one's gone to jail over them, but yeah, you'll be a confidential source.

AN APPEARANCE OF IMPROPRIETY

1st&Goal: Done. What's your endgame?

4thEstatePitBull: You shouldn't know too much, but let's just say I'm lighting three fires on this match, and it's bad luck all around.

Chapter 27

JD ROTATED AND stretched his neck from side to side, seeking to loosen muscles tense from hunching over his keyboard while preparing witness-examination notes. He lifted a half-empty cup of espresso to his lips and downed the bitter brew like medicine.

The TransNation case, set for late April—about four weeks away—charged full speed ahead. But HBA's case listed, dead in the water. Despite the fact that HBA had agreed to a settlement, the agreement circled the drain because HBA had yet to send a check. Now JD had to prepare to go to trial in case the whole thing got flushed out to sea.

He lifted his arms into the air, weaving his fingers together, and stretched to work out the knots in his back. His normal sixty-hour workweek would amp up. Earlier mornings. Later nights. The grind wouldn't kill him, but the crush would waterlog the mock trial prep, and he hated shortchanging the kids. Hadn't been to church in a while either. But if he didn't stand in the gap for his clients, who would? They'd chosen him from all the attorneys in Los Angeles because of the promise he held out—justice.

Monica's words came back to him. *"You can't save them all."* His gut clenched, and he shoved Monica's admonition and his unease down. He had a job to do.

The blare of the internal intercom jarred him, and he stabbed the Speaker button.

"I told you to hold all calls." His words to Monica came out on a bark, and he instantly regretted it. She didn't need to deal with the crash of his overcommitments.

"JD, there is a woman here to see you. Claims she's a friend—her words—from back home and that it's urgent. Won't give her name and won't take no for an answer."

AN APPEARANCE OF IMPROPRIETY

JD let out a sharp exhalation of air. He dragged a hand through his hair. "Bring her back."

Interminable seconds ticked by, and a soft rap sounded at his door. "Come in."

His door swung open. Monica stood aside and allowed a gaunt woman with wispy, frosted blond hair to enter. The woman emitted a rattling cough. JD stared. Recognition hit like a freight train and took him back almost two decades. Forbidden meetups. Youthful promises made and broken.

He clenched his hands into fists out of sight in his lap. "Monica, I'm fine. You can go." He suppressed the quaver in his voice.

Monica arched a brow but left without a word.

JD hesitated, then stood and approached the woman.

"Tammy." He choked back a cough at the powerful smell of tobacco radiating off the woman. "It's been a minute." He bent and gave his high school sweetheart an awkward peck on the cheek. How was he supposed to act here?

He tipped his chin toward his guest chair. "Have a seat." He blanked out all emotion from his face as he took in her ravaged appearance.

"You're looking good, Jimmy," Tammy said, her voice phlegmy and hoarse.

He could not say the same thing about her. She wore tight red leggings and a pink off-the-shoulder T-shirt with "Vegas Baby" across the front. Her exposed shoulder was pointy and covered in age spots. Gold earrings hung from her ears, and her face had the weathered, yellowish tinge of a two-pack-a-day habit. Her telling smirk noted the omission of his return of her compliment.

"Nice office." Tammy's inspection bounced around the trial prep wreckage splayed across his desk. "Heard you made it to the big time. Looks like the rumors were true."

"I do alright." They hadn't parted on good terms. They hadn't parted on bad terms. Their relationship had . . . ended. Without drama. Cleared away like dust washed off the road after a spring rain. JD clicked the end of his ink pen a few times, the noise sharp in the thick silence between them. He'd never returned to Spring Creek after he'd graduated, and seeing someone—anyone—from his old life was like seeing a corpse rise from the grave right in front of him.

A racking cough shook Tammy's slight frame.

"Let me get you a bottle of water." Grateful for the reprieve to think a minute, JD made his way to the mini fridge on the opposite side of his office. He twisted off the top, handed it to Tammy, and sat on the edge of his desk facing her.

Tammy surveyed the room. "No pictures of your wife and kids." It was a question, not a statement.

"Not married. You?"

A hollow laugh escaped Tammy's lips. "Nah. The right one. Well..." She trailed off. A touch of sadness tinted with longing appeared on her sunken face but disappeared as quickly as it had come.

JD eyed his computer and the Code of Civil Procedure that lay open on his desk. Attempting to keep the impatience from his voice, he grasped for words to move the unexpected reunion along. "Look, Tammy, I'm glad you're in town, and maybe we can catch up—"

"I'm dying." She cut him off. Her eyes looked at him, intense and shadowed, before she cut her gaze away.

JD made to stand and flopped back down. Stunned.

"I . . . I'm so sorry." He had not seen Tammy for years, and while he was not experiencing nostalgia, the news still rocked him. *She's too young.*

He crouched beside her and gave her an awkward side hug. Under his hand he felt thin flesh over sharp bones. He moved to the guest chair beside her. Tammy pulled a small package from her purse and popped a stick of nicotine-replacement gum into her mouth.

"I haven't been able to quit yet, but the gum helps. You can probably guess what's gonna do me in. If you haven't already stopped, do yourself a favor and quit while you still have time." Another spasm shook her as she coughed.

The grim situation muddled his thinking, and random possibilities tumbled one over the other. Was she visiting old friends and family before she passed away? Did she want financial help? Perhaps she had an end-of-life legal question. He mentally scrounged around, trying to come up with something appropriate to say in response to her bald declaration.

"You still living back home?"

"Nah, I got out of there soon after you left. That place, nothing but a dead end. You were smart to leave when you did."

A rueful laugh squeezed out of him.

AN APPEARANCE OF IMPROPRIETY

"I made my way to Vegas. Got work as a server at a casino. Worked my way up to blackjack dealer. Not rolling in dough like you, but I did okay."

"How . . ." He stopped himself. Couldn't think of a tactful way to ask what he wanted to know.

"How long do I have?" She connected the dots for him. "Could be a couple of months, could be as long as a year."

"Are they certain?"

"Dead." Her mirthless laugh was punctuated by a coughing spasm.

He couldn't help his flinch and, when she shrugged, knew he hadn't masked his horror.

"Oh, don't look that way. I've come to terms with it. Got right with the Lord several years ago. I don't want to go. Got things I'm still handling down here. But I'm sure when I get there, I won't want to come back."

JD stared at the ground between his feet. His neck and torso felt as though a body builder were pressing him toward the ground. It took intense effort to lift his head.

Tammy looked at him, her gaze wary. "I didn't come here to ask for any money."

"Didn't say that you did."

"I wanted to make sure to put that out there."

Having heard her revelation, he was now willing to give her whatever amount she might need or want. There was no way to scam your way to cancer-ravaged emaciation.

"Well, is there something else I can do to help?" Despite his fatigue and shock, chivalry kicked in.

"Yeah, there is."

"What is it?"

"Have dinner with me tonight."

His desk was pure chaos. A light blinked rapidly on the phone, signaling a day's worth of calls directed to voicemail by Monica. Tammy stood at death's door. Hot emotion roared to life, defeating the gnawing inside about the pile of work on his desk.

He gave his head a shake. Cleared the mental fog. He could cram it all in. Come back after dinner. Pull an all-nighter. Tammy needed him. He would not let her die alone, like he had his mother.

He walked to his desk and jabbed the intercom button.

"Time to shut it down, Monica. We'll get back to work in the morning. Eight sharp."

He clicked off without waiting for a reply.

"Okay." JD checked his watch. "I have a few things to wrap up here. Is seven too late?"

"That'll be fine. My hotel has a restaurant in the lobby."

They exchanged contact information, and Tammy shuffled to the door. She turned. "Seven o'clock."

The look she gave him as she left could have been fear. Maybe relief. He didn't know her anymore.

JD sprawled on his office settee to think. What was it, seventeen, eighteen years since he'd seen Tammy? Theirs had been trailer-park puppy love. She was cute, petite, blond. It was fun and exciting. She'd listened to his dreams about getting out. She'd had her own dreams about leaving their small town as well. They had bonded over stolen cigarette breaks and desperation.

He'd lost Mama a few months before high school ended. Held it together on his own until he'd left for basic training one week after graduation and shipped straight to Afghanistan after that. He'd written steady for a while, but Tammy had never written back, so he'd quit. Their lives hadn't been on the same trajectory anyway.

JD clawed his fingers from his forehead to the nape of his neck. *Man.* She put up a brave front, but what a kick in the teeth.

He walked to the Keurig on a file cabinet, popped in an espresso K-Cup and selected the button for the most concentrated brew. Tonight mandated massive doses of caffeine. He hunkered down to plow through more paperwork before seven o'clock.

***

He arrived ten minutes late at the Sheraton Grand. The lobby's illuminated and sparkling floor-to-ceiling art installation of metallic tubes disoriented his fatigued eyes. He regained his bearings and pivoted toward the restaurant, where he gave his name and was led by a hostess through a maze of tables and booths.

AN APPEARANCE OF IMPROPRIETY

Tammy sat facing him. Sitting across from her, with his back to JD, was a man. Good for her. She had someone to walk her through the progression. She wouldn't face cancer all alone. His newfound fear for her well-being ratcheted down a few notches.

Tammy stood, and so did the tall, gangly guy. As JD neared the table, everything played out in slow motion. Not a man. A teen. JD looked at the boy. His own eyes stared back at him, and disorienting vertigo set in.

"Jimmy, this is Dean," Tammy said. "Dean, this is Jimmy."

Dean stuck out his large hand to shake. After a beat, JD suppressed his shock and reciprocated. He now understood the purpose of the meeting. Completely. He nodded absently at Tammy, his thoughts as addled as if he'd taken an uppercut from a heavyweight champ.

"Well." Tammy's voice sounded tight. She covered her mouth and coughed. "I'm glad that's over. Sit down. Let's eat and talk."

He scraped his chair back and sat down heavily.

They ordered food. The waiter delivered it, but only Dean ate. Judging by the teen's lean stretch of frame, it clearly took massive quantities of food to keep him alive. The boy wore faded jeans, no holes but frayed at the cuffs, and a red T-shirt with "Nintendo" on it.

"Why didn't you tell me?" Confronted by his doppelgänger, JD's mouth worked mechanically, and his voice came off as wooden in his ears. "I could have . . . would have helped."

He'd always trusted Tammy when they were together. She'd had rough spots in her personality. But heck, half of their hometown was some sort of walking dysfunction. She'd been loyal and sweet. Even if none of that had been true, JD couldn't deny Dean was his son. If he found his senior photo lying around somewhere, he didn't think even Tammy could tell the difference between him at age eighteen and her son, Dean. This was no con.

"Psht. I wanted you to get out. No way I was going to crush your dreams. We weren't ready to be parents, and I figured one clueless idiot was enough."

At the square table, JD had a clear view of Tammy to his right and Dean to his left. Dean's jaw was working, masticating a cheeseburger as if his life depended on it.

"What . . . what's he going to do if you . . ." JD fought to put a coherent sentence together. The curry roasted chicken in front of him turned his stomach. He tried to swallow. There was nothing in his dry mouth to make that action work.

"I'm *not* going to make it. Dean here wants to become emancipated by the court so he can live on his own as an adult. I don't want that."

Plate now empty, Dean shifted and glared at JD.

JD squared up to face the boy. "I didn't know about you. Honest. I had no idea. If I had, I would have done right by you." He lifted his hand toward Dean, not sure why, so he dropped it. This kid *had* to understand he would have done the right thing.

"Yeah, Mom told me you didn't know. Look, I can take care of myself." Dean pulled up from a slouch and looked straight at JD. "Don't need any handouts. We've gotten along this far without them."

The words coming out of Dean's mouth echoed the bravado JD used to spout.

"Dean." Tammy gave her boy an intent look. "I'm not asking him for money." She turned to JD, repeating her promise. "I'm not asking you for any money." Her eyes trained on him with a vacant stare, and her words came out as though she were speaking to herself.

"I can't teach him how to be a man . . ." She trailed off. "I'm hoping you two can spend time together. Get to know each other. If something comes of it, good. That's all I ask of both of you." She reached out her bony hands and placed one over JD's and one over Dean's.

***

The spinning in JD's head finally stopped. He took several gulps of water and focused on what Dean was saying.

"College is my next move," Dean said, his tone adamant. "One year living and working in California to establish my residency and save up money. Two years at a community college to do the standard core curriculum. Tuition's low, so it won't cost much. Might even be free. But I'll work, get two or three roommates, eat ramen and beans. Whatever I have to do. After that, all I'll have left is two years at the university level. UCLA's my dream college. If I play my cards right and keep my expenses down, I think the whole plan is doable."

"Looks like you've figured everything out." The boy's thoroughness impressed JD.

"I planned all that before I knew you lived in California. I'm not expecting you to provide anything. Mom and me have been able to make it all these years, the two of us. That doesn't need to change."

Heaviness settled over JD. The boy knew his mother would not be around for any of this. JD needed time and space to think and to talk to someone. Mahalia's face sprang into his mind's eye. A nonstarter for myriad reasons, the least of which was the crushing trial date, about a month away.

"How long you all in town for?"

Tammy continued pushing bits of pork chop around her plate. "A couple more days. Got a girlfriend I want to connect with in the Central Valley, for old times' sake."

"I'll tell you what. Can Dean stay with me for a night or two while you're there?"

The sour squint on Dean's face pulled JD up short. He reconsidered how he'd made the invitation, so he turned to face Dean. "You willing to spend time with me?"

Tammy's face held hope, and her facial expression pleaded with her son. Dean looked at his mother and readjusted from his slouch. "Yeah, I can do that."

Mother and son exchanged silent communication with their eyes. From nowhere, a fresh, stinging rush of the loss of his own mother seized JD, and anxiety and relief crashed in together to douse it. His brain scurried to rearrange his trial prep plans. He could take the bulk of his work home and sandwich in time with Dean during breaks. At least it was something.

JD pulled out his phone. "Give me your number, Dean. I'll text you the details." He typed "Dean Cash" in his address book. One small tap might change the trajectory of his life. Forever. He hesitated, then pushed Done.

Jayna Breigh

***

To: Judge P. Mahalia Jackson
From: ShadowDocket@ZMail.com

Your interactions with Cash are raising eyebrows. The good old boy network plays dirty when there's a promotion on the line. Be careful who you trust. Remember, help is closer than you think.

Chapter 28

"Sorry I've got all this work." JD eyed a stack of papers he'd shoved to the side of his couch to make room for a snack of fried rice and egg rolls for Dean and himself. Twenty-four hours earlier, Tammy had deposited Dean with him and begun her journey to say her last goodbyes to friends. With a little over a day under his belt with the kid, they'd already found their groove. Midnight takeout. JD forked more shrimp fried rice into his mouth and eyed his lanky twin.

Lured by the tempting scent of sesame oil and seafood, Americano deigned to appear to collect a tax of three shrimp, after which she made a beeline to snuggle between Dean's two sock-clad feet. She chewed her shrimp and emitted an occasional satisfied yowl. The boy wore athletic pants paired with a T-shirt with the word "Marvel" emblazoned in white letters on a red rectangle.

"So you got an ex-wife? A girlfriend?"

At Dean's words, JD broke off his rude staring. Couldn't help himself. It felt like he was future Marty McFly running into past Marty McFly at the soda shop. He refocused. "No. Nothing like that."

"Why not? You're rich. You've got this sweet bachelor pad and an awesome cat." Dean snickered and scratched Americano under the chin. "What lady wouldn't want all this?"

JD rubbed the back of his neck, measuring his words. "Well, your mom was my first girlfriend. Teen love, but real." No matter how wrong he and Tammy had been in their actions, he needed the boy to understand he wasn't the product of a meaningless hot-and-sweaty backseat session.

The brackets of tightness eased around Dean's mouth.

"I don't have any idea how much your mom told you about how we grew up in Spring Creek, but it was bad. When I was a kid, the town had poverty and drunks. One of the two main employers had shut its factory and moved all the jobs overseas."

"Remington Textile or Boothe Dynamics?" Dean's brows were knotted in question.

"Thought your mom raised you in Vegas."

"She did. We'd go back every couple of years. Visit family." Dean dished out his third helping of fried rice.

"It was Remington. Boothe held on till I was in high school. They kept downsizing every year. Eventually they shut the doors for good. Those buildings still standing?"

Dean nodded. "Yeah. Only things left are the signs on the front. Buildings are all boarded up. Have been as far back as I can remember."

"After textile jobs dried up, the town fell into a recession. Drinking skyrocketed. When crystal meth hit, the whole thing imploded." JD wiped his mouth and broke open a fortune cookie. *A new adventure awaits you.* The irony hit him, and he suppressed a snort.

"Meth takes you to a different level of crazy. Causes chemical imbalance. Mama and I started out with almost nothing to begin with. We lived in a trailer park full of ex-cons and gamblers. There were some good folks too, people down on their luck. Medical bills, a foreclosure—things like that can push a middle-class family into a mobile home. But after a while, a revolving door of losers paraded through our trailer. Dealers, users. I vowed I would never live like that once I was out on my own. I was going to get a degree, because no one can steal your education from you. And I planned to be my own boss so no company could go bankrupt and take my job."

"What's all that got to do with the fact that you're all alone?"

JD pushed his plate away. "Timing wasn't right, I guess." He shrugged. The dysfunction of his hometown and grief over Mama's death had caught up with him when he'd first entered the service. He'd tried to drown his sorrow and fear with all the wrong vices. The changes he'd made during the war—the promise he'd made to himself. All too personal to share with Dean.

"Well, at least my hanging out with you won't cramp your style."

As much as JD wished he and Mahalia could be an item . . . All these years he'd had a minimal personal life, consumed with work and the Junior Jurors. Now when he was finally ready, his personal life was exploding into chaos. He tamped down a sigh. "Your being here won't cramp my style in the least."

"Can I finish this?" Dean gestured to the remains of the takeout.

JD gave a dismissive wave. "Have at it."

Still chewing, Dean spoke around the rice in his mouth. "Looks like I inherited the freaky-deaky eye thing, but what gives with all the gray hair, dude? You're the same age as my mom. Am I going to inherit that too?"

"Don't know. I could point my dad out in a lineup but never knew him. The hair thing's not that bad, is it?"

Dean gave a laugh. "Whatever you say, old man."

A jab of emotion hit and was followed by heat that suffused his chest. He'd only known the boy for two days, but Dean had already cemented himself into JD's heart like a cornerstone in the foundation of a building. Mahalia flashed in his mind, and his insides wrenched. How could he have a future with her now? Responsibilities already squeezed JD on every side. Who would want to start a relationship with a man who had taken on caring for a teenage child, had a dying ex, and was juggling a sixty-hour week? Dean, work, mock trial prep, Tammy's grim diagnosis. Could he bear up under it all like mythical Atlas? Maybe if he did what he'd always done. Dig in. Work harder. Sleep less. Worry more.

***

JD's tired neurons sputtered and seized. One a.m. and he had made his third trip to the Keurig. No more, or jitters would keep him from concentrating. He jammed his thumbnail between his teeth but yanked it out before he succumbed. Lifting the scalding brew to his lips, he took a sip and focused on his cross-examination prep for TransNation's CEO. *Please, Lord. I need to catch a break time-wise. Somehow.* At this point, if an airplane crash landed and destroyed his condo it wouldn't surprise him.

JD stood and stretched his back. His computer chimed, signaling an incoming email.

Jayna Breigh

> From: Lisa Richards, Esq. Associate Attorney, TransNation
> Re: Request for Continuance of Hearing
>
> Dear Mr. Cash,
>
> Our firm has experienced another unusual and unforeseen turn of events. Mr. Snevelton, along with TransNation's CFO, has severe food poisoning. This is your notice that we will be moving ex parte for a one-week continuance of the upcoming trial based on the prognosis reports provided by the physicians and other resulting scheduling conflicts. Attached are our papers, including a declaration by the doctor and the manager of the restaurant. The hearing will be at 8:00 a.m. the day after tomorrow in Judge Goldstein's chambers.

He knew better than to think someone had jinxed TransNation. He suppressed his elation at the new pocket of time on his schedule. *Thank you, God.* He sent up a prayer for a speedy recovery for his opponents, flipped off his desk lamp, and made his way home. He would call the clerk in the morning to tell her he didn't oppose the motion, and he'd play hooky the rest of the day.

***

Americano lay nestled between Dean's chest and the back of the couch. Turncoat. She was an excellent judge of character, a traitor, or both. Didn't matter. She'd come running back when he busted out the can opener or the ball with a bird inside that squeaked when she batted it.

JD shook Dean to rouse him. "I'm skipping work today. Ready to eat?" Typical teenager-style, Dean had been dead asleep despite the late-morning sun streaming through the windows onto his face. "We're going to the Cheesecake Emporium." Dean startled awake at the mention of the word *cheesecake,* as if a cattle prod had shocked him. JD chuckled and smiled. The boy was over six feet tall but couldn't weigh more than 190 pounds, and he might have another growth spurt in him.

"Wear athletic clothes, because I plan to school you in basketball."

AN APPEARANCE OF IMPROPRIETY

"Give me ten minutes," Dean said.

"You got it." JD smirked at Americano. "Nope, you get the dry stuff today. Already put it in your dish, so come on over, little Benedict Arnold." JD pointed to the bowl on the floor at the kitchen entrance. Without sparing JD a glance, Americano slunk off the couch like high-bred royalty and chasséed to a sunny spot under the windows.

The Cheesecake Emporium was quiet at eleven in the morning. The front case next to the hostess podium held samplings of over twenty different cheesecakes. Blueberry sauce dripped off one, while generous dollops of whipped cream topped by strawberries sat heaped on another. The nut-encrusted carrot cake stood at least ten inches high. Dean wandered over and stared, transfixed by all the desserts.

The hostess started to lead them toward their table, but JD had to call Dean twice before he had the boy's attention.

"How many slices of cheesecake can I have?" Not a trace of humor crossed Dean's face.

JD suppressed a laugh. "We'll see how many desserts you can have when you get through eating your food."

Dean gave a little pout.

He was putty in the kid's hand. He'd have to up his parenting game big time.

They sat, and he opened the large menu, scanning for anything that appealed.

The waitress appeared. "Ready when you are."

They both placed their orders, and the waitress hustled away.

"I'm never out at this time of the day. Usually in court or at the office."

"I'd be in AP Calculus."

"Wow. I'm impressed."

"There was a dude, a college guy, who counted cards. Mom caught him. Card counting is legal, but the casinos hate it. Mom found him outside on a smoke break. Told him if he tutored me in math and went to another casino, she wouldn't rat him out. Turns out he was getting his PhD in mathematics. Using blackjack to pay for his degree. Taught me precalc and statistics."

"Your mom was always good at working the system." JD laughed.

Dean continued to fill JD in on his classes and his school life while JD sipped the coffee the waitress had delivered.

The server reappeared with JD's Caesar salad and Dean's massive heap of corned beef and sauerkraut on rye with a tower of french fries.

"Mind if I say grace?" JD didn't wait but bowed and began. "Lord, thank you for this food, and thank you for Dean. Encourage him and Tammy both. Amen."

JD opened his eyes. Dean sat motionless, staring blankly at his food, his Adam's apple working.

"I want to help you and your mother any way I can. Money for treatment, bills. Whatever you all need."

"Don't you even want a DNA test?"

"We both know there's no need." He lifted and dropped a shoulder.

"Why would you do all that for us?" Dean stared at a spot behind JD's back. "We're not asking for anything."

"It's the right thing to do."

The eyes staring back at JD were glossy with unshed tears. Dean nodded once and tore into his Reuben without a word.

After lunch, JD grabbed his basketball and two bottles of water from the back of the Wagoneer and quick-timed it to the entrance to the athletic club. Inside, a two-on-two pickup game and a pair of guys shooting free throws made hollow echoes on the wood floor. He tossed the ball to Dean, and they jogged to the court. Dean bounced the ball between his legs and behind his back as he walked.

"Pickup or horse?" JD asked Dean.

"Pickup." Dean spun the basketball on the middle finger of his right hand, popped the ball into the air a few inches, and transferred the spinning orb to his left hand.

"I take it you play?"

"Yeah, starting point guard."

They walked to the court, and JD signaled they wanted in next game.

"So'd you play?" Dean asked.

"Varsity. Championship team. North High."

"How many years ago?"

"Nineteen-ish."

AN APPEARANCE OF IMPROPRIETY

Dean's face looked as if gears were grinding in his brain.

"North High doesn't exist anymore. It combined with South, and now they call it Central High."

"How original."

"They brought all the trophies, pictures, and championship banners to the combined school."

JD shucked his half-zip pullover and shot a questioning glance at Dean.

"There was this one picture I stared at all the time. From a regional championship or something. It was from North High. I knew my mom went to North on the rough side of town. All the better-off kids lived on the south side."

JD shrugged. "The reality back then."

"I used to stare at that picture in the trophy case, and sometimes I would wonder . . ."

"Yo. Grandpa, junior. You're in. We're skins. You're shirts. First to twenty-one." A tall, brown-skinned man motioned with his hand. His head was shaved bald. He wore a Michael Jordan jersey and had a ripped physique.

The dude standing beside Jordan Jersey clearly favored LA's home team and wore gold gym shorts with purple piping. He wiped sweat off his face with a wadded-up T-shirt and lifted his head in JD's direction. "All that gray hair, you sure you should be out here?"

The bald dude took a potshot, too. "Ain't no defibrillator around."

"That's Mr. Great-Grandpa to you," JD shot back. Like he never heard age jokes.

Dean stripped off his sweats and tossed them onto the bleachers.

JD knew for certain which picture Dean had noticed. It'd been a magical night. Mama hadn't made it to the game, but Tammy had. He'd been high on life and euphoric after the win. It wasn't the first time between him and Tammy, but doing some math, it was probably the night they'd conceived Dean.

He'd missed so much of Dean's life, but gazing at the strong, confident boy in front of him, something shifted inside. His current life didn't have any bandwidth for a kid. But there was no way he'd let Dean be fatherless for one more day. He intended to make his son a permanent fixture in his life.

He pulled his thoughts back to the gym and jogged beside Dean onto the court. The kid took position to check the ball to Jordan Jersey, who inbounded the ball to his teammate. Dean hustled under the basket, JD grabbed Jordan Jersey's rebound, and Dean rushed to post up. JD made a bounce pass, and Dean hit a layup.

"Not bad for a grandpa. Didn't even need my walker." JD fist-bumped Dean.

With points on the board, the competition heated up. Dean was a trash-talking machine, charging with the ferocity of a lion and never letting up in his intensity. The muscles on his thin frame rippled with exertion. Spinning disorientation whipsawed through JD as he watched the man-boy version of himself.

It was hard fought, but Dean and JD lost by two.

Their opponents came to give them high fives. "Much respect. You two White boys got game."

JD fist-bumped Gold Gym Short Dude. "Next time."

"For sure," Jordan Jersey said.

***

JD lowered the windows to let in some natural air. He shot a glance at Dean in the passenger seat. The boy's eyes were closed, and he had a slight glow from the exertion and the California sun.

"Hungry?" JD flipped on the turn signal.

"Always. Can we do burgers?"

"You bet. We'll hit up world-famous Stop and Go."

JD turned the Wagoneer into the parking lot of the fast-food chain and parked beside a kiosk for car-side service.

"What do you usually get?" Dean craned his neck, trying to see the menu to JD's left.

"Well, seeing as how I'm an old man and all, I've got to watch my cholesterol."

Dean laughed.

A disembodied voice cracked over the speaker. "May I take your order."

"I'll have a ripped burger, no onions, and a Diet Coke." JD turned to Dean. "What do you want?"

Dean leaned over the console toward the open window. "I'll have a double ripped burger, add cheese and extra onions. Upsize the fries and add a strawberry shake."

"That reminds me so much of myself at your age. I could scarf down almost anything, and I'd be hungry an hour later."

JD caught a wistful glance from Dean. The car-side server arrived within minutes and vanished seconds later.

"More napkins?" JD watched a glob of cheese make its way down the side of Dean's face. A gurgling slurp signaled the end of Dean's milkshake.

"So, you shocked you've got a kid?"

JD choked on his sip of Diet Coke. Placed his hand over his mouth and coughed to clear his throat and gain his composure at the abrupt question. He took another swig of his drink to compose himself. "Surprised but not shocked. We weren't careful. It was only a handful of times, but we didn't always have something with us."

Dean's nose wrinkled like he'd sucked a lemon, and he made a gagging noise. "Please. Stop. That's my mom."

"Sorry. I'm . . . new at this." JD ran a hand through his hair. "I grew up without a father. There were bums and abusers in and out of my mother's life. I vowed I'd never be that guy. Yet here I am."

He was afraid to look at Dean. Didn't want to see the abandonment and hurt he'd experienced staring back at him from the boy's eyes. He chanced it anyway and faced the kid.

"I'm here for you. If I'd known, I'd have done right by you and your mom all these years. I want to make up for it now."

"I've got some friends. Their moms and dads are divorced. Or they never had dads. Bad blood between the parents. Their mothers are bitter. But Mom, she never said a negative thing about you. Ever. I'd ask every once in a while. She'd shake her head. Get this air about her."

JD kept his face neutral. Wanted the kid to feel free to open up.

"I tried to hate you. Well, not you, but whoever the guy was. Mom never let me. Said it was for the best. She worked hard. Gave me whatever I needed." Dean shrugged. "Thought you should know."

"I wish we didn't have to talk about this at all. I wish your mom wasn't sick and that I'd been a part of your life. But I can't change any of that now." He tried to catch Dean's gaze, but Dean avoided looking at him.

"Son." He'd not addressed him as son before.

Dean's head snapped up. His eyes, glassy.

"When the time comes, I hope you'll move out here to live with me. Not because your mother asked me to take you in—even though I'd do it for that reason alone. But because I want you to."

Dean gave a small sniff. "I blamed you for everything. For us not having more. For Mom having to work all the time. For her cancer. She loved you. Still loves you. Never would let me bad mouth you or blame you."

JD's heart thudded slowly in his chest.

"Here you are, this great guy." The teen studied his hands and refused to look directly into JD's eyes. "I said to myself, 'Why would he want to take me in? Never met me. Already got his own thing going. I'd be in the way.'"

"No." He made sure his voice was firm. "You won't be." He angled his position until he caught Dean's gaze again and plunged ahead. "Meeting you is one of the best things that's ever happened to me. What I'm trying to say is . . ." His Adam's apple bobbed up and down, holding back the words. "You're the part of me that has been missing for years." He took a few sniffs to damper the hot stinging in the back of his eyes. "And I think you need me too."

Dean nodded a bit and his features relaxed. Like he'd been waiting for disappointment that hadn't come. He cracked a smile. "Yeah, old man—you need me more."

Dean's levity broke the heaviness of the moment.

They gathered their trash into one bag. Dean snatched it up, exited the car, and jogged to a nearby trash receptacle. He plopped back into the car and squarely faced JD.

"In all seriousness. Thanks . . ." Dean coughed. "Dad."

Chapter 29

MAHALIA HADN'T SEEN JD since their working dinner back in March. She'd missed four weeks of Junior Jurors meetings because of a massive contract trial on her docket and a crunch of legislative work on the Litigation and Trial Practice Committee.

Worse, she was months in arrears thanking JD for his calm and support during their near-death experience in the elevator. He'd been a knight in shining armor—handling logistics, keeping her calm while trapped, and defending her against Dinkelman's stalking and harassment afterward. But every time she tried to figure out an appropriate thank-you gift, she remembered that she'd been tempted to press her lips to his, and her obligation to thank him shriveled in the face of worry over potential courthouse gossip.

She shook herself mentally. She'd been off the TransNation case since October, and it was now almost April. Yes, she'd battled with both her fear of death and her desire for an emotional connection while they were trapped, but she had not crossed the line and had not violated the judicial canons. She was an adult, and even though it was delayed, etiquette demanded a thank-you gift for all that he had done for her that night. She let gratitude override her lingering qualms and snatched up her keys.

Whole Foods—or Whole Paycheck, as Cassandy called it, referring to its internet nickname—had an ample assortment of entrees available on a moment's notice. An hour later, after battling aisles packed with Peloton devotees and people looking for organic matcha, she'd purchased a deluxe spread.

As she parked her car in front of JD's condo, the second-guessing circled back around. What was she thinking, dropping by on a Saturday evening? There was 150 dollars' worth of "thank you" in those bags. Stuffed olives, assorted roasted meats to stack on crusty baguettes, flourless chocolate crisps, fruit-flavored bubbly water. Mahalia smacked her forehead and sighed. *You might as well finish what you started, girlfriend.* She hauled the bags out of her car and trudged to JD's door.

She rang the bell and heard the shuffle of footsteps and the clink of the lock.

The door whooshed open, and *those eyes* greeted her. She would know them anywhere—but the face was wrong. It was twenty years younger. The hair was rich brown. It was JD and yet not JD.

"Um, so sorry. I was bringing food for Attorney Cash. Is he here?" As Mahalia took tentative steps into the foyer, Americano appeared out of nowhere to figure-eight around her feet.

"Yeah, he's here. Weird. I thought he ordered pizza. Oh well. Come on in. Drop the bags on the bar." He gestured. "I'll grab the credit card."

She tried not to stare, but disorientation racked her. No? Yes? Looking at the young man from the corner of her eye, certainty locked into place. This was JD's son. Mahalia felt like an iPhone that needed a hard reset to fix a glitchy app.

Was JD married? Separated? Seven hours in an elevator. Foxhole friends, he'd said. Not a word about a teenage son and the next most obvious part, the son's mother.

Mahalia waved the boy off as he approached with the credit card.

"I . . . I shouldn't be here." She stumbled to the door as the scorching heat of humiliation lit her insides on fire.

***

The hot running water sluicing down JD's back did nothing to soothe his nerves. His stomach churned. He'd finally driven a spike into that Dracula of a case, HBA Transit. The ink was still wet, but it was a done deal, and he'd gained space to interact with his son. Dean was a few months shy of eighteen, and if the boy agreed, JD would attempt to form some sort of relationship. He'd been an absentee father because of lack of knowledge, not a lack of desire. Hopefully, Dean would understand and forgive him. If he didn't, JD would just work harder.

AN APPEARANCE OF IMPROPRIETY

JD lathered and shampooed. He was going to hang out in the hot shower until he could get himself together. More lather. More shampoo.

He exited the bathroom, wearing lounge pants with a towel draped over one shoulder, and the doorbell rang. He was almost to the front door as Dean opened it.

"You forget something?" Dean swung the door wide. "Huh, okay. Um, weird." Dean stood rooted in place.

"You paying for this pizza or what?" The bedraggled delivery guy from Sammy's Pizzeria shoved two boxes at Dean.

"I got it." JD grabbed the pizzas. "My credit card still on the counter?"

"Yeah, I put it back."

"Put it back?" Confusion hit for a moment. "Never mind. We'll sort this out."

JD paid the deliveryman and walked the pizza into the kitchen.

Dean sidled up next to him, opened the pizza box, took a slice, and dug in.

"Yer uver schtuff ish over dere." Dean pointed to the grocery bags on the counter, talking around a huge bite of food.

"What?" Dean's words made no sense. JD turned and saw tote bags from Whole Foods. He walked over and pulled items out, examining them. He hadn't ordered any of this. "Who delivered this?"

"Don't know. A lady. Tall. Super gorgeous. Left in a hurry."

Suddenly everything clicked into place. Mahalia's question number seventeen to him when they'd been trapped.

"What are your favorite foods?"

His heart seized in his chest. JD stumbled to his couch in his living room, leaned forward with his elbows on his knees, and hung his head.

"So what's the deal?" Dean propped himself up on the doorjamb to the living room.

"She's a judge."

"On one of your cases?" Dean's lids pulled wide.

"No. Used to be. We're on a community service project together."

"She's super hot." Dean cocked an eyebrow.

"Dean, that's neither helpful nor appropriate. I respect and admire Judge Jackson as a human being. If she were a man, I'd still respect her accomplishments. We're working on a project together . . ." JD trailed off. He was digging his own grave with his diarrhea of the mouth.

"Whatever, dude." Dean's smirk spoke volumes. "She looked upset, so . . . even if you're not dating, maybe a call?"

JD tried calling. She didn't answer. Should he text? What should he say? *I know we aren't dating or seeing each other, and in fact, you used to be the judge overseeing my case, but in case you need to know, that was my son. But I'm not seeing anyone. Never married.*

"Let's eat. I'll figure this out later."

Mahalia had picked out excellent food. Even though JD's appetite had gone the way of the dinosaurs, Dean made short work of the bulk of the items. All JD could think of was that it would have been nice to share the food with her and introduce her to Dean. It would have been a friendly, chaperoned evening. Nothing inappropriate. They were colleagues in the same professional sphere.

"I'm beat, Dean. Turning in early."

"Hope she picks up this time."

***

JD was calling again. Pick up? Don't pick up? Her thumb swiped across the phone. Apparently pick up won. "Yes."

There was a pause. "Um, hello, um . . ."

"Yes, Counselor?" If she kept their interaction formal in the extreme, perhaps she could ease the squeezing in her chest.

"Yes, Your Honor. JD here. Wanted to thank you for the wonderful food delivery." His voice flowed over her like warm syrup.

"You're welcome. It was a thank-you gift to you for . . . spearheading our survival effort."

"Wish you'd stayed to join us."

"You had company." *Your teenage son.*

There was another pause on JD's end.

"That was my kid. I . . . I didn't know I had a son until a few days ago. But so far, so good."

JD's voice petered out, and silent questions rushed in to fill the void. Oh, how she wanted to know the details. Who was this boy's mother, and where was she? Was this woman even now reestablishing herself in his life? Self-conscious prickling heat ran down her spine. Time to cut the call off.

"Glad you enjoyed it. I need to go. See you at the next meeting, and thanks again for the rescue efforts."

"Good night, Your Honor."

"Good night, Counselor."

She would not let the hot, stinging tears fall.

Chapter 30

Mahalia gave herself a stern mental lecture. While her attempt to give JD a proper thank-you gift had careened off the rails, there wasn't anything she could do about it now. Time to pivot and focus on Melvin. The Contender. She psyched herself up for their date.

She checked her outfit in the mirror for the bazillionth time. Despite having a wardrobe full of pumps and power outfits, she wanted to have fun. The close-fitting blue jeans, brown leather jacket, and tartan plaid infinity scarf said "movie date." Low-heeled ankle boots and funky earrings would do the trick. Her fashion goal, mature but on trend.

She pulled her two-strand twists into an updo, tucking and pinning the hair in front to simulate a curly bang. *Rock it, sister.*

She grabbed her cell phone and opened the text messages to take one more peek. Melvin's distorted selfie, snapped moments before he'd boarded his flight, pulled another laugh. He wore a small gold stud in one ear. Not her thing, but it suited him. Circular tortoiseshell glasses gave him a professorial air.

Mahalia swiped up on Spotify and exited the Luther Vandross playlist she'd labeled "Old School Date Mood," grabbed her keys and purse, and headed for the door. Melvin had offered to pick her up, but she did *not* want to do the end of the night "should she or shouldn't she invite him in for a nightcap" tango. He insisted, however, on driving to dinner and the movie. Said he didn't want to lose his man-card. She'd agreed to rendezvous at a central location and take his car from there.

She stopped fiddling with the bracelet on her wrist and glued her mouth shut to keep the idiotic grin off her face. A singsong chant replaced her usual mantra. "Melvin could be 'The One.'" She swatted it away, but the ditty popped back up. She folded herself behind the wheel of her car, and the audio of her phone connected to the speakers. The setting sun hung low on the horizon. She slid her cat-eyed sunglasses on to dim the glare. The rich tones of Lauryn Hill singing "Killing Me Softly with His Song" cemented her "date" frame of mind.

She passed the interchange on the freeway where JD's billboard had stood like a monstrous sentinel. Now, an ad for an exterminator graced the sign. Far less memorable. Her shoulders tingled as she remembered her back pressed to JD's in the elevator. Her whole chest cavity had vibrated when he'd spoken to her in his resonant, soothing voice during their hours of confinement. Later, wrapped in soft blankets on his couch, Americano had kept her company all night, her humming and purring soothing Mahalia's frayed nerves.

That night was the first time she'd let a man besides her grandfather take care of her. JD had been a total gentleman. She'd felt protected and safe. There wasn't anything going on between them. Nothing ever could. So why was she now remembering JD's face as she sped down the freeway toward the man who could be her future husband?

***

JD clapped Dean on the back as he made his way into the condo. "I'm calling an audible. Let's do a men's night out. I'm thinking a movie." After an excruciating wait, the funds from the HBA settlement had landed in his account, and the clients had their share. He'd cut checks for staff bonuses as well.

A pocket of time had opened up on his calendar. He ignored the gnaw in his gut telling him to climb back on the horse and knock out more hours on his other cases. Dean was the most important thing in his life right now. A few hours' break wouldn't hurt.

"Got to have CGI and explosions," Dean said from his horizontal position on the couch. Across his chest, Americano reclined like a queen on her throne. That feline had lost all sense of loyalty. JD gave her the evil eye. Americano took her own sweet time getting down from the couch to greet him.

"Agreed. No chick flicks here. We'll leave as soon as I change." He took a military shower, and twenty minutes later they headed for the car. At the Wagoneer JD cocked an eyebrow and dangled the keys in front of Dean. "Wanna?"

Dean's lids opened wide, and a smile split his face. "You sure? You've never seen me drive."

"I trust you. Just don't kill me." JD tossed Dean the keys.

Once inside, Dean took ample time to appreciate the mammoth wagon, running his hands over the dash and the seasoned leather seats. "Thanks, JD."

He couldn't read the expression on Dean's face, but a hot stinging sensation began behind JD's lids. He broke his gaze away first and brushed away pretend dust from his eyes. "Let's go. Theaters fill up on Friday nights."

Dean's driving skills were up to par with the heavy traffic in LA. He sat bolt upright, both hands gripping the wheel.

"Think I'll put on some music."

"Fine with me." Dean paid assiduous attention to the road.

"Let me introduce you to a group known as Steely Dan?"

"Did they write that song 'Deacon Blues'?"

"That's way before your time. How do you know it?"

"Mom had that song on repeat when I was a kid. Said she knew a guy once who . . ." Dean stopped at the traffic light and looked over at JD. "These moods would come over her. She'd be sad and smiling at the same time. She'd hug me close. Tell me I was the best thing that'd ever happened to her. When I was little, I never understood. There was always happiness with the tears when she'd play this song. When I got older, I figured out the guy must have been my dad. It made her smile." Dean gave a cough.

JD's guts twisted at the sacrifice Tammy had made. She'd driven him away by cutting off communication when he enlisted, knowing she carried his child, and then had raised the boy herself—and done it well. JD would use whatever leverage and money he had to place her into the best treatment center possible and give her whatever she needed until the end. He'd put all options on the table for Dean and Tammy.

The light turned and JD slipped in the cassette, filling the car's interior with the melancholy strains. His heart ached as he listened to Dean hum his theme song.

AN APPEARANCE OF IMPROPRIETY

***

JD and Dean advanced six inches closer to the ticket booth. "Crowd's crazy tonight." JD swiveled his head left and right. "Let's get some junk from the concession stand and call it dinner." The delicious smell from the buttery popcorn made his stomach growl. "We'll never find a table at a restaurant once the movie lets out."

"I'm liking it here more and more every day." Dean rubbed his hand on his stomach in a circle.

The heaviness of the moments in the car shifted to fierce protectiveness toward Dean. He never could have planned the winding road that brought him to this moment, but . . . his son. A bubble of happiness expanded inside him. Joy. *Thank you, God.*

He turned his attention back to Dean. "Remember, when your mother calls, you had broccoli and liver for dinner."

Dean grinned. "And vitamin pills."

They neared the concession stand. Dean jerked to a halt and slapped the back of his hand against JD's chest, stopping his momentum.

"Hey, isn't that Judge Whatshername?"

"Where?" JD angled himself and looked around, not seeing where Dean was indicating.

"Dude, don't be cringe. Stop twisting around and check your nine o'clock."

JD tried to keep his cool as he slowly turned to the left. There she was. Prickly heat zipped down his spine. He looked away and hoped he'd averted his eyes fast enough.

***

A glimpse of silver flashed. She had twenty-forty vision. Didn't need glasses. *Not possible.* In the line buying popcorn and Twizzlers, JD and his son stood as tall as two towering California redwoods. In a city with over ten million people, how did this happen? Mahalia's breath hitched in her chest.

Melvin placed his hand on her back, taking her by surprise, and she flinched. He gave her a gentle pat and steered her toward the last two people on earth she wanted to see tonight. *No, no, no, no.* Melvin propelled her ever forward until she stood right behind JD.

The boy swung around, catching her off guard. "Hey, Your Honor." He jerked his head up once. "'Sup?" The kid had a goofy grin plastered on his face. "JD, look who it is." Dean hooked his thumb in her direction. "The judge."

Mahalia steeled herself as JD took his time turning to acknowledge her. He made a slight bend from the waist. "Good evening, Your Honor."

What's going on? Mahalia rolled her eyes. She followed JD's line of sight, finding it trained on Melvin's arm still behind her. She took a slight step out of Melvin's range.

JD lifted an eyebrow.

"So, Your Honor, I don't think I made an official introduction to my son. Dean, this is Judge Mahalia Jackson and . . ." JD stared down Melvin, his expression unreadable.

"Uh, yes. Mr. Cash." She gestured with her hands toward her date. "Melvin Williams. He's the brother of my stylist. I mean, my stylist's wife. He's my stylist's brother-in-law." Nervous itchiness broke out under Mahalia's arms.

Melvin turned to her with a quizzical expression in his eyes. "And you are?" Melvin addressed JD, but his eyes studied Mahalia.

Mahalia peeked at JD. His expression seemed to say, "Yes, after our adventure in the elevator and a full night sleeping in one of my JAG softball sweatshirts, who am I?"

"This is—" Mahalia stopped. Her neurons were not working fast enough. She tried again. "This is Mr. Jimmy Dean Cash. He's . . . I am helping him with a court-related project, the Junior Jurors, to empower at-risk teens by giving them mock trial experience." There. Nothing wrong with that introduction. More than two random people who worked in the same courthouse, but less than . . . what?

A grim smile played around JD's lips.

"Well . . ." JD coughed. "Make sure Judge Jackson tells you all about our seven hours trapped in an elevator after the recent quake. We had finished a day with the teens and were wrapping things up. Quite an interesting story. Good to meet you. Enjoy your"—he paused—"date, Your Honor." He gave

AN APPEARANCE OF IMPROPRIETY

another bow and turned to the cashier at the concession stand. JD gathered up his order and left with Dean without a backward glance. Dean, however, shot a know-it-all smirk at her as the towering Cash men made their way into the theater.

***

JD and Dean settled into their seats as the annoying pre-trailer advertisements for local plumbers and a bowling alley played on the movie screen. They stashed the supersized bucket of popcorn in the empty seat between them, along with their cache of junk food. JD fumbled around to find the cup holder for his sixty-four ounces of Coke. The two tickets had cost thirty dollars, but the drinks, nachos, popcorn, and two boxes of peanut M&Ms had set him back sixty bucks. Now it made sense that Quincy, Mercedes, and the other Junior Jurors were always crashing at friends' houses to eat microwave popcorn and stream movies rented from Amazon.

"JD," Dean whispered. "You were cool as ice. Handled that like a pro." The cheese-eating grin on Dean's face said the boy was enjoying tormenting JD about Mahalia's date.

"I have no idea what you're talking about." JD refused even to turn in Dean's direction.

"That bit about the elevator. Pure gold. You got that guy eating his heart out." Dean hoisted a fistful of popcorn to his mouth and shoveled it in.

Heat burned the rims of JD's ears.

Dean chuckled and took a swig of his soda.

JD saw Mahalia and Kelvin, Marlin, whoever—no matter—had entered and taken seats a couple of rows ahead, dead center in front of him. *Seriously?* A movie about space aliens and flesh-eating pathogens was what she'd chosen when there was a theater right next door where men in tights with British accents awaited? By a cosmic twist of fate, no one sat in the intervening rows of seats, so he had an unobstructed line of sight. He couldn't concentrate now. She'd unwrapped the scarf from around her shoulders, and he had an unhindered view of the sweep of her neck.

The lights dimmed, and Mahalia gave a peek behind herself. He snared her glance. Wanted her to know his eyes were watching every single moment. She turned around, smoothing her hand over her flawless hair, but appeared to stiffen as Delvin or Derrick pulled the hand-over-the-back-of-the-seat move. Before total darkness enveloped the theater, Whatshisname turned and looked at him. JD countered the dude's questioning regard with his Afghanistan glare. Satisfied that all parties knew where they stood, JD tried to enjoy the previews and his time with Dean.

Chapter 31

MELVIN PULLED THE rented Mercedes up to the valet station and killed the ignition. Heated leather seats and Melvin's woodsy cologne wrapped Mahalia in a cocoon of masculine aura and luxury. The gentle ride of the high-end vehicle paired with the melodic tones of the quiet-storm radio DJ soothed her nerves, while the face of Melvin's expensive timepiece reflected the light from the neon sign hanging above the Roll Baby Roll sushi bar.

Their banter en route to the restaurant had been pleasant enough. Melvin kept dropping names of politicians and celebrities his firm handled. It was impressive, but her renegade brain kept pinging back to JD.

Melvin tossed the key fob to the valet and rounded the car to open her door. He offered his hand, and after she'd exited, he moved it up to her elbow and walked beside her into the restaurant.

"I found this place online. You'd mentioned in passing that you liked sushi. I wanted to surprise you." Melvin's voice held a cultivated quality that under normal circumstances would have checked off a box on Mahalia's "my man must have" list. But tonight, for some reason, it rankled her.

"This place is fine." She'd never heard of it before, but he was putting in so much effort.

The restaurant buzzed with vitality. On either side of the lobby were two large rooms. To Mahalia's left she could see table after table overseen by hibachi chefs feverishly spinning and twirling deadly cleavers, flipping chicken and beef cubes into the air, which landed on the griddles in front of them. With merciless velocity and rapid precision, the table performers chopped the meat, along with seafood and fresh vegetables, into bite-sized portions and drizzled them with soy and teriyaki sauces. With a dramatic flourish, they then plated the items on top of heaps of steaming jasmine rice. Grease fumes rose in the air as the cooking surfaces made loud sizzling noises, almost drowning out the applause flowing from the seated customers.

Melvin hovered close, with his hand resting on her back while they stood in the jammed entryway. Ambient noise made holding a conversation impossible, so Mahalia occupied herself by surreptitiously checking him out. He'd paired tailored jeans with an earthen-colored suede jacket, a brown polo, and driving loafers. Every single detail was right, as though he used a personal shopper or studied men's magazines. He had a cultivated image, not an effortless flair like JD.

Slamming the brakes on her mental reflections, she banished thoughts of JD's giant, pale man-feet and strong, blunt fingers to the mental hinterlands.

A gentleman signaled to them. She tagged along beside Melvin as the host escorted them to the other side of the restaurant. A contingent of intense sushi preparers stood inside an oval-shaped enclosure. The counter-height bar encircled five to six men who churned out various types of sushi and sashimi in rapid succession. The chefs arranged them on plates, which they placed on a meandering conveyor belt that made its way around the bar in continuous circuits.

Melvin and Mahalia sat and ordered green tea and rice bowls. The steaming tea showed up in an instant, pushed forward by one of the busy men manning the assembly line. Mahalia reached out and grabbed a plate of spicy tuna rolls before they made their way past her. Melvin took a plate of salmon sashimi.

Mahalia wanted a professional who could handle himself at posh events. Someone not flummoxed by four courses, three forks, and two glasses. She watched Melvin separate his chopsticks with a deft break and position them in his manicured hands at exactly the right angle. He selected a piece of sashimi and dipped it in his soy sauce bowl before depositing the whole thing into his mouth without one dribble. Table manners and foreign-food test, *check*.

After giving Melvin a chance to chew, she foraged about for a conversation starter. "So tell me more about The Talented Legacy Association."

Melvin's face lit with an intense smile. He patted his lips with a napkin and leaned closer. "TTLA is the brainchild of my fraternity brother Eddie and me." Melvin waved his hand in the air, trying to fill in gaps. "He and I started it together in Chicago. We now have chapters in LA and Atlanta, and one is coming to Harlem."

Mahalia saw the spark of joy and pride in Melvin's eyes. From the title, she was guessing it was a community service endeavor, like JD's Junior Jurors. Mahalia gritted her teeth. Thoughts of JD needed to go back to where she'd banished them. Mahalia raised her bowl of miso soup to her lips. The piping-hot brew stung, jolting her away from dwelling on he-whose-name-shall-not-be-spoken and back to Melvin.

"We take elite African American high school students from well-connected families and do college tours, a coming-out ball, skiing trips. Great fun. The parents network and schmooze, and it shows the kids the caliber of friendships they should develop when they get to campus."

Her back stiffened, and a flush of heat ran up her neck. *The caliber of friendships?* This was *nothing* like the Junior Jurors program. Instead, it reminded her of her cloistered childhood and the Golden Roses. "Aren't there other organizations out there doing similar work?"

"Sort of." Melvin picked up a plate of California rolls as they made their way by. "Over the years, our elite institutions have, how shall we say it . . ."

Did he just use the royal we?

". . . loosened their standards. There used to be tests and rules. Fame has replaced talent and intelligence."

"Didn't some things going on back then get wrapped up with colorism? Weren't there tests back in the good old days that *folk* subjected one another to, like the blue vein test and the fine-tooth comb test?" Heat flushed through Mahalia's chest and face.

Melvin waved a dismissive hand. "You are a trailblazer. Young, beautiful. So what if you're dark skinned? Who cares about some old paper-bag test seventy-five years ago? You've got everything going for you. You are the type of person this group wants. We . . . you and I . . . are the kind of people—"

Mahalia threw up her hand. "Stop." At the mention of her skin tone, anger and hurt welled up and words danced out of reach. "We've told the outside world that intelligence and beauty have nothing to do with pigment levels, yet when the doors are closed and it's only us, we tell a different story."

"It's not like that . . . That's not what I was saying. Is this about that attorney—what's his name? And his Little Lawyer program—"

"Junior Jurors, and . . . no. It's not about JD."

"So now he's JD, not Mr. Cash."

Explosive firecrackers pinged in her skull. "Don't twist this around."

Her thoughts jumbled and swirled together, and shame rushed in like a wave as the cognitive dissonance of her own inner world smacked her in the face. All these years she'd nursed emotional wounds because of colorism, but she'd ignored her own elitist and classist attitudes. *Why do you look at the speck in your brother's eye, but do not consider the plank in your own eye?*

How had she been so blind?

She tried to calm herself. "The Junior Jurors program helps kids who really need it."

Melvin held his hand up in front of himself, palms facing out. "Let's take a step back. Maybe I've . . . I've spoken out of turn." His brows furrowed, and his eyes regarded her with intense concentration. "I like you, Mahalia. I've waited a long time to find a woman as talented, sophisticated, and beautiful as you. The tableau vivant, our calls, your texts. They've been wonderful." His hands fell into his lap. "Here I am blowing it."

Mahalia's muscles relaxed.

"We're still getting to know each other." His gaze was soft and hopeful. "Can we take a step back from trying to solve the world's problems and enjoy ourselves?" Melvin reached out and gave her hand a squeeze. "I'm sorry."

A plate of mochi balls approached on the belt. Melvin took it and placed it between them. "Who doesn't like ice cream? Truce?" He smiled at her.

Here was her Midnight Prince within reach, and she was acting testy and sensitive. She'd been in a defensive crouch for so long that it was hard to relax and let an evening with a man spool out slowly. *Wasn't hard with JD.* She shoved the unwanted reflection into a mental closet, turned to Melvin, and pulled up a genuine smile. He deserved another chance. "Truce."

***

Mahalia gave a languorous stretch, tightening and relaxing her muscles from her head to her toes, as she sat propped up in her bed. The overcast sky outside her window made it a Sunday for sleeping in and lazing around.

AN APPEARANCE OF IMPROPRIETY

She reveled in having a full day to veg out. The Brooklyn Tabernacle Choir played in a gentle hush from a speaker in the corner. She hummed along and reached for her cup of Lady Grey tea. Her conscience pricked. Granddaddy never would have approved of camping out in bed on a Sunday, drinking tea and watching church on a phone.

Pastor Steve had made a real impression. Watching on the internet wasn't the same as going in person, but she'd only missed a handful of Steve's sermons online since she'd visited. She turned toward the bookcase on the other side of her room, where a picture of Granddaddy Henry sat in its antique silver frame. His deep-brown face and salt-and-pepper hair gave him a distinguished appearance, like James Earl Jones. She missed him so much. The rumble of his pastoral baritone remained imprinted inside her. *"Don't forsake the assembling together."* He'd say that when he called her bright and early Sunday mornings when she was in college.

A rattling came from the charging dock on her bedside table, drawing her back to the present. Melvin's name popped up in her text notifications. She turned on her side.

Following their sushi date, they'd patched things up and found steady footing, settling into a routine of weekday texts and weekend phone conversations. Smooth of him. The timing of his weekly Friday or Saturday night call ensured that she wasn't dating anyone else.

> Judge Jackson, I've got a full-fare, refundable first-class ticket to Chicago with your name on it. "A Sunday on La Grande Jatte" is waiting for you at the Art Institute.

She sucked her teeth. Never flown first class. She loved the prestige of being a judge but not the public servant's salary.

And Seurat's painting! The mention of it conjured up images of ladies in bustles and men in top hats enjoying a picturesque, sunny day on the banks of the Seine in Paris.

Jayna Breigh

During the Elevator of Death episode, JD had mentioned that he liked Impressionism as well. There was something soothing about—

Why was she thinking about Attorney Cash right now? A serious contender for the title of "Man Whose Last Name Would Hyphenate Jackson" was proposing a trip to the Windy City to see Monet's *Water Lilies* and she was thinking about someone else? *Girl, check yourself.* She plumped the pillows behind her back as another text dinged.

> If that's not enticement enough, I promise cheese and caramel popcorn for dessert.

He'd put a smiley emoji.

Her relationship with Melvin felt . . . She didn't have the right words. She remained unsettled. Not because of Melvin but because of the shift in her own mind about what to prioritize in her life. Melvin had everything right on paper, but in person there was no zing. She knew that fireworks and excitement often mellowed over time in a marriage, but shouldn't there be some at the start? Shouldn't she be mooning and daydreaming about Melvin all the time?

Pastor Steve's sermons were entering her brain and burrowing below the surface. Like a song you couldn't put out of your head. His words crept in at unexpected moments, pricking and needling her.

"Where your treasure is, there your heart will be also."

What if God was changing her heart and what she treasured? Her Midnight Prince was within reach, but if they rode off into the sunset together, where exactly would they be going? The life Steve kept preaching about looked nothing like the plans she'd been nursing for herself all these years. It didn't look like the life Melvin was living either. Instead, Steve called his congregation to love their neighbors as themselves and embrace hardship and trials as a part of God's plan. And he wasn't talking just about workplace-related hardships as one climbed the ladder of success. He didn't mean trials that came with making it to the next rung on the ladder.

Steve talked about *who* God wanted you to be, not *what*. He'd listed the occupations of Jesus's disciples. Tentmakers, fishermen. Jesus the carpenter. Jesus hadn't collected the best orators or the richest men in the city around himself. Granddaddy had always said, "*All Jesus wants is a willing soul. 'Seek first the kingdom of God and His righteousness, and all these things shall be added to you.'*"

JD sought God's kingdom. Her traitorous brain refused to supplant JD's sad eyes with Melvin's sparkling brown ones. Every time she tried to focus on Melvin, JD would circle back around the mulberry bush like the weasel in the nursery rhyme.

She hovered her fingers over her phone. Her thoughts and feelings were all over the place. Her last conversation with Melvin had given her pause. His words had not only brought back the sting of not fitting inside her own community but also exposed values of her own that she needed to examine. Then there were her work commitments. The Junior Jurors. Mahalia's fingers swiped across her screen.

> Busy calendar coming up, but perhaps in the future?

Her phone dinged in reply:

> Can't wait.

Chapter 32

THE NARROW SEAT in the courtroom gallery gave a loud squeak when JD sat. He'd made it before the first calendar call, so his maneuvering did not draw embarrassing and unnecessary attention to himself. He opened his trial bag and pulled out his papers for today's hearing before Judge Fischer. The rotund man with a port-wine birthmark across his cheek stood in total contrast to Goldstein's Kris Kringle appearance and Judge Jackson's strict, perfunctory courtroom demeanor and distracting beauty.

He glanced at his watch. A few more minutes to review the paperwork on HBA Transit. The case had settled in August, but now in late March it still hung around like a ghost haunting a castle in a movie. Even with the payout to his client in her bank account, the settlement agreement needed an amendment to fix a typo in the confidentiality clause.

No matter. This was the absolute last hearing on the case. Calm washed over him. Additional chunks of time had opened on his calendar, and he wouldn't fill them with work. Instead, he'd block out space for Dean and mock trial prep.

He drew in a breath to focus, and the familiar scent of Chanel No. 5 tickled his nose. He glanced behind him. Wavy blond hair and a peach-colored suit jacket snared his attention. The woman lifted her head. *What's her name again? Kaley, Darcy?* She made eye contact and smiled. *Casey.* She darted her glance to his left and right, stood, and made her way toward him.

"Hello, stranger. This seat taken?"

"Now it is."

He'd made up his mind to set his vow aside. The mental shift had started following the hours spent trapped in the elevator. Layered over that were Tammy's revelations about her cancer and about Dean. This life made no promises, and time ran on swift feet. His job alone no longer satisfied him. What *would* satisfy him? The image of a marinara handprint on the collar of Mahalia's outfit at S'Getti, Soup & Salad floated up. Her cheeks held between pudgy palms for a slobbery kiss. A smile worked its way onto his face.

"What's got you smiling, handsome? Hope it's seeing me." Casey gave a silky laugh.

Though he tried to be attentive to Casey, he couldn't help wishing it were a different woman sitting next to him. But he wasn't the one for Mahalia. For so many reasons, not the least of which was the guy from the theater. His possessive arm had been wrapped around Mahalia for the length of the movie. Not only was Mahalia a judge in his arena, but she also was seeing someone. His stomach gave a sharp twist.

"Do you have a case before Fischer?" he asked Casey, holding back a sigh.

"No. I was down the hall. Saw you come in here. Wanted to say hi. You haven't called me." Casey's eyes implored him to concentrate on her.

Her admission swept away the uncertainty clanging around in his head.

"But you're forgiven." She gave a grimace. "I can be too direct sometimes. I get it. With all the swiping right and left out there, social media, and whatnot." She held her arms up and let them drop back to her sides. "I met someone genuine, intelligent. I wanted to seize the opportunity to connect. Know what I mean?" Her voice pitched up, and she tilted her head to the side.

He nodded. Until Mahalia had invaded his life, his foxhole pledge had been a shield blocking real connection. Now that life's events had chipped away at his desire for solitude, he took a moment to assess Casey. Attractive? No question. Well put together with a pretty smile. He'd seen her perform in the courtroom. She was tough. Quick on her feet.

He replayed Mahalia's visit. Her damp face cloth in his bathroom, her scent left behind on the couch pillow. A touch on his hand drew him back to the moment.

"Lunch. That's all. You've got to eat sometime. Plus, I know a place around here that serves real Southern-style sweet tea."

"All rise." The bailiff's stern words brought a hush to the courtroom.

JD rose to his feet.

"The Honorable Judge Fischer presiding."

He turned Casey's way. She was studying him. There was a vulnerable hopefulness radiating from her.

"Be seated."

He sat at the bailiff's command. "Lunch would be good."

***

"So there I was on this bike in the spinning class, and the ground started lurching and tilting under me." Casey took a napkin and blotted away traces of mayo and chicken salad from her lips.

The little diner she'd picked, A Taste of Home, styled itself as "Deep South meets West Coast" and offered lighter versions of rich homestyle staples. There were pictures of well-known Sunbelt landmarks on the walls—Georgia's Big Chicken, Rock City, Dollywood, and Alabama's U.S. Space & Rocket Center.

"Folks were jumping off their bikes, dropping free weights, sprinting for the door."

"Must have been a madhouse." JD took a swig of his sweet tea. The ice-cold drink tasted like home.

"It was my first real quake. I was sweaty and hot. Terrified. I ran into the women's locker room and ducked under a sink."

"Why under a sink?" He couldn't suppress his laugh while envisioning her crouched in the bathroom.

"I know—it's funny now. I'd read somewhere that all the plumbing and pipes helped."

JD couldn't stop laughing. "I think that's for tornadoes, not earthquakes."

Casey slapped his arm. "Got my natural disasters mixed up."

"Well, you survived, no worse for wear." He took a forkful of the tangy slaw.

"Where were you when the quake hit?"

He halted his chewing. This outing with Casey was supposed to help him forget Mahalia, not recall the moment he'd truly fallen for her. He forced himself to take a methodical bite of the smoky-BBQ sandwich and another long draw of tea. There had been a front-page newspaper article, so there was no use in hiding the story.

AN APPEARANCE OF IMPROPRIETY

"I don't know if you get the *San Gabriel Daily News*."

Her eyes narrowed, but she said nothing.

He shifted around and cleared his throat. "There was a piece about me in there. I ended up trapped for over seven hours in the courthouse elevator."

"You don't say." Her expression was blank.

"I've been to Afghanistan. I had food with me."

Casey leaned forward, "Food. What are you? An urban prepper?"

That pulled a smile. "No. I'd wrapped up with the kids I mentor through a mock trial program. We'd ended for the day. I was hauling out all the materials." He twitched his shoulders up and dropped them. "No biggie."

She narrowed her eyes. "Hmmm." Casey cut her glance away, looking down.

His gut twisted at the omission of the judicial elephant in the room. Time to pivot to every Alabama fan's favorite topic. "You keeping up with Alabama's spring Golden Flake A-Day Game?"

Casey's expression brightened. "You know I am. When the team faces off against itself, it's best-on-best with Bama. I'm hoping another Bulldog will transfer in. If so, Georgia will be crying like babies."

He laughed. Catastrophe diverted—he'd make sure to stay on light topics. The Southern man's obsession with khakis, blue blazers, and loafers without socks.

Their meal wound down, and he walked Casey to her car.

"Now see, that wasn't half-bad, was it?" Casey gave the same pretty, natural smile that graced the faces of homecoming queens from back home.

Casey was right. The grub here was tasty. And with her there were no professional boundaries to tiptoe around—and no hairstylist's-brother-in-law boyfriend. But she didn't send his blood coursing through his veins like a sky-diving adrenaline junkie. He couldn't see his future in her eyes like he did with a certain judge.

He held her car door open as she settled in.

Casey looked up at him. "I think I've got my work cut out for me." She squinted into the sunlight pouring in from behind JD. "But I believe you're worth it. If I don't hear from you in a few days . . ." She gave a cute smile. "Don't be surprised if I call you."

JD closed the door behind her, and she rolled down her window. He hesitated. His heart and mind wrestled over the words to say. He did one more gut check. Yes. He no longer felt the need to hold himself to his monk vow. It was as if boulders fell from his shoulders. He gave himself permission to want more. To seek happiness in a relationship. It was freeing.

"I'll be in touch soon."

***

LA Hearsay Chat Board

4thEstatePitBull: I sent you a file. Did u look at it?

BamaBelle: Yes. I'm holding off for now, but I'll get back to you. Your info was clarifying.

ShadowDocket: Whoever digs a pit will fall into it, just sayin'.

4thEstatePitBull: Nobody asked you @ShadowDocket. @BamaBelle, see you in the DMs.

Chapter 33

JD PICKED UP the vibrating cell phone on the side table beside his living room recliner. A text from Tammy. She'd been in treatment since early April, and it was now almost the end of the month. So, she had a little over three weeks of treatment under her belt. Was that enough time to see a turnaround?

> Oncologist called. Surgery couldn't get it all. Test results show further spread. Checking out next steps. How's it going with Dean?

JD's gut clenched. Despite her current sunken appearance, he could still visualize the Tammy he knew years ago with his letterman jacket slung over her shoulders. Their junior year, that song they loved had looped every day on MTV's *Total Request Live*. She'd jabbered on and on about getting out of Spring Creek to make it as a singer. She'd chopped her own bangs and lightened her hair. He'd told her she was way prettier than that blond girl with all the hit records, and she'd rewarded him with the smile that had done him in.

> So sorry to hear that. I've mentioned the possibility of his moving out here a few times. He's not rejecting it. Like I said before, I want to take him in. What can I do to help?

Jayna Breigh

> My girlfriend found a hospice. Going to pack up a few things and move out of here. Won't need much. She's going to let me stay at her place until, you know. But when it gets bad, I don't want Dean to see all that.

He turned his head. One of Dean's legs hung off the side of the couch. He had an arm behind his head as a pillow, and he was yelling at the ref on the television. JD's protective instincts kicked in.

> We'll cross that bridge when we get there. I'll work on things from this side. Hang in there.

> Thanks, Jimmy.

The halftime buzzer blared, drawing him away from his phone. Bouncy women in gold-and-purple shorts swarmed the basketball court to cheer on the Lakers in their quest for the NBA championship.

JD muted the volume on the TV to escape the bloviating commentators. "Want anything from the kitchen?"

Dean grunted something incomprehensible. Americano, lying on Dean's stomach, wedged her head farther under the boy's chin.

JD felt heavy, weighted, as he stood. He took in his son sprawled on the couch. Like JD, Dean would be without a mother by the time he was eighteen.

He pulled open the cabinet and stared blindly. Ben Kincaide's kids floated in his mind—pudgy hands, lisped-out words, and food stains on every outfit. He'd missed every one of those years with Dean, but he could be a rock for his son now. He liked Dean. They clicked. When he'd taken the teen to scrimmage with Nothing But Net, the kid had talked more trash than DeMarcus. Had helped with sorting papers and shifting boxes of evidence around too.

Even if they hadn't been such a perfect match, he'd do right by him. *Son.*

AN APPEARANCE OF IMPROPRIETY

A giddy lightheadedness inched in for a fleeting moment, but fear kept him from naming the feelings that swelled and ached in his chest.

JD grabbed the bag of chips and jar of dip the grocery delivery service had dropped off. Dean had taken one look inside the fridge, installed an app, and ordered enough food to last JD for weeks.

"Explain again why you're out of school for a full month and my students only get two weeks." He tried doing the math, and he still didn't get it. If Dean was going to live with him, as he and Tammy had discussed, he'd need to work out the schooling details.

"Balanced calendar." The crunching of chips mangled the words.

"And so that means . . ."

"I go to school"—Dean took a huge gulp of Mountain Dew—"year round."

"Even in the summer?"

"Yeah, but we get breaks then too. Ninety days on, thirty days off."

"If you live here next school year, you'll earn in-state residency rates for UCLA."

Dean eased Americano off his belly and sat up. He planted his feet on the ground, elbows on knees and hands steepled under his chin.

JD didn't want to push. A dying mom. Life-altering decisions. Dean had plenty on his plate.

"Look, no need to decide today. Think about it."

A ding-dong chime reverberated through the condo, stopping the conversation in its tracks. Dean shot up from the couch like a released rubber band. His lanky frame made it to the door before JD could leverage himself from his seat.

Dean turned from the peephole, his face scrunched, as if he'd drunk pickle juice. "Bruce, if you keep letting women into the Batcave, eventually the bad guys are going to figure out your secret identity."

JD laughed. Dry, sarcastic. So much like Mama. He walked to the door. "I told you, I have a date." He shot Dean a look and jerked the door open. "Casey. Come in."

Casey glided in. Her wavy blond hair bounced in a becoming way. Nothing bad to say about her appearance. A baby-blue tank top and shorts, long enough to be modest but short enough to be appealing.

She gave him the up-and-down. "Don't you look divine."

He eyed his cargo shorts and weathered JAG T-shirt.

Americano appeared from the kitchen, took one look at Casey, presented her backside, and walked down the hallway toward JD's bedroom. Her tail and head held high, she made her feelings on the matter clear.

His cat needed charm school. Her jealous and territorial shtick was par for the course. *Except with Mahalia.* He shook his head to clear out the unsolicited reminder.

Dean glanced at Casey and shifted his face to teen bored.

This whole thing wasn't playing out like he'd hoped. In the past, to ensure he didn't have any slipups with his post-Afghanistan monk vow, he'd never invited women to his house. But he was trying to give this thing with Casey a real chance. Being around Mahalia had shown him the true cost of his fortress of solitude. He had piles of money, and until just recently no kids of his own. No one to come home to and unwind. No partner to walk beside, encourage, love. Introducing Casey to Dean was a way to take that plunge and commit to a new course of action.

He dragged in a breath and pasted on a smile. "Casey, this is my son, Dean. Dean, say hi to Ms. Chapman."

"Please call me Casey, Dean. I hear *Ms. Chapman* and look around for my mama." Casey gave Dean a fingertip wave. "I've heard great things about you."

JD had sprung Dean's existence on Casey during their lunch, hoping to scare her off. Didn't work. In fact, she'd surprised him.

"I'd be disappointed if you didn't have a few skeletons in your closet. What upstanding good old boy doesn't?"

So far Casey had been nothing but sweet, and she wasn't hard on his eyes. So why did it feel as though every step of this thing was like trudging through wet cement?

Dean stood from the couch, gave a stretch that exposed six inches of his belly, and ambled past Casey. "Nice meeting you." Dean jerked his thumb toward the hallway. "Think I'm gonna Zoom with friends from back home. See you when you get back."

Well, that could've gone better.

The door to the office shut with an echoey click, and the silence between himself and Casey stretched.

"Let's head out, shall we?" He held the front door open.

AN APPEARANCE OF IMPROPRIETY

***

JD picked a hole-in-the-wall that served breakfast 24/7. Locals swore by the huge egg burritos stuffed with peppers, onions, Colby jack, and chorizo sausage. It wasn't swanky, but the place had good eats. The red Formica dinette sets with much-used upholstered chairs, laminated menus, and red and yellow plastic condiment bottles gave a 1950s vibe.

Casey made herself right at home, not turning up her nose one bit at the shabby decor and cracked seats.

"Reminds me of a barbecue place back home." She swept her hair behind her ear and retrieved a napkin from her lap to dab at her lips.

JD nodded as he shoved more burrito into his mouth. Maybe if he kept chewing, he wouldn't have to talk for the whole date. His secret son hadn't frightened her away. One-star dining hadn't scared her off. Casey was setting herself up as a contender.

"Tell me about your practice. What's your caseload like?" he asked.

"Boring. Most of the lawyers at my firm are paper tigers. Never been inside a courtroom at the same time as twelve jurors. We handle cases for corporations. Contract disputes. That's why I'm in front of Judge Jackson all the time. Until Judge Goldstein's accident, she never handled anything except complex litigation cases."

JD worked at attacking a gristly piece of sausage to stall any conversation about Mahalia. The purpose of the date was to get Mahalia out of his system, not to make her front and center.

Casey took a swig of her Diet Coke and dabbed at her lips again. "I'm glad you asked me out, JD. For a minute there, I thought there was something going on with you and Judge Jackson."

"What?" A little piece of burrito went down the wrong pipe, and ice water ran in his veins. He coughed and took a long draw on his tea. "Why would you think that?"

"Well, there was that picture in the paper. I didn't say anything last time we met, but I'd already seen it." She paused. "An . . . acquaintance sent it to me."

There was an out-of-character, closed look about Casey as she spoke. JD brushed it away. "That was an actual emergency. Firefighters pried us out."

"I get it." Casey's gaze remained averted.

He was used to her being brash and forward, but now words appeared to escape her.

She straightened up in her chair. "I didn't tell you before, but I also saw you two having dinner out in the San Fernando Valley. Looked all cozy and personal."

"Casey, we were—"

"I saw the binders and legal pads . . ." Casey trailed off. "But." She gave her head a shake. "It was how she looked at you."

Cold sweat prickled down JD's back. Did Mahalia have feelings for him? He'd been picking up hints, but she was seeing someone. Even when he thought he'd peeked behind her professional facade, she always snapped the curtain closed. Besides, he'd never, *ever* do or say anything to jeopardize Mahalia's professional standing.

"Casey, there is nothing between Judge Jackson and me. We are working on a community service project, nothing more."

Casey looked squarely at JD. The cloud of emotions that had crossed her face were gone. "I'm glad you called me, is all. It isn't often you find an honest, down-to-earth man from back home out here."

Guilt squeezed at JD's gut. The plan had been to date Casey and deep-six his feelings for Mahalia, but Mahalia's essence continued to call to him, like the mythical sirens who lured sailors to dash their ships on the rocks.

***

JD tried to rustle up enthusiasm during the bike ride with Casey. But the relentless glare from the skyscraper windows and his thoughts about Mahalia resulted in stilted conversation. The moderate exercise wasn't working off any of his stress.

They coasted down a hill, and Casey's golden hair shimmered as it streamed behind her. The color and length was the same as Mama's. It wasn't only how she looked. She reminded him of back home in other ways. The slow drawl. The things they talked about. Things he'd spent years trying to outrun. He pedaled harder to make up for lagging and suddenly, in his mind, was riding a different bike on a different day.

AN APPEARANCE OF IMPROPRIETY

His grip had tightened on the colorful paper he held in his hands. Mama hadn't been feeling well, but she'd gotten the little booklet that held the food money and pulled out one of the purple tickets that had a picture of Thomas Jefferson on it and five of the brown ones.

"The store closes in thirty minutes. Go fast as you can, baby."

"Yes, Mama."

He pumped his legs as hard as he could until he got to Gandy's Quick Grocery. Every other letter on the neon sign blinked, and the awning hung down, flopping in front of one side of the big plate-glass window.

He jumped off the bike and flicked down the kickstand. The stitch in his side pulled him up short outside the door. Doubled over to catch his breath, he recited the list to himself again to make sure he brought everything home. Marlboro Lights, two scratchers, a six-pack of Diet Coke, and a mega bag of Cheetos. He still didn't understand how Mama could buy things you couldn't eat with the weird colored money, but he saw people doing it whenever he went to the store for her.

The bell above the door dinged when he entered the dim, cramped space. He immediately zeroed in on the Snickers bars on the bottom shelf of the candy aisle, but . . . no use looking at what he couldn't have.

"Usual order?" Gandy said, not even glancing at him. He wore a dingy tee beneath an unbuttoned Hawaiian shirt. His teeth had ample room, given all the gaps and spaces in his mouth.

"Yeah."

Gandy reached behind himself and grabbed the cigarettes. He turned to his side and punched the buttons on the lottery machine, and two tickets spit out the front. He shoved those across the worn countertop.

JD handed Gandy the coupons. Gandy opened the register and closed it. He never put the food stamps in the drawer. Always put them in a box to the side.

When JD would tell Mama that the math didn't add up on the cost of all the stuff and that Gandy never gave him back enough change, she always gave the same response. "Don't worry, baby. Gandy's trying to help me out. That's all."

He couldn't understand how keeping Mama's change and selling JD things he was too young to buy was helping her out. He turned to leave.

"Hey, boy."

Gandy's voice pulled him up short. The man never spared him a word any other day.

"Tell your mama I'm coming 'round this evening."

Everything inside him stilled. Gandy had never been to their place. When Mama's other men friends dropped by, she was usually sick for a day or so after. Her eyes all glassy. Sometimes acting silly or walking like she couldn't stand up for long. She didn't look after herself like she should. Now Gandy was planning to come around too?

He gathered up the bag with the items. His stomach hurt. They needed out of that trailer park. Needed to live someplace else. Heat pulsed behind his eyelids. He would change this. Somehow. He'd get Mama away from here. Take her far from Gandy and the other losers. He'd have enough money to buy stuff like apples and Snickers, and Mama wouldn't get sick.

It had been a childish promise from an innocent kid.

A horn honked, bringing him back to the present, and he swerved. Casey was already at the bottom of the hill. She had one foot braced on the ground, head turned, looking back as she waited for him.

But Casey wasn't the woman who lingered in his dreams at night. She was his past. He didn't want to go back, ever. Even mentally. She was constantly reminding him of the connection they shared and talking of back home. But he'd walked away from Georgia, never to return.

Mama'd had little when she was alive, and he'd kept even less from his life with her. Scraped together the money to cremate her. Sprinkled her ashes in the town's namesake, Spring Creek. Packed her record player, her music, and the small silver cross she'd worn in a box. That and a few photos were all he held on to.

Back home stood as testament to his failure. His addicted Mama using food stamps to buy necessities or, worse, to trade for oxy or meth. Men in and out, giving her drugs or using them with her. Using Mama. He wanted nothing that reminded him of back home—where he hadn't protected. Hadn't made things right.

But *Mahalia?*

She was strong and confident, and didn't let any man run over her. He could trust her not to let herself spiral out of control. Her strength called to him in a visceral way.

It wasn't fair to Casey. He honestly had been trying to give it a shot, but any more would be stringing her along. He felt relieved at the sight of the Wagoneer parked next to the bike lane ahead.

Restlessness returned and clawed at JD as he walked beside Casey to slot their bikes into the rental dock beside the others lining the sidewalk. A woman walking a half dozen sizes and shapes of dogs squeezed by them on the outside, forcing him into closer proximity with Casey.

Chanel No. 5 mixed with sunscreen washed over him, and he tried breathing through his mouth. Near his condo was a little pocket park tucked between two of the towers next to the on-street parking, and he steered her to a bench.

Taking Casey out had been a disaster. When he wasn't beating back thoughts about Mahalia, he was thinking about Dean and Tammy or cycling through a list of things on his to-do list—returning calls to his 800 number, storing exhibits, recycling trial notebooks. Breaking down the war room for the HBA Transit case now that the settlement was finalized. Final prep for the Junior Jurors mock trial. As soon as the upcoming competition entered his mind, his thoughts would skid right back to Mahalia.

Casey knocked her shoulder against his. "I don't think you've heard a word I said in the last five minutes. What are you contemplating so hard?"

Your constant references to "back home." Restlessness vaulted him to his feet. Casey was his past, not his future. It would be wrong to date her in an attempt to diffuse his attraction to Mahalia. He forced himself to sit again. He couldn't have this talk while looming over her.

"Look, Casey, I'm slammed right now time-wise." He made himself look into her eyes. "A new son, a massive case, a bunch of kids counting on me to coach them through a mock trial . . ."

"Can't someone else step in to help with the kids and assist Judge Jackson?" Red flushed Casey's face.

"I'm not helping *her*. She's helping *me*." He crossed his arms over his chest, realized what he was doing, and forced them down. He felt exposed under her stare and cut away his glance first. "Drop it, Casey." His voice was harsh. "Look . . ." He softened his tone, gazed away, then back at her. "This isn't only about the trial. The timing isn't right. I'm so sorry. Something might change. But right now . . ."

Casey crossed her long legs. Pretty pink polish adorned the toes poking out from her sports sandals, and her intense expression telegraphed her feelings. With her silky blond hair and mesmerizing eyes, she had the ability to bring almost any man to his knees. But he couldn't gin up any interest. He replaced her image with that of a fiery, ebony-skinned judge who ran her courtroom with an iron fist and loved her godchildren with Amazon-like fierceness.

"I understand." Her eyes tightened around the edges, and a little pout sullied her face, then disappeared, replaced by a tight smile.

He'd hurt her. "Casey, I'm so sorry." He reached out his hand but dropped it back down.

"We're good, JD." She stood with a jerk, brushed off the back of her shorts, and motioned for JD to stand so they could walk back to her car. "Everything is crystal clear." Her voice was firm and low.

At her car he hesitated, not knowing how to part. "Friends?" He opened his arms in what he hoped looked like a solicitation for a buddy hug.

Casey appeared to get the hint and came in for a squeeze, accompanied by a couple of back pats. "Friends look out for each other, right?"

"Of course." The knot that had been tightening in his stomach all afternoon loosened by a hair.

"Then we're friends." Casey pulled away first. Walked around the back of her car and climbed in.

JD stood at the curb, waiting for her to drive off. She lowered the window and leaned toward the passenger side.

"Take care, Casey." He fisted his hands and drove them deep into the pockets of his shorts.

"I'm still hoping that timing thing might work itself out. I'll be seeing you around, JD." Casey gave him a soft smile, rolled up her window, and drove away.

Apprehension clawed up his back. Nothing he could point to, but God and his gut had gotten him out of many jams in Afghanistan. *Lord, it's in your hands.*

AN APPEARANCE OF IMPROPRIETY

***

LA Hearsay DMs

4thEstatePitBull: What's your decision?

BamaBelle: Something's rotten in Denmark. The plans a go.

***

Private Facebook Group: The Good, The Bad & The Ugly

Sarah: It's not her turn yet . . . Too young.

Blondie: Agree. But she hasn't stumbled w/the Complex Litigation docket.

Joe: Remind me why we can't shift to Discord.

Manco: Because Preacher is 103 and can't transition off FB.

Joe: 😂😂😂

Preacher: My grandson found some stuff on the LA Hearsay Chat Board.

Joe: How'd you find out about that?

Preacher: A file room clerk mentioned it.

Manco: Sounds like a setup. They steered you right to the dirt.

Joe: We need a judiciary that understands tech. The next ASJ should be younger.

Manco: She handled some of Cash's motions and then was trapped in an elevator with him for hours. Who knows what went on.

Sarah: But she was off the case . . .

Joe: There's a disciplinary case against her. I'll upload it.

Preacher: Those are confidential. How'd you get that?

Joe: We have leaks in the highest court of the land. You think this place is immune?

Sarah: Someone anonymously sent me her 360° reviews too. Staff approves.

Preacher: We're not supposed to know any of this!

Joe: It's about staying ahead of controversy.

Sarah: About the file room . . . I have some concerns.

Chapter 34

Mahalia paced the floor in her chambers. This week she would have her second-round interview for the ASJ position with current Assistant Supervising Judge Aldrich Whitaker. He was supposed to send her the time and some additional information today. Goldstein had told her she was ready. That she could do it. But dread filled her stomach with bile. Over the course of the last few days, the stares from her "brethren" in robes had reached Arctic levels in their coldness. This was more than the normal professional jockeying and office politics, but she had no idea what was going on.

There was a rapid knock, and the door to her chambers burst open. Becky rushed in and halted in front of Mahalia's desk, bouncing on the balls of her feet. The clerk's navy pantsuit was as deliriously frazzled as its owner, who was nodding at Mahalia with a goofy grin on her face. She thrust forward an envelope with only the words "Judge Mahalia Jackson" typed on the outside.

Mahalia's pulse quickened.

"This is a day we've been praying for. I'm always here to help, Your Honor," Becky said, smiling at Mahalia as she backed out of the office.

At the mention of prayer, her conscience stung. She doubted her clerk said actual prayers for her. It was a polite way of offering a kind, generic sentiment. But she knew she herself had spent less than a minute in prayer about this promotion. Her hand holding the missive trembled. She freed a smaller envelope from inside. It was not from the assistant supervising judge's office. It was from the California Commission on Judicial Performance. She opened the envelope and skimmed the page.

Becky's intuition had missed the mark entirely.

"An appearance of impropriety in violation of California Code of Judicial Conduct . . . Further allegation of actual bias in the performance of your duties . . . Compromise to the integrity of the office and the standing of the judiciary in the eyes of the citizenry . . . Per California Commission on Judicial Performance protocol, the name of the complaining party is confidential."

Mahalia wanted to vomit. She bolted the door and slumped against the wall. Ruined. Her entire career was ruined.

Of course the complaints were anonymous. She combed her brain, desperate to remember anything that might have led to this. Why now, while she was in the running for the position of assistant supervising judge?

She plopped down onto her chair, squeezed her temples between her fingers, and fired up her computer. According to the CJP website, some cases were closed after the initial review without investigation of any kind. Consequences advanced from there. The commission could launch an investigation from which a judge could receive private or public admonishment. She might have to appear before the commission or attend a hearing before a special master. Worst-case scenarios—forced retirement, public censure, or outright removal.

Who would have filed this? None of her corporate cases were contentious. The same contingent of stodgy stiffs routinely appeared before her. Dinkelman? What did he have to gain from a complaint? Reporters made their money printing stories, not getting judges disqualified. Did this have anything to do with the Junior Jurors program? Retaliation because of her advice to Mercedes? Something having to do with her intervention for Kyle? It couldn't be the TransNation case. She'd been off that since October.

***

That evening Mahalia sat at her desk after hours. She'd forced herself to attend all scheduled hearings that day but had been unable to make herself do any paperwork. Now that the office was silent, she hoped the headache would recede and that she could get herself back on track. She stabbed at a grape tomato, which skittered around the take-out container until she impaled it on her fork. The violence against the defenseless vegetable was oddly satisfying, given her current mood. She skimmed the Motion to Amend Complaint pulled up on her computer screen. Mega Corporation A sought even more money from Mega Corporation B over some breach of contract.

AN APPEARANCE OF IMPROPRIETY

The FAMU fight song blared from her phone, and the noise caused the pounding in her head to intensify. Her hand moved toward the phone and retreated. She stretched her hand out again, hovering but not picking it up. It wasn't Melvin's fault, but she wasn't in the mood to chat or text with him tonight.

Melvin was saying all the right things when they spoke on the phone. He had tickets to the Black Film Festival in Atlanta early in the summer, and he'd invited her to his family reunion in Chicago over the Labor Day holiday. Whenever they spoke, Melvin's voice, like a radio DJ on the midnight to 3:00 a.m. shift, lulled her with the promise of high-end vacations and hobnobbing with the elite. She shook her head and picked up the phone.

> Checking to see if you got
> the delivery I sent today.

Two dozen blush-colored roses sat in a genuine crystal vase beside her computer. Her hand freed the card from the envelope to read it again.

"To the future."

The blast radius from the impropriety complaint overshadowed any thoughts of her future. She'd been waiting for years for someone with Melvin's résumé, charisma, and pedigree. But she had never let her guard down with him. Never shared her dreams. Her fears. She hadn't thought to call him all day to help her process and work through the complaint filed against her.

A real relationship required transparency and vulnerability, but she hesitated to let him into the places she kept to herself. The weak places. The scared places.

During their more personal moments, she'd broached her gnawing faith questions. How things Granddaddy Henry said were coming back to her now, swimming in her head when she lay down at night and again when she woke up in the morning. How Steve's sermon on knowing God's will ate at her conscience. Melvin, quick to see the humor in situations, usually managed a joke about pastors who showcased their sneaker collections on Instagram. Try as she might, she couldn't get their interactions to turn to deeper matters of faith and meaning.

If she couldn't talk to him about a simple sermon, how could she tell him about the ethics complaint? The charges left her feeling exposed. Vulnerable. What would Melvin do if he knew she might be reprimanded, sanctioned, or worse? If she wasn't formidable, would he still want her?

Faces drifted through her mind. Kyle, José, Quincy, Langston. They needed mentors like Melvin. She'd tested the waters, but Melvin had given a gentle, but permanent, brush-off.

She held the phone in her palm. She couldn't think of a response to his text. A pair of intense, serious eyes floated in and out of her mental frame. The rumble of a calm voice in the terrifying dark of an elevator. How she'd been transparent and shared her pain, her fears. A man comfortable lifting his hands in church during a praise song and whose Bible had underlining and coffee stains.

Mahalia hadn't even prayed while trapped in the elevator with JD. Hour after hour. Not a single prayer while they'd dangled in the shaft. Sure, she'd promised herself she'd go to church after they'd been rescued, but she'd dragged her feet on that as well. Instead, she'd slotted herself right back into her routine and kept on keeping on until her friend Cassandy had forced her hand.

Throughout her life, she'd striven for the brass ring of affluence and status to throw back in the faces of the people who had wounded her with their taunts and hurtful comments. In her dreams she and her educated, charming, financially secure husband were at the top of the social pecking order, commanding, directing, controlling. Hot condemnation stabbed at her conscience. Granddaddy Henry had said King Jesus held exclusive right to the throne.

"Oh, you can go your whole life thinking you are sitting high and mighty. But on judgment day, every knee will bow and every tongue confess who the real King is."

Today, every one of her achievements could come crashing down without a moment's notice.

Raw shame and disappointment coursed through her. Rooted in her seat in her chambers, surrounded by walls adorned with plaques, a framed *State Bar* magazine cover, and her diplomas, her life looked like the path leading to destruction that Granddaddy Henry had always warned her about. Thoughts

AN APPEARANCE OF IMPROPRIETY

she'd been too hardheaded to entertain before now poured in like water over a breached dam. She wanted off the broad road. She'd made idols out of her fictional vision for a man and out of her now-crumbling social position.

She sealed her eyes shut and asked God to give her the words she needed to say.

For what will it profit a man if he gains the whole world, and loses his own soul?

The phone fell from her grip and plopped onto the desk as she realized she was going to let her Midnight Prince ride off into the sunset without her. She pressed the heels of her hands to her eyes to keep the water from leaking out. Her dream, what she'd been hoping and praying for, would voluntarily slip through her fingers. She was about to bid him goodbye. Send him on his way. And for what? There was no future with JD. Those thoughts only led to a dead end.

But other thoughts could free her if she surrendered her will to God's. Took herself down off the pedestal and acknowledged that he was the only one entitled to stand on it. Stopped using advancement and achievement to undergird her sense of self, and instead made God the foundation of her life.

She bowed her head and surrendered her old dreams. Thoughts and whispered words mingled together. "I am sorry for spending the last decade thinking anything or anyone but you could satisfy. Forgive me for my ungratefulness, my vanity, my pride."

The words of one of her grandfather's favorite hymns came to her.

> *All to Jesus I surrender,*
> *All to him I freely give;*
> *I will ever love and trust him,*
> *In his presence daily live.*
> *I surrender all.*

Pain and regret welled up and flowed out. The hurt and insults she'd tried to vanquish with accomplishments pounded inside, trying to pull her back into her fortress of self-accomplishment.

"No! I surrender all."

She held her fisted hands in the air. The strain eased out, and she uncurled her fingers one by one. She let it all go. Relinquished it all. Prayers rasped out. "You are on the throne. You've always been there. I surrender all. I trust you and thank you. Give me the words. Please." Another shuddering breath, and she swiped Unlock on her phone.

> Thank you for the roses. I'm thinking our schedules and lives won't mesh during this season. So sorry to let you know like this, but it's for the best.

She hit Send and turned off notifications. She'd speak to Melvin in person. Soon. But not today. A cement block lifted from her chest, and cleansing breath entered her lungs. The date for the mock trial was fast approaching. She straightened her spine and pulled her shoulders back. She would be 100 percent professional and distanced. JD and his kids would get the absolute best that she had. Nothing less.

And after? When the competition was over? When the meetings ceased? JD would move on. She'd move on. And with God's grace, her heart would recover.

***

To: The California Committee on Judicial Performance
From: Rebeckah Collins, Clerk to the Honorable P. Mahalia Jackson

To Whom It May Concern:

There is a private chat board where courthouse staff, reporters, and others trade information, helpful tips, and gossip. I have reason to believe that sensationalized information was supplied to the commission to destroy Judge Jackson's career. See the attached screenshots. This letter is to support Judge Jackson. I offer my help in any way and am willing to testify.

Chapter 35

"All rise. The Honorable Judge Arnold Goldstein presiding."

Mahalia rose as well. She'd tucked herself into a corner of Goldstein's courtroom to watch the start of the TransNation case. More bodies than usual crammed every crevice in the seating area, making the courtroom stuffy. Even JD's son, Dean, had a seat.

She surveyed the packed gallery. Dinkelman sat front and center in the area reserved for the press. She restrained the urge to say bad words about him in her mind. She hoped Goldstein would hold Dinkelman in contempt of court if he even dared to pull out his phone and snap a picture.

A woman entered the courtroom and sat next to the reporter. Mahalia dredged her memory, but no luck pulling up the blonde's name. A vague picture of the woman sitting by JD on a bench drifted through her thoughts. Her brain blared an insistent alarm, like a fire station doing a full rollout, to no avail. Hundreds of lawyers paraded before her. The dots wouldn't connect. But the niggling feeling that had dogged her since she'd received the ethics hearing letter crept back in. Finally the name came to her. Casey Chapman. Pink pantsuit. The attorney who'd given her a rough time at a hearing. The one who'd had lunch with JD under a palm tree. The woman was now glued to Dinkelman's hip.

A fuzzy mental picture zoomed into focus. The dinner at the San Fernando Seafood Grill. Chapman had been the fair-haired partner of the duo of women ushered out by the owner, Vinnie.

The woman ran the tips of her dusty-pink manicured nails through the hair that had cascaded over one brow, smoothing her fingers through the tresses and flipping the ends. Dinkelman's gaze followed every movement like a cat watching a laser pointer.

Why was she at this hearing? And sitting next to Dinkelman, no less. Had she filed the ethics complaint for the appearance of impropriety against Mahalia? Constructing career-damaging accusations out of a working dinner in full view of the public? Why would she?

Chapman turned her head and glanced at Mahalia. A sheen of tears filled the woman's eyes, and she blinked them away. She pulled her bottom lip between her teeth and trained her gaze, heavy with longing, on JD at the front of the courtroom.

Realization landed like a left hook. Chapman had *feelings* for JD. Had she perhaps launched a ballistic attack to fight off a potential romantic rival?

In this moment, sitting so close to another woman who clearly cared for JD, the reality of Mahalia's own feelings stood out in stark relief. Illuminated like thousands of stars on the clearest of nights.

The bailiff escorted the jury panel to their seats. It was too late for a graceful exit to the hallway to compose herself. She directed her attention to the front, hoping her face did not betray her emotions.

Goldstein had told her JD's billboard had turned the process into a hot mess, with TransNation's attorneys grumbling about not being able to seat a fair jury and filing yet another motion to change venue. The jurist had settled their ire by promising to admonish the jury, even though a third of the prospective pool had seen the monstrosity and two women had JD's 800 number memorized.

She cast a long look at the back of JD's glorious silver head. He was nothing like the caricature portrayed on his sign. From what she'd observed of his interaction with the Junior Jurors, he was a man of the highest integrity, and he genuinely cared for people. She'd seen it in the elevator the night of the quake. Then he'd taken in a son he never knew he had without any apparent hesitation. She searched her mind for what Goldstein had said about him.

"*He's on the angels' side.*"

Yes. He was also a man of deep, genuine faith. She drew in a prolonged breath and shoved aside her emotions about the ethics complaint to focus on the proceedings.

The jury held the bulk of the power from this point forward, but Goldstein would run a tight ship. The two motions she'd ruled on months ago were water under the bridge at this point unless there was an appeal.

Her heart cracked at the sight of the Hunt family, whom she'd gotten to know a bit from all the paperwork when she'd been the judge on this case. Ann Hunt and her two young children, Caylee and Dylan, sat in the front row of the gallery, behind JD. Beside them sat a grandmotherly looking woman with her arms around little Dylan. The young boy wore a brand-new-looking navy V-neck sweater over a polo shirt. His sister was clad in a yellow floral print sundress covered with a cardigan, her long hair in a tight ponytail. What a horrible reason to get new outfits. But she understood. Their presence would help solidify the tragedy in the minds of the jurors. In profile, the children's faces were masks of somber defeat.

"Counselors, are you ready to proceed?" Goldstein bellowed out.

Mahalia focused on the defendants' table and the phalanx of TransNation attorneys jammed together like sardines. A sea of navy-blue suits. They nodded in unison.

"Mr. Cash?" Goldstein asked.

"Yes, Your Honor." His charcoal-gray suit was impeccable. Not a hair was out of place.

"Mr. Cash, your opening statement."

JD rose from his seat in a confident, smooth motion, strode toward the jury box, and stopped a foot away from the first row. He clasped his hands behind his back.

"Ladies and gentlemen, seated behind my table over there"—JD pointed to Ann, Caylee, and Dylan—"are my clients. The wife and children John Hunt left behind when he died in a horrific crash. The evidence will show that my clients are here today because of the reckless conduct of the executives of TransNation Trucking Corporation." JD moved his head left to right, appearing to take in every person on the jury.

"If you drove here today, you no doubt saw one, two, maybe three TransNation trucks making their way down the road. The facts are easy to understand. TransNation skimped on vehicle maintenance. They encouraged tired drivers to remain behind the wheel and counseled them to use stimulants to stay awake. Impaired drivers experiencing excessive tiredness have slow reaction times. Fatigue causes hesitation, which can be deadly when equipment fails or when there are dangerous road conditions."

So far, JD's presentation had been flawless. No theatrics. From Mahalia's vantage point, not a single juror looked bored.

"Last year on January twentieth, tragedy struck. The driver in this case, Walt McClatchy, could have avoided the accident caused by shoddy maintenance procedures if he had been alert and not driven to the breaking point by TransNation's efforts to save pennies per mile."

JD strode back to his table so the jury would focus on the Hunt family in the gallery behind him. "You will hear from the CEO of TransNation himself about the depths to which the company sank in order to wring out every bit of work possible from their exhausted drivers and their overtaxed, under-maintained equipment."

JD's opening statement struck the right balance between a matter-of-fact presentation and tugging on the jury's heartstrings. He didn't overstate and didn't lay it on too thick. Mahalia forced her head to remain still, but she wanted to nod in agreement. Those TransNation trucks barreled down the freeway and often drove erratically. She'd seen it firsthand.

"TransNation may offer evidence intended to smear my clients' deceased husband and to cast doubt about the company's liability. They have attempted to silence the driver, Mr. McClatchy, and will question his motives. I don't fault them. But this is not about Mr. Hunt or Mr. McClatchy."

Smart. Pointing out potential weaknesses in his case before TransNation raised them.

"If I were facing a potential multimillion-dollar verdict, I would expect my lawyer to use every tactic and strategy in his arsenal to deflect any culpability my company might have. I have confidence, however, that after you have heard all the testimony, you will enter a verdict against TransNation and in favor of my clients to send an unmistakable message about the absolute need for safety on our roads."

JD once more scanned the jury. He didn't look at the TransNation table as he made his way back to his seat.

Mahalia eyed the twelve citizens seated and ready to pass judgment. It seemed by their expressions that JD held them in the palm of his hand. Only twenty minutes into the case and TransNation was flailing in quicksand.

Chapter 36

Mahalia sat in the outer vestibule of Assistant Supervising Judge Aldrich Whitaker's chambers. The keys of the computer manned by his ancient battle-axe secretary tippy-tapped at a feverish pitch. Mahalia squeezed her forehead between her fingers. As the outgoing ASJ, Whitaker had the right to interview his successors.

This morning marked day two of the TransNation trial, and she'd hoped to slip out in a gap between her own hearings to catch at least a little more of the proceedings. But this interview took precedence over everything else.

A click of the doorknob and the squeak of a rolling cart jerked her attention back. The door opened, and Tanner's mom entered with a cart full of files.

"Oh."

Mahalia saw the woman's throat working.

"Judge Jackson." Ms. Kane's eyes widened, and her face flushed.

"Just put those files over there," Judge Whitaker's secretary told her.

Tension vibrated off the file clerk, and she avoided Mahalia's eyes as she deposited several accordion files onto a side table and exited. Mahalia had never thought about it before, but file clerks had almost unfettered access to the courthouse and its paperwork.

The feverish typing stopped. "Judge Whitaker is ready for you now." The secretary pointed toward the door behind her desk.

Mahalia's pulse raced. Seeing Tanner's mom gave her an odd feeling, but she didn't have time to process that now. She stood, pulled her shoulders back, and checked her outfit one last time. It had felt wrong to select what had been her "lucky" pantsuit. She did not need luck anymore. Instead, she had thought of Just Steve, said a small prayer, and picked a royal-blue ensemble with a crisp white blouse and a scarf tied around her neck.

On the walls in Judge Whitaker's chambers were pictures of the last ten ASJs, going back to the 1990s. Would she be on that wall? Her hands were clammy, and her mouth was dry.

"So, Judge Jackson, you want to take my office and do my job?"

"I . . ." The interview was not starting as she had expected. Maybe all those rumors about the old guard circling the wagons were true. She mustered her thoughts. "I want to carry on your standard of professionalism, efficiency, and excellence as the manager of the courthouse."

"The assistant supervising judge is the face of this building and everyone in it. The person in this position must have the absolute confidence and respect of all the other jurists and administrative personnel who support them."

She was up for the challenge, but this felt less like an interview and more like an attempt to either dissuade her or tell her she was not qualified.

"The staff in your courtroom have given you high marks. Unlike some judges, you've not had any defections, and your clerk has been with you since you have been on the bench."

The knot in her gut loosened a smidge. She was not friends with Becky, but the longer she worked with the woman, the more she realized Becky had her back. Her clerk worked hard to make sure that nothing dropped through the cracks. Had she been taking her staff for granted? *Help is closer than you think.* It was, and she'd been missing it. She made a mental note to take the whole staff out to lunch to thank them for their loyalty and support, no matter the outcome of this meeting or her bid for ASJ.

"However, I've also received some unsolicited, confidential input regarding your temperament as a judge."

Who would've sent something like that to Whitaker? The rarefied world of complex litigation, at least on the surface, played nice. It wasn't until she'd handled Goldstein's caseload that she had seen alley-cat lawyering.

"There is a whisper campaign against you. A picture is circulating. I realize it is fake, but that it exists at all calls the court's reputation into question. I've also learned that someone filed an ethics complaint against you."

Wait! "How do you know there's an ethics complaint? They're confidential."

AN APPEARANCE OF IMPROPRIETY

"Someone is taking the time to, piece by piece, undermine your authority and credibility as a judge. I've seen anonymous notes. So have other committee members. There are people outside this courthouse as well who have a vested interest."

Her heart jerked, and she willed herself to settle down.

"Are you going to give me an opportunity to defend myself?" She struggled to keep her composure.

Whitaker's stiff professional demeanor relaxed. "Look. I shouldn't be telling you this, but I'm going to recommend you for the position. Among other reasons, technology is advancing quickly, and the court is slow to catch up. We need someone in an administrative position who can act as a bridge between the older judges stuck in their ways and the court staff champing to be on the cutting edge."

Her mind pinged to her mentor and his abhorrence of all things digital.

"But what you need to know is that you have enemies, and they are fighting dirty. I've been around this courthouse long enough to know that ninety percent of these types of accusations are not true. But it's the other ten percent you have to watch out for. I would encourage you to make sure your house is in order if you want this job."

Whitaker stood and gestured to his door. "I wish you the best of luck."

***

As Sidwell approached Ann Hunt in the witness box, JD concentrated on the jury and forced himself to relax his face muscles. Ann had done a masterful job during his direct examination of her earlier in the day, and he didn't want the jury sensing any stress rolling off him. This cross-examination would cement the jury's impression of both Sidwell and the Hunt family.

He studied the twelve citizens sitting in the box. The timing on Ann's cross-examination worked in her favor. Stuffed bellies from a catered spread, combined with the still air in the courtroom, created a brew of boredom and impatience. Sidwell would have an uphill battle capturing and holding the jurors' interest during his cross. The man adjusted a pair of cheaters on the end of his hawklike nose and fiddled with the paper he held in his hands.

"Mrs. Hunt, I am so sorry for your loss." The words coming out of

Sidwell's mouth didn't match the tight line of his lips and the calculation in his eyes.

Ann gave a single nod.

"I'm sure this must be difficult."

Ann plucked several tissues from the box on the corner of the witness stand but did not dab her eyes. Instead, she wrung the tissues in her hand.

JD regarded the jury. Not a single person appeared to be buying the false sympathy. In fact, a couple of jurors had their arms crossed. Excellent.

"A question, Mr. Sidwell. Now," Goldstein admonished.

JD hadn't objected, but Goldstein was right to cut off the attempts to butter up the jury.

"Yes, of course." Sidwell turned back to Ann. "Your husband left no life insurance, did he?"

"No."

"He had no 401(k)?"

"No."

"Was he in the military long enough to qualify for a pension?"

"No."

"And you don't work, do you?"

JD had prepared Ann for this question.

"Especially now, my full-time job is raising our children." Ann shifted her focus to her kids, sitting behind JD.

"Indeed." Sidwell pursed his lips like an old schoolmarm. "You're suing for several million, but between you and your husband, you've never had a net worth greater than ten thousand dollars. Even that resulted from the boom in the housing market over the last few years. You basically were living check to check?"

"Yes, we've never had much."

"So several million dollars would be a significant change, isn't that right?"

"Several million dollars won't bring John back."

"Move to strike as nonresponsive," Sidwell spat out.

"Objection sustained. Mrs. Hunt, you need to answer the question he asked." Goldstein's voice was gentle. Not scolding.

"Withdrawn. I think the jury knows what's going on here."

JD sprung to his feet as anger flared in his chest. "Objection, Your Honor. Mr. Sidwell is testifying."

Goldstein glared at Sidwell. "You're getting close to the line."

"I apologize, Your Honor."

Sidwell spun and walked back to his counsel table. He riffled through a notebook, removed a piece of paper, and resumed his questioning from that location.

"You stated during your direct examination that your husband was on his way home on a break, to eat?"

Ann's eyes welled. She gave a curt nod. "Yes."

"Not headed to meet his Alcoholics Anonymous sponsor?"

Rustling and a stifled gasp emitted from the jury box. The startling question had jolted them.

JD's hopes of defusing John Hunt's former drinking problem were poised to implode. He slammed his palm on the table. He had to get the jury's focus back on TransNation. "Objection. Move to strike, and sidebar, Your Honor."

"Caution, Mr. Cash. No need for an outburst." Goldstein narrowed his eyes at him.

"Sorry, Your Honor." He reined himself in. Too much drama and the jury would think JD and his client had something to hide.

"You may approach."

Sidwell curled his lip as both men made their way to stand at the corner of Goldstein's bench farthest from the jury. If he ran across Sidwell in an alley tonight, he'd have to work hard to restrain himself from pummeling the arrogant tool.

"Your Honor, you previously ruled on our pretrial motion to exclude any evidence of Mr. Hunt's prior drinking problems. Further, the toxicology reports indicated the absence of alcohol in Mr. Hunt's system." JD spotted perspiration on Sidwell's upper lip. *Weasel.*

"People fall off the wagon all the time." Sidwell shrugged. "I think the jury should know this man had a drinking problem."

"The operative word in your sentence is 'had.' The toxicology report found no evidence of alcohol in his system. Further, the officer on scene determined no inebriation on his part contributed to the accident. Your Honor, this is ridiculous."

The glint in Goldstein's eyes could have cut glass. "I agree, Mr. Cash. Objection sustained. Stick to what you can prove, Mr. Sidwell."

"Yes, Your Honor."

"Now step back.

"Ladies and gentlemen of the jury, you are to disregard Mr. Sidwell's last question."

Heat flushed JD's face, and he clamped his jaw hard, trying to keep his expression neutral. The jury could not unhear the question. Better to let the thing smooth itself over.

With the issue of John's drinking behind him, there was nothing left for Sidwell on cross-examination. JD had already made a preemptive strike on direct examination about John's speeding tickets, and Ann had offset any damage by testifying about his defensive driving classes. Satisfaction suffused JD. Ann had held her own and not hurt the case.

Would some of today's rulings have turned out differently if Mahalia were still the judge? Or would her assistance with the Junior Jurors, or anything else, have prejudiced her against him? No way for him to know. Right now he needed Goldstein to hold a tight rein and keep TransNation from any more tricks.

Chapter 37

WITH THREE HOURS of sleep under his belt, JD had never been more ready for an examination of a witness in his life. Snevelton was an adverse witness, so JD was free to use every cross-examination trick in his tool bag to eviscerate the man's testimony. The courtroom buzzed with an expectant air. A half dozen reporters filled the press section, and the jurors sat upright and attentive.

TransNation's CEO sat in the witness chair, his middle-aged paunch straining the buttons of his dress shirt. With his drab-brown hair combed straight back and held in place by shiny gel, Snevelton looked like he sold snake oil for a living. JD's gut churned at the simpering smile on the CEO's face. The man was practically a murderer, and he didn't care.

JD planned to set the trap and let Snevelton tangle himself in a web of his own lies. He reviewed his notes one last time and approached the stand. "Mr. Snevelton, you've been in the trucking business how long?"

"Going on twenty-five years." Snevelton gave a curt nod, as if to punctuate his achievement.

"And for this region of the country, where would you rate TransNation in terms of safety?"

Snevelton stuck out his chest. "I would say we're in the upper ten percent of all trucking companies."

In his peripheral vision, JD spotted a male juror in the back row rolling his eyes.

"Last year more than five thousand people died in accidents caused by tractor trailers on our nation's freeways, close to fifteen people a day, every day of the year. Do you know how many accidents had a TransNation driver behind the wheel?"

"No, I don't. But I'm sure you'll tell me."

"You're right. I will."

Sidwell was on his feet in a nanosecond.

"Withdrawn." JD faced the jury for a beat. He held eye contact with one female juror, then a second. Their faces telegraphed that they didn't like Snevelton's snarky comeback.

"TransNation trucks killed or injured a hundred and fifty people, three percent of all serious big-rig mortalities."

Snevelton fidgeted in his seat.

"But you knew that, didn't you?"

"That figure you quoted was from two years ago, I believe. I don't keep that type of information in my head."

"Sounds like you do."

"Move to strike." A vein pulsed near Sidwell's collar. "Mr. Cash is testifying."

Goldstein pointed the business end of his gavel at JD. "Mr. Cash, you're pushing it."

The judge was right. In fact, he planned to push even further.

"Withdrawn. Moving on. Let me refresh your recollection with Exhibit 13." JD strode to his table and grabbed a sheet of paper. "This is an email to you from Congressman Berber of Arizona. Do you recognize this email?"

Snevelton took the document from JD's hands and read it. His face flushed red.

"Never seen this before. When you look at it, you can tell that the email is not addressed to me."

"Oh, right," JD said. "Well, I already admitted the document into evidence, and I had a witness authenticate it. So let's read what it says for the jury."

JD seized the document from him.

"'I can't keep covering for you with the DOT. Your company needs to get its annual fatalities down. I'm not sticking my neck out for you any longer.'"

Snevelton raised a single eyebrow in contempt. "The document clearly shows it is addressed to the president of our corporation. He doesn't work for us anymore. I fired him. As I stated, I've never seen the email before."

"Your Honor," JD said, "I ask that you strike the last statement from the record. There was no question pending to the witness."

"Sustained. Ladies and gentlemen, please disregard the witness's last statement."

JD retrieved another document from his table. "Mr. Snevelton, I'd like to hand you Plaintiff's Exhibit 14 and ask if you've ever seen this document before. It was also previously admitted into evidence."

Snevelton tossed the document onto the witness stand with a dismissive air. "Nope. Never seen this one either."

"It's to that same fired president. I'm going to read some sentences to make sure you've never read it."

JD strode toward the jury box, faced the jurors, and held the letter up to read it. He made intentional eye contact with a juror whose facial expression telegraphed his dislike for Snevelton.

"'*Citrus aurantium* herbal tea is an effective stimulant. Although it will pop on drug tests when used in excessive quantities, it is legal. Please tell all drivers about the effectiveness of this stimulant when combined with caffeine. Also, please notify all drivers of the locations of herbalists who supply the tea along their routes.'"

He lowered the letter and turned his head toward Snevelton, careful to remain near the jury box so Snevelton would have to face the jurors. "But you've never seen this before, correct?"

"As I said, I have never seen that email before. My name is not on it. It is between the former president, whom I fired, as I stated before, and the local dispatch office."

"Right. And why did you fire him?"

An attorney at TransNation's table shot to his feet, "Objection. The firing of that employee is not relevant to the current lawsuit concerning Mr. Hunt's accident."

"Sustained." Goldstein's face was a blank mask.

JD raised an eyebrow. The question was within Goldstein's latitude to allow. JD was going somewhere with this line of questioning, but he would have to attack it from a different direction.

"Mr. Snevelton, under the law, what is the duty time limit for a driver in a day?"

"Eleven hours, per DOT regulations."

"And how many hours in any week?"

"Weekly limits are either sixty hours in seven days or seventy hours in eight days."

"Any of your drivers ever drive longer than eleven hours in any day?"

"In all honesty, there are drivers who put their own safety at risk by occasionally driving longer than the regulated hours. But not at our company's insistence. They're violating our regulations, and if we find out, we will terminate them."

"Is that so?"

"Yes."

"And you've never encouraged drivers to exceed the eleven-hour-per-day maximum?"

"Never."

"How do you keep track of the total hours a trucker has driven in a day?"

"Simple. We have software installed on every truck to log every hour our drivers are on the road."

"No way a driver can disable that software?"

"Nope. Not possible."

He strode back to his own table. Glanced at his legal pad. "Mr. Snevelton, is it your assertion that TransNation is not liable for the accident that killed Mr. Hunt?"

Snevelton turned and faced the jury but did not look at Ann Hunt. "I'm sorry this happened. But my company was not at fault. I am not at fault."

JD angled himself so he had the jury in sight. "Mr. Snevelton, my client is not located over there by the jury. She's seated behind the counsel table."

Two attorneys for TransNation jumped up at the same time. "Objection."

Goldstein slammed his gavel down hard.

"Withdrawn." JD stared down Snevelton. "I have no further questions, Your Honor, but we reserve the right to recall him on rebuttal."

"Fine. The trial will resume at one o'clock tomorrow."

Chapter 38

ONE O'CLOCK IN the afternoon and the trial would resume at any moment. JD flicked a glance at the jury and at the press pool. It was day three. The jurors were maintaining their poker faces, but JD's gut told him the Hunt family had their sympathy.

The gaggle of reporters in the gallery had thinned out, but the diehards on the business beat remained, tracking his every move in the courtroom. Good. He wanted trucking companies to read news articles about the trial so their shareholders would pressure management to revise safety protocols. Unfortunately, the press pool also included Dinkelman, who sat front and center watching the trial from gavel to gavel.

"Let's start today's proceedings," Goldstein said. "Call your next witness, Mr. Cash."

Twenty minutes earlier Goldstein had stunned JD and dealt the Hunts' case a harsh blow.

As expected, before the trial began, TransNation had filed a flurry of pretrial motions in limine. Goldstein denied all of them—except one. He'd deferred his ruling on the motion to exclude the testimony of Walt McClatchy—the driver of the rig that had killed John Hunt.

Today Goldstein had decided—the non-disclosure agreement stood, and McClatchy was out.

JD jammed his thumbnail between his teeth and yanked it back out. Before trial TransNation had tried to shut the case down with a summary judgment motion based on the NDA—and failed. But motions in limine played by different rules. With this new decision, the magnitude of Edgar's testimony was now multiplied by a factor of ten. It was up to the hacker to carry the day.

"I call Mr. Edgar Martinez."

After the oath had been administered, JD approached the witness box. Didn't want the jurors' attention ping-ponging between himself and Edgar. As requested, the hacker had complied with JD's request to tone down his geekiness by ditching the tech-themed T-shirts for a black mock neck. He was also wearing more conservative ear gauges. The combat boots remained.

"Mr. Martinez, please tell the jury what you do for a living." JD faced Edgar and clasped his hands behind his back.

"I'm a white hat hacker."

"Whoa, you mean like WikiLeaks?"

"No. Not like WikiLeaks."

"Explain what you mean." JD intended to ward off any attack on Edgar's credentials by bringing out his hacker activity up front.

"White hat hackers work to help corporations and the government defeat the bad guys who are out to misappropriate state secrets, take down power grids, steal identities. Stuff like that."

"Where did you get your education?"

"I have a degree in computer science from Caltech, and I was a contractor for the DOD for two years. The rest I learned OTJ."

"And by DOD and OTJ, you mean what?"

"Department of Defense and on-the-job training."

"Mr. Martinez, what work did you do for my firm?"

"You asked me to go through various hard drives to recover any emails sent to or from the CEO of TransNation."

"And did you find any?"

"No. I did not find any."

"Objection, Your Honor," Sidwell bellowed. "This line of questioning is not relevant. Mr. Snevelton testified that he did not see any of the emails Mr. Cash showed him. And now Mr. Cash's own expert is testifying that he had no knowledge of any emails sent to or from Mr. Snevelton."

"Mr. Cash, where's this going?"

"Only a few more questions, Your Honor."

"You have exactly two questions, Counsel."

"Thank you, Your Honor. Mr. Martinez, witnesses are not allowed in court to view the proceedings until after they have testified. I will now bring you up to speed so we can discuss the testimony of a prior witness."

Edgar nodded for JD to proceed.

"During his time on the stand, Mr. Snevelton testified he had not seen Exhibit 13 or Exhibit 14. Did you find evidence to the contrary?"

"Yes, I did."

"What did you find?"

"I found proof of delivery and opening of blind carbon copies of Exhibits 13 and 14 on a computer owned and used by Mr. Snevelton."

A collective gasp rose from the observation gallery, signaling to JD he was extracting information the jury needed to hear.

"Order in the court." Goldstein slammed his gavel on his bench several times. "There will be order."

"Objection, Your Honor. No evidence shows Mr. Snevelton was the one to open and read these documents."

"We'll get to that, Your Honor," JD countered.

"Objection overruled."

In the delay and disruption caused by their mass food poisoning drama, TransNation had dropped the ball and blown the deadline to examine Edgar under oath before trial. Now JD was going to reap the payoff from Judge Goldstein's ruling denying TransNation the right to depose Edgar. Big time. "To refresh you, Mr. Martinez, Exhibit 13 was a document that said, 'I can't keep covering for you with the DOT. Your company must reduce its annual fatalities. I'm not sticking my neck out for you all any longer.' And Exhibit 14 was about *Citrus aurantium*, the herbal stimulant. How do you know Mr. Snevelton viewed these documents and not someone else?"

"Every computer I analyzed from TransNation had a unique password."

"How can you be sure someone else didn't log on and view these emails? How can we prove Mr. Snevelton viewed them himself?"

"Well, Mr. Snevelton's computer had an additional layer of security. He also had a fingerprint scanner. My review of his computer showed he never opened an email without the combination of both the password and fingerprint."

"How were you able to circumvent the fingerprint requirement during your review of the computers?"

"Someone turned off that layer of security when the computers were donated to a charity."

JD gave the jury a pointed look to make sure they were tracking with Edgar's testimony.

"And how did you determine Mr. Snevelton opened the blind copies of these emails?"

"Because although someone tried to erase all the files, it was clear from bits of data I was able to retrieve from the hard drive that someone opened them using a fingerprint plus the password. My examination also confirmed Snevelton replied to the emails."

JD walked over and stood by the juror closest to Goldstein's bench. "Mr. Snevelton also testified his company uses a computer program to track drivers' hours. Did I ask you to review anything regarding that?"

"Yes."

"And what did you find?"

"I found anomalies."

"What were those?" He looked at the jurors. A couple of them returned eye contact.

"I found evidence of systematic tampering with the underlying computer program to decrease drivers' times."

JD scanned the jury. One woman in the front, who'd said she was a widow on the juror questionnaire, and who'd been scribbling notes throughout the trial, sat up straighter and shot a glare at Snevelton.

"By how much per driver were the logs undercounting the time?"

"In any week, TransNation undercounted a driver's time by five to ten hours."

"Over the course of a month . . ." JD started.

"It added up."

"Mr. Martinez, how do you determine the actual time TransNation trucks were moving?"

"TransNation also had a GPS tracking system on all their vehicles, separate from the time-clock system. I developed an algorithm to cross-reference the GPS data with the time log and calculated the difference. Easy."

JD gauged the jury's reaction to Edgar. The widow pressed her lips into a thin line, and the accountant avoided looking at Snevelton or his attorneys.

AN APPEARANCE OF IMPROPRIETY

"Easy indeed. No further questions."

"Ladies and gentlemen," Goldstein said, "we're going to break for the day. Remember, don't discuss anything you've heard today with anyone, including other jury members. Also, please do not decide the case and do not form any conclusions until you've heard all the evidence."

The widow juror raised a worn and knobby hand.

Goldstein nodded, giving the juror permission to speak.

"Your Honor, you said if we have a question, we can ask you. I have a question before we go home."

"The way it works is that you submit your question in writing, and I decide how to handle it."

"Okay, Your Honor." The woman flipped a few pages on her notepad and scratched something out in a flurry.

The deputy took the folded paper from the juror and gave it to Goldstein. The judge opened the paper. His lids pulled wide, and his shoulders rose, but he quickly blanked out his expression. He refolded the paper and tucked it into a portfolio on his desk.

Prickles clawed up JD's back.

Goldstein pinned him and Sidwell with a stern scowl. "Counsel, I need you both in my chambers tomorrow at nine o'clock. Sharp. And I want your clients and all decision-makers in the courthouse. Ladies and gentlemen of the jury, we previously informed you that there would be a half-day session tomorrow to accommodate a witness. Now you will be free all day."

Goldstein scanned the gallery. "Everyone is dismissed. Have a good evening." He slammed his gavel down, rose, and exited the courtroom without a backward glance.

Goldstein's curt behavior sent ice water running through JD's veins.

Chapter 39

Fear tightened JD's insides as he entered Judge Goldstein's chambers the next morning to find Sidwell already present.

"Mr. Cash, Mr. Sidwell, are your respective clients here on the courthouse grounds today?"

"Yes," JD said.

Sidwell nodded.

"Good. Here's the note from the juror." Judge Goldstein handed the juror's note across the desk for Sidwell and JD to examine at the same time.

> In the bathroom, I heard two jurors discussing the case. They were saying things like "punitive damages" and "liability." It sounded like they'd already made up their minds, but I'm not sure. Wanted to bring this to your attention.
>
> Respectfully,
> Althea Broadnax

This could mean a mistrial. JD scrolled his mind back over Goldstein's instructions to the jurors. The judge had handled them perfectly. He'd admonished the jury before every break and at the conclusion of each day to keep from forming opinions and to refrain from discussing the case with anyone.

During jury selection, Goldstein had quipped to both Sidwell and JD that thanks to *Law & Order* reruns and Court TV, it was harder and harder to find jurors on high-profile cases who followed the rules. The temptation to branch out into their own investigations was especially appealing if there was a chance they could parlay their stint into a book deal or a reality TV guest spot.

"Gentlemen."

Goldstein's words drew JD back into the moment.

"Let me put on my problem-solver hat for a minute. This juror's note confirms that Mr. Cash is scoring major points in the courtroom. If talk of punitive damages is being bandied about, the jury has already determined liability against TransNation."

"Well, Your Honor . . ." Sidwell's face gave away every emotion inside his head. "The jury has disobeyed your instructions. It's clear a mistrial is in order."

"Maybe, maybe not." Goldstein raised an eyebrow. "But you think about this, Mr. Sidwell. The writing is on the wall. Your defense stunk."

Sidwell gave a sharp exhale.

Goldstein folded his arms across his chest, "Second trial, third trial. Won't matter. Your client's going down. And you know it."

JD saw his chance. "Besides, Sidwell, the Hunt family has nothing more to lose. She doesn't have any expenses to pay until the next trial's over because of my contingency agreement. That's the way my cases work. And I might increase my punitive damages request."

"Gentlemen, I'm pulling an old trick out of my playbook. I'm giving you a hard shove toward settling. I want stinkers off the docket and only want to try cases worth the expense of taxpayer money and time."

Smart move on Goldstein's part. A settlement might hurt TransNation a bit, but not like a multimillion-dollar punitive damages verdict. For JD, it would be a win and would give the Hunts the money they needed to fill the financial wreckage left behind by John Hunt's death.

"Agreed, gentlemen?"

He and Sidwell both nodded.

"Now go out in the hallway and don't return until you settle this thing."

***

JD sat immobile in his Wagoneer. Time drew out. He'd thought the floor would split open and swallow him when he'd read the juror's note. Sidwell's face had gone ghost white. Settling a case was always deflating—even for multiple millions of dollars. No denying there was an adrenaline rush swashbuckling through a trial in front of twelve jurors. But the reality? Ninety percent of all civil cases ended in settlement, many on the courthouse steps minutes before trial.

A mistrial could mean months at the back of the line waiting for a new trial date. It took many sessions with clients to drill into their minds that a jury verdict was not the finish line. If TransNation appealed the decision, they would use every procedural trick in the book to drag things out. And time was not on Ann Hunt's side. Bills needed payment. More importantly, her family needed all her attention, unburdened by concerns about a protracted trial.

Was Ann denied her movie-style ending with a thundering closing argument? A decisive moment of truth for the world to see? Yes. But by agreeing to forgo the legal drama and by opting for the mundane formality of entering the settlement into the record, she'd secured a future for herself and her children.

TransNation had agreed to $5 million—five times what she'd hoped to recover. The corporation's resident bean counter had told the CEO it would be a bargain if they could cut their losses.

With prudent investment, college tuition was secure for Ann's children and grandchildren. She could stay home, focus on healing. The money, however, would never fill the hole left behind.

Finality.

God had answered his prayers for the Hunt family. The system had done what it could. Ann Hunt had walked out of that courtroom knowing she could breathe again.

JD pushed down the gnawing feeling that always surfaced when he cleared a boulder off his caseload. There was another widow out there. More messages piling up on his 800 number. His instinct was to dive right back in, but for the first time, he suppressed the incessant baying that always urged him to take on another case.

This settlement opened a window of time in his life giving him a chance to change how he operated. Dean needed him. Scratch that. His *son* needed him. Hospice loomed for Tammy. The mock trial prep needed work. It was not his job to save the world.

AN APPEARANCE OF IMPROPRIETY

Wait. Where had that come from? He sat with the notion for a while.

JD had been grinding and hustling for so long. He'd carried on his back all the burdens of his clients and the students, as though every part of the outcome depended on him. Trying to atone for his mother's death and outrun the hurt. Outrun his trailer-trash background. Outrun the worry. If he stopped moving, stopped working, stopped doing, the whole thing might implode. But would it really?

God was the one who orchestrated all events for his purposes. It was God's job to save the world. And by trying to play God, JD had taken on a responsibility far too heavy. He couldn't possibly do everything, and yet he worried about every person who needed help.

Who of you by worrying can add a single hour to your life?

Honestly, JD had been so busy trying to save people that they'd become projects, not real humans that he needed to relate to on a transparent and personal level. Until Mahalia, he hadn't felt his own need for relationship. Realization came crashing in. His monk vow. The punishing workload. He'd isolated himself. Willing to put others first, but never truly getting close.

You do not even know what will happen tomorrow. What is your life? You are a mist that appears for a little while and then vanishes.

Dean, Tammy, the settlement . . . Mahalia. All off-ramps to a new road. A fresh way of looking at things. Shrugging off the past and embracing the future.

He turned the ignition over, listened to the low rumble, put the Wagoneer in Drive, and put the past in his rearview mirror.

Chapter 40

The early May marine layer left a gray cast in the morning sky. Mahalia's chamber door swung open so fast it made a breeze and startled her. Becky stood in the doorway, murmuring to herself as usual, with a legal-sized envelope in each hand.

Doomsday was here.

Becky bounced on her toes, a hopeful, expectant smile beaming at Mahalia.

The two stared each other down. Mahalia gave a delicate cough, and another.

"Right. I get it." Becky twiddled her cross necklace. "You want to have this moment all to yourself."

Becky gave a diminutive wave and backed out, closing the door behind her. Mahalia flinched at the *click*, her nerves taut as piano wire.

She held an envelope in each of her own hands, moving them up and down. Weighing them as if she were Lady Justice with her scales. She closed her eyes, said a brief prayer, and chose the letter in her left hand. Not peeking at the paper while she unfolded it. Wanting to take the whole thing in at once.

> The legal system is a sacred trust between the citizens, judges, attorneys, and all other court personnel. We must maintain every effort to ensure that all our citizens feel that they received due process under the law. The facts in your case at first appeared to show what some might deem lapses in judgment. However, after careful consideration, we find no credible evidence that you have violated any provisions of the California Code of Judicial Ethics. We consider this matter closed.

AN APPEARANCE OF IMPROPRIETY

The apprehension drained out of her. The letter was not a ringing endorsement, but she stood exonerated.

Her insides squeezed as she stared at the second envelope and tried to guess the contents. Mental images of Just Steve and Granddaddy Henry rushed in. She could hear both saying there was more to life than appearance and status. When she'd applied for the ASJ position, her motives had been centered on the standing she would have and how it would reflect on her. She had given no thought to the importance of the job to the legal system or to society at large. It was just another stepping stone for her.

She paused. *Will the contents of that envelope really change my life?* If she didn't land the position, would that make her a failure? Had she asked herself these questions six months earlier, the answer would've been a definitive yes. She would have viewed herself as a failure for not attaining the highest position available in the shortest amount of time. But now things were different.

Working with the Junior Jurors had reminded her that not everyone was advancing from a position of stability and love like she had. Not everyone had a tight-knit family system to push and drive them. Working beside JD on the program, she'd learned about compassion for others and the value of small victories. She'd learned that being a role model entailed connecting with people mentally and emotionally.

Thinking about Kyle, Aisha, and Mercedes warmed her insides. Her impact on the lives of those kids meant something—not because she was a judge but because she was someone who cared.

She tilted her face toward the ceiling, raised a balled fist, and opened her fingers one at a time. "I surrender all" floated out in a whisper.

> We regret to inform you that the committee has not selected you for the assistant supervising judge position. This decision does not reflect upon your ability as a judge. After careful consideration, we've selected a more seasoned jurist. Given your strong credentials, we encourage you to apply at the next opening.

I surrender all.

Jayna Breigh

***

"We're back from the midday recess. You may cross-examine the witness who was on the stand before the break." The judge presiding over the mock trial spoke into the microphone before him.

Mercedes stood tall and proud at the defense counsel table. "Mrs. Minerva Spittaker, please step forward." A teenage girl wearing a gray granny wig and oversized spectacles gingerly stepped forward and sat in the witness chair.

Mercedes held a legal pad in her shaky hands. She paused a second and launched into her cross-examination.

JD drew back his suit cuff and checked his watch. Again. Still no Mahalia. He had wanted his son to see this as well, but Dean had flown back to Vegas to pack up and ship his things out here. He'd be back the day after tomorrow, but JD missed him.

In about three hours, closing arguments would be over and the mock trial case would be in the hands of the jury. No coaching from the sidelines allowed. He couldn't use any hand signals, and he couldn't pass any notes. His gut tightened. He'd been jammed up in Afghanistan, sure, but thinking about how much this mock trial meant to his kids was nerve racking.

From his vantage point in the first seat of the visitors' area, he surveyed the theatrically solemn faces of the six high school students selected to act as adjudicators in the mock trial case—not a smile or a trace of boredom anywhere.

The Sherman Oaks Prep student playing Mr. Spittaker, seated next to his attorney at the counsels' table, also sported a gray wig. He used a pencil to scratch beneath the sling over his arm. The cane propped against the table further added authenticity. Sherman Oaks Prep took the top honors almost every year.

Quincy bent his torso toward Mercedes and furiously scribbled on a legal pad. JD scanned the courtroom again, seeing it through the eyes of his kids. He'd make sure they sent a thank-you note to Mahalia for cashing in a favor and securing a courtroom that was on the National Register of Historical Places. He closed his eyes and visualized Gregory Peck as Atticus Finch thundering away in the courtroom scenes of *To Kill a Mockingbird*.

AN APPEARANCE OF IMPROPRIETY

The fine woodwork and hulking judge's bench gave the proceedings the solemnity needed to give the mock trial experience authenticity.

Quincy turned toward the gallery and pointed behind JD to Aisha. The girl scurried forward. Quincy whispered in her ear, and she scuttled back to her seat, where she reached into a box that held exhibits. She hustled back to Quincy, who took the piece of paper from her, read the document, and gave her a fist bump.

JD's chest swelled with pride as he watched the kids working together more smoothly than drive-through attendants at a Chick-fil-A. He turned and glanced back. Brittany, José, and Langston sat behind him.

He made a mental note that the teens needed to send Rhoda McNally at Kids Camp Charity International a thank-you note for the top-quality secondhand clothing she had supplied. The favor had only cost him the promise of an added year of paid high-speed internet service for her charity and a couple of top-of-the-line computers capable of handling programs with heavy graphics capacity. He'd also added KCCI to the list of charities his trust funded, and Rhoda would be none the wiser.

Langston wore a well-fitting suit, but judging by the beat-up Air Jordans on his feet, Rhoda hadn't been able to locate any shoes big enough.

He checked his phone and reread his earlier text to Mahalia. Still no reply. They'd gone over the calendar weeks in advance. She'd been AWOL since the Hunts had settled with TransNation. Only had time for conference calls on mock trial preparation matters. Wouldn't meet with him in person. He was trying to keep his nose out of her business, but she was co-adviser. She'd promised to come to the competition.

> We're about halfway finished.
> Think you can get here in time?

His finger hovered over Send. A door clicked behind him, and his gaze locked on Mahalia, who was making her way into the courtroom. A band loosened around his chest. He tilted his head toward the empty seat beside him, but she selected a seat farther back in the gallery. Posture rigid, eyes forward toward the judge on the bench.

His gaze soaked her in while she fixated on the students carrying on the trial. As always, her outfit complemented. Today she wore a turquoise-colored pantsuit worthy of royalty.

Was she still dating Mr. McHandsy from the movie theater? His heart hoped not. He wanted her beside him today, tomorrow, and every day after that. They could pass notes like kids. Root for the team from the gallery. He observed her posture. Her stony facial expression. Was she cutting off all contact?

There was still the awards banquet tonight. The kids were looking forward to it. He wanted her there even more than here. Once the mock trial was over and Goldstein returned to the program, there would be no reason for them to keep in touch.

Zero barriers stood between Mahalia and himself. Not TransNation. Not the competition. But no more reasons existed for her to remain in his life either. Except his gut screamed at him that he'd fallen for her. Full stop. No going back. And that his feelings weren't all one-sided. He'd cut back the dating to zero before Casey, but his radar still worked fine. Mahalia had been throwing off subtle signals for a while now. He was certain. Or had the last few months been a fever dream?

For weeks, the possibility of taking her in his arms during the dance that followed the awards ceremony tonight had given him more jitters than his first kiss. But looking at her now, after all their hard work together, ice water ran in his veins. Were they going to treat each other as strangers?

***

Shame, hot and painful, held Mahalia glued in her chair. Eyes forward. Chin up. Shame that someone had filed a complaint against her. Even though she'd been vindicated, being called to the carpet like that stung. The empty seat beside JD beckoned her like the first glimpse of home after a long journey. Like Granddaddy Henry's expansive lap that she'd crawl into when she'd skinned her knee.

Granddaddy would wrap her up tightly in his arms. His drugstore Aqua Velva would wash over her, and she'd let go of her tears, leaving them all on his shirtfront. He'd produce a handkerchief from his pocket, wipe her eyes and nose, give her a firm squeeze, and whisper, *"Everything's going to be alright, baby girl. Granddaddy's got you.*" But there was nothing Granddaddy or JD could do for her. Her pride was battered. She missed unconditional love, the kind Granddaddy gave her. The security. The safety net.

It was between her and God now. Repairing her tattered dreams. Reconfiguring her life now that she realized all the climbing and striving had taken her down a path to nowhere.

The action in the courtroom dragged her out of her self-flagellation and back to the moment. Quincy stood close to the witness box, the way she'd taught him. His hands shook. But he was getting his questions in and making a record for the jury.

Her traitorous eyes turned toward JD. He sat like a proud father. The half smile on his lips and the softness in his eyes radiated how much he cared for the kids. She thought she'd seen hints of that care directed toward her. The dinner at San Fernando Seafood Grill had clearly been a mistake. Too intimate. Cozy. The accidental church date. She'd seen him as a man rather than simply the mentor for the Junior Jurors or an attorney working a case. Is that what had clouded her judgment in her conduct with him? Was she even now questioning her commitment to The Rule?

She refocused, and her gaze tangled with JD's. He mouthed, "Everything okay?"

She straightened her back and gave a curt nod. An expression that she couldn't read crossed his face, and she looked away. After the ceremony tonight, they'd go their separate ways. Goldstein had completely healed and could return to mentoring the mock trial program in the fall, so that was off her plate. Plus, JD had a son now. Caring for his ex-girlfriend, even remotely, would take up more time. All of this on top of his caseload. She only had to hold herself together for a couple more hours. She tried to focus, but her reflexive mantra would not come. Prayer flowed instead. She gave in, and the words poured out. She had nothing to lose and everything to gain. *Lord, please help me.*

Chapter 41

THE STAFF AT the beachside hotel off the Pacific Coast Highway in Santa Monica had gone above and beyond JD's expectations. He'd delegated the decorating for the mock trial awards ceremony and dance to the concierge, and the hotelier had come through with flying colors. Each table in the ballroom had a stack of old law books topped by a mason jar with a candle. Propped next to each jar was a gavel. Back-in-style hits from the 1980s blended in with Taylor Swift and Beyoncé.

The kids were all doing a line dance he'd never seen before and couldn't imitate. Satin and taffeta shimmered on the gyrating girls. The used prom dresses had also been contributed by Rhoda.

Then there was Mahalia. A vision. The only way to describe her. His mouth had gone bone dry when she'd walked in, glowing in a dandelion-colored dress. Or maybe it was daffodil. Regardless of the name of the color, she wore it well. As he watched her on the dance floor, her dress flowed and moved and wrapped around her, accenting her willowy curves in a classy, timeless way.

"Mr. Cash, you gotta come out here," Destinee squealed, while Aisha bopped from foot to foot next to her in time to the music.

"I don't know . . ."

Devin popped up to his right. "Ain't scared, are you?" The kid gave him a smug grin. "You *can* dance, right?"

No. "Yes."

"Come on. Let's see it." Langston materialized to his left.

The classic "Footloose" came on. At least he recognized the music. Kevin Bacon had killed it on the dance floor in that movie, but there was no chance JD could do anything even close.

AN APPEARANCE OF IMPROPRIETY

His kids joined him in a scrum. One giant circle of arms and legs moving in time—or not—to the music.

With Dean transitioning to living with him full time, JD would step back for a year from the program. He took a mental picture of this moment to hold in his heart forever. Sherman Oaks Prep had taken home the trophy and the win, but Langston wore the ribbon for Best Attorney around his neck. Kyle, who'd stopped ditching class, had even talked to Edgar about applying to Caltech.

Satisfaction mingled with sadness. He rubbed his hand over his heart and tossed a wave at the kids. "I'm done." He walked his way through the klatch. José and Mason fist-bumped him, and Brittany gave a shy smile.

He flopped onto a seat beside Mahalia.

"That was hard to watch." She was fake coughing to cover her delightful laugh.

"Leading by example. Awkward, gawky example. You know, not all of us were fortunate enough to inherit the rhythm gene."

"Pshhhh." Mahalia sucked her teeth and gave a delicate wring of her neck. She was killing him with all her cute little ways. He smiled to himself. Between Mahalia and Americano, he had his hands full with the saucy women in his life.

She caught him staring.

"You know," she said. "Brittany has a crush on you. Be gentle when you let her down."

Whoa! Where is this coming from?

"What makes you think that? I treat her like all the other girls in the program. She never tries to spend isolated time with me. I've done nothing inappropriate." JD shrugged. "Besides, I don't know what I would say."

"Well, I see it clear as day. I wouldn't want you to run into any problems down the road." She studied her water glass, one slender finger circling the rim.

The night had taken a left turn and was now barreling toward a cliff. "Well, Your Honor, what do you recommend I do?"

"You need to have a conversation with her. Nip it now."

His insides clenched. The last thing he needed was a high school girl with a crush. He suppressed a groan. "Would you be willing to talk to her for me?"

***

He'd pinned her with . . . those eyes . . . when he'd asked. When he focused on her with intensity, like he did now, she was powerless to object.

"Of course." What had she gotten herself into? She could kick herself for not expecting the awkward outcome. Who was she to think she could get all maternal? She'd only dipped her toe in the teenage waters with Mercedes and Kyle. An involuntary groan escaped from her.

She walked to the table where Brittany was sitting with Aisha and Mercedes. The girls radiated with beauty this evening. Their postures and bearing regal. The pride at having fought hard during the competition and the joy of dressing like princesses for the dance glowed on their faces.

Nervous prickles ran down Mahalia's arms. She shoved down her jitters and plunged ahead.

"Brittany, do you mind taking a walk with me?"

The girl scrunched her face. "Do you feel sick, Your Honor?"

"No. Everything's fine. I wanted to have a little woman-to-woman chat."

A wrinkle formed between Brittany's brows. "Okay with me."

"Oooooo, you're in trouble," Devin said.

"Shut up, Devin. You're jealous because you wish the judge was talking to you."

"Roasted," José said. He slapped Quincy's hand multiple times and guffawed.

"You can laugh all you want," Devin grinned, "but the judge promised me a slow dance. Isn't that right, Your Honor?"

His antics calmed Mahalia's nerves a bit. "Yes, I did. After I get back."

Langston's face held awe. "You the man, dude. You the man." He fist-bumped Devin.

Mahalia turned her back on the playful hijinks and hormone-driven antics.

"Let's walk a little." She moved toward the exit to get air and steel her resolve.

AN APPEARANCE OF IMPROPRIETY

Brittany walked quietly beside her.

Cool salt-tinged air moved past on a soft breeze, and she wrapped her arms around herself to ward off a chill, nerves, or both.

"So what's up, Judge?"

Why was this so hard? Because she could understand why this girl, or any girl with two eyes and half a brain, would fall for JD. She had. And he had no clue. Worse, he'd never know. Ever. Her world had been upended the minute she'd seen that billboard, and her life had not been put right since.

"Your Honor, I'm from the neighborhood. I can take whatever you've got to say." Brittany looked at her squarely. "Just spill."

"You're right, Brittany." Somehow, confronting Brittany about her obvious affection for JD exposed Mahalia's feelings for the same man. *Stop stalling.* Time to put on her big-girl pants and get this done. JD deserved her complete support and help. Best to give Brittany an easy letdown.

"I want to talk to you about Mr. Cash."

"Sure. What's up?"

Something was off-kilter. Brittany showed no signs of discomfort, but Mahalia's own insides were churning. She'd expected evasion, but the girl was eager to talk.

She took a deep breath and stumbled on. "Sometimes, when an adult does something generous for a young person, certain feelings can grow."

The girl jumped right in. "Do you mean, like love?"

"Um, yes. Well, no. A person may *think* they are in love, when what they feel is admiration or gratitude." Mahalia grasped both Brittany's hands. "Does this make sense?"

"Well, of course I love Mr. Cash."

At the girl's bold, straightforward declaration of love, something cracked open inside Mahalia. Love. Love described what she felt for JD. Not admiration. Not respect. Not attraction. She'd fallen for everything about the man. His care for the kids and fierce protectiveness for his clients. His chivalrous way with her. His integrity and faith. She'd been waiting all this time for a Midnight Prince—the status, the position, the external trappings validating her worth. JD needed no external props. Everything holding him up was invisible—his honor, his commitment, his God.

She pushed the startling revelation back. Brittany's features were both expectant and quizzical. Stinging pricks hit the back of Mahalia's eyes. She had grown to care for these kids, and an ache formed in her heart at the possibility that her next words would crush Brittany's feelings.

"You understand that he can't return your feelings." She peered into Brittany's eyes. "It wouldn't be right."

Brittany gaped at her as though seeing her for the first time. Her eyebrows rose, and she held her mouth in a quizzical half smile, half frown.

"Wait a minute." Brittany freed her hands from Mahalia's grasp. "You think I'm in love with Mr. Cash?"

"Aren't you?"

A high-pitched keening squeal burst out. Brittany doubled over.

Panic gripped Mahalia. She moved closer and wrapped her arms around the girl. "Are you okay?"

Brittany snorted and stood back up. Tears were streaming down her face. She opened her mouth, a honking noise came out, and she slapped her thigh with her hand. "No way. He's. So. Old." The girl swiped under her eyes with her thumb and let out a few breaths. She regained her composure. Her face turned serious.

"Well, I . . . I mean . . ."

Brittany cut her off. "Look, Judge, Mr. Cash's done so much for me and my family. Did you know my mom works at one of his former client's offices? She'd been cleaning houses for years, but it was breaking her body down, hauling all the cleaning supplies, the long hours. He got her on as a receptionist at first. Now she's an administrative assistant."

Unexpected tears welled in Mahalia's eyes.

"He paid for my SAT prep class and wrote a college recommendation too. Someone like me, where I'm from, with a lawyer recommending me . . . If I didn't have Mr. Cash and his program, I probably would've been a mom by now myself, and a dropout."

The infernal stinging hit Mahalia's eyes again. She willed the tears to stay put.

"I tell you what I wish, Judge. Sometimes I lay on my bed at night and wish he was my dad. That's why I love him. He's the dad I always wanted."

"Oh, sweetheart." Mahalia threw her arms around the girl's neck, then held her out at arm's length.

AN APPEARANCE OF IMPROPRIETY

"So no, I'm not in love with Mr. Cash. But this is what I *do* think." Brittany lowered her head, paused a second, and raised it. "He's crazy in love with you."

What? She tried to push back the fluttery feeling of happiness in her chest, but her mind began a rapid inventory of words and events. The door opening. His attentiveness when they were working on the mock trial. *No. Not possible.* After seven hours in the elevator, they were foxhole friends, nothing more. Colleagues in their public service. This camaraderie explained the snatches of deeper feelings that sometimes shone in his eyes, right? Besides, he was seeing—she choked on the name—that Chapman woman.

She fussed with her strand of pearls. "No, that's not true. We're professional colleagues. Sort of friends. Nothing like that."

"It's on blast, he's so into you. The way he says your name, the way he looks at you. And I think you like him back." Brittany nodded.

"You're mistaken. We respect and appreciate each other as professionals." Even as she said the words, hope bubbled and buzzed inside her.

"No disrespect, but, *whatever*, Your Honor." The girl screwed up her lips in humorous scorn.

Mahalia stroked her neck. "I think it's time I got back inside. I'm glad we cleared the air, and sorry for the misunderstanding."

"Okay, Your Honor. I'll be right in."

Mahalia made her way toward the door, stopped, and turned back to Brittany one last time. Brittany had whipped her phone out of her bag, and her thumbs made frenetic jerks as she typed, a secret smile on her lips.

Mahalia spun back around and walked inside. A tornado of emotions ripped through her.

***

Mahalia sat down facing JD, cleared her throat, and gave a little grimace. "I was wildly off base about Brittany." She clapped her hand over her eyes and peeked at him through splayed fingers. "So sorry about that."

The knot of low-level fear, which had coiled in his belly since Mahalia had told him her suspicions about Brittany, loosened. "Glad to hear it." He sat back in his chair, not sure where to go next with the conversation.

"I don't want to go into too much detail about what she and I talked about. But can I say, what you have with these kids is priceless." She smiled, and crinkles formed in the corners of her eyes.

Her approval warmed his insides like sunshine. "It is. I'll miss them." He leaned forward, bracing his elbows on his knees. He found himself careening toward a major life detour.

"What's happening?" Her eyes trained on him.

"My son, Dean, is going to live with me." He tapped his fingers on the table in a random beat. His emotions backed up on him, and he worked to push the words out. "After . . ."

Mahalia placed a hand over his and gave a squeeze.

The song ended, and seconds later Sinatra's distinctive take on "I've Got You Under My Skin" began to play, drawing adult mentors out onto the dance floor. A couple of dads took their daughters out as well. JD looked at Mahalia. Couldn't tear his gaze away if he tried. He closed his eyes and took a deep breath, working up his courage. But he opened his lids only to see her back as Devin led her away. In her high heels the boy's head barely reached her chin. His timing with Mahalia—still off.

The rustle of taffeta made him look to his left. Brittany stood beside him, a slight blush on her cheeks. "Mr. Cash, can I have this dance?"

"Of course."

Dancing to fast music wasn't his forte, but he had a little two-step under his belt from back home that would work. He gave Brittany a twirl, placed her a respectable distance from himself, and worked his way around the dance floor. Sinatra ended and was replaced by the plaintive violins and soaring first line of "At Last." There was another tap on his elbow, and Devin, his arm still around Mahalia, asked to cut in. Before JD could gather himself, Devin whisked Brittany away, leaving him standing there in front of Mahalia.

His heart thudded in his chest. He held his hand out. "Your Honor."

"Counselor."

He pulled her in, rested one arm on her waist, and held her slender hand in his.

"Let's hope your slow dancing isn't as awful as your fast moves."

Lightness infused him. "Let's hope you're right."

Silence settled over them while Etta James sang about the end of loneliness and shipwrecked dreams. The lyrics flowing out of the speakers, heavy with longing, stoked his yearning for a future with Mahalia.

In her heels, her eyes almost met his straight on. He had prepared no words for this moment. He held on and savored her willowy height, her delicate floral scent, and her closeness.

As the final melancholy notes died off, the lights turned up. Pulling away from her felt like cleaving his body from his heart.

The squawk of feedback over a microphone pierced the air and broke the spell. "Congratulations again to all the teams that competed. Thanks to Mr. Jimmy Dean Cash for securing this location and for supervising the decorations. Good job, everybody. See you all next year."

The students gathered around him to collect their stuff off the tables.

Devin came alongside. "Mr. Cash, we were wondering if we could go to the Santa Monica Pier and ride the Ferris wheel?"

Kids. He couldn't suppress his laugh. Not too long a walk. Only a few blocks.

"Devin when we planned this awards dinner and dance, I asked you guys if you wanted to include the pier, and you told me, and I quote, 'The Ferris wheel is whack.'"

The kid had the decency to look embarrassed.

"Well, that was then, Mr. Cash. This is now. I heard from my boy Langston that Brittany wants to go to the prom with me. You wouldn't hold a brother back from going after a girl, would you? Plus, everybody knows girls think the view from the top of the Ferris wheel is romantic."

Devin lowered his head. When he raised it, his shy, hopeful face revealed all his emotions.

JD sucked in a laugh and patted Devin on his shoulder. "You convinced me. Can't stand in the way of love."

As the word escaped his mouth, his gaze landed on Mahalia, and tenderness spread through him. He closed his eyes briefly. Maybe he'd take a clue from Devin tonight. Make his intentions known as they took in the view of the ocean. Throw his hat into the ring.

"Give everybody a ten-minute warning, and we'll go."

"Thanks, Mr. Cash." Devin turned, whipped his phone out, and moved his thumbs around rapidly.

What was with all the texting tonight? They were all together in one place. Why not talk to one another?

***

A cool breeze drifted off the Pacific as they strolled down Ocean Front Walk toward the Ferris wheel. The kaleidoscope effect of the rotating wheel on the waves was hypnotic. JD took a deep breath, filling his lungs with the unmistakable smell of ocean mixed with popcorn and cotton candy.

Kyle, Langston, and Devin took the lead. Brittany had her arm linked with Aisha, their heads close together. The others followed behind. Their giggles and boisterous boasting mingled and floated over him. Mahalia had taken a position in the middle of the pack, her leisurely stroll like a model's. He hung back, bringing up the rear to catch any stragglers.

Thoughts pinged around but didn't coalesce. After tonight, he had no natural ties to Mahalia. Time to stick his neck out there and see what happened.

Mahalia dropped back and walked beside him. He strolled next to her in silence. She gave an abrupt pitch forward. On instinct, he shot his arm out to steady her.

"Guess I'm not wearing sensible shoes for a walk," she said.

He savored his hand on her waist for another moment and found his opening. He moved his arm and offered the crook of his elbow. "Just so we don't have any unfortunate mishaps. Wouldn't want to have to sue the City of Santa Monica for defective sidewalks."

She peeked at him, gave a brief nod, and snaked her arm through his. As she walked, she kept her head down and examined her steps. He sensed uncharacteristic shyness. Hope rose, and blood pounded in his temples.

Her face wore a bashful expression.

With superhuman restraint, he kept his face forward. His eyes were trained on the kids, but Mahalia's presence had every nerve ending on high alert. The sweet scent of her. Her graceful arm through his. Her height in those ridiculous heels bringing their eyes within a millimeter or two from level.

AN APPEARANCE OF IMPROPRIETY

He kept his mouth shut and soaked in her presence. The night felt custom-created for romance by a Hollywood studio.

Her weight shifted, and she bumped against him.

"Someone filed an ethics complaint against me. I've been dealing with that for the last few weeks. It consumed me."

The heat rushed from his body. "I . . . I'm speechless. Who could ever find something of any substance to file such a charge?"

A series of emotions scrolled across her face. Sadness. Shame. Protectiveness? She averted her gaze for the briefest second, then looked at him squarely.

"It was Casey. Casey Chapman." Her words were soft, but they hit him with the force of a bomb.

He ground his teeth and bit back words he hadn't used since the military. "I'm lost." Tightness banded his chest. "Do you have more details?"

"It was a lot of things all piled on top of each other. Dinkelman's picture from the earthquake. An Instagram post I never mentioned to you. But Casey was there in San Fernando at Vinnie's. When I saw her at the opening day of the TransNation trial, I realized why she seemed so familiar. I put two and two together after remembering what Judge Whitaker said at my interview about courthouse gossip. There's no doubt it was her."

***

Despite her feelings about the woman, Mahalia had held back the fact that she'd seen tears in Casey's eyes. JD was a man worth caring about deeply, and she could not fault the woman for that. Still, he radiated tension, and Mahalia instantly regretted having said anything at all. Why had she opened her mouth? He was seeing Chapman, and the ethics complaint had been dismissed.

His jaw tightened. "What were the grounds for the complaint?"

What reaction had she hoped to pull from him by telling him? She didn't even know. Some kind of crazy feeler? Testing the waters to see what was going on with him and Casey? She waited for his arm to drop, but he tightened his elbow instead, drawing her closer.

"Appearance of impropriety." It stung afresh, letting those words leave her lips.

His steps faltered momentarily. "I'm so sorry . . ." His caring eyes swam with regret. As always, his chivalry won the day.

Regret or shame or some idiotic desire to protect him, or maybe herself, kept her mouth running. "I'm not mad at Ms. Chapman. The committee dismissed the case. And I'm happy for you two. You make a lovely couple. With all that you do for everyone else, you deserve to be happy."

His brows pulled up. "Wait, what? What makes you think Casey and I are together?"

"I got that sense."

He shook his head, lips pressed together in a line. "We went out a couple of times, but we're not together."

How did she feel? Her thoughts swirled. Relief? Sadness for him if Casey was the woman he wanted? What should she say? She peered at him and decided to ask what any good friend would. "You okay?"

"It was never serious. A few dates." He looked at her, and the intensity caught her off guard. "She's not the one."

His admission lightened her mood. She was glad Casey hadn't hurt him. She'd give herself this one last night to enjoy his company and what could have been. A thin thread of hope tugged at her heart, but he had so much going on. It seemed like the timing wasn't going to work out.

Her thoughts shifted back to the ethics complaint. "Do you want me to tell you the whole story?"

"Not tonight. Tonight's a night to enjoy what we've all accomplished."

Relief washed over her. She really didn't want to rehash it all here and now.

The Ferris wheel came into view, and they joined the line. The kids were jostling to partner off in the gondolas, two or three to a car. Just in front of them, Brittany and Devin got into a car together. Mahalia felt JD gently nudge her forward to join them, but Devin jerked the door closed.

"Sorry, Judge, this one's full." The boy winked at JD.

JD turned to her. "We don't have to ride. I know you don't like elevators and such."

"This is different. Not boxed in. I'll be fine." After being trapped in an elevator with him for seven hours, a Ferris wheel overlooking the ocean would be a sweet farewell.

He glanced at her, gave her a crooked smile and gestured to the gondola. "After you."

The car swayed as JD helped her in, and reflexively, she gripped his knee.

"You'll be with me, Mahalia." His eyes, full of something she couldn't quite believe, held her gaze captive. Steady, sure.

Yes, she was safe with him. Safe to be herself. Safe to have flaws and fears. When terror had gripped her in the elevator, he'd used a bag full of tricks to keep her calm and help her save face. When she'd been stiff and awkward with the students, he'd rolled with it, not pointing out her discomfort. She wouldn't have to strive and climb. Even if he only offered friendship, she'd take it. She wanted more. So much more. But the approval, the understanding . . . She could breathe. Her strivings could cease. He accepted her, warts and all.

The car began its ascent, and she stiffened. He put a comforting, friendly arm around her, so she turned to him.

"I want to tell you how . . . nice it's been getting to know you, JD. Your work in the courtroom is outstanding, at least what I saw of it, and your love for the Junior Jurors is inspirational. I'm glad I can call you my . . . foxhole friend." The moon cast its silver glow on the ocean expanse in front of them.

She tried to smile, but her lips trembled, and tears threatened to spill. She cared for this man from the depths of her being. Never had she ever met anyone like him. The hue of her dream man no longer mattered.

Any fool could see JD was a rare find. His compassion and care. The way he put others' needs before his own. His calm steadiness. She closed her eyes. *Please, Lord.* A gust of wind jostled the car, and her elevator panic gripped her. His other hand rested in his lap, and she seized it, clutching and squeezing so tight that his knuckles were white from the pressure. She mashed her lids shut to ward off the panic.

"I've got you." JD's breath tickled her ear. The tone held more meaning than she had a right to expect. She opened her eyes, and his soulful brown ones stared back at her. But for the first time she saw his eyes in a different way. Not sad but radiating affection and concern. Steadfastness.

Commitment. He was loyal and determined. His eyes carried the weight of a man of character.

She squeezed her lids together again. Fighting back the powerful attraction that scared her in its intensity.

"Open your eyes, Mahalia. I'm right here."

She opened her eyes. His hand gripped hers. His arm held her close. A small gasp escaped as she watched his lips descend and pause. His eyes scanned her face, waiting. *Yes, today. Yes, forever.* Before she could formulate the words, a raucous laugh from the car above them broke the spell of the moment, and she pulled away briefly.

JD released her. His eyes, which seconds before had burned with emotion, were shuttered, and she felt cold down to her bones. Had she mistaken his compassion for something else? Had he come to his senses after a brief moment of madness with the gentle sea air and moonlight?

The car rocked to a stop, and the attendant opened the door. JD withdrew to another universe. He took her hand to help her from the gondola but released it immediately and kept a respectful distance from her, making no effort to breach her personal space again.

***

What was he thinking? Good thing he'd come to his senses in time. They'd had no conversations. He had no idea where her head was at. She'd been super vulnerable with him about the ethics complaint, and he'd almost taken advantage of that moment to get physical.

JD walked with the boys at the front of the pack to the stretch Hummer limo. He angled his gaze toward Mahalia as she slid into the vehicle. He'd blown it. She'd sought security and reassurance because of her fears, and he'd decided it was the perfect time to get up close and personal. Yes, they were colleagues and even had a friendship, of a sort. Was movie-date-dude a factor? He had no idea what the status of that relationship was, but he'd gone in for a kiss. He'd paused, waiting for her to give him the green light. But she hadn't. That was his answer. She'd have met him halfway if she'd been interested.

A subdued hush filled the limo on the ride back to City of Angels. The boys surfed on their phones. Some dozed. Brittany and Devin sat side by side. Not talking, but hands touching. Santa Monica and West LA scrolled past his window, giving way to the grittier northwest downtown area the teens called home.

The kids spilled out of the limo and into awaiting cars. As they passed, some patted him on the back. A few embraced him. He watched as the girls threw themselves at Mahalia, who gave warm hugs to them all. She'd impacted them, no question.

Mahalia was a force to be reckoned with, and she'd upended his entire life. Now he wanted a wife. He wanted a family, and he wanted it with her. His new situation crowded into his brain. A teenage son with a dying mother. He'd let go of his vow, but the timing was all wrong.

He waited until all the kids got off. Kept his distance. She waved from afar before sliding into her vehicle. She gave a short toot and drove away, taking his heart with her in that clown car.

Chapter 42

Mahalia dragged her arm from under the comfy throw blanket and held her wrist in front of her eyes. Five fifteen on Sunday morning. Turner Classic Movies continued in muffled tones on her TV. She'd drifted off watching *Witness for the Prosecution*. Now Popeye Doyle sprinted after someone on a congested New York street in *The French Connection*. Restlessness had dogged her all night, punctuated by random movie dialogue.

She stretched and readjusted. It had been two weeks since the awards banquet. An interminable span with no contact between herself and JD. She missed his quiet sense of humor, his steadfast care. The way he challenged her to want more from life than padding for her résumé. In fact, she was giving genuine consideration to carrying on with the program, even if JD quit his involvement.

She righted herself, fished around in the blanket for her housecoat, and planted her feet on the ground. The always-present early morning sounds in her neighborhood—the rumble of a car, a random airplane headed for LAX—held something else. Some animal was making weird snuffling sounds. Better not be a raccoon looking to paw through her trash.

She rushed to the door and yanked it open, but pulled up short. Not a raccoon. Sitting on her stoop, hunched over, was a woman. Mahalia hadn't even grabbed her cell phone. Should she call the police? The woman looked harmless enough. "Excuse me. Are you okay?"

The squatter turned, and Mahalia instantly recognized her. Tanner's mom, Angie. Tears flowed down Angie's emotion-blotched face.

"Judge Jackson."

"Angie, why are you here? Are you hurt? Do you live nearby?"

AN APPEARANCE OF IMPROPRIETY

"I came . . ." Angie sniffed several times and wiped under her nose with her sleeve.

None of this made any sense. "Do you want to come inside?" Mahalia wasn't sure whether she should move closer or step back from the distraught file clerk.

"No. No." Angie sniffled. "This is a mistake."

Things had changed for Mahalia. She viewed people differently now. Her compassion muscle had grown stronger. This woman was hurting, and she'd take the time to understand. She cinched her housecoat tighter around her waist, tucked it under her bottom, and sat beside Angie.

"Must have been hard when Tanner got kicked out of the program."

"You have no idea." Angie's laugh was rueful. She looked at Mahalia, eyes awash in remorse. "I found a scrap of paper in Tanner's room with your name and address on it."

This whole situation was disorienting. "What?" Neighbors were emerging from their cocoons. A cyclist. Someone picking up their *LA Times* from the end of the driveway. She didn't feel unsafe, but this was all so weird.

"When I saw your personal information in his room, that's when I knew things had gone too far." Angie rotated to face Mahalia. "Tanner's got issues. My ex reappeared out of nowhere when he thought Tanner had some money prospects." Angie shook out her shoulders. "I got caught up in the money fever too. And when Tanner lost it all . . ." She dropped her head. "Anger ate away at me. And Tanner absorbed the poison I was spewing."

This was a lot to take in. "Do you want some water?"

Angie shook her head. "Here's the thing. When the school yanked Tanner's scholarship, I thought college was out the window. He'd get a dead-end job. We'd continue to scrape by. Trying to get out from under the bankruptcy . . ." Angie looked off into the distance.

Mahalia gave the woman time to compose herself.

"About a month ago, out of nowhere, your clerk, Becky, invited me to the lunchtime prayer the chaplain's office puts on. Said something weird like, 'Help is always closer than you think.' I went, and they prayed for me. All that praying worked. God worked. I figured out I'd become a monster. Not the mom my boy needed. I knew I had to change."

Amazement smacked Mahalia in the face. Becky. A prayer warrior. Tears sprang into Mahalia's eyes as well. Oh, how she wished she could tell Granddaddy Henry about this. God had provided for her all along. This whole time she'd had someone who knew all the forces arrayed against her and who stood in the gap for her with prayer. She blinked to chase away the stinging in her eyes.

"But . . ." Mahalia still didn't understand. It was dawn on a Sunday. "Why are you here?"

Angie trained her gaze on Mahalia. Worry and hope filled her eyes. "To apologize."

***

Angie's emotional confession had drained Mahalia, but for the first time in her career, she felt true contentment. She hadn't made it to the next rung on the ladder and had received a mild scolding from the Council for Judicial Performance, but somehow those things didn't matter as much as she'd expected. She wasn't the same judge she'd been nine months ago—and that was a good thing.

Even with the lack of sleep, she was full of restless energy. She'd puttered around the house, straightening and dusting until about nine, when she'd logged on to catch Just Steve preaching at the first service. Now she went to the kitchen to rinse out her teacup and rustle up an early lunch. Granddaddy would have been proud of the way she'd handled the woman's confession this morning. She was sure of it. What would JD think if he knew? Would he care?

A rolling sensation, like that of being on a ship's deck in rough water, jarred the room, sloshing the water in the teacup. Two sharp jolts shook her house, and panic surged through her. An aftershock. Seconds passed. Another sickening bump. She scrambled to her doorframe. More minutes ticked by. Nothing. The clock on the other side of the room said eleven thirty. Her heart pounded. Her mind flashed to the terror of being in the elevator. The memory of how JD had calmed and protected her the entire time.

AN APPEARANCE OF IMPROPRIETY

She felt compelled forward by one urgent imperative. *Get to JD*. She had to see him. Didn't matter that this moderate quake was a flimsy excuse. Her fear of the tremblers drove her to the one place where she knew she could find security.

Did you feel that?

The three seconds until his response drew out like an eternity.

Yes. You?

Can I come over?

Of course.

***

JD shooed Dean from the living room back to his home office. His son groggily complied.

The aftershocks had been mild, but he could see how Mahalia would be spooked. Maybe he'd suggest night church. It was only a few hours away. Follow that up with dinner and marriage. *Get a grip*. She was simply reaching out to her foxhole friend.

JD ran around like a dervish tidying up Dean's nest of fast-food bags and energy-drink cans. His focus had shifted since his son had moved in. The relentless drive had eased, and he was becoming comfortable with the more manageable pace of his life. He put on a kettle for tea as well. One package of chamomile left. He hoped it would calm her nerves. Americano sensed something was up and made herself a tripping hazard.

Ah yes. One more thing. He hustled to his office to grab an impulse purchase from eBay. He ripped the package open and placed the items on the floor by the entryway.

He waited for a beat after the knock at his door, collecting himself. His heart hammered in his chest.

He opened it, and there she was. She wore jeans and a soft-looking sweater. And her sky-high heels.

She entered and stood there before him with her soft scent wafting over him. The light from the kitchen illuminated the angles and planes of her face. He closed the door with a small *click*.

She made no move toward the living room. Americano hummed and made figure eights around her ankles. Mahalia's gaze trained on JD. Intently. There was emotion behind her eyes. It was hard to read. Not fear or panic. If he wasn't mistaken, he saw tenderness and care. For him. Americano continued her display of affection.

His condo made a rocking motion following a small aftershock.

He drew nearer and looked down at the circling feline. "You like her, girl, don't you?" He lifted his head back up and stared straight at Mahalia's beautiful face. He could see her feelings for him shining in her eyes. "Me too. I like her a lot."

She was so tall. In the tottering heels, she matched him almost inch for inch. "You're not wearing sensible shoes for an emergency." A slow smile pulled at his lips. "Why don't you try on those shoes down there? You'll be more comfortable." He gave a pointed look to a spot next to the door.

She drew in a sharp intake of breath. "You remembered."

"The bunny slippers? Of course I remembered."

A radiant smile graced her face. She moved closer to him.

Her pull on him intensified. He regarded her trembling lips. He gripped her waist with one hand, spanned the other across her back, and pulled her close. Anchoring her to him. Everything in her eyes and on her face said this was what she wanted. All he had to do was tip her head.

Up close, her isolated features were magnified. The inky darkness of her eyes, the angles of her face and narrow chin, the velvet of her skin. She gave the briefest nod.

He brushed his lips across the smooth, broad forehead that housed the brilliant mind and fierce emotions of the woman he loved.

Several heartbeats thudded between them. He felt the glide of her cheek sliding up his. He waited for her to determine the pace. Then . . . the gentle press of her soft, full lips.

AN APPEARANCE OF IMPROPRIETY

***

Mahalia smoothed her hands over JD's shoulders and slipped her fingers into that glorious gray mane. It was like spun silk, like she'd dreamed it would be. She pressed into the kiss, willing him to take the lead.

And he did.

He was possessive, commanding, and tender. It was everything she knew him to be. A man with a fierce protective side and who put others' needs before his own. Even now he wasn't taking. He was giving. His heart and feelings were on display, demonstrating that he'd cherish her.

He slowed the kiss and eased away.

"Precious Mahalia." Her full name on his lips held the promise of forever. "I love you." He ran his hand up her nape and tucked her head into his neck.

Fear tried to take over. Tried to make her back away. The words came back to her. *"I surrender all."*

She'd never taken a leap this big. She'd never envisioned her future like this. She breathed in the familiar scent of his shower gel and breathed the fear out as he cradled her close. "I love you too."

A door cracked open down the hallway. Dean popped his head out. "Finally, old man."

JD laughed and pulled her close again. Americano gave a gentle purr and cuddled up on Mahalia's feet.

> *Whoever dwells in the shelter of the Most High*
> *will rest in the shadow of the Almighty. . . .*
> *. . . He will cover you with his feathers,*
> *and under his wings you will find refuge;*
> *his faithfulness will be your shield and rampart.*
> Psalm 90:1, 4